The Girl in the Glass Tower

The Girl in the Glass Tower

ELIZABETH FREMANTLE

MICHAEL JOSEPH

an imprint of

PENGUIN BOOKS

MICHAEL JOSEPH

UK | USA | Canada | Ireland | Aust.
India | New Zealand | South Africa

Michael Joseph is part of the Penguin Random House group of companies whose
addresses can be found at global.penguinrandomhouse.com

First published 2016

001

Copyright © Elizabeth Fremantle, 2016

The moral right of the author has been asserted

Set in 13.5/16 pt Garamond MT Std by Palimpsest Book Production Ltd, Falkirk, Stirlingshire
Printed in Great Britain by Clays Ltd, St Ives plc

A CIP catalogue record for this book is available from the British Library

Hardback ISBN: 978–0–718–18046–1
Trade paperback ISBN: 978–1–405–92005–6

www.greenpenguin.co.uk

Penguin Random House is committed to a
sustainable future for our business, our readers
and our planet. This book is made from Forest
Stewardship Council® certified paper.

For Raffi

There's an inherent limit to the stress that any material can bear. Water has its boiling point, metals their melting points. The elements of the spirit behave the same way. Happiness can reach a pitch so great that any further happiness can't be felt. Pain, despair, humiliation, disgust, and fear are no different. Once the vessel is full, the world can't add to it.

Stefan Zweig – *The Post Office Girl*

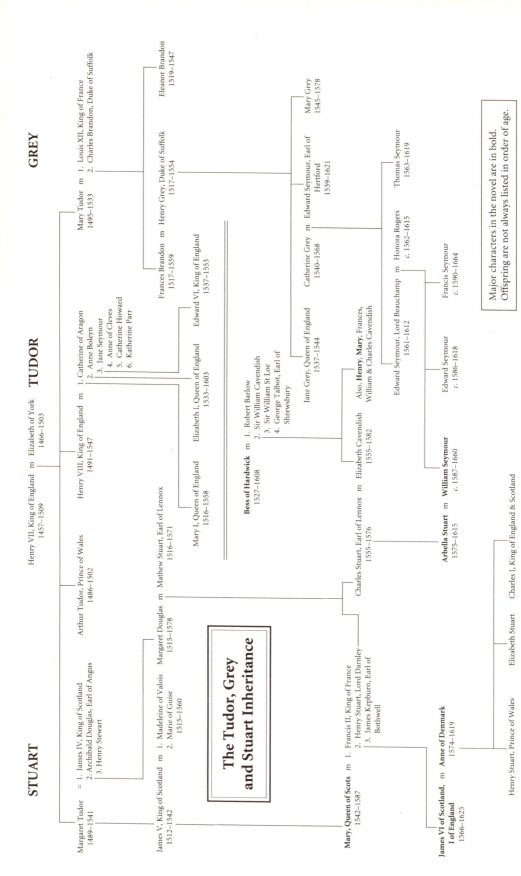

STUART

TUDOR

GREY

The Tudor, Grey and Stuart Inheritance

Henry VII, King of England m Elizabeth of York
1457–1509   1466–1503

Margaret Tudor = 1. James IV, King of Scotland
1489–1541   2. Archibald Douglas, Earl of Angus
   3. Henry Stewart

Arthur Tudor, Prince of Wales
1486–1502

Henry VIII, King of England m 1. Catherine of Aragon
1491–1547   2. Anne Boleyn
   3. Jane Seymour
   4. Anne of Cleves
   5. Catherine Howard
   6. Katherine Parr

Mary Tudor m 1. Louis XII, King of France
1495–1533   2. Charles Brandon, Duke of Suffolk

Eleanor Brandon
1519–1547

Frances Brandon m Henry Grey, Duke of Suffolk
1517–1559   1517–1554

Edward VI, King of England
1537–1553

James V, King of Scotland m 1. Madeleine of Valois
1512–1542   2. Marie of Guise
   1515–1560

Margaret Douglas m Mathew Stuart, Earl of Lennox
1515–1578   1516–1571

Mary I, Queen of England
1516–1558

Elizabeth I, Queen of England
1533–1603

Bess of Hardwick m 1. Robert Barlow
1527–1608   2. Sir William Cavendish
   3. Sir William St Loe
   4. George Talbot, Earl of Shrewsbury

Jane Grey, Queen of England
1537–1544

Catherine Grey m Edward Seymour, Earl of Hertford
1540–1568   1539–1621

Mary Grey
1545–1578

Also, **Henry, Mary,** Frances, William & Charles Cavendish

Edward Seymour, Lord Beauchamp m Honora Rogers
1561–1612   c. 1562–1615

Thomas Seymour
1563–1619

Mary, Queen of Scots m 1. Francis II, King of France
1542–1587   2. Henry Stuart, Lord Darnley
   3. James Kepburn, Earl of Bothwell

Charles Stuart, Earl of Lennox m Elizabeth Cavendish
1555–1576   1555–1582

Edward Seymour
c. 1586–1618

Francis Seymour
c. 1590–1664

Arbella Stuart m **William Seymour**
1575–1615   c. 1587–1660

James VI of Scotland, m **Anne of Denmark**
I of England   1574–1619
1566–1625

Henry Stuart, Prince of Wales

Elizabeth Stuart

Charles I, King of England & Scotland

Major characters in the novel are in bold.
Offspring are not always listed in order of age.

PART I

'The name of a successor is like the tolling of my own death-bell!'

Elizabeth I

Is the hammering inside my head?

Tap, tap, tap, in the soft place beneath my temple, in the matter where my thoughts live.

Something, someone tapping, wants to be heard, to escape.

It is a subtle and prolonged species of torture, this noise, reminding me of the impossibility of freedom.

I am the pane in the window overlooking the courtyard; I am cracked in two places but still manage to hold my form. Through the glass the world is distorted, divided into three parts, each with its own perspective, none of them quite true.

Tap, tap, tap.

It is the sound of my youth. For months and months they have been renovating the rooms beneath mine. I try to keep my mind on the clean smell that drifts up: whitewash and freshly sawn timber. My maid surprises me on the floor, nose pressed to a crack in the boards to breathe it in. It takes me far into the past and somewhere back there I believe I will find a way to make sense of things, of the shape of my life, the shape of me.

I am taken back to another tower, the little Stand Tower at Chatsworth; I was nine. I know that because it was the year the boy to whom I was betrothed died. He was the Earl of Leicester's son, not even out of babyhood; I never met him but there was much talk of it among the servants. They said that since Leicester, despite all his efforts, never achieved the throne by marriage to the Queen, then his son might instead, by wedding the Queen's most likely heir – that was me.

The walls inside the Stand Tower were cool to the touch

and left a powdery residue on the tip of my finger. The door was propped up to one side, waiting to be fitted. Everything was coated in a film of fine sawdust and the stone flags were scattered with pretty curls of shaved wood. I picked one up and threaded it on my finger, holding up my small hand to admire. Noticing the dirt beneath my nails, I imagined the fuss Nurse would make later, glad Grandmother was away in London on business, otherwise, never mind my grubby nails, I would not have dared to be up at the Stand Tower without permission and with only a stable lad for company.

I poked my head out from the entrance to ensure Tobias was not peeping, but he was seated on the bottom step humming tunelessly, with his back to me, as good as his word. The ponies were tearing at a tussock of grass nearby; everything was green and full of promise. Or was it? Surely it was late summer then and the land must have been parched – though perhaps there had been rain, for I feel sure I remember the soft squelch of mud underfoot.

Memories are like that cracked pane of glass with its subtle distortions. *Tap, tap, tap.*

I stepped into the shady interior and unbuckled my satchel, pulling out a crumpled pair of breeches pilfered from the laundry, giving them a shake. Little eddies of dust danced and wood shavings skittered over the floor.

I remember clearly the thrill that passed through me as I held those breeches up to my body. 'If only you'd been a boy.' Grandmother's refrain circled about my head. I stepped into them, tugging them over my shoes, not caring about the mud that smeared up my white stockings. Bunching my layers of skirt in one hand, I tied the breeches' tapes as best I could. They were much too big, puffing out wide and cuffed above the knee.

The idea had come to me from a troupe of players that had visited Chatsworth in the spring. I was allowed to stay up that night and watch them perform a comedy with a girl disguised as a boy – though truly it was a boy actor pretending to be a girl disguised as a boy – which had us all, even Grandmother, laughing until our cheeks ached. I had thought a good deal about it, tried to imagine what it might be like to be a boy, to go about unencumbered by skirts, to ride astride, to be at the heart of things instead of on the edges, to be listened to even when you spoke nonsense, like my baby boy cousin whose infant burblings were a source of wonder for Aunt Mary and Uncle Gilbert.

I fumbled with the fastening of my skirt; the knot was too tight, tied double and wouldn't undo. I was tempted to ask Tobias for help but didn't dare; it was enough already, persuading him to go up there with me; though he didn't seem to mind that it might have caused him misfortune if we were caught. Exasperated with the stubborn knot, I yanked hard; something gave, with a crack of broken threads, and the skirt, petticoats, bum-roll and all, fell to a heap at my feet.

I began to experiment with my newfound liberty, striding back and forth, one hand on my hip as if perched at the hilt of a sword, drawing it, lunging forward with a jabbing motion towards an imagined adversary. Girding myself then, I sidled out to stand at the top of the steps. Tobias was busy scraping mud off his boots with a penknife. I hollered, a kind of battle cry, as much as a nine-year-old girl can make such a sound, and took the steps two at a time, making a final running leap to land before him.

He jumped up in shock and then, seeing me, clapped a hand over his mouth. Only then was I aware of the sight I must have been, my boned satin bodice atop the voluminous creased breeches and my filthy stockings all wrinkled about my ankles.

'Highness!' was all he could manage.

'Don't call me that. Just for today can you not pretend I

am any old girl playing dress-up?' I secretly wanted to tell him to call me Charles, to make-believe just for an hour that I was a boy and named after the father who was an empty space in my memory.

He looked aghast, as if I had asked him to denounce God. 'What should I call you, then?'

'Call me whatever you want, anything but *that*.'

He opened his mouth to speak but said nothing.

Not knowing what to do with the awkwardness, I sprang at him, thrusting with my imaginary sword. '*En garde!*'

He laughed then, drawing his own pretend blade from its pretend scabbard, raising it to meet my own. We danced back and forth, slashing and swiping until he saw his chance and pounced forward. '*Touché!*'

I collapsed to the ground, clutching my chest with a terrible howl.

He was still laughing, quite red-faced with it, as I prepared to mount my pony. Dancer tossed his head, rattling his bridle, sensing my excitement.

I whispered into the hollow of his ear, 'Just you wait, boy, together we're going to fly,' then realized with a thud of disappointment that of course he wore a woman's saddle. There would be no flying, just the usual sedate lumbering canter. I began to unravel, as if a thread had been pulled somewhere inside me, and didn't know what to do so I did nothing, just stood looking into the valley, fighting my distress.

I had a clear view of Chatsworth. I could see Uncle Henry in the mews with the head falconer, I recognized his bright blue cape. I liked Uncle Henry. He said he had 'magic hands' and could make things disappear. When he got his cards out and began flicking and flipping them, people were drawn to wager he couldn't, but he could; I had seen it with my very own eyes.

Someone was shaking a red Turkey carpet from one of the

windows like a flag and threads of pale smoke rose from the chimneys in the forbidden wing where the Queen of Scotland was housed. Her convoy had arrived from Wingfield a few days before, under heavy guard, and the Chatsworth staff were all grumbling about the extra work. I could see the day-watch in the courtyard below her apartments and a mounted pair, with muskets slung over their shoulders, patrolling the east entrance.

All at once I knew what to do; I unbuckled Dancer's girth strap, lifting that wrong-shaped saddle off, propping it on the steps.

'Are you sure?' Tobias had the same look of concern he'd worn when I'd asked him to accompany me to the tower. 'What if some harm should befall you? Riding bareback is –'

'You may be four years my senior, Master Toby, but I am at least as good a rider as you and you know it.' It was true; I was a natural in the saddle, everyone said it. 'Besides –' I was about to remind him that he was obliged to obey me but stopped myself, for I had stepped into a place where the normal rules didn't apply.

I led Dancer to the steps and swung my leg over his round, piebald rump, marvelling once again at the freedom the breeches offered. 'Good boy.' I leaned forward, resting my cheek against his neck, whispering, 'You'll fly like Pegasus.'

Once out of the copse and on to open land we picked up our speed, galloping faster and faster, hooves thundering, the wind in my face, hair streaming in my wake. Pleasure simmered in me; it was as I had imagined, exactly: being a comet shooting over the sky, an arrow fired from a bow, a bird soaring, a lead bullet whistling. In that moment I was untouchable; I wanted to wrap the feeling in my handkerchief and keep it in my pocket for ever. The sensation returns to me across the years – the illusion of freedom is so complete I feel as incorporeal as a current of air that could blow through the crack in the window.

We slowed eventually to a walk as we reached the cover of trees. Tobias, who had been following on his own horse in anxious pursuit, drew alongside me, saying, 'Why did you want to do this?'

'I don't know . . . to know what it would be like.' I couldn't find adequate words to describe the sensation of joy, of liberty, of vigour, but he seemed satisfied. I realize now, after all this time, the thing I always sought above everything, above the crown, above love or matrimony, was freedom.

'You won't tell anyone?' I said, but didn't really need to ask, for Tobias had already pledged his silence and he was good at keeping secrets; he had kept secrets for me before. He'd said nothing when he'd found me once on the roof leads after dark. I had gone up there to look at the moon, or so I told him, but truly I had gone there out of curiosity and too much curiosity was not supposed to be a good thing in a girl, or so Grandmother liked to remind me. I hadn't thought to ask Tobias what *he* was doing up there, when he belonged in the stables. Nurse said I was a secretive child. Which I took to mean that Nurse thought me dishonest, but there is a difference between keeping secrets and telling lies.

'You have my word,' he assured me.

'Let's not go back just yet.' We were already at the Stand Tower, dismounting. I wanted to eke out that moment of stolen freedom before having to truss myself back into my dress and return to the house where my tutor awaited with his book of Latin verbs. 'Let's go up!'

The staircase was tightly spiralled and steep and unlit. I mounted cautiously with one hand on the wall, which was cool and damp as pastry. I imagined I was a knight rescuing a maiden. Round and round the stairs went, until we arrived at a chamber flooded with light from four large curved windows. There was a rotten stench from the corner.

It was an ordinary, small, brown speckled bird, lying belly up, its twig claws clutched into tiny fists.

'Nightingale,' said Tobias. He picked it up firmly as if shaking someone's hand. 'Must have flown in through an open window and not found its way out again.'

I couldn't get the thought of that small bird out of my head, flapping wildly, bead eyes swivelling, flying terrified at the panes, mistaking the glass for sky and eventually losing all hope. *Tap, tap, tap.*

Tobias opened the window and threw the little carcass out. For some reason I had expected it to float down like a feather but it dropped hard, as if its bones were filled with lead. We stood for a while in silence.

'You been up here before?' he asked.

'Yes.' I could see the guards searching a delivery cart in the Chatsworth courtyard. 'Before this tower was built. With my mother.' Remembering Mother felt as if someone had tied a rope about my heart with a slipknot. 'She's dead.'

Tobias lowered his head and, after a silence, pointed towards the house. 'She's your aunt on your father's side, isn't she?'

I didn't understand immediately that he was talking of the Queen of Scots until he added, 'It's a terrible thing that she should be shut away for all those years and her own son sitting on *her* throne.'

It was not clear to me how the Queen of Scots' situation had come to pass; I only knew what Grandmother had told me, with lips pursed in undisguised disapproval: 'She was foolish in love and paid insufficient heed to good advice. Given half a chance she'd push our queen off her throne and take it for herself.'

What I did know was that she had been in my step-grandfather's custody, at one or other of his houses, for a very long time. She used to have greater freedom and walk in the gardens, even ride out and hunt occasionally under guard. But things had changed and she was now kept under close watch with no visitors and had to take her air on the roof leads. Those were the orders of Queen Elizabeth.

'She'd like to see you' – Tobias was whispering, despite the fact that there was no one to hear – 'I promised I would bring you to her.'

'But it is forbidden . . .' I stopped. Was this why he had so readily agreed to accompany me up to the Stand Tower; he wanted a favour in return? 'Do you serve her? I thought you served my grandmother.'

'In a manner of speaking.'

I didn't question him further, for it was clear from his crossed arms and floorward gaze that he wouldn't say more. Suddenly I felt very young, too young to understand things, but I could not deny my desire to see the Scots Queen, and what greater temptation is there than that which is forbidden?

As I slunk across the great high chamber, a sound startled me, sending my heart thudding as if it had a mind to burst right out of my chest, but it was only a log falling in the fire. Once in the long gallery I moved faster, keeping close to the wall. I stopped, holding my breath as I heard the unmistakable slap of slippered feet. Ducking behind a tapestry, I waited as the steps moved past, their rhythmic *pat, pat* punctuating another sound, a *clickety-click* that conjured in my mind the chink of Grandmother's fat pearls that she wore in four heavy strands to below her waist. But no, Grandmother was in London. All sorts of imagined scenarios assaulted my thoughts: a change of plan, a lost wheel on the coach, plague in the capital. Only as the sound was receding did I dare peep to see the back of one of the laundry maids with a creaking basket of linens. Relief gushed through me; but I sensed myself drawn to the danger and the idea of having a proper secret, something real and important.

As Tobias had told me, there was only a single guard outside the forbidden apartments. I suppose, now I think of it, it must have all been carefully arranged, but at the time my understanding was slight. He knocked on the door with the butt of his halberd; three sharp knocks in quick succession, a pause, and then two slow ones. It opened and a hand reached out, beckoning me into the room. The latch clicked shut behind me.

The chamber was dimly lit and there was a general rustling as the women, who were scattered about, put their embroidery frames and books to one side and dropped to the floor, heads bowed. I felt a laugh pressing at my throat. I was used to the servants' deference but these were well-born ladies and I a mere child. Unsure of the correct way to behave, I stood gawping at them for what seemed an age, wondering if I was supposed to give some command, a gesture, to indicate that they were free to go about their business. Then by some invisible cue they all rose and returned to their needlework or whatever it was I'd interrupted.

I cast my eyes around for the Queen, who was said to be a great beauty; one or two of those women were comely enough but I reasoned that a queen got on her knees for no one, save God. A pebble of disappointment dropped into me. I had expected to find her glorious, seated beneath a canopy of state, festooned in jewels and haloed in gold light, like in the cobwebby paintings of the saints that were stored away in the cupboard at the back of the chapel. Grandmother had scolded me for 'putting my nose where it didn't belong' when I'd asked her what they were doing there. I was puzzled by those paintings, for I knew it was wrong to revere the saints and supposed that must have been the reason they were gathering dust in the dark.

There was a movement in the corner and a woman I hadn't noticed heaved herself up from a prayer stand, stepping into view. She was tall as a man and stout with it. 'Ah,' she said, opening her arms wide. 'Let me look at you; come, my eyesight is not what it was.' Her voice was odd, not quite French like the dance master and not quite Scottish like the head falconer, but a mixture of the two.

I stood rooted to the spot, unsure of how to behave. This great lumpen matron dressed in black was surely not the beautiful Queen of Scotland. That pebble of disappointment seemed to swell. But then I saw something, a haughtiness in her demeanour, a spark of pride in the eyes, which made me drop in a curtsy all the way down to the floor.

'Up, up,' the Queen said. 'Come and sit with me.'

The ladies hustled round, procuring a pair of chairs, which they placed by the hearth. The Queen lowered herself into one, fitting her bulk tightly between its arms, and patted her lap with the command, 'Up, Geddon,' for a small dog to jump on to it.

'Mary, would you bring us something to drink,' she said. 'We have three Marys here: Mary Devlin,' she pointed to a woman who was filling two cups from a ewer, 'and two more there,' she waved an arm in the general direction of the embroiderers. 'And *I* am Mary, of course. There is your aunt Mary Talbot too, though we never see her these days. It's a shame. I was fond of her.'

She crossed herself, something I had only ever seen done once by one of the stable lads; the head groom had cuffed him for it. 'All named for the blessed Virgin.' She waved her arm towards the prayer stand, where a painting of the Virgin, puce-cheeked with a brilliant blue gown, dandling a plump, haloed baby, was hung. Only then did I notice a large jewelled crucifix in a corner and the rosary beads that hung from all the ladies' girdles. Everybody knew the Scottish

Queen was Catholic but, seeing those prohibited objects, things the household chaplain denounced in his sermons as the tools of heresy, reminded me of the strangeness of that other faith.

I couldn't help but think about the stories I had heard the servants whisper, of Catholics who tried to poison Queen Elizabeth, who sought to destroy all we knew to be good and right, and the priests being dragged from hiding places hardly bigger than rat holes and taken to the Tower for interrogation. My maids often sat in my bedchamber when they believed me asleep and discussed what happened there. I would spread my limbs out in the bed and try to imagine what it might be like to be stretched on the rack. I had never questioned the wickedness of Catholics, but the Scottish Queen, smiling and petting her dog, seemed as far from an enemy as a robin from a raven.

'Your parents chose a Scottish name for you; not really a name you think of for an English queen, is it? But just as well you are not a Mary too. That would be most confusing, though I would like to think you had been named for me. I suppose that would have been too much to expect, given that I am such a wicked woman.' She emitted a small, bitter laugh. 'But I am so very glad to have this chance to see you, Arbella.' She reached out and squeezed my hand tightly.

My first instinct was to snatch it back. It had been drummed into me from infancy that I, as royalty, must never be touched without permission, but I reasoned that would not apply to a queen and so left it sitting limply in hers. She smiled openly and warmly. Grandmother never really smiled, though she often told me she loved me; she said a smile made a person seem meek. I wondered about that, for the scriptures said meekness was a virtue, that the meek would inherit the earth, but Grandmother was not to be questioned.

She was strict and inflexible and capable of turning a

whole room to her attention just by clearing her throat. By contrast, the Scottish Queen's smile made me feel safe and, in some peculiar way, though that royal aunt of mine was a complete stranger and an enemy of sorts, profoundly loved.

'I am to be moved to Tutbury and it occurred to me that we might never be under the same roof again.' She sighed, sinking into her seat, like an ancient house settling. 'Tutbury is hell itself.' She crossed herself once more.

Leaning in close enough for me to smell the aniseed on her breath, she continued, 'You see, I have always thought of you as something like a daughter. My son' – her voice cracked as she said it and I was aware of all the women craning in to listen – 'I fear my son is lost to me.'

'I am sorry for that.' I meant it from the bottom of my heart, thinking of my own mother and how even death could not break our bond.

'My little James, your cousin, the King of Scotland' – her tone was momentarily hard and then softened – 'what a bonny infant he was.' She gripped my hand very hard. 'His mind has been poisoned against me.'

I didn't know how to reply, just repeated, 'I am very sorry for that.'

'Now, I *know* you have been raised in the new faith, my dear, but you are yet young. What age are you? Nine, I think. Am I right?'

I nodded.

'Fresh as a new shoot.' There was that tender smile once more. 'I want you to remember this. Whatever you have been taught to believe, the Catholic faith is the true faith; it is the only path that leads to the Kingdom of Heaven.' She placed her palms together as if in prayer. 'Despite what has befallen me, I know it is God's plan and I have faith in His wisdom. If He had meant for me to have the throne of England, then it would have been mine – I suspect He has other plans for me.'

I had never heard anyone talk of God in such a way; it was as if the Queen knew Him intimately, as if He was her own father. God for me was something intangible and frightening.

'It is my hope that one day, my dearest child, you will see what a comfort the true faith is. Ask your Aunt Mary, Mary Talbot, she will tell you.'

'Aunt Mary?' My head had begun to churn with all that new information.

'If the English throne was not my destiny then it is surely yours and when you have achieved it, I will be up there watching over you and your Catholic England.' She had a beatific look on her face as if she had been visited by a host of angels. 'You are my hope, Arbella.' With that she released my hand again and took something out from beneath her gown, a small wooden box, which she opened, removing a flat elliptical object from it. 'I want you to have this, as a reminder of our meeting.'

I took it. It was like a ring without its shank; one side was a smooth disc of red stone, on its other, set into a bed of gold, was an oval of translucent milky substance bearing the impression of a lamb. I didn't know what to say; it seemed so very precious.

'It is an Agnus Dei,' she told me.

'The Lamb of God.'

'You know your Latin. Good girl.' There was that smile again, deep and inviting. 'It has been blessed by His Holiness the Pope,' she whispered, 'and will protect you. But do *not* let anyone see it. I'm afraid these days an Agnus Dei can visit trouble on its owner.' She sighed and the smile disappeared. 'But earthly trouble is sometimes the price we must pay for heavenly grace.'

I wanted to ask what she meant, how could it at once protect and visit trouble; but I said nothing.

Less than three years later the Queen of Scotland was gone. I wondered if she had been executed because she no longer had the protection of her Agnus Dei.

Tap, tap, tap.

My fingers wander now to the silk purse that hangs from my girdle containing my treasures: the weighted die that Uncle Henry gave me once, to remind me things aren't always as they seem; the tiny bell from Geddon's collar; the fold of parchment containing a lock of my husband's hair; the smooth crystal drop from the glassworks at Hardwick; the scrap of paper bearing Mistress Lanyer's poem; it is about me, but a me I no longer know. Right at the bottom, beneath everything, is the Agnus Dei, blessed by the Pope. It has not protected me very well.

Tap, tap, tap.

Clerkenwell

A sheaf of papers lands on the table with a thunk, sending out a billow of dust. It is tied with a length of faded ribbon that might have once been crimson. Motes jig and twirl as if alive in a shaft of sun that falls through the open window. Ami feels a sneeze build then dissipate at the back of her nose.

'What are they?' She puts the loaf she is carrying by the window to cool and picks up the papers.

'Smells good.' Hal reaches out to break a piece of bread off. She slaps his hand away, laughing.

He smiles that bright smile of his and taps the papers in her hand. 'From Lady Arbella's effects.'

'Lady Arbella.' She carefully lays the papers back on the table, fearing they might disintegrate beneath her fingers.

Her son seems distracted now, whistling and searching for something, patting down his doublet, then delving in the large leather bag that hangs on the back of the door, then in the chest, his head disappearing. 'A man I know was charged with clearing out her rooms.' His voice is muffled. 'He thought you might be interested in them; said he remembered you'd dedicated a poem to her. I told him you knew her once. You did know her, didn't you?'

'That's right,' she says.

Her mind wanders back to the last time she saw Lady Arbella. An image springs up from the past, that distant gaze, the russet frizz, an echo of the old Queen, scraped back and tamed beneath her cap, her sharply pronounced clavicles and thin graceful arms. They were in the stable yard at Richmond Palace; it must have been more than a decade ago. Lady

Arbella rarely looked directly at anyone which earned her, wrongly, a reputation for aloofness, but she had cast an indecipherable look at Ami and asked, 'Are you my friend?'

Ami remembers the formality of her reply: 'My Lady, I would never presume to call myself your friend, but you have my firm loyalty and love.' A flash of sadness had scudded over the other woman's face. It made Ami realize how lonely life must be for one so highborn, how much she must have yearned for ordinary friendship, and she regretted having not simply said, 'Yes, I am your friend.' Friendship had seemed impossible in the gulf of hierarchy that separated them, but there was no doubt that that was what it was.

Ami feels the old tangle of remorse; deep in a neglected part of her heart she knows it was she who caused the final misfortune – the greatest one. She had longed to beg forgiveness but it was not to be. In the end she failed her friend. She can hear those words, can still hear the rage in them: *If this fails, I will never forgive you.*

Hal continues, pulling her out of the past: 'He said he'd get nothing for them, so you may as well have them.'

'Are they letters?'

'I don't know, not letters, just scribblings, I think.'

If not letters then Ami feels sure she knows what they are. It was she who suggested to Lady Arbella that she take Book VI of Ovid's *Metamorphoses* and turn it into a drama. They had discussed it many times and Ami had sent her early drafts of her own poetry, but she had never seen a word of Lady Arbella's *Tragedy of Philomel*. She'd concluded it was never written. But here it is.

She takes a cursory look at one or two pages and lifts the sheaf to her nose, imagining some vestige of her friend's scent has remained, but the prevailing smell is of dust. The dense text is a painful reminder of how long it is since she herself has set down words in any meaningful way. Not since her book was published four years ago has she been able to write, no matter how great, how desperate, her desire. It is as if her muse has deserted her irretrievably.

She has suspicions that the thicket of guilt entangling her is to blame; but with the arrival of this – a bubble of hope expands in her – she might find a release from that and with it the inspiration to write once more. She is tempted to sit down now and make a closer study, but would rather wait until she is alone, for she is sure that once she starts to read she will not be able to stop.

Hal continues to rummage, still whistling. She is struck suddenly by his looks; he has become a man, dark and chiselled, whilst her back was turned.

'What are you looking for?'

'Those new strings for my lute.'

'I strung it for you yesterday.' She crosses the room and takes the lute down from the high shelf where it lives with a jumble of other instruments, passing it to him. She cannot play very well, though she should, for she is the daughter, sister, widow and mother of musicians, but she can string and tune a lute faster than any of them.

'What would I do without you, Ma?'

'I'm sure you would manage.'

It is *she* who would not manage, were Hal to go. He is bound to want to wed before long and then what will she do? She cannot bear to think of herself as one of those burdensome mothers-in-law, sharing these two cramped Clerkenwell rooms with her son and his bride. She pushes that worry aside; Hal has no mind to marry just yet.

'Look,' he says. 'The tabby's caught its first mouse.' He is pointing to the corner where the cat is eviscerating a small carcass. Hal had rescued the tabby a few months ago from the water butt and brought it back to life, letting it suck milk from the corner of a linen cloth at hourly intervals.

'She'll be earning her keep soon,' Ami says. 'Come on, you mustn't be late for the music master.' Taking Hal's hand, she can feel the calluses on the pads of his fingers, the result of a decade of teasing sounds from catgut.

As he throws his coat on she sees a flash of his father in his profile, not her husband, Alphonso, who died three years ago and left her deep in debt, but his true father, the man she loved and spent her reputation on.

She still feels a sense of loss when she thinks of Henry Hunsdon, though he is long gone; she never garnered that depth of feeling for her husband. But Alphonso gave her respectability and a name for her son; for that she is grateful. Mind you, he was paid handsomely for the favour. She often wonders if she was right to keep Hal ignorant of his true origins. And that is not all she hasn't told him; he is not aware that Alphonso left her without two pennies to rub together. That was the reason she had to leave the spacious house in Bishopsgate for these mean lodgings, though she'd told Hal the old house was too much for her to manage and too full of ghosts. She doesn't want him beset with worry when he has the chance to make his mark in the world.

She will manage – she always has – but in the time since Alphonso departed, her debts have escalated and the trickle of money that came from the sales of her book has run dry.

'Have you packed everything you might need? Not forgotten your clean stockings, your blanket in case it's chilly at night?'

'Ma!' He is disgruntled. 'I'm not an infant!'

'I can't help worrying.'

'Well, don't. I can very well look after myself. I am only going to court, not to the moon.' His tone shifts and he adopts a look of concern. 'You won't be lonely, will you?'

'No, of course not.' She takes a breath, girding herself for his departure. 'This will keep me occupied.' She points to the papers on the table, feeling a whirr of anticipation, wondering what they might contain.

'They said the Lady Arbella was cracked in the head, is that right?'

'You don't want to believe everything you hear. Now go. You'll be late.'

She carries his lute to the door for him and, picking up the cat, stands watching as he walks away, feeling her heart tighten.

Goodwife Stringer lumbers by, hefting a large basket of apples, and flashes a slanted look Ami's way. The houses on this street are pressed tight up against one another, like crowded teeth, and their neighbour cannot keep herself to herself. Barely an hour goes by without an encounter with Goodwife Stringer.

'Boy left home, has he, Widow Lanyer?' she says, putting her basket down with a huff of breath. Her sculpted features make her the sort that might be described as handsome, but the effect is spoiled by a permanently welded scowl.

'He's only going for two weeks.'

There is something a little hostile about the woman's tone, which puts Ami on her guard. Goodwife Stringer is well known in the parish for putting her nose in other people's business.

'All on your own, then?' she pauses. Ami says nothing, just maintains her position in the doorway, straight as a sentry. 'I s'pose you know that a witch is to be hung later.' The woman's eyes move slowly from Ami's face to the tabby in her arms and back again. 'They say *she* had a cat that spoke to her.'

'I doubt that's true.'

Goodwife Stringer is silent and continues boring her through with that stare.

'If you have something to say to me . . .' Ami can feel

tendrils of wariness reaching up her body. There has been a frenzy of suspicion about witchcraft since the Scot James took the throne and it can catch like wildfire. Any nail that sticks up must be hammered down.

'I *do* have something to say to you, Widow Lanyer.' Her eyes fix on Ami's. 'I suppose you won't be happy till you have turned the world on its head with your *poetry*.' She says the word as if it is an expletive. 'If Eve is free of sin, as you choose to believe, then why did God give us women the pain of childbirth? I ask you that.'

Ami knows it is futile to engage in theological exegesis but can't resist asking, 'Have you read my book, then?'

The woman stutters, clearly wants to say that she has but can't quite seem to allow herself the lie. 'There is no need to read it. Everybody knows what it says.'

'Well, if you know what it says then you will be aware that I do not suggest that Eve is without sin. I merely propose that Adam is the more culpable for being the stronger and yet still allowing himself to be led to temptation.' She shouldn't really bother, for such women will think what they want. Besides she doubts whether Goodwife Stringer can read more than a grocer's bill, so her opinions must be based on hearsay, and there has been enough of that.

It was inevitable that her book, like the women in it, would be misunderstood. In court circles it was celebrated for its subtlety of thought, amongst the women at least. But four long years have passed since she visited court.

The Chief Minister, Salisbury, had taken her aside and told her: 'The King does not welcome women who get above themselves. Your poems have caused offence to His Majesty and, acting on his royal command, I am expelling you from court.'

Queen Anna had shown Ami some kindness, told her she was very sorry, that she and all her women found her poetry 'marvellous', but that she had no influence with her husband and his decision was final. As a consolation the Queen had offered her a jewel, a large ruby set with pearls, as a parting gift. A 'nest egg' she had called it. Ami keeps it safe, beneath a floorboard under the bed. It is the one thing the debt collectors will not get their hands on.

Goodwife Stringer has begun to shuffle from one foot to another.

'I am sure you are busy,' Ami says firmly. 'I wish you a good day.'

'Indeed!' The woman seems incapable of even forcing out a goodbye as she picks up her basket and trundles off, muttering something under her breath.

Ami shuts her front door, having to use all her self-control to resist slamming it, but as she remembers the sheaf of papers on the table her anger disperses. She opens the shutters fully to allow in more light and cuts a slice of bread for herself. It is still warm and soft enough to need no butter, which is just as well for there is none. She crams it into her mouth and takes another slice, enjoying the fact that she is alone and has no witness to her greed; it is a comfort and she has blessed few of those these days.

The shaft of sun has shifted and falls directly over the papers on the table as if they are haloed. In a moment of fancy Ami sees it as a sign, laughing inwardly at herself for indulging such whimsy. She turns over the sheaf, where is written *The Lady Arbella – TO BE DISCARDED*.

She sifts through the ream, casting a cursory glance over each page. It is not the *Tragedy of Philomel* she'd expected, that is immediately clear. Some of it is written in a beautiful precise hand, but most is tangled and illegible, scrawled manically as if written in desperation to expel something. Like an exorcism; Ami is surprised at her analogy, wonders where it came from. There seems to be no chronology but some of the pages are dated and she tries to impose a semblance of order over them.

Excitement begins to prod at her, for this document is better than that unwritten tragedy. The disjointed and barely decipherable pages seem to recount a life, Lady Arbella's life. It slowly dawns on Ami that she might discover, somewhere in these pages, what truly became of her dear friend. Also, hope springs up suddenly – and with it those excoriating words: *If this fails, I will never forgive you* – these scrawls, like a code to be broken, could reveal whether Lady Arbella had ever found a shred of forgiveness for the friend who failed her.

Hampton Court

Dodderidge, who had accompanied me on the journey from Derbyshire, came to a halt at a pair of carved doors and consulted the piece of paper on which a steward had drawn a crude plan of the corridors of Hampton Court.

'I believe we are here, My Lady,' he said, and must have seen the anxiety on me for he added, 'Don't worry. The Queen won't be there, just some of her ladies, and besides, your aunt will be arriving from London within two hours at most.'

'Can't you come in with me?' I knew full well it was a futile request, that one didn't invite one's retainer into the Queen's rooms. Grandmother had made sure I understood the courtly protocol to the letter. We had made a brief visit to court the year before, when I was still only twelve and might have been forgiven for not knowing exactly how to behave. Anyway Grandmother had stuck to me like gum Arabic to ensure all went smoothly. But this was different; I was to stay for three weeks with Aunt Mary for company. It was on our arrival that a messenger came to announce my aunt's delay on the route from London.

On the long ride south I relished the idea that Grandmother thought me old enough to conduct myself properly alone. I felt fully adult, mounted on my new horse, Dorcas, a coal-black mare, a hand higher even than Dodderidge's imposing mount. Dorcas was young, too big for me and too wild according to almost everyone, though when I rode her she was docile as a kitten and made me feel capable of anything. But the minute I dismounted in the yard and Dorcas was led away by a groom, my nerves gathered.

'No . . . wait,' I called to the lad, who stopped, turned and dipped his head, sliding his cap off. I ran over. 'She will need a good drink before she has her oats, and not too many as she's prone to colic if she eats too much after a journey . . .' I was babbling. When the horse dealer first brought Dorcas into the yard at Chatsworth and she sidled over to me, whickering and nudging her soft muzzle into my shoulder, I knew she was mine. They say you know instantly with a horse, like finding a kindred spirit. Grandmother had taken some convincing but had relented eventually on seeing how obliging the mare was with me, how at the slightest command she would do my bidding. Riding her was the closest I could imagine to flight.

'Understood, My Lady,' said the boy, who, I noticed, was tapping an impatient foot. It hadn't occurred to me that he must have had a dozen other horses to see to and that the delay might bring him trouble. I hadn't been raised to think of others' needs and was blithely inconsiderate back then. I wrapped my arms about Dorcas's broad black neck and rested my head against her, breathing in her scent, leather and sweat, closing my eyes for a moment before allowing the lad to lead her off towards the stables, feeling the wrench of her departure.

Had I not been where I was I would have followed them. Grandmother had said I was too old to always be larking about in the stable block, that I needed taming and to learn how to comport myself like a lady. That meant being shut inside most of the time doing needlework as far as I could tell. My embroidery skills were frustratingly poor, so I'd begun to spend more and more time with my tutor, translating passages from Latin to English and then to Greek, which Grandmother approved of. Since I was to be queen one day – though at the time the idea seemed both intangible and, if I thought about it too deeply, quite terrifying – my education was of the greatest importance. But even my fascination for learning didn't quite eradicate the lure of the stables.

Dodderidge was waiting patiently – I never knew a more patient man. He was scrutinizing the plan, occasionally glancing up towards the building as if to assess which windows matched up with the route we were to take to the ladies' rooms. A man approached him to ask where my luggage was to be taken. Dodderidge towered over the fellow. (Dodderidge towered over everyone and, though he was still quite young then, he walked with an old man's stoop that only served to make him seem taller still, and meant that his fine fair hair flopped forward permanently into his eyes.) He counted the bags and chests as they were carried off towards my aunt's rooms and sent my two maids in their wake.

He and I marched side-by-side up the steps and into the great hall, where a crowd had gathered about a troupe of musicians, and on past the guards, who nodded us through into the watching chamber, where groups of well-dressed men played cards and dice and servants threaded their way about busily. Beyond was a clamour of people all seeking entry where we were going, their way barred by more guards who stood aside sharply to admit us when Dodderidge informed them who I was. The long gallery was tightly packed with milling courtiers dressed up like a muster of peacocks. As we moved through at a funereal pace I became aware of the curious glances and could hear two girls in whispered conversation behind me.

'Who is she?'

'It's the Lady Arbella Stuart.'

'Looks like a Tudor with that red hair.'

'All the Stuarts are Tudors; didn't you know?'

'How so?'

'Her great-grandmother was Margaret Tudor, the eighth

Henry's sister. She was wed to a Scottish king – surely you know that?'

It was a strange thing, hearing myself talked of like that, and as Dodderidge shepherded me through and people dipped as I passed, I sensed myself fill with importance, beginning to understand what I had been raised to know but had never yet felt: my elevated position in that courtly melee.

Once beyond the long gallery and past more guards the place became quite empty of people, save for the odd scurrying servant. The web of corridors necessitated frequent consultation of the plan, and as we passed into ever more private areas my nerves began to prod. I might have turned and run but the carved doors were opening and Dodderidge was handing me in to the usher, who announced me loudly – 'The Lady Arbella Stuart' – so there was no going back.

The room was of quite modest proportions and contained a dozen women, none of whom I had set eyes on before. They were all decked magnificently, making me understand why my maid had insisted I wear the embellished gown I was trussed into, and I thanked her silently for her bullying. I was hustled around, inspected thoroughly by curious eyes, and introduced to all present, but my nerves made their names slip out of my head. I wished desperately for the formidable presence of Grandmother – Grandmother who knew all the rules – when only minutes before I had been luxuriating in my freedom from her.

'How is dear Lady Shrewsbury?' said someone.

'She is exceedingly well,' I replied.

'Too busy building houses to join us at court, I suppose.'

'She *is* very busy,' I replied. Someone less green than I was then might have noticed the slightly disapproving tone. People, I learned later in life, could not quite reconcile themselves to success, particularly in a woman, and always sought subtly to undermine it. Those women would have been acutely aware that Grandmother, though she was the countess to one of England's greatest earls and a friend of long standing to the Queen, was born a Derbyshire squire's daughter, albeit one with a canny instinct for making the right connections: she had married-up four times and amassed great wealth with her astute dealings. Despite her humble origins, she had the ultimate trump card in me, for none of those blue-bloods at court had a granddaughter who was heir to the throne. But I was oblivious to that complex web of hierarchy then.

I finally landed on a bench.

'Aren't you to be matched with the Duke of Parma?' my neighbour, an ancient lady, the Countess of somewhere, had asked me.

I couldn't think of a satisfactory response. It was the first I'd heard of such a match and my insides began to shrivel at the idea of being sent off to a foreign court to wed a stranger. I was floundering for a response when, thankfully, the ancient countess continued. 'I thought the idea was that a marriage contract between the Queen's heir and the Spanish King's cousin might put an end to his plans to invade.'

'That is likely,' I said, pleased with my non-committal answer. No one had spoken to me directly about marriage or anything else, but Grandmother had impressed upon me the importance of always appearing as if I knew exactly what was going on and to 'act like the heir to the throne and don't smile, it will make you seem meek and ingratiating'. The talk of imminent invasion had even reached Derbyshire and the servants chattered about it constantly, but then I suppose they'd all known the Queen of Scots in one way or another and the Spaniards were, by all accounts, bent on vengeance for her death. She had died a traitor, or a martyr, it depended which way you saw it.

That day, a year earlier, when the news arrived of the Scottish Queen's execution was indelibly inked into my memory.

I'd overheard my step-grandfather, the Earl of Shrewsbury, who had witnessed the event, discussing it with his steward: *. . . butchered her, hacked at her neck. It was inhuman. To do such a thing to an anointed queen . . . I will be damned for it. I wish she had never fallen into my orbit.* I was horrified – that kindly woman I'd once met, hacked at as if she were nothing more than a length of timber. The earl had her little dog beneath his arm. I recognized it, remembered it sitting on her lap and her hand squeezing mine, the warmth of her smile. Nausea washed up my body. *And this creature,* the earl continued, *will not leave off pining. I can't bring myself to drown it.*

I still, even after all these years, have the bell from Geddon's collar in my bag of treasures – small objects that bring me a thin kind of comfort.

The ancient countess was looking at me, waiting for me to say something else. My vague response was clearly not enough for her. 'I'm not entirely sure I would relish marriage to a Catholic,' I offered, feeling rather pleased with myself, for Grandmother had pressed upon me the importance of advertising my faith. The old woman nodded approvingly.

Another voice entered the conversation. '*Something* must be done, for that Spaniard's armada is almost built, and he will send it our way; you mark my words.' This was my neighbour on the other side, who was fidgeting with her fan. Fidgeting was another trait that, like smiling, revealed weakness and which Grandmother insisted I conquer.

'We are to hear a story from Ovid, I believe,' said the countess, ignoring the fidgeting lady as if she hadn't spoken at all.

I knew a little of Ovid, enough to be aware that most of the stories were deemed unsuitable for someone of my age, and so a little flame of anticipation lit in me. At thirteen, any glimpse into the mysteries of the adult world is a thrill and I was not to be disappointed.

A woman walked forward to stand at the centre of the chamber with an open book in her hands.

'I don't know her. Who is she?' asked the countess.

'Henry Hunsdon's mistress. Musician's daughter, I think,' replied the fidgeter.

'Gracious me, she's young enough to be his granddaughter.'

I found myself captivated by that woman who was someone's mistress, a fact that made her seem to my young and cloistered self immediately a little dangerous. Her hair was black and thick and glossy as Dorcas's mane, and her eyes too were dark, set deeply above the angular planes of her cheeks and framed by arched brows. In contrast, her skin was pale, but nothing like as light as the almost blue-white complexions of most of the women in the room. Her difference to them was striking, making it hard for me to tear my gaze away from her, and I wondered if that was beauty.

She began to recite. Her voice, as richly captivating as her looks, drew each woman listening into the story, as if falling under a spell. The poem told of the marriage of the King of Thrace to Procne, one of a pair of sisters. It was not a myth I knew, which gave me hope that it might be one of the unsuitable ones, and as it unfurled it became clear that this was so. The King of Thrace's uncontainable attraction to his wife's lovely sister, Philomel, led him to ravage her. I felt a forbidden thrill tug at me, the story winding about my imagination, as Philomel vowed her vengeance: *for this wickedness full dearly thou shalt pay . . . my voice the very woods shall fill.*

I felt the room garner behind that imaginary heroine, each one of us inside her mind craving revenge, willing her to shout her attacker's crime from the treetops. But the reader paused, leaving us suspended an eternal second, before continuing.

... That drawing out his naked sword that at his girdle hung,
He took her rudely by the hair, and wrung her hands behind
   her,
Compelling her to hold them there while he himself did
   bind her.
When Philomel saw the sword, she hoped she should have
   died,
And for the same her naked throat she gladly did provide . . .

A shift of timbre in her voice and all at once the entire
listening company had flung their hands over their mouths in
shock.

... And with a pair of pincers fast did catch her by the tongue,
And with his sword did cut it off. The stump whereon it
   hung . . .
Did patter still. The tip fell down and quivering on the ground
As though that it had murmured it made a certain sound . . .

The fidgeting lady to my left emitted a horrified howl, 'He
cut out her tongue,' and grabbed at my arm.

I snatched it back, shaking her grip away. 'Don't touch
me!' It came out as a shout, sufficiently loud to silence the
room. All eyes turned, causing my face to burn and my heart
to clatter and making me wish for Grandmother's wing to
hide beneath.

'Why ever not?' asked the countess.

Grandmother's careful schooling ran through my head
and I quoted her verbatim: 'Because I am to be queen and it
is correct to seek my permission before touching my person.'

A few snorts of laughter erupted around the chamber and
the countess said, '*That* is not how we do things here at court.
Almost every one of these ladies here has royal blood of one
kind or another . . .' She continued, talking on about Edward
III and his thirteen children, but I wasn't listening. All I was

aware of was my burning skin and the whispers and cupped hands and flickering glances.

'*Noli me tangere*,' blurted someone with a burst of laughter.

'She's only royal, not divine,' laughed another.

I yearned to disappear and considered running out, back through the tangle of corridors to the stables and Dorcas – riding her all the way Derbyshire at a gallop. How could I have known then how that odious term would stick to me? I would for years, well beyond Elizabeth's reign, be known as '*Noli me tangere*' – 'Touch me not'. Never to my face, of course, but I would not be allowed to forget that initial humiliation.

It was Lady Rich who came to my rescue. I didn't know who she was then but she appeared as if from nowhere. 'Leave the poor child alone.' She crouched down to my level and smiled broadly. Grandmother's voice passed through my head: *Don't smile, it will make you seem meek.* But there was nothing enfeebling about Lady Rich's smile; on the contrary, it was dazzling and made her seem like the only person in the place worth looking at.

'Ignore them,' she said quietly. 'They'd all kill each other to have a drop of your blood, so hold your head high and make for the door. I will be right behind you.'

Once we were out of earshot she said: 'What a collection of small-minded old crows, they are. Don't listen to them.' She laughed in an abandoned burst, throwing her head back before turning to me. 'I am Penelope Devereux, or Lady Rich for those who prefer, and your aunt sent word asking that I keep an eye on you until she arrives.'

'Then your father is the Earl of Essex?' I said, glad to remember the Devereuxs in Grandmother's great book of the peerage.

'Was,' she replied. 'It is my brother who is now the earl.'

'I'm so sorry.' I felt crushed at having made yet another

faux pas – how could I have forgotten the famous, young Earl of Essex – but she smiled that dazzling smile once more.

'For goodness' sake, how would you have known. You've not been here five minutes. You've never seen my brother.' She paused and I noticed how people gawped at her as we passed. If I had wondered about the dark woman's unusual beauty I was sure of Lady Rich's. It was not only her obvious qualities – the tumbling golden hair, the bright black-star eyes that the poets had written of – it was also her sheer presence that seemed to diminish all those around her. 'Wait until you do,' she added. Making me wonder if the brother was at all like her.

'It's a shame we missed the end of the poem,' she continued. 'Do you know the story?'

I shook my head.

'No, I suppose you're thought too young for such things.'

We walked on in silence until eventually we arrived at my aunt's rooms, where my maids were unpacking and Dodderidge was checking items off on a list.

As Lady Rich made to leave I asked, 'How does the story of Philomel end?'

She looked at me for a moment as if deciding how to phrase her response. 'Well, let's just say the sisters got their revenge but the price was high and the gods turned Philomel into a nightingale to save her from her brother-in-law's wrath.'

I wanted to ask more, to know what Philomel's revenge was and its high price, but she had disappeared down the passage before I could form my question.

I did not have to wait long to find out if the Earl of Essex was like his sister. He was seated to my right at supper and she was on his other side. They were a gilded pair, as if God had used up all His quota of charisma when making them. I hardly dared look at him.

The Queen was to my left. Of course I had been filled with trepidation on encountering her but she made a great fuss of me, which made *me* feel gilded too. I felt quite at home in her presence, for she was intimidating in much the same way as Grandmother – strict, self-possessed, guarded – so I knew exactly how to behave to gain her approval. She talked to me of Grandmother with fondness, told me she had known her almost all her life and that she hoped she would accompany me to court the next time.

'Your grandmother is one of the most astute women I know,' she said. 'I admire her greatly.'

The Queen ate with her gloves on. I had never seen that before, all the grease soaking into the chamois making it dark. They were replaced swiftly, by a servant, between courses, allowing me a glimpse of her age-spotted hands. She, like Grandmother, didn't really smile, though her brown eyes flashed occasionally if something amused her. Supper was a sedate affair, a musician strumming quietly nearby, the soft babble of conversation, and the Queen carefully sipping watered wine and eating little.

The presence of Essex on my other side pulsated, igniting in me a kind of profound and inexplicable embarrassment. I had never been at such close proximity to such a creature. He smelled of flowers, a thick scent like hyacinths, I had never known a man to smell like that, not even Uncle Henry, whom Grandmother always said was 'given to flamboyance'. His hair fell in glossy dark tendrils and his eyes, though I didn't dare look at them properly, were a piercing violet blue. His manner with the Queen was shockingly casual. He spoke across me to her, saying something to the effect that she was looking comely, as if she were some wench in the laundry and not the Queen of England.

She leaned over and pinched his cheek, quite hard, leaving a pink blot, saying, 'Bad boy,' whereupon he laughed, murmuring, 'You know you're fond of it.'

The French ambassador and his wife were presented later in the evening and she said, placing one of those gloved hands lightly on my head, 'One day she will be even as I am.' I noticed a whisper pass round the chamber as her words were repeated from mouth to ear. I saw Lord Burghley and his unprepossessing son Robert Cecil nod between themselves in approval. I knew them as great friends of Grandmother's. She had told me that the court danced to Burghley's tune but that it would not seem so. That was his gift, she said, to seem innocuous, and that I was to make a good impression on him and his son, for it would set me in good stead.

As I was distracted watching that seemingly innocuous pair, Essex leaned in to me and said very quietly, 'I hear you are a cold fish, Arbella Stuart,' not using my title, as he should have. I was quite light-headed with the whiff of that lush floral scent and grappled for a response when he added, 'My sister says you don't like to be touched.'

I didn't know if he was mocking me.

'Lost your tongue?' he said.

I was reminded of Philomel – inevitably – and her severed tongue.

Then, beneath the table, he took his index finger and stroked it slowly over the back of my hand. I dared not move a hair. The place where his finger had met my skin felt seared, as if he had branded me. 'But your birth and blood give you the right to remoteness and, cold fish or not, I plan to wed you when you are old enough to –' He stopped mid-sentence and turned away to speak to someone else, leaving me hanging.

I racked my brains to think of what he might have meant

to say. Did he not know I was to be promised to the Duke of Parma, whoever that was? I saw that Robert Cecil had his eyes fixed firmly on Essex as if he had been trying to lip-read. The look on his face was stony and he turned to say something to his father, who in turn looked towards the earl. It made me suddenly feel out of my depth and I was glad when Aunt Mary finally arrived and asked permission that I might retire for the night.

As we were preparing for bed and I stood in nothing but my thin shift while my maid rummaged in the trunk for my nightgown, Aunt Mary said, 'Look, sweeting, you are becoming a woman.' She pointed at me. I followed the direction of her finger down to my chest, where the outline of my new bud breasts was visible through the fine linen. I crossed my arms firmly over them, turning away, pretending to look for something so I didn't have to meet her gaze. I didn't want to become a woman. All the talk of marriage had unsettled me.

'Have your monthlies started?' she asked, oblivious to my discomfort.

'No.' I pretended to search for something in my jewellery box, removing its contents and replacing them item by item.

'May I?' she asked, holding up a comb.

I nodded, allowing her to stroke it through my hair. It was a familiar ritual, the asking and granting of permission, and seemed entirely natural, but I was reminded of those taunting women and felt an echo of the earlier humiliation. Then a question surfaced in my mind: would my husband have to ask my permission? Just the idea of it – the act – mortified me.

'Do you eat properly?' asked Aunt Mary as she teased a knot out of my frizz of hair. 'If you don't eat properly it can prevent your monthlies from starting.'

I said nothing but my mind was whirring. She had unwittingly given me a solution. I would not become a woman.

We settled into the bed and she said, 'You did well this evening, sweeting, acted far beyond your years. The Queen was impressed, Burghley and Cecil too; that counts for a lot.' She was quiet a moment and I felt glad to have her beside me. In the dim candlelight I could see my mother in her face, her uncomplicated gaze, her generous mouth and the cloud of wild chestnut hair that was escaping from her nightcap. 'What did Essex say to you?'

I thought I oughtn't tell her but did. 'He said he'd marry me one day.'

She huffed out a sigh. 'I wouldn't listen to that, if I were you. It won't be Essex who decides where you will wed.'

'Am I to be wed to the Duke of Parma, then?'

'Heaven knows,' she replied. 'I suspect the Queen is trying to win him over with a promise she has no intention of delivering.'

'So I won't be wed to him?'

'It's unlikely, I'd say. I doubt she'd want you married to a Catholic and producing heirs of the wrong faith.'

I wanted to ask her more but she sounded slightly bitter, I didn't know why, and then she leaned over to snuff out the candle before saying in the dark something I'd heard more times than I could count from Grandmother: 'Shame you were not born a boy, things would be much more straightforward.'

I touched my fingers to the bud breasts, pressing them hard as if to push them back inside.

Clerkenwell

A bang at the door wakes Ami. She is momentarily disorientated and realizes she must have fallen asleep reading. There is another bang, this time accompanied by a shout. She assumes it is Hal, until she remembers he left for court the day before. Lady Arbella's papers are spread over her lap. *Shame you were not born a boy*: the memory of what she was reading before she'd dropped off sidles back to her.

It had been slow going; the papers were half destroyed and barely legible in places, scrawled as if written in urgency, the ink smeared and smudged. She has found no sign yet that she was forgiven. But to find herself briefly there – her younger self – was like a glimpse of her own half-obscured reflection in a window. She'd been nineteen and acutely aware of her lack of nobility among those terrifying women, who looked down on her for her low birth and perceived loose morals. They resented being forced into grudging politeness, for Henry Hunsdon was the Queen's first cousin and it wouldn't do to upset his young mistress. They'd all assumed she'd be discarded in a month but she hadn't been. Six years she'd loved Henry Hunsdon and he her, confounding them all.

Ami remembered the incident. Lady Arbella – just an unsmiling, big-eyed girl of thirteen then, with nobility stitched through her – abruptly leaving the reading. She hadn't understood at the time what had happened, didn't know what to make of the biblical snippet of Latin: *Noli me tangere*. Perhaps the child was frightened by the story. Truth be told, she'd been glad that the girl hadn't had to hear about how Procne murdered her son and served him up to his father. Those Greeks, the lengths they would go for revenge!

She is pondering on the coincidence that she'd thought the writings might be that very same tragedy transformed to drama by Lady Arbella when another bang jolts her properly awake.

'Widow Lanyer. You know the reason I am here. My patience is wearing thin.' She hates being called 'Widow'; it makes her feel as if her time is spent. She may be forty-six years old but there is life in her yet. There is a currency in widows, but they must be either young or rich and she is neither.

'Widow Lanyer!' It is Mansfield here for payment – again. One of his men replaced a number of tiles for her last winter and made some other repairs to her falling-down dwelling. Mansfield is respected here in Clerkenwell; a man who has pulled himself up by his own boot straps. She doesn't want to get on his wrong side but there's little she can do; she knows she hasn't the means to settle the bill.

She continues to sit motionless, hoping he will assume she is out, but can't help thinking of the bucket half filled with rainwater that sits in the upstairs bedchamber – testimony to yet another lost tile. She supposes that Hal will be paid for his services at the palace. Thanks to Queen Anna's inexhaustible enthusiasm for masques and entertainments, there are opportunities. But it will be a pittance; most of the musicians have their own means, or a benefactor of one kind or another, and play at court for the status. It will go no way to settle the debts that are building up. Mansfield is not her only creditor.

He is knocking at the window now; she can see his outline through the thick glass. She can no longer afford the fine panes she was once accustomed to and her mind turns to wondering whether the chance opportunities of her youth have left her unprepared for the straitened circumstances she finds herself in. Thinking back to the comforts of her childhood under the wing of a countess, a woman who saw in Ami, lowly born as she undeniably was, some spark of intelligence that pleased her, she cannot help but feel a sense of loss. Ami's father had been her lutenist; she'd taken pity when both he and Ami's mother had died in the same week.

She consoles herself with the reminder that she may no longer have the luxuries of her early years, nor the illustrious connections and the sense that doors would open with ease, as if well oiled, but what she will never lose is the education that the countess had invested in her. And what is education if it is not a means to opening doors?

Mansfield has his face pressed right up to the glass now, his forehead flattened and yellow. 'I can see you there. Open up!'

She puts the papers to one side and pulls herself out of the chair, still fuzzy with sleep, making for the door which she opens ajar.

'I'm so very sorry, Mister Mansfield, but I haven't the means to pay you.'

'Every time! What is your excuse now?' His tone is bereft of sympathy.

'I have no excuse –' She is about to tell him of Hal's employment at the palace but he shoves the door open, pushes her aside and steps into the room.

He is a broad man with a shock of straw-coloured hair and large hands. Mansfield started as a labourer and now has several working for him. He's known as a grafter; people like him and she supposes it is for the fact that he is a living demonstration that it is possible, with hard work, to go up in the world.

'I'm so sorry,' she says. 'Can I offer you something to drink? A cup of beer perhaps.'

He nods and makes a grunt of assent, seating himself

uninvited at the table. 'I find it hard to believe you are lacking in funds. Isn't there a book with your name on it?'

'I wish I could say my poems earned me a living, but sadly that is far from the case.'

'It is put about that you have noble patrons – ladies and countesses. Surely they will not see you go short?'

She pours a measure of beer into a leather cup and hands it to him. 'That may have once been true, but it is no longer so.'

'What is it about then, this book of yours?'

'It's about Eve.' She sees little point in explaining to him that the aim of her work was to excuse womankind's sins and his response proves her right.

'A book about a wicked woman? I'd have thought you wouldn't be able to print them fast enough.' He grins at her.

'It is not the kind of book you imagine. Do you think if it were as popular as you say, that I would be going about in a dress such as this?' She lifts her arms to show her sleeves where they are almost worn through at the elbows and scarred from where the pearls have been snipped off and sold. He clasps hold of one of them, stroking the threadbare fabric, allowing his hand to move further up, so the back of it skims her breast. Her breath stutters. It is a long time since she has been touched by a man in such a way.

'Perhaps, then, you can pay me in kind.' His mouth is slightly open and he inhales abruptly, as if attempting to keep control of himself.

Pulling her arm away, she says, 'Do you have some musical instruments that need mending? That I can do for you.' She is being disingenuous. She knows what he's getting at.

'I do have an instrument that needs attention, as it happens.' He brings a hand to the front of his breeches, laughing, seeming pleased with his joke.

She doesn't laugh. 'What is it? A lute? A viol?'

'Don't be coy with me.' He stands, grabbing her by the waist, and pushes her up against the table. 'You know exactly what I mean.' He is right up close so she can smell the beer and tobacco on his breath.

She turns her face away sharply. 'Take your hands off me, or I will shout for the neighbour.'

She doubts whether Goodwife Stringer would even respond, and if she did, seeing her in this unwanted clinch would only serve as evidence of Ami's perceived immorality and add fuel to the woman's suspicions.

'So you don't mind whoring if the man is noble enough, but not for scum like me.' He is growling tight to her ear, has pushed his hand right up under her skirts and is touching her. She struggles to get out of his grip. 'Your legs only open to access the court. Is that what you are saying?'

She will not dignify his comments with an explanation. His fingers continue to excavate her private parts. She crosses her legs tightly.

'I've heard it said that the nobleman who made you his mistress' – with this word a little shower of spit lands on her cheek, causing her to flinch and him in turn to grip her more tightly – 'was old enough to be your grandfather.'

There is barely a soul on this earth who believes the truth: that she loved Henry Hunsdon deeply despite his age and that she would have loved him just as much if he'd not been who he was.

'Remove your hands from me. I will not say it again.' She is surprised at how steady and firm her voice sounds.

He pushes himself up to her further so the hard edge of the table presses into the back of her thighs. His skin has the sharp yeasty smell of mouldy bread.

'Do you truly want this on your conscience? What will you say of it come Judgement Day?'

He steps back, dropping her, as if she is hot from the oven, turning away, hiding his shame.

She is at a loss to know who to turn to for help. If Hal knew, he would drop everything, take on labouring work to help pay the debt, but she will not draw him into this. He has a foothold at court and it could take him somewhere. Hal has a gift and soon it will be recognized; there will be some noble patron who will want to sponsor his talent. Were it not for her he could live with barely a care in the world, instead of having to keep a roof over his mother's head. She thinks of the Queen's jewel, the sole thing that has shored her up against destitution. It would fetch quite a price at one of the Cheapside dealers, though they would doubtless try to fleece her.

'If you give me a little time . . .' she begins, but stops herself. Even if she sells the jewel she doubts its price will cover her husband's debts. That jewel can surely serve her better.

She inwardly curses her dead husband for frittering away the money Hunsdon had bestowed on them. It was a large sum; vast, some might say. That is what it costs to buy a husband for your pregnant mistress to save her from public shame. She has often wondered what might have happened if Hunsdon had lived a few years longer.

Alphonso never liked her, always resented the circumstances. He loved the money, though, fancied himself as a gentleman, and it is surprising how short a time it can take for such a sum to disappear if you are determined to compete with the wealthy. He had invested what wasn't spent on gaudy fripperies in a hare-brained building scheme.

It makes her physically sick to think of it, for he not only lost everything but also found himself, through his own foolishness, owing a large sum to the blackguards who took his money in the first place. The only reason they are not beating her door down is the fact that they know she cannot pay them, but were she to sell her jewel and pay off Mansfield and his like, word would get out and they would soon be at her door. All this is running through her head while Mansfield eyes her from across the room.

'Time, you have had time enough.' He has his arms crossed over his chest and his gaze is direct to the point that she feels stripped naked. 'If you come to me willingly and give me what I ask, in a mere half-hour you will owe me less. We could make a regular thing of it.' He steps closer to her once more. She takes a stride backward.

Her mind continues to seek a solution. A half hour, it is so short a time? He is muscular beneath that jerkin, and strong, and is a good decade her junior. Would it be so very bad?

'Be your whore?'

'I wouldn't use that word. "Mistress" might serve us better.'

'Whatever you call it, it would be the same. Besides, do you not think you will be judged for adultery as much as for' – she cannot quite bring herself to call it rape – 'the other thing.'

'There would not be space enough in hell if all adulterers were sent there.'

Her thoughts are spinning in a vortex. What has she to offer but this?

Greenwich Palace

'By all accounts the Parma match is off again.'

Robert Cecil was talking quietly with Grandmother in the gardens of Greenwich Palace. He was a man so neatly put together, nothing out of place, he seemed to have walked directly out of a portrait. I wasn't supposed to hear; they thought me absorbed in my archery practice. But they were talking about me. My proposed marriage to the Duke of Parma had sunk along with the Spanish Armada four years before, but it had been raised again recently.

'Does she think no one sees her game?' said Grandmother bitterly. 'Now she is too old to be wed herself, she is using the promise of Arbella's hand as a makeweight in her foreign policy.'

It was true there had been a number of matches proposed for me, none of which, thank goodness, had come to fruition. I still assumed Essex would come for me, though why I believed that or even desired it I have no idea. Perhaps it was because I was sixteen, an age that brought with it such feelings of confusion and contradiction, making me at once abhor the idea of marriage and all that came with it yet harbour a secret desire for a man like Essex whom I had met only once.

Cecil had taken the end of his cape and was rubbing vigorously, fabric to fabric, at a small smear of dirt on his sleeve. I never saw Cecil wear anything but black and he was an odd-looking man, small and tidy though rather crookbacked and birdlike, with thin legs. He unsettled me, despite the fact that, according to Grandmother, he was a powerful friend to my cause. Even *Cecil* had touted himself once as a potential husband for me. 'So crooked Cecil sees himself wearing the crown matrimonial, does he?' Grandmother had said of it, clearly amused by the suggestion, for Cecil may have been the son of England's foremost statesman and Grandmother's greatest ally, but he lacked good enough blood for Lady Arbella Stuart.

It was my first visit back to court since the rout of the Spanish fleet. I'd been excited about it, felt I was on the brink of something, had an idea in my head about fulfilling my destiny, but as we were filing in to be presented to the Queen, I'd noticed some of the women firing glances my way and whispering. I thought I heard someone hiss, '*Noli me tangere*,' and was immediately catapulted back to that earlier, humiliating episode. Within hours I was wishing myself back in Derbyshire, where I could easily escape Grandmother's strict regime with daily rides into the hills. I had developed a bond with Dorcas that was unbreakable. My maid Margaret thought me daft for my love of that horse but Dorcas had become my friend and my confessor, and when I was with her out on the heath, with the wind in my face and the thunder of hooves the only sound, I felt invested with a supernatural power, as if I were a divine, sexless Artemis harnessing the forces of nature. It was a seductive feeling.

I continued listening: 'You can't disagree,' said Grandmother to Cecil. 'You know what the Queen is like. She's been manoeuvring pieces on the European chessboard for near on thirty-five years. She knows exactly what she's doing with all these marriage negotiations.' From the corner of my eye I saw her flick a hand in my direction.

I took aim. The bowstring was taut beneath my finger and it took all my strength to pull back. I lined my eye down the shaft of the arrow and released. It whistled as it took flight in a high curve and met the outer edge of the target.

'I'm out of practice,' I said, turning to Aunt Mary, tugging at the waist of my dress. 'This gown is too tight. I cannot move properly.' I'd had a whole new wardrobe made for court, which necessitated stillness and straightness, for the minute I slumped even slightly, hidden bones would dig at me, despite the spareness of my body, despite the hunger pangs I had learned to love as evidence of my ability to control the secret ministrations of my body. Margaret had begun to grow plump, fleshy mounds overspilling her dress. I saw it as a sign of weakness.

'I can adjust it for you,' said Margaret. 'Loosen your laces a little.' Her expression was sweet and guileless and I wondered what she must have thought of court and all the hard people there.

'I'm blaming my dress but I am a bad shot really.'

'It doesn't matter,' said Aunt Mary, looking at me across her own bow with a half-smile. The feather in her hat was broken, its end dangling. I reached forward and plucked it off, handing it to her. With Aunt Mary nothing ever seemed to stay in its right place, always a glove missing, or a fan misplaced, or hair rebelling against its style. 'There are better things to have a talent for. You may not be a good shot but you can speak Greek fluently.' She released a snort of laughter. 'My dear clever niece.'

We heard the rattle of arms and marching feet. Turning, we saw the Queen's guard tightly surrounding a group of women, making their way towards us through the gardens. Craning my neck, I saw a glimpse of the famous marmalade wig in amongst them. We all fell to our knees. I imagined finicky Robert Cecil distressed about the state of his silk stockings on the damp grass.

The royal party stopped, the guards parted and the Queen emerged. The sun was bright and clean in the wake of a recent shower and it lit her starkly, revealing things that were invisible in the candlelit interiors of the palace: the gaunt hollowness of her cheeks, the crêped texture of her skin, her jutting breastbone and the lines framing her thin lips, making them seem drawstring-fastened. I knew she was younger than Grandmother by six years; but she seemed older by far and had aged greatly since I was last at court.

It was no wonder people whispered that her end was nearing. It was dangerous talk; even I knew, naive as I was then, that it was treason to discuss the Queen's demise. I felt the wet soak through my dress to my knees, and kept my gaze firmly on the lavishly embroidered royal skirts.

Grandmother's eyes bored into me and I could hear her refrain in my mind: *Carry your head high. Eyes down for the Queen until she instructs you otherwise; anyone else, gaze beyond their shoulder. They must recognize they are beneath you from your bearing alone.*

Once instructed to do so, we rose and Grandmother complimented her on the loveliness of the gardens at Greenwich, saying how she would like to emulate them at Hardwick.

'I hear you are making extensions to your house there,' the Queen said. 'Do you never stop building, Bess?' She laughed and so did Grandmother, making them seem like dear old friends, which I supposed they were, even if they were rarely in each other's company.

Two of the Queen's maids were whispering, and one pointed at two men walking towards us from the river.

'Look,' said Margaret in my ear. 'Look who it is.'

It was Uncle Henry, who winked at me, but with him was the Earl of Essex, radiant in sky-blue satin. The sight of him caused a flush to run up my body as if I'd been dipped in a vat of soup. He smiled briefly at me. I turned away, remembering, as if it were only the day before and not four years, the burning trail of his finger on the back of my hand. Despite Aunt Mary's words I had thought of Essex often, had secretly imagined all sorts of scenarios in which he would arrive and fulfil that promise of marriage. What else was I to think about, tucked away in Derbyshire? Young girls will have such thoughts with the slightest encouragement, and I was no different, not then; it was an ordinary obsession I suppose.

Margaret stared at him open-mouthed and the two whispering maids giggled.

A page was offering a plate of sweetmeats, exquisite things glistening with sugar. They were stuffed into mouths with delighted 'mmmms' and 'ahhhhs' and half-mast eyes and everything suspended for a moment of pleasure. I shook my head as the page neared with the platter, a sense of invisible power welling from my resistance. The boy looked at me as if I were a miracle or mad or both and returned to offer more to the whispering women whose mouths were already engorged.

Uncle Henry came to stand beside me, still chewing, smelling of marchpane, reaching a hand out, burrowing it in the back of my ruff, pulling out a silver coin. 'I'm too old for those games, Uncle Henry.'

'Never too old for magic.' He tossed the shilling in the air and caught it, then opened his palm. It was empty; the coin was gone. I had seen him do it a thousand times.

'How did you do that?' gasped Margaret.

'Like I said, magic!'

Margaret's eyes were bright with wonder. She was the sort to believe in magic.

'Honestly, Brother,' said Aunt Mary. 'Will you never grow up?'

'Don't you find her impossibly bossy?' he whispered loudly to me, winking at his sister. 'What about Essex? He looks fine, don't you think?'

I shrugged as if I'd barely given the earl a second look but he *did* look fine. Inside I felt my heart bloat. I suppose I believed myself in love, there, in that moment, fool that I was.

The shilling had reappeared, dancing between Uncle Henry's fingers, flashing silver. He came in close, talking quietly so as not to be overheard. 'Essex was in terrible trouble with –' He nudged his head in the direction of the Queen. 'Banished for a few months. Got one of the Queen's maids in the family way. Married the girl; God knows why. Tried to keep it a secret.'

I remember the feeling clearly, just as when I had taken a fall out riding and winded myself. I'd thought myself dead, couldn't catch a breath. I wanted to shout: *It's not true, Essex is mine – he's mine!* That was the moment I grew up.

'Enough of that, Brother. Arbella doesn't need to hear that kind of inappropriate talk.'

If I'd been another kind of girl I might have cried, but I never cried. I picked up my bow and arrow, lifting it, lining it up with my eye, feeling my dress pulled exasperatingly tight across my shoulder.

'You haven't got it quite right.' I did not turn to look at Essex behind me, too close. 'Here, let me show you.' He took me by the elbows. All I could think of was that he was married; I wanted to slither away out of his hold but he had me tight, pressing his body against my own, suffocating me with that infernal hyacinth smell. I looked around for Grandmother, waiting for her to tell him I wasn't to be touched, to insist he release me, but she didn't appear to have seen. 'Lift your arm higher. Bend it more. That's right.' His face was pressed to mine, cheek-to-cheek, skin-to-skin, as he looked down the length of the arrow. Panic began to fizz up in me. 'Pull back!' He held my hand firmly – 'Keep your aim!' – pulling with me. 'Now release.'

As the arrow flew, he let me go and my panic frittered away. It landed with a twang at the very heart of the target. Margaret let out a squeal. Aunt Mary and Uncle Henry had begun to clap. 'That's how it's done.'

I looked round. The Queen had me in her sights, directing a steely frown in my direction. I stepped abruptly away from Essex, half tripping on a tussock of grass, righting myself on Uncle Henry's arm. He shoved me in the direction of Aunt Mary, as if I were leprous. Grandmother was frowning. I had done something wrong but I didn't know what. 'Give it to me,' the Queen said, reaching out for my bow. I felt all the eyes turn on us. 'Want to see it done properly?'

She took a lace handkerchief from her sleeve and handed it to one of her pages, who stooped to pick up a pebble from the path, wrapping the square of lace around it. Everybody watched in baffled silence as the lad strode several yards away towards the target. The Queen stepped up to the line, pulled an arrow from the sheath and lifted her arm high. She adjusted her stance minutely, seeming unencumbered by her gown, which was considerably stiffer and more voluminous than my own, her ruff a great, frilled, hampering cartwheel.

The gathered crowd fell silent. 'Hoy!' she cried, and the boy down the field tossed the little parcel high into the air. The stone fell but the handkerchief hovered momentarily as the Queen drew and released in a single swift movement. The arrow sang as it flew, capturing transitorily the floating white fabric and moving on through the air to meet the target with a decisive whump. My own arrow was dislodged and fell to the ground, disappearing into the long grass. The page held the handkerchief aloft so we could see the hole pierced through it. A cheer went up.

'*That* is how it is done!' She smothered a private smile and gave Essex a long hard look before moving off, the guards encircling her once more, to continue her perambulation.

'Does she really need such a guard?' Aunt Mary asked her brother.

'There have been whispers of another assassination plot.'

'Goodness, not again.'

'Catholics.'

Aunt Mary looked away into the distance towards the target. 'Poor her, it must be hell.'

'She's used to it.'

Aunt Mary wore a strange, contorted expression and was twisting her ring round and round her finger as her brother spoke. I wondered if she was thinking of me and whether I would be under such constant threat when I took the throne. It was foremost in *my* mind.

A man in royal livery ran across my line of sight, stopping in front of Cecil, who had joined the royal party. The man was gesticulating wildly and I noticed another consignment of guards, marching, halberds up around the corner of the palace, moving our way. The tray of marchpane fancies was abandoned on the grass, its contents scattered. Something was happening.

The Queen's armed huddle appeared to tighten and move towards the building, suddenly reinforced by two pairs of men with muskets. The atmosphere sharpened, like the air before a storm. Other men, heavily armed, were heading our way and several mounted guardsmen were cantering along the perimeter wall. Aunt Mary was holding tight to one of my elbows; Grandmother had the other. 'Stay calm,' she said several times. The colour had dropped from her face and she didn't appear at all calm herself.

'Come with me,' Essex said, reappearing from nowhere, with a pistol in his hand. 'Cavendish, are you armed?' he asked Uncle Henry, who pulled out his own weapon from the folds of his cape. 'Take the rear.' The guards were upon us and he began barking orders at them to surround our party.

Margaret was crying and asking repeatedly, 'What's happening?' in a voice shrill with fear.

'For goodness' sake, pull yourself together,' I said, catching a glance of approval from Grandmother. 'Nothing can befall us with all these armed men.'

Margaret's usually milky complexion had taken on the transparency of whey. 'Help her, will you?' I said to Essex, fearing she was about to faint. He tucked his gun inside his doublet and scooped her up.

My heart was thumping, not because I was scared but from the thrill of danger, making me aware of every last crevice of my body, as if it had been turned inside out. I found myself imagining what it might be like to wield a pistol, what would it feel like to have the ability to protect myself in such a way. It made me understand the Queen's practised skill at archery and I wondered if she was equally adept with a firearm.

Once inside, we were conveyed to Aunt Mary's rooms. Essex was ordering the guardsmen to make sure all the doors were properly protected.

'Would you kindly enlighten us as to what is happening?' asked Grandmother in her most imperious tone.

'There appears to be a threat posed to Her Majesty and your granddaughter, My Lady. Specifically what, I do not know.'

'Well, no harm can come to her in here,' said Uncle Henry, before calling for wine. Grandmother glared at him. 'We might as well amuse ourselves if we're going to be cooped up for a while. Who'll play me a wager at dice?' He settled himself on to a stool by the table in the window. 'Sister? Arbella?'

Essex eyed me from beneath his dark curls, making my belly feel loose, and sidled over, saying, 'You can still count me as your champion, My Lady,' before making for the door.

Grandmother watched him with a slanted look and Aunt Mary said, 'Give our best wishes to *Lady Essex*,' rolling her eyes and muttering the word 'irredeemable', as the earl left the room.

'Keep away from that one,' said Grandmother once the door had shut behind him. 'Now he's wed, he's of no use to us.'

I wanted to ask what she meant by that but she made it clear that the topic was closed by turning to one of the pages with a list of orders.

The following day we headed back to Derbyshire in an unwieldy, slow-moving train, with triple the usual guard. Strangely, I was more disgruntled than afraid. I was made to travel curtained in the coach with Grandmother and Margaret rather than on horseback, and had to watch through a crack in the hangings as Dorcas was led on a halter by Dodderidge. It was just past Whitsun, the best time of year, when the trees wear their spring blossom, the birds are in full song and the sun caresses everything gently. But all that was frustratingly obscured; the birdsong smothered by the grumbling roll of wheels; the fresh hope-filled light filtered to us in frustrating slivers and the blossom barely visible. I had the sense, as our party lumbered north, that a heavy drape was being drawn around my life.

Grandmother, Margaret and I sat close together, bolstered by cushions against the rocking of our vehicle. She laid a stiff, gloved hand on my skirts. 'I will do all in my power to ensure you are safe, my jewel.' I imagined myself closed in a velvet-lined box, with an indented shape that exactly fitted my body. My head lolled and jigged and my mind turned inevitably to Essex, silly girl that I was, but the forbidden had such an allure – it was ever thus for me. I don't know what I thought would happen to his wife were my dreams realized, and I'm not sure I ever allowed my thoughts to go as far as what it might mean to desire marriage; knowing he was my champion was enough.

A letter had arrived as we were leaving, and I'd thought he

might have written to me, but it was imprinted with Cecil's seal and addressed to Grandmother. She had turned her back to read it and stiffened visibly about the shoulders. When the motion of the coach lulled her to sleep, I plucked it carefully from her purse, feeling sure that if anyone had the full picture of my situation it was surely Cecil. I had come to realize, even young and green as I was then, that Cecil knew everything.

Most esteemed Dowager Countess,

Alas I must report to you of an intrigue of profound seriousness, which has put the safety of Lady Arbella under great risk. The Questioning of a Jesuit rat whom my men pulled from a hole lately, has revealed a complex and dangerous plot involving the abduction of your granddaughter to the Continent, where there is a plan afoot to there mount an invasion intended to overcome Her Majesty and replace her on the throne with Lady Arbella. There is some sense abroad that, given her tender years, she might be malleable to be bent to their faith and married to one of theirs.

I advise you to spirit yourselves away under guard to one of your Derbyshire houses – Wingfield is a place well fortified, I believe. Was the Scottish Queen not held securely there on many an occasion? Keep your granddaughter safely, watch her, do not let her walk alone, only in sight of the house, and I counsel strongly, never beyond the walls; guard her chambers and vet all your staff and visitors for traitors. One can never know when there is a Judas in one's midst, so take the utmost care with strangers. You have my and my esteemed father's wholehearted and thorough support in this. We cannot allow Lady Arbella's claim to be sullied.

We must be mindful of the future and, I assure you, I intend to do all I must to ensure that the Queen's good will towards your granddaughter is maintained; but she is reluctant, as ever, to make her intentions regarding her successor fully clear with an official declaration, though she has, as you are well aware, insinuated Lady Arbella's suitability on many occasions.

Without such a pronouncement we must maintain the utmost vigilance. I hardly need to tell you there are others who would see themselves in her place, not least her cousin, James of Scotland, though I fail to see how a Scot might circumvent that old decree omitting foreigners from the English throne. However, nothing is impossible.

My eyes are everywhere.

I cannot impress upon you enough the seriousness of this threat, my dear Dowager Countess, and insist you destroy this missive. We must not let this wicked attempt to abduct your girl prevail, nor any other.

R. C. On the thirtieth day of May, in the year of Our Lord 1592

It seemed as if Cecil, with his talk of kidnapping and insurgency, were discussing a person I didn't know, someone far removed from myself, teetering on a knife edge, surrounded by silent threat. But it was I, and beneath the placid surface of my life there was – and always had been, I realized – an unseen turbulence which had revealed itself only in the events of the previous day.

'I should like to learn how to fire a pistol,' I said, when Grandmother had been jolted awake by a pothole and the letter had been stealthily returned to her purse.

'Whatever will you think of next? Perhaps you'd like to go and fight the Catholics in Flanders?'

I imagined the weight of the thing in my hand, feeling all its explosive possibility, how it would kick back at me on firing like an angry pony, how it would smell of burning and gunpowder and potency.

It was on the final day of our journey, several hours on from Wollaton Hall, where we'd spent the night, that our coach lurched to an abrupt halt, throwing us violently back in our seats. There was a loud volley of shouting, the words indistinct, and the unmistakable scrape of weapons being unsheathed. Grandmother looked at me. I had never seen fear in her eyes before but there it was, the same fear that was flailing about suddenly in my own belly. Margaret's face had turned grey and she was gripping the edge of the seat with a white-knuckled fist. Someone called out, 'What is your business?'

'You are both my maids,' whispered Grandmother, still looking at me. 'If they ask, you are called Mary Temple.'

I nodded, repeating, 'Mary Temple.'

'Take these off.' She indicated my jewellery. I unclasped my necklace and pulled off my rings, handing them to her. She stuffed them down behind the upholstery and urged, 'Your gloves and ruff too. The lace is too fine for a servant.' Margaret, with visibly shaking hands, helped me remove the ruff and crushed it into a ball, stuffing it under the cushions. I noticed Grandmother pull Cecil's letter from her purse and slide it under the seat.

There was more shouting outside and a shot was fired, making us jump; Margaret screamed and a horse squealed. I was sure it was Dorcas. Grandmother had her hand tightly round my upper arm and her eyes were shut, her mouth moving. She was praying. Through the crack in the curtains I saw that the guards had crowded close round us. All I could think of was Dorcas, out there, petrified.

'What are your intentions?' I recognized Dodderidge's voice. 'Declare yourselves.'

There was a response. 'What did he say?' asked Grandmother, but neither of us had heard.

Someone dismounted and Dodderidge's head appeared round the door. 'They are after valuables, that is all.'

'I wouldn't trust what they say. This is the valuable they'll be wanting.' She nodded towards me. 'How many are there?'

'Only three,' he replied.

'Three thieves wouldn't attempt to overcome a train as well guarded as ours. There must be more to it. There may be others up ahead. Is there anything on them that reveals their faith?'

'Not that I have been able to see.'

'How is Dorcas?' I asked.

'Don't you worry about her,' he replied.

'For goodness' sake, this is not the time . . .' Grandmother said over him.

There was a scuffle and another shot rang out, then further jostling and the sound of something slumping heavily to the ground, followed by horses turning and galloping off.

'Oh God,' I said, pressing a fist to my mouth, biting hard into my finger.

'One is shot.'

'Dead?' asked Grandmother.

'Looks to be the case.'

There was nothing on the dead man to suggest he was anything other than a common thief, no incriminating Catholic paraphernalia, but as Grandmother said, we couldn't be entirely sure in what guise they might come. It all seemed so far-fetched; how could anyone think I might be taken and easily persuaded into a faith that was not mine, as if I were not a person in my own right? It was the first time I had a palpable understanding of the price of my royal blood and a true sense of the danger that came with it. It gave me a glimpse of what it might be like to be queen; a glimpse I would rather not have seen.

Margaret was in a terrible state, cowering in a corner of the carriage, and even the guards were jittery. They slung the corpse over poor Dorcas. I watched her skit and buck in protest at her lifeless burden, as if she was spooked by his ghost, but Grandmother wouldn't allow me to soothe her, deemed it too great a risk, as did Dodderidge. The body must have served as a warning to any others who might have threatened our convoy, for the rest of our journey was mercifully uneventful.

Clerkenwell

Ami and Mansfield stand opposite each other watching, motionless, as if on the brink of combat. His words ring in the silence: *There would not be space enough in hell if all adulterers were sent there.* The violation of his fingers on the soft parts of her body, just moments ago, has left an imprint of disgust and all she can think of is sluicing herself clean, washing off his smell and the disturbing sensation of his touch. She would give him a piece of her mind but knows that if she allows her temper free rein she will have lost the battle. Taking a deep slow breath, she draws in her willpower, resolving not to squander the fragile moral high ground she has gained.

A thankful interruption comes with a tap at the door. He shifts, head down, towards the hearth, turning his back to the entrance. She skirts round him to answer it, finding a boy on the stoop with a grubby face and filthy hands, proffering a letter. It is from Hal – news of his safe arrival, she hopes. The boy waits for a tip she can ill afford but she notices a line on the back by the seal: *Messenger paid.*

'Go on, be off with you,' she says, stuffing the letter into her apron pocket and stooping to pick out an apple from the basket nearby, tossing it to the boy, who grins and takes a bite. Goodwife Stringer stands watching, leaning against the jamb of her open front door.

'I see you have a visitor,' she says once the boy has gone.

There is something vaguely menacing in the woman's tone that puts Ami on the defensive. 'Only Mister Mansfield, come to settle an account.'

'Is that so?' the goodwife replies.

Instead of simply wishing the busybody good day and

closing her door, she says, 'Of *course* it is so.' Her voice comes out shrill.

The other woman merely raises her eyebrows and after a pause says, 'Went to that hanging. What a thing it was. She mewled something awful on the scaffold, begging for mercy. You should have heard the howl as she died, her body twitching and shaking and all. They said it was the devil leaving her.'

'Good God,' says Ami involuntarily. 'What a world we live in.' She'd seen the so-called witch often at the market. Poor woman was just a widow who sold trinkets for good luck – she was harmless.

'What a world indeed,' the goodwife replies. 'We must all be vigilant. There's dark forces all round us.'

'Yes, vigilant . . . yes.' Ami is flustered. 'Well, better be getting on.'

'Don't want to keep Mister Mansfield waiting.'

Ami doesn't rise this time, just bids the woman a bland goodbye and closes the door to face the other threat within. But the sight of that grubby little messenger has caused an idea to percolate quietly in her mind.

'You have several children, don't you?' she asks Mansfield.

He has his back to her and doesn't turn. 'What of it?'

'Your family must produce a quantity of dirty linen. I could take in your laundry, do your mending.' She tries not to think about her lack of skill with a needle, reflecting on the irony that her privileged upbringing may have given her the means to produce a book of verse, recite tracts of philosophy in Latin, consider the meaning of life, but not to earn her a living.

'Laundry, mending.' He looks amused, as if she has told a joke. 'What do you think my wife is for?'

'But . . .' She searches for a response, something to salvage this idea of hers, which is the only thing between her and a descent into whoredom – the thought horrifies her – or selling her jewel, which is worse.

Her mind finally alights on a possibility: 'A man like you, who is going up in the world' – he turns; she has his attention now, can see his pride is engaged in the slight smile that ripples over his mouth – 'might be well served in sending your laundry out. It would leave your wife . . .' She lets her words hang, hoping he will fill in the blank with the idea that his wife might be more available for his own needs.

'I suppose she *is* busy enough. We have six children and she is calving again.' He pauses. 'Very well, I shall bring you our laundry on Monday.' With that he leaves, calling out, 'Good day to you, Widow Lanyer,' before the door bangs shut behind him.

Ami leans against the table and closes her eyes, remaining there motionless for some time before laughter catches in her, provoked by relief more than humour. She submits to it until she is heaving and wiping her eyes on her apron. Only then does she remember Hal's letter in her pocket.

It is short and perfunctory, so unlike her demonstrative son, and outlines his news in a few short sentences. His final words explain the brevity of the rest: *Someone asked me if I was Lord Hunsdon's bastard. I said I wasn't, of course. Why might they have thought such a thing, Ma?*

'Oh God,' she breathes, slumping on to the bench. Regret prods at her. She ought to have told him the truth long ago but she was tied into a lie that was not hers alone, it was her husband's too and ensured their public respectability. She takes out her writing box, dipping a worn quill into the dregs of the ink, scribbling out a response: *I can't think why, my love. Someone jealous of your good fortune, perhaps?* It strikes her, the way a lie must breed more lies, and shame creeps over her. The truth seems so complicated and shouldn't come in a letter; she will tell him, but not now.

Beneath the slot for the inkbottle is a secret compartment. It holds a small portrait of Henry Hunsdon, wrapped in an old offcut of velvet from a dress she had years ago, in a time when velvet was what she wore all winter. The miniature was made for her by Nicholas Hilliard, one of the old Queen's portrait painters. She fishes it out. Inspecting the familiar image, she is reminded of going with Henry to the artist's studio at the top of a building off Cheapside and watching as the tiny likeness took shape. Hilliard had painted one of her too, for her lover. She wonders what became of it when he died. His widow destroyed it, she supposes.

Looking at the thick sludge of ink in the base of the bottle and the tatty state of her pens, she feels a sense of loss for those times of possibility, when she'd first begun to compose verses and inspiration was everywhere. Writing used to be a thrill that swept her up and carried her along. But that was the past.

Lady Arbella's papers are calling. Despite the difficulty in deciphering the text, the story has begun to bewitch her, and though reading it pricks her guilt she feels compelled to return to those scrawled words, hoping they will offer absolution. If nothing else they provide a distraction from the thicket of woes that seems to have encroached upon her.

She'd thought she'd known Lady Arbella, or at least had a clear sense of who she was, but there is so much she didn't know. She never spoke of her youthful obsession with Essex, nor the way she was irrevocably shaped by her grandmother's rules, nor had she ever mentioned the all-pervading sense of danger that coloured her youth. But Lady Arbella was not a woman to talk of her past or of her feelings, and that was part of her enigma. Ami *had* known of her courage, for she saw it first hand, but what girl, when held up at gunpoint on the road, is more concerned with the welfare of her horse than her own safety?

64

As she reads and untangles, she begins to sense a curious new affinity with Lady Arbella, for although they may have always been separated by position, they were both women denied the destiny their upbringing and education promised. Until darkness falls, she picks her way on through the pages, eager to find the places where her own story intersects with this one, feeling sure that these scrawls will eventually offer up the answer she has been searching for.

Wingfield

I crept silently through the upper corridor, feeling my way along the walls in the dark, finding the indent in the panelling marking the door to Grandmother's study, lowering my hand down and across to meet the latch. Its click sounded loud as a gunshot and I stood, breath held, to make sure I was alone.

Embers glowed in the hearth; I fumbled for a candle and touched its wick to them, grateful for the vague light it threw out. Grandmother's desk was a mass of papers and somewhere amongst them was a letter from my cousin James of Scotland. Dodderidge's whispered words repeated in my mind: *It is in the pile of correspondence to the far left*. He had said there might be something of interest for me contained in that letter but that he had been unable to get his hands on it without arousing suspicion.

In the five months I had been at Wingfield my universe had shrunk to the size of a dolls' house and, like a dolls' house, the front of my small world could be removed and its inner workings thoroughly inspected. I was watched constantly: Grandmother watched me and Cecil watched her watching me and the Queen watched Cecil watching her watching me. I supposed that the Catholics intent on spiriting me away watched invisibly too. That threat was to lurk interminably in my life.

Under this regime of scrutiny I felt impelled to shed light on events obscured from me. My secretive nature blossomed and I became adept at spycraft, seeking information, listening to the servants' gossip, loitering outside half-open doors, finding ways to cast my eye over Grandmother's frequent private correspondence with Cecil before it was balled up and tossed into the hearth.

Dodderidge, who believed it my right to know what was being arranged on my behalf, helped me in this espionage, acquiring information on Grandmother's paperwork for me. She occasionally enlisted his services for letter-writing, giving him access to her private papers. My security was much discussed, and my education, as was the question of who was to pay for it.

I shuffled through the stack of letters, listening with one ear for sounds outside, eventually finding the royal seal of Scotland. I scanned my eyes down the neat paragraph: *The Lennox inheritance will remain under my jurisdiction* – he referred to my father's bequest, which by rights should have come to me years before – *for the time being. It is not without problems . . . there are others who might be have equal right to it . . . the Lady Arbella is not of age . . . It is a Scottish title and she was not born here in Scotland so the inheritance is problematic . . .*

It would seem he intended to continue withholding my patrimony. Perhaps he felt it was a way to pull my strings. But I perceived an irony at the heart of his words, for the fact that I was born in England made *me* Elizabeth's heir rather than him, despite his being male. I replaced the letter, disheartened. This espionage gave me the illusion of power but truly was nothing more than an exercise, for I was incapable of changing my circumstances.

Beyond the window it was still dark but the first birdsong told me dawn was imminent. I blew out the candle, careful to leave everything exactly as I'd found it, and crept from the room and back into the pitch-black corridor. Surprising myself, instead of turning left towards my bedchamber I turned right and took the stairs, carefully, one hand clutching the banister. I could hear the night-guard's snores and saw him, in a pool of light from his lamp, slumped forward over the table, head cradled in his arms, halberd propped beside him.

I slunk past and, not giving a thought to the fact that I wore only my nightgown, slipped silently as a ghost out through the door. Clinging to the darkest corners under the walls, where even the trickle of moonlight couldn't reach, I made my way, as if magically drawn, towards the stable block.

A reassuring earthy smell assaulted my senses as I entered. Horses shifted in their stalls and one or two of them looked out, curious as to who was skulking about in the gloom. But Dorcas knew me; she puffed out a low whinny as I approached – it was not the first time I'd paid her a clandestine visit.

Once I was in her stall she pushed her muzzle into me, her usual greeting, puffing hot breath, nostrils flared, into the crook of my neck. Gaining a foothold on a joist, I climbed up on to her broad back, lying forward to rest my head against her withers, humming quietly, imagining the pair of us galloping over the heathland alone, sensing her excitement as she lifted her head to scent the breeze. Her body rolled beneath me as she got into her stride and soon we were one creature, flying towards the future. My fantasy reached an abrupt halt, interrupted by the reality of my situation. 'I can't stay long, girl,' I whispered, 'or they'll notice I'm gone.'

My days of riding out had come to an end. Very occasionally I was allowed to put Dorcas through her paces in frustrating circles in the home paddock, under the careful eye of the head groom, the steward and several others. There are limits to the enjoyment of performing a passage or a capriole or a perfect lead change when there is no opportunity to take a gallop at the end. It was for my own safety. I was not to walk beyond the garden walls and even within I was to be accompanied at all times. The stables, though inside the walls, were out of bounds because of the constant deliveries and comings and goings. It was thought someone might find opportunity to snatch me away.

A distant door banged and footsteps approached, a stable lad up early, I supposed. I slipped silently off Dorcas's back and pressed myself into the gloom. The footsteps neared. Dorcas shifted and scuffed a hoof, sensing tension in the air. I folded myself further into the recess.

The bolt shot back and there before me in the half-light was Grandmother, white-faced, with her rotund steward, Mister Reason, at her side, rubbing sleep from his eyes.

'Good grief, Arbella, we've been worried sick. I have a dozen men out looking for you. And in your nightgown. You'll catch your death.' She turned to Mister Reason, barking, 'Fetch a blanket, for goodness' sake.'

The man scurried off and I emerged from my lair to face my fate, mumbling an apology.

'Dear girl, you are blue.'

I looked at my hands and saw she was right – I must have been out there longer than I realized. Only then did I feel the October cold and began to shiver uncontrollably, holding my arms about my body. Reason returned with a great itchy horse blanket. 'Not that filthy thing,' said Grandmother, removing her own shawl and wrapping it round my shoulders.

'This really has to stop,' she said as we crossed the yard towards the house. She didn't sound angry, just concerned. 'What on earth were you doing out there this time?'

'I miss Dorcas,' was my reply.

'What, that horse?' She seemed astonished that I could have developed such a fondness for a dumb quadruped, but how could I explain the sense of peace and comfort I had in Dorcas's company? There was no logic to it, and Grandmother liked logic. I knew my secret visits to the stables were over. 'Mister Reason, would you see to it that Lady Arbella's bed is moved into my own chamber.' She turned to me again. 'It's for your safety, you know that, don't you.' It was not a question.

I felt my world shrink further – aged seventeen and I was to spend my nights in my grandmother's chamber.

'We'll talk about it later, dearest,' she added as we entered the hall. 'There is something I must see to.'

In my rooms Margaret was on the edge of the bed, crying, her face buried in her hands, shoulders hunched and quivering. Ten-year-old Cousin Bessie looked at me with a shrug and upturned palms, indicating she had no idea what the matter was.

Margaret was a passionate girl, given to tears, but emotional incontinence unsettled me. I hovered over her, unsure what to say when she blurted, 'He's leaving, I can't bear it.'

'Who's leaving?' I asked.

'Morley, of course!' She revealed her face, wet and red.

'Morley's leaving?'

'I can't bear it,' she wailed again.

Bessie was rubbing her back, saying, 'Show us how you can take off your shift without removing your gown,' to distract her from her misery. It was Margaret's trick and never failed to make her laugh.

'What will I do?' Nothing was going to ease Margaret's despair.

Morley was my tutor, and though we had never particularly warmed to one another I admired his quickness of mind. He had given Margaret a few lines to recite in one of his elaborate staged productions and she had talked of him unceasingly, blabbing nonsense: *He looked at me a certain way; he dropped his handkerchief deliberately for me to pick it up – you were there, Bessie, you saw; he sat next to me at prayers.* Margaret had grown into one of those wholesome girls with an unthreatening prettiness and top-of-the-milk skin who attracted cow-eyed looks from most of the young male staff but never from Morley, though she refused to acknowledge his indifference.

During those one-sided conversations, Essex lurked in my thoughts, surprising me occasionally. I was sure he would come one day and everything would change; he would rescue me from my captivity and from the inevitable marriage to a stranger in a foreign court. I don't know what I thought would happen to his wife. I don't think I went so far as to wish some misfortune would befall her, but perhaps I did – I can't remember. The callow longings of youth pale once a few years of life have been lived, but back then, at Wingfield, I had so few small joys to attach my thoughts to and Essex was one of them, Dorcas another. Each, I realize now, represented some kind of freedom.

'Why is he leaving?' I asked.

'I don't know,' sobbed Margaret.

'I think –' Bessie began and then stopped herself.

'What, Bessie?' I was suddenly curious, as her expression was a puzzling combination of embarrassment and fascination.

'I can't say it.'

'Go on.' Even Margaret had stopped blubbing to listen.

'He was caught in an embrace with' – she was speaking through her fingers and couldn't look at us – 'the gentleman usher – the tall one.'

'It's not true!' exclaimed Margaret, wearing a look of disgust.

I said nothing but thought it seemed plausible. I'd seen him exchange looks with that usher several times and had once watched the fellow pass Morley a letter in the garden after nightfall and conduct a furtive whispered conversation, which I was too distant to hear. I had read the Greeks and was more accustomed to such things than my companions.

I went to the window and, as if it had been staged, could see Morley clamber up on to a loaded cart in the stable yard. 'He's on his way.' I said. The girls joined me to watch as he trundled slowly off, with Margaret leaking more tears and muttering about not even having said goodbye. I was not sad to see him go. He was a good enough tutor but I never felt he really cared much for my education. His mind always seemed to be elsewhere – on the gentleman usher, I supposed.

Later, Grandmother called me in. She'd been at her desk, over which were the unrolled plans of the New Hall at Hardwick – her great project. It was to be the emblem of her success, a towering palace of glass, lording it over all of Derbyshire.

She stood and moved to the front of the desk to stand before me. Morley had behaved in an 'unacceptable manner' was all she said of his departure. 'But never mind about that, what I am concerned about is you, my dear.'

Behind her, meeting my eye, hung the portrait of me aged nearly two. I was square-faced and tightly trussed into a dress that I thought I remembered, being unbearably stiff and itchy, though surely I'd been too young for such a memory. In a fat paw I clutched a doll in the form of Queen Elizabeth.

For years that miniature queen lived on a high shelf in the nursery, far out of reach. I coveted her like nothing else. I had other dolls, beautiful creatures, exquisitely wrought, but I didn't want other dolls, even then there was no allure for me in girlish playthings and I took greater pleasure in imagining a stick was a sword or a broom a hobbyhorse; but I wanted the miniature queen. My infant mind had long machinated on how to achieve my aim and one day the perfect opportunity offered itself. When Nurse and all the maids were called to the kitchens to help with some drama, leaving me alone, I dragged up a stool and climbed on to it, stretching as far as I could to get the tips of my fingers to the edge of that little queen's skirts. She fell, exposing a wooden stump where a pair of legs should have been.

Looking at the portrait of my younger self I was revisited momentarily by the overwhelming sense of disappointment I'd felt on discovering that the little queen's exterior perfection was not matched by what lay beneath – a plain peg of wood, barely even sanded. I hid her and later gave her to Grandmother's favourite hound Apollo, who took her out into the paddock, shredded her fine clothes and gnawed at her shapeless timber body until she was unrecognizable. The miniature queen's disappearance became a nursery mystery that was never solved.

'I know it has been difficult for you, with all the restrictions,' Grandmother said. Her pearls, outsized and sheeny, clattered as she poured them from one hand to the other. Her voice was soft, the voice she rarely revealed to anyone but me, and sometimes to Aunt Mary and Uncle William, her favourite child, a fact she never sought to hide.

'I understand why it has to be like this.' An image of Dorcas with that cadaver slung over her back came to me and with it the palpable fear on Grandmother's face in the carriage as that shot was fired. 'It's just' – I felt I had to say it – 'I feel like the Scottish Queen shut away . . .'

She looked at me and tilted her head. 'Dearest, it is not remotely like that. She . . .' – Her tone changed, was suddenly laden with disapproval – 'that woman was a traitor, a Catholic who sought to unseat our Queen with her treachery.'

A vivid memory of the Scottish Queen swilled through my mind, her warm smile and her words: *The Catholic faith is the true faith; it is the only path that leads to the Kingdom of Heaven.*

'But how is it different? I have lost my liberty as she did.'

She sighed. 'I know it is a difficult burden to bear, but bear it you must. Your position comes with great responsibility; you are no ordinary girl; as the Queen's precious heir you must be protected.'

I realized then, looking at the serious dark-grey eyes of the two-year-old me with that doll in my pudgy fist, that the image was an illusion, for it was I who was the doll and it was the Queen who had me clasped in her hand and could do what she wanted with me – even throw me to the dogs if she pleased.

'How will I learn to be queen if I am never at court?' The idea of my becoming Queen of England was too daunting to ponder on properly. 'I will never be prepared for . . .' I couldn't articulate all the things I feared. Despite my copious learning, I felt I knew nothing of statecraft; I had the sense too that my house arrest at Wingfield was perhaps a preparation in itself, for to be queen meant living a life watched and restricted and under constant threat. 'How will I command loyalty?'

'Listen to me!' Grandmother's face almost broke into a smile, but not quite. 'Managing my estates is much like running a country. It requires the same tenacity and attention to detail, the same respect from one's staff. Watch me, and you will learn all you need.' She stopped a moment and I remember wishing I could be more like her. She was the strongest person I knew. 'You must know,' she continued, 'that Elizabeth was denied a place at court for many years before she took the throne and look how great she became. Everything will be different when we move to Hardwick.' She said it as if Hardwick were Paradise and not just another more beautiful place where I would be held prisoner. She let her pearls fall to her lap and reached out for my hand, asking in an old ritual, 'May I?' I nodded and she took it in both of hers, which were chilled and papery. 'I know it is difficult and I am here to help you. I understand you miss your horse and

74

the freedom of riding out. I understand how fond one can become of an animal; I do not have a heart of stone, as you believe, but my foremost care is for your safety – it must be.'

I nodded. I understood. I had witnessed the threat at first hand.

'You are my most precious jewel, Arbella, and I will protect you if it is my last act on earth. The risk I took to bring your parents together –' she let her words hang. I'd heard it often; the jeopardy of marrying her daughter, without royal sanction, to Charles Stewart, Earl of Lennox, a prince of the blood, and how she had been obliged to negotiate delicately with the Queen to avoid the fate of Charles's mother, who had found herself in the Tower for aiding and abetting a potentially treasonous match.

I felt my frustration well. 'And *you* never give a thought to the greatness you stand to achieve as the Queen's grandmother?' The words erupted from my mouth unbidden and laden with anger.

'Your sarcasm is unbecoming, Arbella.' Her expression was tight and I sensed her temper rousing too.

'I am nothing but the final brick in your empire, the means by which you can make your elevation complete.' I was shouting now. 'And I must sleep in your bedchamber like an infant. So your investment is protected.'

She gave me a cold, hard stare. 'I fear I have made a monster.'

'No! It is your ambition that is monstrous.' The painted girl was staring at me. 'I'm not a thing that you can wind up to do your bidding.'

'I know, I know.' She had gained control of her anger, while mine was still boiling. There was not even the faintest tremor in her voice. 'I know you are not a thing. I love you very much.'

She was completely calm as if those angry words had never been said.

I stormed from the chamber, stopping outside for a moment to allow my rage to subside and to regain my poise. Whispers were coming from the pages' room, a welcome distraction.

'They said he kissed the gentleman –'

'You are wrong,' interrupted someone. 'Morley is a Catholic spy; that is why he was dismissed. No one's supposed to know.'

'How do *you* know then?'

'I just do.'

I crept away with the sense of encroaching danger. The threat had always seemed something exterior, lurking outside, abstract, but this news of Morley brought the menace within. My already small world shrank further.

In the narrow space between my bed and Grandmother's was a small table cluttered with objects. A much-thumbed bible atop a stack of books, a carved facsimile of the Talbot coat of arms, a dish containing various small items, pearls and buttons, a silver thimble, a pin cushion and other nameless things.

I picked up the oval miniature that lay amongst those objects. On one side, behind a perfect curve of glass, was Jane Grey, the executed queen, dark and sober, and on the other was her sister Katherine, golden with rosebud lips and teasing eyes, the opposite of serious Jane. Katherine's fate was no less tragic than her sister's; she'd been separated from her beloved husband and sons and died of grief.

I had been captivated as a child by those doomed girls who'd lain beside Grandmother's bed for as long as I could remember. Jane had been willing to die for her faith – brave to the last, they said – and her death was recorded in the great Book of Martyrs that lay on the table outside the chapel. But it was Katherine who was the greater puzzle, whose fate was more obscure, draped in shame, it seemed to me. It was whispered she starved herself to death. I imagined her forfeiting nourishment as a last act of resistance, when she had no other way to take hold of her own destiny. I too knew how to befriend the pain of hunger, to feel the seductive power of resistance, to force the body into submission. There was no place for Katherine Grey in the great book, but to me she was a martyr – the cause she stood for: free will, or something like it.

'Why do you keep the Grey girls here?' I asked Grandmother as she got into bed.

'To remind myself that even the best-laid plans can go awry,' came her reply.

'What do you mean by that?'

'You can never know which way public opinion will fall when a childless monarch passes on.' She paused and sighed deeply. 'Not enough care was taken in the choice of Jane Grey's husband. That was what led to her downfall.'

I didn't fully understand what she meant but it was clear she didn't want to be drawn out, for she extinguished her candle and drew her bed curtains.

Her words circled my head as I lay awake in the dark of my own curtained space, imagining those two tragic girls with their royal blood like mine and wondering if Morley truly was a Catholic spy and whether that, rather than my dawn wanderings, was the reason for the new sleeping arrangements. My only comfort came from the churning pangs in my gut and running my hands down the grille of my ribs and over the sharp jut of my hipbones.

It was not long after Morley's sudden departure that my new tutor arrived. I remember clearly my first encounter with Starkey in Grandmother's withdrawing chamber. I awaited his arrival sitting quietly in the window alcove with Margaret and Cousin Bessie. Grandmother was being read to across the chamber by one of her women and Mister Reason was playing chess with Dodderidge. Margaret was embroidering a complicated woodland scene; she was deft with a needle and was always working on something spectacular. Grandmother used to say it was her only saving grace, for she wasn't bright, but she was kind and loyal and I was fond of her. She was curious about the new tutor's arrival. She hadn't said anything but I could tell by the way she'd worn her best lace partlet and pinched her cheeks surreptitiously when we heard horses outside. I hoped for her sake he wouldn't be some ancient parson; all I knew of him was that he was a chaplain.

Starkey turned out to be a fey young man with hay-coloured hair and a solemn demeanour; he was of a similar age to me, as far as I could tell. Entering slowly, he progressed diffidently across the floor, holding his hat in his hands. Margaret made a disappointed sigh and went back to her needlework – he was no dashing Morley, that was manifestly clear. His black clothes were spattered with mud and he apologized for it, seeming mortified.

Grandmother put him at his ease, insisting he draw up a stool beside her and tell of his journey. Despite her formidably intimidating presence she knew how to get the best out of a person and soon Starkey was describing the floods near Leicester and the high winds as he'd ridden over the ridge. He had an air of concentrated seriousness, as if he thought very carefully before speaking, and I knew instantly that I was going to like him, in much the way I'd known in moments that Dorcas and I were a match.

We were left alone, more or less, in a corner of the large chamber to discuss my studies and I suggested taking some air on the roof leads. Mister Reason was dispatched to keep an eye and mounted the stairs behind us, up and up to the top, wheezing and grumbling about the weather.

The wind was up, plucking at our clothing, and a procession of angry clouds scudded past. We came to a halt at the parapet's edge, from where we could see the river coiling away into the distance and the mill far down in the valley, its wheel turning.

'We might be birds perched up here,' said Starkey. 'If you could choose, what kind of bird would you be?'

I had never been asked such a question, hadn't thought to consider such a thing, and replied without thinking, 'A nightingale.' As I said it I was reminded of the story of Philomel, which hadn't crossed my mind since that time at court, and also that dead bird in the Stand Tower, how it had fallen.

'Ah, the night singer,' he said. 'That's a rather sad choice. Isn't it always thought of as a lament?'

'Not always; the nightingale heralds fine weather.' I was determined to make something good of it. 'Its song is the most beautiful. And you, what would you be?'

'Oh, I don't know. I'd like to think something like an eagle or a buzzard but I'd more likely be something a great deal more commonplace – like a pigeon.' He puffed up his chest and acted out a passable impression, cooing and strutting along the roof. Mister Reason looked over, perplexed, watching us laugh.

'Why a pigeon?' I asked.

'I come from ordinary stock,' he replied.

'Yet you are not ordinarily educated or Grandmother would not have employed you.'

'I suppose we shall see if I meet her standards.' He looked away a moment into the distance, giving me a chance to inspect him unobserved. His doublet was ill-fitting, as if it had been intended for someone else, and had been carefully mended in several places, but his linen was crisp and white despite the fact he'd been on the road. It was his eyes that drew my fascination, though; they were thickly lashed, quite lovely, and had an intensity of expression that suggested great depth.

'Nothing wrong with ordinary stock.'

He turned to me. 'If you were a commoner and had to have a trade, what would you be?'

I was struck by the way he seemed not to think of the fact that I was a woman. 'A groom, perhaps.'

'Ah yes, a fellow in the stables said you had a gift with horses.'

'Though I only ride in the paddock these days.'

We fell silent for a time, and though we'd only made each other's acquaintance minutes before, I was entirely at my ease with Starkey. I felt instinctively that he was someone who didn't want anything from me, only, with his questions, to know what I was truly like. I was unused to that.

He turned those eyes on me after a while – his hair had blown awry in the wind – and asked, 'What kind of queen do you intend to be?' It was something else I had never considered; all I ever really thought of was my own inadequacy and whether I was up to the role.

On seeing my hesitation, he apologized. 'I didn't mean to confront you with a difficult . . . on our first meeting . . .'

'No, you are right. It is something I must think of.' I was running through all the great monarchs of England in my mind, pondering which I might emulate, when it came to me as a moment of epiphany, in a single word. 'I will seek to be just. Yes, a *just* queen, that is what I want to be.'

'Ah, then' – he rummaged a hand beneath his clothes, procuring a volume of Plato's *Republic* as if from nowhere – 'we must look to Socrates first, I think.' His eyes flashed bright and he stroked the book as if it were sentient and might respond to his affection.

Though Starkey served as chaplain in our household as well as tutor, and often reminded me that when I was queen I would be God's envoy on earth, I never saw him touch a bible with the fondness he showed to that volume of Plato.

Clerkenwell

Ami arrives at the backfield, heaving the Mansfields' dirty linens. The washerwomen eye her up and down and seem to approve as they introduce themselves and offer to share the hot water from their large communal vat that hangs over the brazier by the river. A number of small children scurry about collecting kindling and dry wood to keep it stoked. Their children, she supposes, which makes her feel her years. The other women are robust, with sturdy bodies, and half her age.

It is hard, physical work, layering the linens in the bucking tub, filling it with water, hefted by the bucketful from the vat and adding the lye, so sharp it stings her eyes and the back of her nose. As she labours she thinks of the irony that once she disguised herself as a laundress. She wonders whether she will be mentioned masquerading in Lady Arbella's story. Donning the garb of a laundry maid hadn't prepared her for the sharp reality of the back-breaking work. That familiar remorse prods at her, for failing her friend – but it was worse than that. Failing makes it sound accidental. Perhaps this work she does now is a penance. Hal also hovers about her thoughts. He hasn't written back. It has been four days. Worries peck at her. She fears he hasn't accepted her inadequate explanation and that he might have come to the truth about his paternity. But perhaps he is simply too busy to write.

Once her linens have been well soaked the women make space for her at the row of trestles, where they beat the dirt out of their whites together. It makes a rhythmic, thwacking sound, a music of sorts. They laugh as they go along the tables, taking it in turns to confess who it is they imagine is at the other end of their washing bats receiving a beating. When it is Ami's turn she says Alphonso's name, and finds there is some satisfaction in this make-believe.

They exchange gossip and stories, local matters mainly: who has a fancy for whom, who's been caught with their fingers in the pot, who's having a baby that isn't fathered by the husband. Ami doesn't say much, afraid that her refined turn of phrase, learned from those years at court, might set her apart.

Inevitably talk turns to the big scandal: the court proceedings in which the King's fallen favourite and his wife, the Earl and Countess of Somerset, are being tried for murder. It has captured the public imagination: a mysterious death in the Tower, the implication of a countess and the woman who'd been hanged for it already, a whiff of witchcraft, corruption seeping upwards through the court. Ami recalls meeting the Countess of Somerset, she was Frances Howard back then – a striking creature even at the age of twelve, with confidence beyond her years, the kind of girl who inspires envy.

Ami imagines telling the women that she has known the illustrious accused, laughing inwardly, for they'd doubtless assume she was spouting nonsense and think her half demented like Mad Dot, who wanders Clerkenwell looking for her dead babies – it is said they all died in a single night. It forces Ami to remember how far she has plummeted in the world, but there's nothing to be done about it and the hard labour provides a distraction.

With the beating finished there is rinsing to be done, and then everything must be spread out on the grass to dry. Despite the ache in her back she feels a glow of satisfaction to see the neat rows of bright white linen against a carpet of green. The sun is shining but she wonders what she will do when the weather is not so good. She pushes the thought away – there is no space for pessimism here.

She sits back with the women in the shade of the big oak and they pass round a flagon of small beer, still discussing the trial. She wonders if they gossiped about Lady Arbella out here, when that scandal was in its throes. Of course they did, everybody did. No one talks of her any more though. It is as if she never was.

'Did you go to the witch hanging?' There is silence and she realizes that all eyes are on her, waiting for her answer.

She stops herself blurting, *Why ever would I want to watch an innocent woman suffer?* saying instead, 'I was not able.'

'Shame,' says Birdy, a dough-faced, stolid woman who couldn't have been less like a bird if she'd tried. 'It was quite an occasion.'

'Next time come with us,' says Dill. Ami has noticed that the others always agree with Dill. 'P'raps they'll hang that countess. I'd like to see that, but she'll be done in private, I s'pose – not for the likes of us.'

Their eagerness is monstrous. Ami feels the gulf between her and these women and understands the depth of her loneliness since Hal departed for court, for though it is a mere two-week absence it signals the beginning of a more permanent departure. She cannot hold on to him for ever.

After the long day she has no energy to eat more than a hunk of bread with some dripping and, anyway, she is impatient to get back to her reading. But soon it will be too dark to read and candles are an expense she can ill afford. She considers using some of the dripping to make rush-lights, which would offer a few minutes of sputtering flame, but she has no rushes. Anyway, she finds herself dropping off even before darkness has fallen. She dreams that Lady Arbella is right there in front of her, speaking, saying something of great importance: *I want you to know that* . . . She is on the brink of knowing, but the voice fades and she can hear nothing.

The next evening it is the same, and the next; her exhaustion gets the better of her and she makes excruciatingly slow progress with her reading. It is as if the manuscript bewitches her to sleep rather than revealing its secrets. But at least Mansfield is off her back.

When she arrives for the fourth consecutive day at the backfield, Dill says, 'Four large loads in a week; that's a lot of washing for one household, particularly as you live *alone*.' The way she says it, with narrowed eyes, makes it clear that she is thinking more than she lets on.

'Looks to me like she's taking it in,' says Birdy, looking directly at Ami, though addressing Dill.

Birdy had been glad to help Ami lift a heavy load of sodden sheets out of the bucking tub only the day before and had given her a gentle ribbing for her fine manners and all her 'pleasing and thanking', as she'd put it. She hadn't meant it unkindly and had said, 'Anyone can find themselves on hard times, wherever it is they might have started off.'

Ami understood that, however hard she tried to blend in, she was as rarefied in the eyes of those laundresses as the noblewomen at court had been to her. She knows only too well that difference at best causes curiosity but more often can be the source of suspicion. With the reception she gets on that fourth day, she realizes that while she was assumed to be nothing more than a woman fallen on hard times and having to do her own household linens, she was welcome in their ranks. But now they suppose her to be an impostor, a person after their trade, it is a different story.

Ami wonders if censorious Goodwife Stringer from next door has been gossiping about her impoverished circumstances, or worse. She called out from her stoop as Ami passed the previous day, with a load of dirty laundry, and fired off a volley of questions which Ami answered evasively. The women in the field have closed ranks on her, that much is clear. But ignoring the sideways stares and disapproving whispers, she makes an attempt to light her own fire, scrubbing in the undergrowth for kindling and dragging logs from the nearby copse. She takes a light from the big fire under the hard gaze of Dill.

She labours on in silence, doing her best to ignore the huffs and whispers.

Once her whites are all laid out, she goes to the bushes to answer a call of nature, coming back to find someone has flicked ash over the lot. She forces back tears of exhausted frustration as she sets to work once more, knowing that if she shows weakness it will be the end of her.

Concealing her feelings is a lesson Ami had learned among the women at court, who could be every bit as cruel as these washerwomen. She tries not to cast her mind too far into the future, for a day at a time the work and the women are tolerable and the exertion leaves little time to worry about Hal's continued silence; plus there is satisfaction at least in keeping her creditors at bay.

Hardwick

'Please stand still,' said Margaret, crouched on the ground, her mouth full of pins. 'I will never get this hem straight if you keep moving.'

'But I'm so cold. Could we not move closer to the hearth? I know you need the light but . . .' It was the sheer size of the windows that made the rooms at Hardwick impossible to heat. I secretly longed to be back at Wingfield, where the windows were of more modest proportions. But Grandmother seemed impervious to the chill and could not hide her delight at her vast shimmering rectangles of glass, fit for a cathedral, the talk of all Derbyshire.

We had been in the New Hall at Hardwick for three years, living in a cacophony of sound, stonecutters, carpenters, glaziers, plasterers, scaffolders, roofers, welders, all combining to ensure that from dawn to dusk there was never a moment's peace. A permanent film of white chalky dust sat on every surface, finding its way into even the finest crevice, making our hair tacky and our eyes itch.

Just as she was resistant to the cold, Grandmother appeared immune to the dust and noise. I always had the impression that Grandmother's constant building – for there was not a time I could remember when she was not overseeing the construction of one great house or another – was driven by some kind of intangible, transcendent hope, as if those grand edifices would shore her up against her own demise.

None of us understood why we had moved into the New Hall so soon, though I suspected it was because the garden walls were high, the stable block distant from the house and the setting, perched as it was atop a high point, offered views into the distance. Anyone approaching could be seen long before they arrived.

'I don't suppose you will ever be cold at court. Remember the great hearths at Greenwich?' Margaret's eyes were bright in anticipation of my return to court, the reason for the new gown, and several others, being tailored for me.

'How many years is it since we were there?' I was counting back in time but there was so little to distinguish one month from another.

'Nearly ten years,' she said.

'A decade!' I felt a sudden sense that time had been stolen from me, all those years, the years of my blossoming, spent out of sight; almost twenty-six years of my life gone and nothing to show for it. But I was to return to court soon and take my place. I allowed myself to imagine the journey there; I would ride Dorcas again, at last, whom I had only seen recently at a distance, riding out with the grooms. Starkey and Dodderidge would ride with me, and Margaret, who was a nervous horsewoman, would be stuck in the luggage cart with the other maids.

Margaret stood and began to peel the pinned-together garment away from my shoulders. 'Take this off, so I can finish it.' She slid it down my arms, careful not to let the pins prick me, and set it aside, then dragged the fur blanket from the bed, wrapping it around my shoulders. 'What's the matter?'

'I'm just surprised so much time has passed.' I was thinking, too, of Cousin Bessie, who had been betrothed a few months since and had returned to her mother's house to prepare for marriage. 'They all grow up and go.'

'Don't think of that. You will be at court soon and everything will be different.'

I settled into a chair by the fire, closing my eyes, feeling the heat on my face. 'At last.' The summons came at Epiphany. Grandmother had held the letter up and waved it triumphantly like a banner. 'Your time is coming,' she'd said. 'The Queen wants you at court once Lent is over.' Fabrics were ordered and a lavish new wardrobe planned as meticulously as she had planned the building of Hardwick New Hall.

As Margaret set the dress to one side, the sweep of the skirt knocked a stack of papers to the floor. She crouched to pick them up, passing them into my outstretched hand. I shuffled through the pages, reading a line here and there. I had been attempting a drama – Cleopatra – intended as an homage to the Queen, to offer her on my arrival at court, but I was struggling as to how I might convey the Queen of Egypt's death without causing offence. Starkey and I had argued over Cleopatra's demise. He claimed it was honour that had driven her to take her own life; I believed it was guilt; she had failed her people, after all.

'What is it about?' asked Margaret.

'What, this?' I tapped the papers. 'Nothing really, just some ideas. Something to present to the Queen.'

'Just think, by spring we will be at court.' She picked up another dress from the bed, holding it up to her body. 'It's lovely, this taffeta. What colour would you say it was?'

'Hmmm?' I was still thinking about Cleopatra and her death, imagining how I might invoke the drama of the snakebite when I had never seen more than a common adder. What colour was an asp, I wondered.

'Peacock blue, I'd call it,' she said, momentarily confusing me. 'It needs altering too, would you mind?' She was brandishing her needle.

I reluctantly left my fur cocoon and she helped me into the garment. The fabric was stiff, and edged with gold braid that scratched at the skin under my arms.

'I'm going to have to take it in.' She sighed. 'You have thinned down since we last tried it.'

'It's Lent!' I snapped, regretting my tone, adding, 'I suppose I'd be bound to lose weight during Lent,' to sound less as if I was defending against an accusation. If I'd told her I liked the way my body was, lean and flat, or that I enjoyed the feeling of my clothes being loose, like a boy's, she would have thought me out of my mind.

'I'll add some tucks. That should do it.' I watched her as she worked. There was nothing thin about Margaret, Lent or not. She had grown into a soft-cornered woman who was watched by men and pretended not to notice.

'Never mind,' she continued, her voice muffled by a mouthful of pins, 'think of the feasting at court. We will be well nourished there.' But I was thinking that, with so many people dining together at court, it would be more difficult for anyone to monitor what I was or wasn't eating, as they did at Hardwick. 'I *will* be coming?'

'To court? Of course, you are part of my household.'

'Do you remember the Earl of Essex carrying me when I fainted?' She sounded breathless when she said this and I wondered if she had been conjuring up abstract fancies in her head about the earl, as I had for more years than I cared to count.

'How could I forget?'

'Will *he* be there?'

'Didn't you know? He is to be tried for treason.'

'Treason?' Her mouth was an O and I could see her dreams crumbling in the forlorn expression she wore.

'He tried to raise an army against the Queen.' I left it at that, though the situation was far more complicated. The near decade of my incarceration, so interminably long to me, suddenly seemed such a short time for the earl to have risen so high and fallen so low.

I had discussed it at length with Starkey. 'There are rumours Essex has chosen to back James of Scotland's suit for the English throne,' he'd said.

'I very much doubt that,' I'd replied. Essex wanted me on the throne; I knew it in my bones. He was my champion; he'd said it himself.

'Anyway, if it is true, the earl's demise weakens your cousin James's suit for *your* crown.' There was a quiet passion in Starkey for what he termed my 'cause', which I suppose was what it was, given I was not the only one who believed themselves to be England's heir. There was my cousin James, of course, but he was a foreigner, and the Seymours, whose legitimacy was in question; my flaw was being female, I supposed. That my claim was the strongest never seemed in doubt and I didn't consider then the fact that the small world of Hardwick was not representative of the wider world outside its gates.

I never once had the impression that Starkey's support of me was motivated by self-interest, it was more his desire for justice and the proper order of things – virtues which he held in high esteem. He talked often and with conviction about Socrates' death; a noble end, he called it, 'an end that upheld justice above all'. He believed Essex should do as Socrates had done and end his own life.

'And damn his immortal soul?' I asked, deeply shocked by the thought.

'He is already damned,' was Starkey's blunt reply.

'The Queen will forgive him.' I felt sure of it. She had already forgiven Essex more than once and I was sure she would do so again, refused to entertain any other possibility. 'It is said he is like a son to her.'

'The Queen has been too magnanimous with the earl,' he'd replied. 'There was always a sense of inevitability that he would eventually turn on her, as Caesar's favourites turned on him.'

'When I am queen, I too hope to be loved rather than feared,' I said. 'Do you suppose that is a failing of femininity?'

He had laughed at that. 'A failing? I don't think so.'

'But women tend to forgiveness.'

'Do you love God or fear Him?' Starkey surprised me with his question.

'Both, I suppose,' was the answer I came to.

'As God's envoy on earth you will inevitably be feared. It is how you choose to wield the power of it that will determine the kind of queen you are. That is your challenge.'

His words made me feel my exile painfully. My lack of an example to emulate had become a constant concern; I had only theoretical notions on which to base my beliefs and still feared I might abruptly find myself on the throne and at a loss. Had I been at court, I might have become accustomed to the everyday machinations of statecraft, groomed for the role I would one day take, rather than having to glean my knowledge from watching Grandmother run her estates, or from books and thousand-year-old exemplars. I questioned the sense in educating me so vigorously only to keep me in the dark about matters that had me at their heart but Grandmother seemed to feel I was still a child. It was as if she hadn't noticed the time slip away. Perhaps from her great age there was little difference between fifteen and twenty-five. But at last I was going to court and all that would change.

'Will he go to the block?' asked Margaret. For an instant I didn't realize she meant Essex; I had been too caught up in my own thoughts.

'The Queen will pardon him, as usual.' An image of Essex, splendid and smelling of hyacinths, swooped down on me. It made me think of the myth in which Hyacinth died, trying to catch a discus, in an attempt to impress Apollo.

Margaret said nothing, going back to tacking tucks into

my dress, silently, with only the gentle hiss of thread pulling through stiff fabric.

A soft knock interrupted us. 'My Lady?' Margaret opened the door and Dodderidge swiped his cap off, revealing a sparse growth of hair, a visible indication of time passed. 'I'm terribly sorry to disturb you.' He seemed afraid he might be disrupting something grave and important rather than the mundane business of fitting dresses. 'But your grandmother would like you upstairs. The pictures that arrived yesterday are being hung.'

Grandmother was pacing the great high chamber, wrapped in her favourite fur, a white stoat with unnerving ruby-set eyes. She was not alone; a couple of her women were inspecting the newly painted panels, two men were lugging a crate through into the gallery and my little cousins, Wylkyn and Frannie, were whispering and giggling about something to one side.

'Margaret, would you take the children next door,' Grandmother ordered. 'I'd like a word with you alone, Arbella.' She sent the women with Margaret and Dodderidge was to help oversee the unpacking of the pictures. 'Make sure the men handle them properly. I don't want any damage. Mister Reason is there but . . .' She left her words floating. Reason, though fiercely loyal, had become elderly and ponderous and we all knew he couldn't be relied upon to supervise properly the efficient unpacking of Grandmother's precious artefacts.

The chamber was a vast square space as high as it was wide. New rush matting had recently been laid, giving it the scent of late-summer meadows, which was quite at odds with its grandeur. That scent pervaded Hardwick and whenever I caught a whiff of straw in the years to follow I was always transported back to those cold and splendid rooms.

The immense windows flooding the space with light made

the greatest impact, even in February when the sky was blanketed with a thick layer of gruel-grey cloud and the sun hadn't been seen for months. They framed a vista that rolled away for miles, making the house seem perched on the edge of the world with a view of infinity. The room had an effect, a way of making its occupants feel intimidated, except, I supposed, for Grandmother, who must have looked out of those windows and known she was queen of all she surveyed. Derbyshire was her realm.

She said, 'Can't you put some gloves on or something?'

I held my hands out, opening my fingers. They were covered with ink.

'I don't know what you find to write about.'

'Just poems, stories . . . things.' I wrote primarily to fill time in those empty days that stretched out for ever, creating worlds to inhabit in my mind, places where things happened. 'I have been writing a play about Cleopatra to offer to the Queen.'

'I wouldn't do that,' she said through pursed lips. 'Can't you embroider her a pair of sleeves or gloves instead?'

I didn't reply.

'I wanted to talk to you. There have been things on my mind and with you going imminently to court . . . well . . . you have been so long here, I wonder if you are fully prepared for the . . .' She hesitated, closing her eyes as if to search for the right word. 'The potential dangers you could face.' She shuffled her pearls.

I still said nothing. I knew well enough that there were moments when Grandmother was not to be interrupted.

'I have been thinking of Katherine Grey, your mama's godmother. She was a dear friend, God rest her soul.' I tried to imagine Grandmother with such friends, women to whom she might have confided her secrets, but the idea would not fit. 'It's many years ago now, but you must know

94

her story.' I nodded and followed her to the dais, where there were two embroidered velvet chairs set under a canopy. We took one each, I balancing tentatively on the edge of mine, she seeming enthroned, her years belied by her poker-straight posture. 'Like you, she had royal blood, a quantity of it, her sister Jane had been queen after all . . .' She paused, seeming to cast her mind back. 'In the end Katherine Grey was a little fool, driven by passion. She wed herself to the Earl of Hertford and went to the Tower for it, carrying his son. It is treason when a princess of the blood weds without permission.' She stopped to clear her throat before fixing her gaze firmly on me. 'Desire is a demon; it will possess you, my girl, if you don't take pains to resist it. Katherine Grey was lucky not to go to the block like her sister.'

I wanted to say she was not lucky, not lucky to sink to such despair as to bring on her own slow death. I'd heard the story many times: the Queen was incensed; so afraid of being pushed off her throne by Katherine Grey's royal son, she had the marriage denied. The infant, little Lord Beauchamp, would have had a stronger claim than mine had he not been deemed illegitimate. I would have had another life – it was impossible to imagine a different destiny, or whether I might have preferred a more ordinary path. Hindsight cannot unravel and reweave a life to a different pattern.

'The Queen still hasn't truly forgiven Hertford,' continued Grandmother.

I remembered meeting Hertford once when I was a child. He seemed a genial man, but what can you tell from a brief encounter? He'd admired my hands, said they reminded him of someone's and looked suddenly sad, which made me think he was talking of golden Katherine Grey, trapped for ever behind her oval of glass on Grandmother's bedside table.

'At court you'll find people who will try to take advantage of your position.'

I wanted to shout at her, ask her if she thought me a little fool too, but kept on nodding.

'Give them short shrift. No one will seek to know you for yourself; remember that. If the Queen chooses to broker a match for you then we must play along but . . .' She hesitated a moment. 'Cecil and I are of the mind that we should hold off any wedding until . . . until later.'

She steepled her fingers, as if about to pray. 'It will always be possible to delay, whilst appearing to acquiesce . . . if necessary.' I fixed my gaze on the stoat's ruby eyes. 'Look at me, Arbella. I need to know you are listening.' I did as she bid, focusing on the thin line of her lips. 'Cecil has given me his word; he will be watching out for you.' She softened then. 'I know you will make a dazzling impression, dearest.'

'I will do my utmost to see you proud, Grandmother. I assure you I have no intention of making a bad marriage, nor will I allow anyone to take advantage of me.'

'Good; I'm glad you understand.' She stood and led the way towards the door. 'Your Aunt Mary will be with you. She knows how to manage court life and you will be sharing her chambers.'

The thought of those women around the Queen, remembering my long-ago faux pas – the snatched-back hand and the whispers, the sidelong glances of disapproval, the cold shoulders – made me shrivel. I supposed many of those women would be long gone but that was little comfort, for I was awake to the fact that I was not one for easy affinities with those I hardly knew – the likelihood of my making a 'dazzling impression' was slight – so I was glad to know that Aunt Mary would be there as an ally. I was close to my aunt; she was often at Hardwick, though there was a certain amount of tension between mother and daughter, for

Grandmother had taken against Uncle Gilbert; it was something to do with money. With Grandmother it was often to do with money; in her world profligacy was the ultimate sin and an unpaid debt, even between close kin, was a profound dishonour.

'I suppose Margaret will be coming?' I said.

'Didn't I mention, I've had an approach for Margaret's hand. I'll be sorry to see her go.' She stroked the stoat's pale fur. 'She's a good girl, and has a talent for needlework, but we can't keep her for ever.'

'Margaret is to wed?' I was wrong-footed, wondering how, with my careful surveillance of Grandmother's correspondence, I knew nothing of it. 'What does her father say?'

'I have written to him but he will not turn down *this* offer. It is from a much better family than theirs. Apparently the Byron boy saw her here at some hunting party or other and has set his heart. I can't imagine why, for she is not exactly a spring chicken.'

'Oh.' I couldn't think of what to say. 'First Cousin Bessie and now Margaret.' I could feel the dejection spreading through me. The world was moving on and I had been left behind in a childhood I had grown too large for. But, I reminded myself, I would be at court soon and, hostile women or not, my life would begin.

'People seem to set so much store in love these days,' Grandmother carried on. 'It seems like madness to me, but this is a good match.'

I questioned the idea that happiness was to be found in wedlock. I had seen the misery of Grandmother's final marriage and the extent to which she and the earl loathed each other by the end, but then Grandmother was not a woman given to compassion and even I, with my limited experience, understood that forgiveness lay at the heart of a good marriage.

'Did you never love *any* of your husbands?'

'Cavendish, I loved Cavendish' – her voice was clipped, as if I'd made an accusation – 'the father of my children, *your* grandfather.' She looked at her pearls. *Pitter-patter*, they went, like rain on glass. The stoat stared on at me with red eyes. 'Yes, I loved him. But don't you be fooled by love. You are destined for greater things.'

'I am not the type to be taken in by love.' I said it, but still somewhere buried deep in me, in a place I barely dared to look, was a notion that love might offer some kind of transcendence, a way to invest meaning into life and paradoxically a path to freedom. But I knew little of love. For Grandmother, love, even of her children and grandchildren, was a transaction. I was not so naive as to think that her affection for me wasn't bound up in what I, or more accurately my royal blood, might add to her carefully constructed empire. That was just her way and it was impossible not to admire how she had employed it to best use.

'Perhaps not,' she replied. 'But you have a tendency to be unpredictable.' She closed the conversation firmly by standing and moving to the door, giving me no opportunity to defend myself.

There were a number of workmen busying themselves in the gallery, which was a mess of open cartons and strewn packing straw. Paintings were stacked against the walls; I saw familiar glimpses, a painted dress I vaguely remembered being worn by Mother, Aunt Mary's neat, be-ringed hands, half the Queen's face.

For a moment Grandmother and I stood in the doorway unobserved. Margaret and the two women were down at the far end, sitting on the floor with the children, Wylkyn strumming at a lute and Frannie singing in her sweet, reedy voice. Dodderidge and Reason were about halfway down, standing in front of that portrait of me as an infant, with the miniature queen in my hand. They appeared to be in disagreement about where it should hang, with Mister Reason complaining I should be on the right-hand side of my father rather than the left.

I had never seen the portrait of my father before, wondered which of the Shrewsbury houses it might have hung in. He was a stranger to me and looked young, which he must have been, for I knew he had died aged only twenty-one. At first glance it appeared as if his heart was bleeding but it was a rose embroidered on his doublet, a Tudor rose, I realized, noticing its white centre, stained yellow with age. That was to remind the world he was the great-grandson of the first Tudor king. So in a sense the rose did signify blood, the blood that was mine too.

'She is crooked. She needs to drop an inch on the right,' said Grandmother, pointing at the picture of me.

I shivered and wrapped my shawl more tightly round my shoulders. The gallery faced east and held sixteen of Grandmother's immense windows, so even the fires raging in the two great hearths seemed to make little impression on the February cold. Casting my eyes about the space, at all those painted relatives, I imagined that tangled web of kinship, into which I was tied, like a knot that was impossible to undo.

'I don't want that in here.' Grandmother pointed to a portrait of the Scottish Queen propped against the panelling. Dodderidge swiftly turned it to face in.

No one spoke of the Queen of Scots and it was Starkey who had explained to me what really had happened to her, how she had been the focus of Catholic conspiracies to oust Queen Elizabeth and had been deemed too great a risk to remain alive. I wondered if the same fate might befall me; after all, was I not also incarcerated for fear of insurgent plots? He must have seen something scribbled over my face as he'd said, 'It is different for you. She instigated the insurrection that brought about her downfall and, besides, you are not a Catholic.'

'But people still seem to think me malleable enough to be converted.'

'If they knew you they wouldn't think such a thing, would they?'

The Scottish Queen's words ran through my mind unbidden: *The Catholic faith is the true faith; it is the only path that leads to the Kingdom of Heaven.*

'None of them know me.' I'd replied. 'I am something they conjure up in their heads.'

Margaret began to sing a round with the cousins. I caught her eye and she smiled, making me sad with the thought of her imminent loss. Through the vast window I saw a wagon lumber round the curve of the drive in the distance, watching its slow trundle towards the stable block. As it neared I recognized the horses. 'Your things from Chatsworth have arrived.'

'My tapestries.' Grandmother clapped her hands together.

Dodderidge whispered to me, 'Your uncle Henry will be furious.'

I pictured Uncle Henry's handsome face, livid, watching on as the last of Chatsworth's treasures were bundled on to the cart and tied down with canvas. Grandmother had been stripping Chatsworth to furnish Hardwick for years.

'Chatsworth must be quite emptied out,' I said.

'The contents of that house belong to *me*,' snapped Grandmother. 'They are mine to do with as I wish.'

'But Uncle Henry —'

'Don't talk to me of your hopeless uncle. He's a wastrel, as you well know. Had I not brought those things to Hardwick they would have already been sold to fund his habits.'

Nobody spoke, though Reason rearranged his big hands and murmured a noise of agreement in the dense silence.

I could never understand Grandmother's loathing of her eldest son, for to me he bristled with charm, much more so than his dull, upright younger brother William, who was inexplicably the favourite. I missed the Uncle Henry of my childhood, who would burst into a room, captivating its inmates, always with a surprise of one kind or another: an unusual feather, a puppy in need of an owner, a new card trick.

Since the great schism between mother and son, the exact source of which remained obscured to me, I rarely saw Uncle Henry. Though I was the recipient of secret letters, just affectionate and newsy missives, but prohibited nonetheless. I hoped there might be one in the hands of the carter bringing the tapestries.

'Would you excuse me, Grandmother?' I felt suddenly oppressed by my illustrious relatives watching me from the walls. 'I should like to take some air before it turns dark.'

'I suppose so.' She seemed reluctant. 'Mister Reason can accompany you.' I saw Reason shift uncomfortably at the thought of trailing his bulk round the damp gardens with me.

'Could I not go alone with Margaret, just this once?'

Grandmother sighed. 'I don't see why not. Mind you wrap up, though; I wouldn't want you coming down with something. You are far too precious.'

Margaret and I made our way around the perimeter wall of the gardens – a walk tedious in its familiarity. I glanced towards the house, where I could see the ever-present shape of Grandmother watching from the window. No doubt looking out for armed men bent on my abduction, concealed in the surrounding woods. After nearly a decade of what amounted to imprisonment, I questioned whether such a thing was likely, though Grandmother never let her guard drop. I supposed she was not prepared to risk the prize fruit she had waited a lifetime to ripen.

'First to the hedge,' I cried, picking up my skirts and running into the long grass, more for the pleasure of irritating Grandmother than for the simple joy of feeling the wet blades about my ankles. I could imagine her indignant huff leaving a cloud of condensation on the window and knew it would not be long before Reason was dispatched to curb our fun.

We ran for the partial cover of the yews. I could hear the puff of Margaret's laughter at my shoulder but I was too fast for her and pulled away towards the dark shape of the ancient hedge. The garden passed in a blur; I felt the pleasing hammer of my heart and the chill air kissing my cheeks, imagining Grandmother: *A young lady must conduct herself sedately.* What if I'd not been born a lady, if I'd been a tinker's daughter, or a farmer's I wondered, would my life offer more joy?

I asked myself if I would give up the pleasure of reading and writing for an ordinary life – of course not and, besides, a farmer's daughter was no more free than any other woman. It was men who had freedom. My foot caught on a root. I landed in the soft mulch, unhurt, bursting with laughter and then laughing more at the thought of Grandmother's disapproval. I rolled over and lay flat, looking at the sky through the mesh of branches.

'Are you hurt?' Margaret cried, breathless from running.

'Not at all.' I was grinning like an idiot in my bed of dirt.

'Your dress!' She had fixed her eyes on my overskirt. 'It is covered in mud.'

Sitting up, I saw the pale silk was smudged with black loam and that it was clogged in the embroidered border. I laughed but Margaret didn't join me and I realized that perhaps she was sad to see her fine needlework ruined. 'Never mind, it will brush off.'

'May I help you up?' She offered a hand tentatively.

I nodded, and she pulled me to my feet.

'You are too thin,' she said, reprising her refrain from earlier. 'You don't weigh a thing.'

'I cannot help that.'

She pulled back to arm's length, meeting my gaze with raised eyebrows. 'Your courses have stopped; you can't hide it from me.'

'Nature does as she pleases,' I replied, but it was a lie, for I had tamed nature to my own ends by sheer force of will, imposed androgyny on my body. The thought of it made me feel capable of anything.

'You are to be wed,' I said, to change the subject.

'What do you mean?'

'It seems quite clear to me.' I felt suddenly bitter about it all, not pleased for Margaret in the least.

'But I mean, to whom?' She looked as if she'd been slapped.

'Some local boy, a Byron, good family. He has *seen* you somewhere.' I pictured it, Margaret, allowing her gaze to flicker minutely towards some faceless fellow, catching his desire like a hooked fish. Margaret was that kind of girl; I was not.

'Oh.' She plucked at her cuff. 'So I am not to go to court?' She wouldn't look directly at me. 'And you.' Her eyes became shiny with tears, dissolving my acrimony. 'Who will keep an eye on you?'

'There are plenty to do that,' I said, knowing that was not what she meant. I led the way to the arbour where there was a bench, only slightly damp. 'You will have a house of your own and infants.' She had talked of these things almost con-stantly: *When I have a home and a string of babies*, she would stuff a pillow up her dress saying, *I think I shall make an excellent mother-to-be.*

If *I* thought too long on the idea of something growing in me it made me cold with panic.

'But what about you? We will be separated.'

'When I am queen, I shall make you a lady of the bed-chamber. How would you like that?' I said it to reassure her and this it seemed to do, for she wiped her eyes on her sleeve and took out a scrunched square of linen to blow her nose.

'I should like that very much indeed.'

A memory popped into my mind of those solemn girls who had sat day in, day out with the Queen of Scots, as much prisoners as their mistress, and shivered as if someone had walked over my grave.

'*You* will be matched soon,' she continued.

'Perhaps.' I did not repeat Grandmother's caution about marriage.

I could hear Mister Reason calling for me. 'I suppose we'd better go in.'

The cart from Chatsworth was being unloaded as we approached the house. All the warmth generated from running had dissipated, leaving me, in my drenched shoes and stockings, cold to the bone.

While Reason's attention was elsewhere, I whispered to the carter, 'Anything for me?' He shook his head. Disappointment spilled into me; the forbidden letters from my flamboyant uncle were small highlights in my dull existence and made me feel connected to the world outside.

The great hall was busy with people, a group of pages loitered to one side, eyeing up the maid who was sweeping away the mud that had been trodden through; a scribe hovered with a stack of papers that probably needed signing and Grandmother was at the centre of it all, inspecting the tapestries – scenes from the trials of Job – which had been partially rolled out over the long table.

There was the sound of someone dismounting outside

and a messenger rushed into the hall. He was panting, filthy from the road, and must have travelled quite a distance, judging by the state of him. He dipped in a bow before Grandmother and fumbled with the fastening of his satchel, having to remove his gloves to untie it. Eventually, with us all watching in silent expectation, he pulled out a letter. I instantly recognized Cecil's neat hand. Grandmother took it and gestured to Reason to give the fellow a coin and direct him to the kitchens for nourishment.

She turned her back to open the letter, little shards of the seal scattering about her feet. I remember tension in the air, though there couldn't have been, for a letter from Cecil was a regular occurrence and none of us knew in that moment the extent to which things were to change as a result of that missive's contents.

I noticed Grandmother's body stiffen as she read. Then she turned, plainly seething, her eyes hard as pebbles, and said through gritted teeth, 'There has been a change of plan. You will not be going to court as arranged.' She cast me a look of accusation that I didn't understand. I waited for an explanation, watching her ball up the paper tightly and throw it into the hearth, seeming not to realize that there was no fire lit. It was unusual for her to be so distracted. I kept one eye trained on the screwed-up letter for fear it might disappear if I looked away. 'Oh, and Essex is dead,' she added. 'The day before yesterday.'

Margaret gasped and began to make little choked sobs.

Grandmother swept off without another word.

Clerkenwell

Mansfield walks in and sits himself at the table uninvited as if he is the master of the house. Ami hurriedly puts a lid on the pot of dripping and shoves the sheaf of rushes out of sight. She has been making rush-lights and doesn't want him to see that she has been reduced to lighting her evenings in such a humble way. She is aware that, given he knows only too well her diminished state, it is a futile gesture, but she can't help wanting to preserve the little pride she has left. She thinks of the bees-wax candles she grew up with, their clean, silent, odourless light, and feels for the first time in some years the loss of the countess whose household she was raised in. Were she still alive, she would have taken Ami in, of that there is no doubt.

Dumping a sack on the floor beside him, Mansfield says, 'Linens for you.'

It is stuffed full; Ami's heart sinks, for it has been raining and she has nowhere inside to hang that quantity of washing, not with all the rest she has. She has started taking in linens from elsewhere too, to earn a little more for necessities.

She is nearing the end of her second week as a laundry maid and she can feel the dull ache in her body from all the lifting. The washing bat has rubbed her palms sore; her hands are chapped raw and blistering. She is unravelling with the exhaustion. In her head she has a picture of Mistress Mansfield and her numerous children clad in brilliant white like a host of angels – they must all have clean linen at the very least once a day, given the rate she has been washing for them. Last week was the same. 'Those are done.' She indicates one of the neatly folded stacks of clean sheets that she set near the hearth earlier to air.

'Good girl.'

She takes a breath, resisting the urge to snap back at him to mind his manners. Whether he is mocking her or belittling her or both she cannot tell, and part of her wants to laugh, for it is a ridiculous thing to call a woman of her age – unless, the thought surprises her, it is said in the throes of passion, when foolish things are often whispered.

'Don't suppose there's a cup of small beer for me, is there.' It ought to be a question but it is not. She was woken that morning by the gentle *plink* of rain dripping into the bucket upstairs. He still has not sent a man round to mend that tile.

'I might have some dregs left.' She can feel his eyes on her as she bends to lift the heavy ewer from the corner. 'My roof still needs mending.'

'Tomorrow.'

She tips a measure of the cloudy liquid into a cup and hands it to him.

'Your boy coming back soon?' he asks.

'Yes, soon.' In truth she doesn't know exactly when Hal will be back; he still hasn't written. 'He's due back Sunday.' This is the truth, at least, but whether he will turn up or not, she doesn't know.

'I see that playwright fellow met his end.' He taps at the papers on the table. 'Did you know him? You being a woman of letters – thought you might have.'

'I did once, as it happens.' Her mind is cast back to the old days when she was surrounded by musicians, players, writers; her youth was made up of them. It was Will Shakespeare who had encouraged her to put her own pen to paper in the first place. She has him to thank for that. No one knew of him back then but everyone believed he would make something of himself. He could work magic with words like no one else. His death is a great loss to that world but it is a world she is no longer a part of.

Mansfield picks up one of Lady Arbella's papers as if to read it, though she knows he cannot. Despite her desire to discover what has been written – about her, about that cauterized friendship – she has hardly managed to read a thing since she began the washing work. Reaching to take the paper off him, she finds her hand captured in his. Looking at it, he draws in a breath through pursed lips. 'Must be sore.' He softly brushes her raw skin with the pad of his index finger.

She snatches her hand away, tucking it in the folds of her apron. 'It's the starch.'

'Not used to hard toil?'

She doesn't answer but meets his gaze directly.

''Spect you've always had someone to do your housework for you.'

She still says nothing and remembers how life used to be before she'd had to let the servant girl go – all that time to think and write. If only she could write now, she might feel closer to the person she used to be, but she hasn't even time to read. Her mind drifts way back; when she was Henry Hunsdon's she wanted for nothing. Her greatest chore was to read to him – 'you have a voice pure as running water,' he used to say – or accompany him to the theatre – if she closes her eyes she can still hear the roar of the crowd and the laughter – or entertain him in the bedchamber – 'You make me feel immortal,' he had told her once. She had all the time in the world then to compose poetry. When you are eighteen you have no idea of the finite nature of things. She senses time bearing down hard on her.

'Ten days ago you had fine hands.' The softly spoken compliment sounds odd on Mansfield's coarse lips.

'I still have eight fingers and two thumbs; that's what matters.'

He takes a swig of his drink and she watches him. His own hands dwarf the cup, one of his nails is black and she notices for the first time that he is missing the tip of his left little finger, astonished she hadn't seen it before, for it seems now startlingly apparent. She wants to know what happened, feels a kind of sympathy. He is not entirely an unattractive man; rough, yes, but not unattractive.

'There is no *need* for you to labour in such a way.' His voice has dropped an octave.

Not this again, she thinks. But in spite of herself she is imagining those hands – that stump of a finger – on her naked flesh. A shiver grabs her.

'It is not such great hardship,' she says. 'There are worse ways to make a living than doing laundry.' For some reason she thinks of the smell of the lye, so pungent it makes her retch.

'I suppose it is convivial, if nothing else.'

'It is that,' she replies. She will not give him the satisfaction of knowing how the washerwomen have ostracized her and make him believe she will weaken and relent to becoming his whore. It is clear he still hopes for that, even after her firm rebuffs, though she fails to see why he would want a woman of forty-six when with his money he could pick up a wench down in Southwark on any day of the week, even Sunday.

'But a woman like you is not cut out for such work . . . An educated woman.' She thinks she can detect a note of disapproval beneath his words.

'Sadly, my education has not well prepared me for a real life. There is not much call for a female clerk.' She emits a sour laugh.

'There *is* another way.' He has adhered his gaze on to her breast, though she has crossed her shawl over and tucked the ends into the waist of her apron so there is not an inch of flesh visible. 'Surely it's not *such* a terrible prospect.'

'It is not *terrible*, no,' she says. She knows well enough that a man whose pride has been dented can become vindictive and that is the last thing she needs. 'But neither is it a prospect I can consider.'

She doesn't look at him, keeps her eyes fixed on her blistered hands and wonders if it shows on her face that she is lying, for she *is* considering it. She thinks of her time liberated for reading, imagines Arbella's papers offering up their secrets. Acquiescence is beginning to seem inevitable.

Hardwick

Essex is dead! It reverberated in my ears. More than anything, more than the sorrow that was twisting its way through me, I felt a fool, for I believed I had known Essex, but all I had known was an imaginary creature conjured up for my own comfort.

Crouching down, I plucked Grandmother's discarded letter from the ashes in the unlit hearth, secreting it up my sleeve before going to comfort Margaret, who was crouched over the table, spilling tears on to Job's dead woven children.

My hand hovered over her head, not quite touching. 'Don't cry. You barely knew Essex.' Her tears were delaying my opportunity to discover the contents of Cecil's letter and my impatience began to loom.

'It's just . . .' she snorted into her handkerchief. 'It's just that everything's about to change and there's nothing I can do to stop it.'

'Things cannot stay the same for ever.' As I said the words I was struck by the thought that for me life *was* to stay the same for ever. My world, on the brink of opening, was to have its lid rammed back on. I was to continue waiting for my real life to begin.

I had the urge to scream at her, tell her how lucky she was that her life was in motion, but pushed that thought away and mustered some sympathy. 'You always talked of wanting a husband, infants.' I found my arms opening for her and, without questioning, she leaned into my awkward embrace. Her body felt unpleasantly soft in contrast to my own, and the thought of her damp tears and oozing nose meant it took all my strength of will to sit still. I wanted, I tried, to be warm but simple affection felt so very difficult to me; I was unused to it, I suppose, and that letter was burning a hole in my sleeve. Once her sniffing had abated, I said: 'Why don't you go to the kitchens and fetch some sweetmeats? That will cheer you up.'

I hustled her off and took the stairs to the first floor. I felt my life shrinking once more, as if soon it would be too small to accommodate the whole of me at one time – perhaps, I thought, I would have to hack off pieces of myself to fit.

Grandmother was in the withdrawing chamber, sitting in the half-light, tapping her fingernails on the arm of her chair.

'Shall I light some candles?' I said.

There was no reply, only the thrum of those fingernails.

'Would you like me to fetch you something?'

Tap, tap, tap.

'A drink, perhaps?'

Tap, tap, tap.

It was as if I no longer existed, and for a moment I wondered if I had become invisible, silent, transparent, like her windows.

'Grandmother,' I said, approaching, standing so close she couldn't ignore me. 'What is it? What have I done?' My mind was churning with possible reasons for this sudden withdrawal of affection, things that might have been revealed in the letter in my sleeve. What did other people do in such circumstances, I asked myself. Do they get on the floor to supplicate, leaking tears, do they beg and paw and cling? I didn't know.

'Don't,' is all she said, with a small dismissive flick of her wrist.

I hoped my dejection wasn't apparent in my expression. Grandmother couldn't bear a weakling, so I stood tall and walked on through, leaving her in the gloom.

As I was half out of the door I heard her utter those familiar words, 'If only you'd been a boy.'

To get to my own chamber I had to pass through hers, for the other door, which led to the corridor, was kept locked for my protection. I occasionally allowed myself to imagine armed men scaling the building in the darkness and spiriting me away. At first it was a petrifying thought but over the years it had transformed into a kind of hope, driven by a fantasy of escape. I never allowed myself to imagine the full consequences of such an event – marriage to a Catholic, an army raised, the Queen ousted, or worse, an executioner looming above me. No, it was just the escape itself, with Dorcas, galloping away into the night.

In Grandmother's room there were two men dismantling my bed. Its blue and white canopy was loosely folded on the floor and they had set about taking apart the frame.

'What are you doing?'

The two men turned to me, removing their caps. 'The dowager countess instructed us to put it in your own bedchamber.'

'My bedchamber?' I said stupidly, as if I didn't quite comprehend, pointing at the connecting door.

'That is correct, My Lady.'

'Well, carry on then, I suppose.' Paradoxically, I felt devastated, rejected, though I had dreamed for years of being liberated from sharing Grandmother's chamber.

My own chamber was smaller and I wondered how they would fit the big tester in, supposing they would have to remove the existing bed, where Margaret slept with one of the other maids.

I sat on the floor by the crackling fire, pulling the paper out. It left an ashy smear on my frilled linen cuff from where I'd plucked it from the dead hearth. I opened it up and, angling it towards the remaining light, began to read.

Most esteemed Dowager Countess,

Essex met his end this morning and there has been little grief. The events of the past month have wrought changes that we could not possibly have foreseen. The political climate has altered irrevocably and it would seem that Her Majesty has turned her thoughts for the succession away from Lady Arbella and towards King James. Nothing has been said, but with my knowledge of her, I feel I am well placed to interpret her feelings and actions on the matter.

Speculating upon her intentions, I can only imagine she feels England has no appetite for another of her own sex on the throne; there seems no other motive to elevate a foreigner above a legitimate English heir. It is for this reason that I regret to announce the indefinite withdrawal of Her Majesty's invitation to the Lady Arbella to court.

It is my greatest desire, dear Dowager Countess, that you can find it in yourself to understand I have had no choice but to bow to Her Majesty's desires in this matter. But my regrets run deep, for, as you know, my greatest wishes have long lain with your granddaughter.

The best we can now hope for is that your jewel is matched favourably with the Queen's blessing and I assure you I will work tirelessly to achieve such an end. There are a number of foreign princes desiring of an allegiance with our royal house who might make appropriate potential suitors for her hand.

R. C. On the twenty-fifth day of February, in the year of Our Lord 1601

'My Lady.' It was the men dismantling my bed outside the door. 'Would it inconvenience you greatly if we brought the bed through now?'

'No, of course.' I touched the corner of the paper to the flames and held it, blazing, until it threatened to burn my fingers, only then dropping the last fragment into the fire.

I stood, smoothing the front of my dress with my palms.

My world was spinning and I felt that if I moved I would tumble right off the edge of it. The trajectory of my life had been altered irrevocably but I was still the same person and didn't know what to do. Gathering my thoughts, I resolved to find Starkey. His counsel would help. The men returned holding candles, looking ghoulish in their light. For a moment I imagined them catching the hangings, flaring up, flames licking at the fine plasterwork ceiling. I made to leave.

The miniature of the Grey sisters was on my desk. The men must have put it there, supposing it mine. An old conversation flashed through my mind:

Why do you keep the Grey girls here?

To remind myself that even the best-laid plans can go awry.

What do you mean by that?

You can never know which way public opinion will fall when a childless monarch passes on. Not enough care was taken in the choice of Jane Grey's husband. That was what led to her downfall.

I remembered not really understanding what Grandmother meant by that at the time, but now I was beginning to get a sense of the jostling for position as the Queen aged and it was clear that I had been elbowed out of the way.

I gave my head a little shake in an attempt to dispel the image which had appeared in my mind of Jane Grey blindfolded, kneeling at the block.

I don't know how I made it to the schoolroom downstairs without falling but I must have found some inner resource of steadiness. Starkey was in there as I expected, reading in the dim light of a single flame. Though I was not supposed to be with Starkey unchaperoned, I found it easy to circumvent this restriction and the schoolroom had become a sanctuary where he and I passed many hours together, sometimes in silence, separately scribbling our thoughts on to paper, sometimes engaged in a lively exchange of ideas.

'You will ruin your eyes,' I said, taking a taper and lighting more candles as a means to calm my inner turmoil. 'My trip to court has been –'

'Postponed,' he interrupted. 'Yes, the servants were talking about it.'

'Not postponed, no. The invitation is rescinded.'

'What is the reason given?' He was frowning.

I sat and explained the contents of Cecil's letter, forcing myself to remain steady and not allow the frenzy that was moving through me in waves to break my surface.

'This is a setback, that is all. You know that, don't you?'

'I'm not so sure. The Queen seems adamant, according to Cecil.'

'Listen to me; you were born to take your rightful place, it is not a question of choice. Remember Socrates: for a just society each must perform his ordained role. Doctors must heal, soldiers must fight, rulers must –'

'Rulers must rule.' I was always reassured by Starkey's ordered version of the world, in which everything took its proper place, but I had begun to suspect that, in the face of outside forces, such an ordered world might be less straightforward than I'd once believed. 'But Cecil . . . Cecil is the man who decides. You know enough of him to understand that. He may insist it is the Queen's wish that my cousin takes the throne, but he wears his ambition too close to the surface. Even I, who know so little of men, know that. If he believes there is advantage to him in James becoming king then that is what will happen, despite what he has said in his letter about it being solely the Queen's wish.'

'Have faith. God has His plan for you.' There was a quiet fervour in him, in his eyes and the way he pressed his palms together and was moving them back and forth like a supplicant. Between God and Socrates, Starkey had built around me an impregnable edifice. It was a refuge, with its own certain logic, in which we had existed comfortably.

'Your cousin,' he continued, 'is a foreigner. He has no right to your throne, no matter what Cecil' – he spat the name as if it were the devil's – 'wants. It is what God wants that will come to pass.'

'And the Queen? If it is *her* wish then that must reflect God's desire, for she is His emissary.'

'It is –' His mouth opened but he seemed unable to force a sound out of it. Sudden as a sneeze the words came: '. . . *not* her wish.' He then repeated it calmly. 'It is not her wish.' Starkey's unwavering confidence had a powerful allure that drew me in tightly and he regarded me with a beatific smile that seemed filled with love. 'God has shown me in a dream . . . you know this anyway.'

'Your dream of me crowned.' When the barren years were stretching out and I was despairing of ever being recalled to court, Starkey had spent a day in prayer, begging for a vision of the future. When he slept, that was his dream. 'I wish I had your faith.' I banged my fist down on to the table, hard enough to bruise the knuckles.

'Don't,' he said. 'Please.' He offered his hand like a question. I nodded my assent and he took my bruised fingers very gently, inspecting the damage.

'Cecil is seeking a foreign match for me.' I was thinking of the conversation earlier with Grandmother about marriage and how it was to be avoided until I was on the throne, but everything had been different only a few hours ago. My world was like a reflection in a convex mirror, nothing quite as it should be.

'There will be ways to prevent that.'

He seemed so sure. I longed for his unassailable conviction.

Hardwick, twenty-two months later

'My Lady!' A shard of light fell through the gap in the curtains, reigniting the pain that had been hovering. I scrunched
my eyes shut. 'My Lady!' Joan's voice was needling. Joan was
Margaret's replacement, in a manner of speaking. I say that,
for she was more jailer than companion. She had thrown a
stack of my papers on the fire not long before. 'You don't
want all this nonsense cluttering up your chamber,' she had
said of it. I suspected spite but it might have been sheer
ignorance.

I buried my head beneath the covers, trying to imagine
Joan away. 'I am not well.'

Joan made an exasperated sigh. 'But your grandmother
requires you to join her. She's waiting.' I could hear the worry
in her voice and suspected it was more her fear of displeas-
ing Grandmother than concern for my health.

'A minute. I need a minute.' I could hear her tutting but
ignored it, concentrating only on taking several long deep
breaths. The pain in my head sulked like an ignored child. I
circled my temples with the tips of my fingers, remembering
the pilfered ewer of Grandmother's best French wine that
Starkey and I had imbibed in the schoolroom on the previous evening.

Such indulgence was not a regular occurrence and Starkey
had needed persuading to break his advent fast, but we were
commiserating his imminent departure. Grandmother had
dismissed him; it was under the guise of his being offered a
congregation elsewhere, but in truth it was a dismissal – part
of the slow whittling away of those closest to me. Thinking
of it caused my hatred to flare. Soon, I feared, she would find

a reason to be rid of Dodderidge, rendering my isolation complete.

Fragmented memories of the previous evening returned. We had made toasts, all sorts of toasts, to Socrates, to Plato and the Stoics, even to dear Dorcas, if my memory served me well. We had laughed and laughed until we could barely breathe, neither of us wanting to think of the fact of his imminent departure.

I could hear Joan riffling through the papers on my desk. 'I don't know what she finds to write about,' she said to herself, though loud enough for me to hear. 'And what's the point if no one ever reads it.'

I held my breath to prevent myself from snapping at her. Slowly, as my thoughts assembled, I remembered the letter Dodderidge had secreted between the leaves of a book left on my pillow the previous evening. As I was retiring, stupid with drink, I had read it, or tried to. *The petals are falling from the rose and it is time to gather our forces in preparation*, Uncle Henry had written, but beyond that my memory was a blur.

All I knew was that it contained something important and deeply secret concerning my future. I racked my brains to remember where I'd put it, fearing I might have left it exposed on my desk, where Joan was now nosing about. But then I had a vague memory of having read it in bed, with a candle, whilst Joan was snoring on the truckle, of dripping wax on my coverlet, could feel the smooth discs under my fingertips. I searched amongst the bedclothes to no avail but, sliding my hand beneath my pillow, my touch met with the rough surface of the paper and relief flooded through me.

The day burned red through my closed eyelids as I surfaced, but the headache had receded to a distant throb. Squinting, I could see the sturdy shape of Joan standing over me with the light behind her, making her expression unreadable, though her impatience registered in the clearing of her throat.

'Better?' Her tone suggested I had wasted her entire morning, though she had waited a couple of minutes at most for me to emerge. She folded her arms firmly beneath her great shelf of a bosom, which stretched the fabric of her dress perilously tight.

'Yes, better. Thank you.'

'You *do* look off colour, I must say.'

I swung my legs out of the blankets to sit upright, regretting the sudden movement as my head swam for a moment and nausea loomed; but I sat absolutely still on the edge of the bed until it died away. Warmth was spreading out into the room from the hearth. I touched my fingertip to the hidden letter once more to be sure it was truly there and I hadn't burned it for caution whilst in my cups. *Your time is nearing.* Only fragments came back to me.

I stood, nodding my assent for Joan to help me into my underclothes. Lacing my bodice, she pinched the skin of my waist, hard enough to hurt but not to bruise; that was her way. 'You are all skin and bone.'

'It is the way God made me.' *Better than your great hefty shape*, I thought.

'No more shapely than a lad.' A bud of satisfaction opened in me on hearing that.

'I should like to wear the green velvet today.' I said this knowing Joan would have to fetch it from downstairs. 'I would like to look my best for Starkey's last day.'

'You two are thick as thieves. You'll miss him,' she said with a sly smile. 'Why don't you wear the rose damask? It suits your complexion better than the green. Particularly as you look so unwell today.' Joan was mistress of the backhanded compliment.

'It must be the green. Green is Starkey's favourite colour.'

This was a lie, I had no idea what colour Starkey preferred; we had far better things to discuss.

'Anyone would think you were sweethearts, the way you talk.' It was framed light-heartedly but not meant so. Perhaps she believed that was the reason for his departure.

She made a final, half-hearted attempt to promote the pink dress, fully aware that I was not often amenable to persuasion, and left the chamber muttering 'stubborn as a mule' under her breath.

Once the door had closed behind her I took the letter to the window. Uncle Henry's florid hand brought a smile to my face but the content was serious.

My dearest and most beloved Royal niece,

It is my understanding that Cecil is negotiating to wed you abroad and my mother is inexplicably in his pocket. This will undermine any hopes of you ever fulfilling your purpose. We must prevent this if your cousin James is to be overcome in his hopes to take the throne that is yours.

Our perfect solution lies in a proposition from Lord Beauchamp. He has offered one of his sons, probably the oldest, Edward, for marriage. A match such as this would seal your claim incontrovertibly.

The Seymour boys have enough royal blood to make a suitable union with you. As the grandsons of Katherine Grey and the Earl of Hertford, they are the only Englishmen I know of who do. Two Tudor lines would be entwined. The Seymour line may be illegitimate, though I happen to know Hertford is determined to prove it good. He would know if he was properly wed to Katherine Grey and there are many others who believe the union was sound.

The petals are falling from the rose and it is time to gather our forces in preparation. There will be a window of time when the rose is almost withered in which you can wed with no risk of repercussion, for heads will all be turned the other way. If your cousin is proclaimed it will be too late and too dangerous.

I can only assume, and hope from deep in my heart, that you are willing. Your time is nearing, a mere matter of months, I'd wager, and you must be prepared to leave Hardwick at a moment's notice. I will have everything in hand. There are a number of influential nobles who, when it becomes necessary, will gather to counter Cecil's faction and the Scottish claim and back yours. Few will want a foreigner on the English throne. I will begin discreetly mustering support and plan to gain the Earl of Hertford's favour; that will shore us up and doubtless bring others to our cause.

I ask you to send what things of value you own to a safe place, as you may find yourself in need of funds once away from Hardwick.

I await your word of agreement, your loving uncle, Henry Cavendish.

XX Dec – AD 1602

A buzz of anticipation traversed the nape of my neck. We had heard of the Queen's failing health from the usual lines of communication between the court and Hardwick – a constant back and forth of messengers on the Great North Road. The entire country had been quietly on tenterhooks, waiting, preparing.

I imagined that 'window of time', a period of limbo when the Queen would be reaching out to death, not quite gone but neither in a position to crush my Seymour marriage with her practised force and before Cecil had a chance to bundle my cousin on to the throne. For the first time my fate seemed tangible. It was my window; I was perched on its ledge, ready to fly from it to meet my future.

Casting my gaze out across the gardens I saw a pair of doves cooing to each other on the roof of the gatehouse. It seemed like a sign, though I was not a great believer in omens. Thinking about Hertford and his own doomed marriage to

Katherine Grey, I wondered whether his intentions in that had been driven by ambition or love. But things are never so clean cut, for surely love and ambition are often bedfellows. I had cause to believe he would be sympathetic to my situation, having lived through something similar himself. I did not know him, had met him briefly once at court, but felt an affinity which I assumed he shared, for did I not have the same Tudor blood as his long-dead wife running through my veins?

The idea of fighting for my legitimate claim had ignited a spark in me. After all, I had been raised knowing it was the sole purpose of my existence. What truly stirred me too, aside from the idea of the crown, was the adventure of such an endeavour, the fact that I, who had lived a life entombed, with no jurisdiction over my future, was taking hold of my own destiny.

I watched the pair of doves take flight, their tail feathers fanning out beautifully as they opened up their wings. I was stimulated not by the notion of marriage in and of itself but by what such a union would bring me. It would raise me to my rightful station and even if it didn't succeed in setting me on the throne it would set me free.

I destroyed the letter and, with those funds in mind, took up my casket of jewels, emptying it on the bed, picking out the few prized pieces; they were all the wealth I owned. Had I come into my father's lands on my majority, as I was meant to, I would not have needed that meagre collection of trinkets. It was my cousin James who persisted in keeping my inheritance from me. Grandmother had petitioned him on my behalf for years. I reasoned that James didn't see it in his interests to furnish me, his rival, with sufficient riches to buy the kind of influence that might challenge his own ambitions.

I bundled up the jewels into a small cloth bag, tucking it beneath my petticoats. Then, taking up a length of linen and my embroidery scissors, I sat hunched on the floor and carefully made a small incision above my ankle. It was a monthly ritual. I squeezed the lips of the cut, catching a few drops of blood on the linen, watching it blossom out into the weave of the fabric.

After mopping the tiny wound, I discarded the bloody cloth in the linen basket, and was putting on my stockings as Joan returned. I smiled at her. 'You seem better,' she said as she helped me into the green velvet.

'I do feel a little more like myself.' She tightened my laces while I plaited my hair and coiled it to my head, fastening it. All the time I could feel the pouch of jewels pressing against my thigh.

'There you are.' She handed me a lace-edged cap. 'Lovely.' To see us you might have thought we were the best of friends.

As I'd anticipated, she picked up the linen basket, holding it on her hip, sifting through its contents with her opposite hand.

'Can't the servant maid do that?' I said.

'Yes, I suppose so.' She had the bloodstained linen between the tip of her finger and thumb. 'Your courses are on time to the day. You *are* lucky. I can never tell from one month to the next when mine will appear.'

The idea of Joan's monthlies horrified me. 'I have been blessed with regularity.'

She had no idea that my courses had stopped long since. Joan was saying something; I wasn't listening, was watching the rolls of her chin wobble as she spoke. The sight of her flesh made me feel cast in steel, slender and deadly as a sword. In my life, as it was then, with its margins so narrow, such a seemingly small deceit as the pretence of my courses was a great triumph and its effects poured into me, filling me with courage to execute the greater deceit that was looming.

*

As I entered the withdrawing room, the dogs greeted me, tails waving lazily. Grandmother was silhouetted in the window and there were various members of the close household scattered about the room. Starkey was reading, Dodderidge was in conversation with Mister Reason and the little cousins were playing draughts in the alcove.

As I approached Grandmother she snapped, 'You missed morning prayers.'

'I've been out of sorts.'

She looked me up and down. 'You seem perfectly well to me.'

In the garden below some men were busy reshaping the winter beds, transforming one of them from the form of an A into an E, so they spelled out, rather than AS for Arbella Stuart, ES for Elizabeth Shrewsbury – Grandmother's initials.

I couldn't help saying, 'How convenient that both Stuart and Shrewsbury share an initial. It will save the men a good deal of work,' and made no attempt to hide my sarcasm.

She sighed with pursed lips and ran her hand down the length of her pearls, reminding me of my own treasure cached beneath my skirts. 'I trust you are feeling better now.' There was not a splinter of sympathy in her tone, only irritation, but what use was sympathy to me anyway. 'Let's eat. We have all been waiting.'

We gathered at the table and Starkey said grace. I felt Grandmother stiffen with annoyance when he stumbled slightly over one of the prayers.

'This is the last grace you will say for us,' I said once we were seated, feeling intensely the tug of imminent separation.

'I wish you would stay longer,' said Wylkyn.

'An opportunity has come up.' Starkey was falsely bright. 'And in life opportunities are to be gr—'

'Grasped with both hands.' Wylkyn was unable to resist finishing Starkey's oft-used saying.

'We can't keep him here for ever,' I said. 'That would be selfish.'

'Will we have a new tutor, then?'

'Not some fellow who is fond of the birch,' Frannie pleaded. Starkey was known for his lenience with the children.

Grandmother masticated slowly in silence, seeming impervious to the sentiment about the table.

'There is a new man coming in January,' I told the children. 'But in the meantime *I* will be keeping an eye on your studies. Isn't that right, Starkey?'

'Wylkyn, will you vow to speak only Latin with Lady Arbella until the new man arrives?' he said.

'*Voveo*,' said Wylkyn.

'*Promitto* or *spondeo* might be more correct for such a promise,' I corrected.

'Will you teach me Latin too, Cousin Belle?' asked Frannie.

'Don't be silly, Frances. Girls don't need anything more than the most rudimentary Latin,' said Grandmother, taking a slice of manchet bread, inspecting it closely, picking out some tiny impurity and sniffing it as if it might have been poisoned.

'But Cousin Belle knows Latin,' pleaded Frannie, refusing defeat.

'It is different for her. She will be . . . well.' She stopped, and I thought that in that moment Grandmother no longer knew what I might be. 'It is different.'

The secret of my escape simmered beneath my skin and I wondered when my indomitable grandmother had lost her fight.

'But different why?' Frannie had not accurately read Grandmother's mood.

'Enough,' she barked, silencing the child. 'The sooner the new tutor arrives, the better. Arbella has more important things to do than conjugate Latin verbs.'

What things? I wanted to shout, for nothing filled my empty days.

I rubbed at the little incision on my ankle with my foot. In some small way that sensation, the intense momentary sting of it, reminded me that I was the governor of my destiny, that I had mastered a convincing illusion that had taken in even prying Joan. It reminded me that I had the courage to set myself free whatever the cost.

I filled my plate and, breaking my food into small pieces, quietly slipped some to the dogs. They had developed the habit of lurking about beneath the table near me, where the pickings were rich. Hunger prodded insistently at my belly but I refused to acknowledge it and it skulked off like a demon in the face of a saint. No one noticed that I ate almost nothing, for the impression I managed to create was the opposite. I had learned that it is easy to make people imagine they know what they are seeing, just as Uncle Henry liked to do with his tricks.

Looking back, I have often wondered what made me thus. Perhaps it was that I had been educated for a more stimulating kind of life, prepared for greatness, and found myself an adult woman of twenty-seven, kept in perpetual girlhood, in a world bereft of even jurisdiction over my daily walk in the gardens. That feeling of emptiness, that glorious hollowness, and the artifice that achieved it, gave me a sense of accomplishment, perhaps even of pride.

Once we had left the table I made my way down to the schoolroom, seeking a moment alone with Starkey before his departure. I shut the door and, noticing last night's empty flagon of wine in the corner, said lightly, 'You look as if you've seen better days.'

He didn't take my cue and tell me I was hardly a picture of health myself, as he might have done on any other day. 'I can't endure this.' He turned his back as if he couldn't bear even to look at me.

A silence fell, punctuated only by the faint clamour coming from the great hall where the rest of the household were finishing their meal. Grandmother employed a large entourage; she liked to think of Hardwick as her own personal court. I could hear the clatter of dishes being cleared, followed by the scrape of a table being pushed back against the wall.

'You must make the best of it,' I said eventually, to his black worsted shoulders, so straight; Starkey had perfect bearing. 'Think about it; you will not be stuck here with . . . You can find a nice girl to be your wife.' My voice cracked slightly.

'A nice girl is the last thing on my mind.' He turned back to me then. 'I have never had any other ambition than to serve you.' He looked like a man grieving.

'I wish . . .' I didn't continue.

We both looked at the floor, not knowing how to fill the silence, but then I found myself surprised by a sudden and overwhelming desire to reach out and take his hand. It was cold and stiff. I rubbed it between mine to warm it up as one might a child's. His desolation was written all over him and I had to resist the urge to blurt out the plans for my marriage; to tell him that we would soon be reunited and away from the auspices of my grandmother, that he would be my chaplain in my new life – my imminent new life – that we had a shared future to look towards; to tell him that Uncle Henry was mustering armed men to aid my escape. But I knew well enough that I might endanger him with such knowledge if my scheme went awry. The idea of Starkey withstanding a grilling from Cecil or his henchmen chilled me to the core.

'When things have changed' – he must have supposed I meant at some obscure point in the future – 'I hope you will take the position of my personal chaplain.'

'May that day come soon.'

It may come sooner than you think, I said silently, then, 'You never know.'

'It grieves me to leave you here with so few friends. You will be at the mercy . . .' His words faded away.

'Come now, have you not spent hours drumming into me the advantages of stoicism?'

He smiled then; it was a wan sort of smile but it gave me a splinter of joy. 'You are right. Stoic I shall be.'

'I am more resilient than you think, and though I may be bereft of friends within these walls, save for Dodderidge, I have many elsewhere.' I began to count them off on my fingers. 'Aunt Mary and Uncle Gilbert, Uncle Henry, Cousin Bessie. And there is you.' I smiled then too. 'Wherever you are in the world, I will always think of you dearly.'

He was gazing at me with a strange intensity and then, without warning, he flung his arms around me, holding me tight. I could feel the thump of his heart against my own. I had never been held in such a way; it was the way a child might cling on to its mother before a period of separation, or even the clasp of a lover. I allowed my head to rest on his shoulder; the worsted wool was rough against my cheek. I closed my eyes. Time slowed. Our hearts matched in rhythm. I inhaled as he exhaled, as if we had a pair of lungs in common, like those conjoined twins you hear of, who only live a matter of hours.

I emitted a strange, faint moan and he broke away from me abruptly. 'I'm sorry, so sorry. I don't know what came over me.' His cheeks were painfully red and he could not bring himself to look my way.

'No! I'm . . .' – I stumbled over the words – 'I'm glad of it.'

I willed him to meet my eye and read my sincerity. 'You are the nearest thing I have to a brother.'

'A brother,' he snorted with sudden derisive laughter. 'Please God, not a brother –'

I interrupted him; afraid of what he might have been about to say. 'There is something I need you to do for me.'

'Anything, anything – it would be an honour.' His eyes lit up and I wondered if he was relieved that I'd prevented him from finishing his previous statement. 'Tell me what it is I can do.'

I began to fumble beneath my skirts and was reminded suddenly, strangely, of that time back in my childhood when I changed into those voluminous breeches in the Stand Tower at Chatsworth. Catapulted briefly back to the feeling of riding astride, bareback, the force of the wind filling me with the potent sense that nothing was beyond my reach.

I pulled out the linen-wrapped package of jewels, placing it on the table beside us. 'These are all I have of value. I cannot keep them here, for I fear Grandmother will commandeer them. Will you take them to Cousin Bessie? Did you know she's with child? It will be nice for you to see her again.' I was rambling to prevent myself from spilling out the true reason for this service I was asking of him.

I held out the parcel and Starkey took it with the solemnity of someone receiving the sacraments, clasping it in both hands carefully with a look of reverence. 'What shall I tell her?'

'To keep them safe, that I'll be in touch and to tell no one.'

'I am honoured that you trust me with so delicate a mission.' He had become stiff and formal but the memory of his body pressed up to mine hung in the air.

'I might need funds one day.' This was the most I dared tell him. The less he knew, the less likely he would be endangered. 'You must not breathe a word of it to anyone –'

We were interrupted by Wylkyn clattering in, calling out loudly to his sister to hurry up. He stopped and must have sensed intrigue in the air, for he said, 'What are you doing? What is that?' pointing at the linen bag in his tutor's hands.

Starkey looked petrified, as if caught out by the devil himself, and a new flush crept over his face. It should have occurred to me then that he was unsuitable, too nervous, too fundamentally honest, for such a delicate and possibly dangerous mission. He opened his mouth to say something but I spoke over him.

'It is a leaving gift from me. I thought Mister Starkey might like a few trinkets for his new home to remind him of his time at Hardwick.'

Starkey was staring at me aghast, perhaps fearing he too might be required to lie; he was a man of the cloth, after all. Or perhaps the realization was alighting on him that the task he had agreed to fulfil might somehow put him at risk.

'What are they? May I see?' The boy was plucking at the corner of the bag with eager fingers.

'No, Wylkyn,' I said, trying to keep my voice firm and steady. 'It is to be a surprise for Mister Starkey. Don't you think it will bring him more pleasure to open it when he has arrived at his destination and then be reminded of us all at Hardwick?'

'I suppose so.'

Only then did I notice Frannie leaning on the doorjamb watching us, sucking on a strand of hair that had fallen free of its ties. 'What? What will be a surprise?'

'Nothing,' said her brother with a dismissive wave. 'Come on, let's go.' He reached up to a shelf, taking down a measuring stick. 'We are going to measure the long gallery. Mister Reason and Mister Dodderidge cannot agree on its length,' he added, before rushing from the room with his sister in his wake, leaving me hoping he wouldn't mention my supposed gift to Grandmother.

'Don't make too much noise,' I called after them, mindful of the fact that Grandmother had forbidden them from going up to the gallery unaccompanied. 'And don't forget we are supposed to be conversing in Latin.'

'Are you truly willing to do this?' I asked Starkey, once we were alone again.

'I couldn't be more willing.' He seemed to have gained a new composure, which gave me confidence. 'You know I am ever your most loyal servant.' I remember having the fear then that I might never live up to the expectations he held for me.

I have thought often about fate. When you have been bred for a particular destiny, it is hard to change the course of it, like an arrow, once aimed and fired its flight is predisposed unless something should stray in its path.

'One day I hope to be in a position to reward your loyalty.'

He was holding the jewels pressed to his chest as if they might have imparted some special power to him.

'I do not seek personal reward, only that you find your rightful place.' Despite everything, Starkey had never given up his belief that the throne would one day be mine. But the idea of wearing the crown, embedded in me from infancy, had become an abstraction; it was the hope of liberty that drove me. Uncle Henry's marriage plot was my lodestar; indeed, my desire to escape the confines of Hardwick was greater than my fear of the grave potential consequences of the plot's failure.

I watched as Starkey cached the jewels on his person. That done, we stood a few feet apart, enveloped in awkwardness. I wanted to step towards him and return to that glorious embrace in suspended time, but a spontaneous act cannot be repeated and I found I couldn't muster the courage.

'It will be cold on the road. You will take care not to catch a chill, won't you?' The bathos of my words made me sad and all at once I couldn't bear the idea of him spending Christmas with strangers – not with me.

'At least it will be frozen rather than muddy.' He seemed pleased too, to be able to resort to banalities about the weather.

Unfamiliar emotion was ballooning in me, threatening to make itself known. 'Have you packed your things? I could send Joan to help you.'

'That old witch?' He looked at me in mock horror and his eyes glinted briefly with humour, forcing a laugh from me.

'Write to me,' I blurted out.

Neither of us wanted to leave first, as if by doing so we might destroy something fragile, like new-blown glass shattered, but I girded myself and moved towards the door. 'I shall watch you leave from the gallery window.' I felt my resentment build at the thought that I wouldn't be able to ride the length of the drive with him, nor even see him off at the stables. As consolation, I clung to the thought of my imminent freedom with dear Starkey back by my side.

Someone is whistling in the street. 'Hal,' says Ami under her breath, rushing out of the door. And there he is strolling along, bag slung over his shoulder, lute hanging from his hand.

She waves, calling out to him, noticing how he stiffens at the sight of her. 'If you'd sent word you were coming, I'd have been better prepared.'

'I thought you knew I'd be back today – two weeks.' He shrugs, allowing his dark hair to hang forward, so he doesn't have to look at her as he passes by to enter the house.

'Without word I wasn't absolutely sure . . .' She follows him in and shuts the door. 'I didn't expect you so early. I've no small beer and I haven't started making the bread yet.' She is thankful that she finished off the final load of laundry and delivered it to Mansfield's house before Hal arrived.

He makes a cold little huff in response as he lets his bag drop to the floor. She takes his lute, placing it carefully on the high shelf. She'd like to hug him but senses it is not a good idea.

'I'm not staying long. Been asked to go on progress with the King's party. Leaving at dawn.'

'But that's wonderful news.' She pastes on a big smile and throws her hands up to hide the disappointment – though how would she have hidden her penury and her new working arrangements if he were to have stayed? She would have found a way to explain, but there is no need now. Besides, she *is* happy, for this is a great honour. 'I knew they'd recognize your talent.'

He goes to the cupboard, opening it, picking up a piece of elderly cheese. 'There's nothing to eat here, Mother.'

'No, I was saying, if I'd known when you were coming . . .'

He leans against the table and begins to pare the rind off the cheese. 'You never told me you were dismissed from court by the King.'

'It was a while ago.' She senses she must tread carefully. 'It didn't seem to matter.'

'And that's not all you've kept from me, is it?' It was surely impossible that he knew the other reason for her dismissal. 'Rumours about my paternity.'

Ami swallows, partly relieved that it is not the other thing – mired in shame – that she has to explain. 'I wouldn't listen to them if I were you. You know how people will invent stories – particularly at court. Just nonsense.' Why is she lying? She has become tangled in her own untruths.

'So I am *not* Lord Hunsdon's bastard?'

'Hal, please.' She can't bring herself to deny it fully. 'Please don't be like this. Let's not allow some idle tittle-tattle to spoil the fact that you are home.' She stops short of reminding him he is all she has – he knows that. But she sees something shift in his demeanour. The tautness drops off him. He flicks his hair back and smiles, bright as lightning. He has chosen to believe her. He was always like this, could never hold on to a sulk for long, and it makes her quite giddy to see that smile again, the ghost of the gappy, babyhood grin that melted her heart every time. It's the same even now he is a young man, that welling of love, that feeling that she must rein it in for fear of smothering him.

'You know they talk of you a good deal in Queen Anna's chambers. Your poetry is greatly admired there. I didn't realize you were so . . .' He stops and seems to puff out a little. 'You are well known, Ma.'

'They still talk of my work at court?' It fills her with joy to think of her lines being read, thinking of the Queen's women still discussing her poetry even after such a long absence. It makes her feel she is still part of it all.

'It made me so proud, Ma. I wanted to butt in and tell them I was your son.'

'I hope you didn't.'

'Of course not; I know my position.' He smiles again. 'But' – he pauses – 'why, if you are so celebrated at court, did the King dismiss you?'

'He was offended by the content of my work. That I sought to defend Eve and other women he deemed indefensible.' Hal has a crease of incomprehension running vertically between his eyes. 'And King James doesn't approve of educated women. His wife is not of the same mind.' It is only part of the truth but she cannot tell him the rest. Her secrets and lies press down on her.

The tabby jumps on to the table and Ami reaches out to push her off but Hal grabs her wrist. 'What's happened to your hands?'

Ami tucks them away beneath her shawl. But Hal pulls the garment aside, exposing them, chapped and raw as hunks of meat and this only after two weeks of washing.

He looks at her, questioning.

'It's nothing.' She wraps him into a hug, so he can't see them. 'How happy I am to have you back.' She is always struck by the size of him, for in her imagination he is still the small boy she raised. 'So you are going on progress with the royal party. I am so proud of you.' She leans away to look at him. 'To think, my little boy playing for the King.'

Fleeting annoyance passes over his face, reminding her that this truce is fragile. He will not have liked being called a little boy. She wants to ask if he will be paid for his services but is afraid he will read the worry written all over her if she brings up the subject of money.

'Just as your grandfather did. It was King Henry on the throne in those days.'

'The music master has increased my fee by a ha'penny,

which is not much but I feel sure that it will lead to patronage of one kind or another. There are one or two noblemen who have made noises. It is my flute-playing they like, rather than the lute. The place is overrun with lutenists but pipers are more rare.'

'None play as well as you, of that I am sure. Those lords and earls will be falling over themselves for your talent. Be patient, my darling.' She lets him go, still taking care to keep her hands hidden. 'I have a few eggs. I'll boil them for you to be going on with. I hope they're feeding you well at court.'

'You should see the quantities of food they serve, whole sides of venison, great knuckles of pork, poultry I never knew existed, and every day, not only on feast days.' His eyes are bright with it all.

'I *have* seen it. Oh, I remember the banquets in Queen Elizabeth's day. Goodness, you couldn't have conjured up such sugar artefacts . . .' She is struck by the memory of a sugar castle – its fine detail, each roof tile a separate painted square, each window a minuscule transparent pane, the delicate turrets topped with tiny banners, so lifelike they appeared to flutter in an imaginary breeze – demolished, as if destroyed by cannon fire, by the end of an evening.

They compare stories of excess, each trying to outdo the other, and Ami is glad the attention has gravitated away from her secrets. There will be more washing tomorrow; she can feel each great basin of water hefted from the Fleet, all the wringing, all the beating, all the heavy lifting, her aching bones and those awful women making it all the more difficult.

She is thankful Hal won't witness any of it if he is leaving at dawn. She remembers the royal progresses, the bustle and excitement of them, the servants run off their feet, packing and unpacking, dismantling and rebuilding furniture, their great convoy trundling through towns and villages, people lining the road, hoping for a glimpse of the royal party. How she loved to explore the unfamiliar houses, losing herself in winding corridors, happening upon libraries with books stacked to the ceiling, where she'd steal a half-hour alone. She remembers, too, the conversations with Lady Arbella, in stolen moments, in which they would discuss poetry and writing, exchange their work. Ami sought advice about her defence of Eve and between them they would scrutinize all the biblical stories about wicked women to tease new truths out of them. They talked of Philomel too, and how that tragedy symbolized the ways silenced women found to be heard. It was a perfect project for Lady Arbella, who always seemed to her to be a woman with much to say but to whom no one listened. Thinking of her leaves Ami hollow for the absence of that affinity. The loss of a friendship can be every bit as devastating as the loss of a love. Particularly when it is lost through one's own fault.

'We shall have a feast of our own, Ma. I shall go out to the market and buy one of those pies you like so much.'

Inexplicably she feels tears pricking at her eyes and moves to busy herself by the hearth so he doesn't see.

'Did you find anything of interest in those papers?' he asks.

'Goodness me, yes.' She thinks of little else as she scrubs and squeezes and beats the dirt out of endless stacks of filthy linen. Her raw hands are the proof of her shame. But the lack of candles and the density of the text means she is making interminably slow progress. She is like Tantalus, the fruits at her fingertips yet just out of her grasp. 'It's not what I'd thought.'

'What had you expected?'

'A drama. I knew she had worked on one once – a tragedy.'

'What is it, then?'

Ami is at a loss as to explain exactly what it is. 'Scenes

from her life, I suppose. Very personal . . . and sad. It would bring tears to a glass eye.'

'You *are* funny, Ma, taking such pleasure in misery.'

She had never thought of it like that. 'It's not that I enjoy the misery; but it brings inspiration.'

The cockcrow wakes her. She hears something, someone, moving downstairs. It is not the cat; the tabby is beside her curled on the pillow. Fear paws at her; she imagines an intruder, wondering how she will defend herself, until she remembers, through the fog of sleep, that Hal is home.

She lies a moment, luxuriating in the warmth of her bed, refusing to think about the three loads of washing that will be delivered in a while. Instead she thinks of preparing a breakfast for Hal before he goes on his way and drags herself down the stairs.

'Good morning, my darling boy,' she says as she stoops under the lintel at the bottom. But the place is empty, Hal's bag is nowhere to be seen and his lute is not on the high shelf. 'Hal?'

She goes to the door, looking up and down the street. But it is empty, save for a few chickens pecking about and a stray dog sniffing in the gutter. She walks along a little and calls his name again.

'He went off with his bag.' She turns to see Goodwife Stringer, who has appeared from nowhere, standing arms folded. 'Did he not bid you goodbye?'

She gathers herself. 'I expect he didn't want to wake me.' The woman looks unconvinced. 'He's going on the royal progress.'

'Even so, you'd have thought he'd bid his ma goodbye.'

Goodwife Stringer is looking at her intently, waiting for her to say something, but all she wants is to get inside and see if Hal left her a note. 'I'm very busy, please excuse me.'

Inside, there is no note but there placed, accusingly, at the middle of the table is her miniature. It has the inscription

Henry Lord Hunsdon ♦ *Aetatis Suae 68* ♦ *Ano D 1593*

spelled out in gold on a bright blue background running round the curved edge of the image. She sinks on to the bench, looking at her grotesque hands, dropping her face into them, and begins to weep, feeling her fragile world crumble to extinction.

Hardwick

Though he had been gone barely a week, I was bereft without Starkey and thankful that Hardwick had begun to fill with relatives arriving for the Christmas season, with Aunt Mary amongst them. My aunt's permanent air of chaos, things forgotten, things in disarray, things mismatched, teamed with her tendency towards unrestrained enjoyment and raucous laughter, provided a welcome disruption to the rigorous order of Hardwick.

On the day she arrived we braved a walk round the icy garden, where she slipped me a letter from Uncle Henry, telling me, 'I know about your plans. I intend to do what I can to help.'

I read it as we walked together; it was bitterly cold and our breath hung in clouds.

On reflection I think it should be you to canvass Hertford's support, rather than I. A plea directly from you will have an air of authenticity, demonstrate you are a willing party, a driving force in this, and not simply a pawn in your favourite uncle's power games.

'Have you read it?' I asked her.

She nodded. 'He showed it to me before it was sealed.'

We were conscious of Grandmother watching at the window and instinctively spoke in whispers, as if she were able, through some kind of supernatural force, to hear us.

'I see he wants to shore himself up against mishap. It's reasonable, I suppose.'

'The risk *is* great to any who choose to aid you, should anything go . . .' She let her words hang seeming unwilling to utter out loud the possibility of mishap.

'He'll be able to distance himself from the whole affair, say it was entirely my plan and that he was simply doing my bidding.' I may have been headstrong and naive at times, and unprepared, cloistered as I had been, for the cut and thrust of the real world, but I was not so stupid as to believe that Uncle Henry was plotting for familial affection alone. He stood to gain much by our ultimate success.

'You know Henry,' she said. But I didn't really know him, just the memories I had of the dashing uncle with the magic hands. I was aware, though, that he was as much a means to achieve my freedom as I was a pawn in his game of politics.

'Whom should I send to Hertford with my petition?' I asked.

'Dodderidge is the obvious choice. He's trustworthy to the bone. Mind, you will need to instruct him well.'

'Dodderidge? Shouldn't it be someone of higher standing? Might the earl not be insulted?' I couldn't bear the idea of losing Dodderidge, who'd been with me since childhood, even for a few days. I suppose I'd been hoping she might suggest her husband; a petition from one great earl to another was sure to have traction, but my hope was futile for I knew Uncle Gilbert wouldn't dirty his hands in such treason.

'Dodderidge knows how to handle himself, and we can easily invent an excuse for his departure. Perhaps his sister near London will fall ill and want him by her side,' she suggested.

'You're so much more resourceful than I.' I felt inadequate beside my aunt, who seemed to have a practical understanding of the world that couldn't be found in books.

'It is hardly surprising since Grandmother has had you holed up here for most of your life. You are all education and no experience. My dear girl, once you are out there you shall find your wings.'

'Why are you helping me?' I had a sudden urge to understand why she was prepared to embroil herself in treason on my behalf.

'Because I love you, of course.' She laughed then, in a sudden uninhibited burst.

'I'm glad to have seen the back of that dull little man, aren't you?' said Grandmother as we all sat to dine later. We were quite a crowd, with the Christmas arrivals.

Mister Reason had droned out a lengthy prayer. We'd been taking turns to say grace in Starkey's absence and a man from the village was coming up to oversee matins and evensong every day until the new chaplain arrived in January.

'On the contrary, I miss Starkey.' As soon as the words were out of my mouth I regretted them. It was ill-judged to show dissent, given I was secretly preparing for flight.

'Do you think he's arrived yet?' asked Wylkyn. 'Do you think he's opened your gift?'

'A gift?' said Grandmother. 'I knew nothing of this.'

'There is nothing to know. I merely offered him a knick-knack as a memento of his time with us here.'

'Did you?' The room fell silent save for the crackle of the fire and she gave me a hard stare. 'You were far too familiar with him – the son of a tradesman.'

'They spent a decade together here, Mother.' Aunt Mary sprang to my defence. 'Of course they would have grown close. They were of a similar age and shared a love of learning.'

'Well, I have spent a lifetime with Mister Reason, haven't I?' Grandmother looked over towards her old retainer. 'How many years is it?'

Reason gulped down a mouthful in order to reply. 'Something approaching forty, My Lady.'

'And I wouldn't dream of developing a fondness. It simply

wouldn't be appropriate. It would embarrass him, wouldn't it, Mister Reason?' Reason looked quite embarrassed enough as he nodded his agreement.

Dodderidge rose to refill our glasses, catching my eye and flicking a look towards the ceiling. I would miss my ally when he went off to deliver my proposal to Hertford, with Starkey absent too. Starkey had written; he had been pondering on Socrates, he wrote, and how it is not merely life but a good life that has value. The parish he'd been promised now seemed less certain, and though the tone of the letter was bright, beneath it I detected something else, not quite sadness – more like wistfulness; perhaps he was missing me as I was him.

'Mother, you are so old-fashioned.' Aunt Mary was the sole person who dared tease Grandmother. Uncle William, an undemonstrative man with a tidy ginger moustache who was father to my little cousins, sat stiffly as if awaiting an explosion. Aunt Mary winked across the table at me as she added, 'Will you be inviting Henry for the festive season, Mother?'

'That profligate son of mine?' Grandmother's indignation prevented her from reading her daughter's playful provocation for what it was, and she began to list Uncle Henry's failings.

'There are worse things than profligacy,' said Aunt Mary, wiping a dollop of something off her chin with a finger and then licking it. Grandmother wore a look of disapproval as she watched her daughter. 'Perhaps he needs to be brought back to the fold.'

'There will be no prodigal-son stories where Henry is concerned.' Grandmother's response was emphatic and came with a sour look, which caused an uncomfortable silence to fall over the table. The dogs gathered around me, hopeful for titbits. I ate mouse-sized morsels of white fish the texture of wool. Even for someone like me, who was never seduced by delicious fare, the advent meals were unappetizing.

'I had a letter from Margaret Byron,' I said to change the subject.

'What is her news?' asked Grandmother, but I was aware this was pretence as my correspondence had been read; I'd seen the hairline crack on the seal where it had been opened.

'She had a baby.'

'What did she call him?' Grandmother had made a rare slip-up; she could only know the baby was a boy if she had seen the letter. I felt a small surge of inner power to be a step ahead of her.

Once the meal was over I found a moment alone in my chamber to write a letter of introduction for Dodderidge to present to the Earl of Hertford. I truly believed, then, that Hertford's own miserable history of secret marriage would make him sympathetic to my cause and thought about mentioning it in my letter, but caution prevailed. Anything incriminating was to be avoided, so my note was brief and plain: *I send My Loyal servant, Mister Dodderidge, and beg you to hear the news of importance he brings,* and so on.

Folding the paper, I held a candle beneath the wax cradle, tipping a little of the viscous liquid on to the join. With all the letters passing between my uncle and myself the acrid smell of hot sealing wax had become associated in my mind with the idea of freedom, and so ignited in me a spark of optimism. As I pressed my seal, the creak of a floorboard behind me sent a pulse pattering in my temple. I turned. Grandmother stood in the doorway with Joan behind her.

'To whom are you writing?' She was wearing a benign expression but I was not fooled.

'I thought I'd send a letter to Cousin Bessie, wishing her a peaceful festive season, since she won't be joining us.' I turned to face them, matching Grandmother's insincere look and, as deftly as Uncle Henry performing one of his conjuring tricks, slid the offending note beneath the mess of books and papers on my desk. She approached, casting an eye over the clutter.

'You haven't written anything.' She ran a finger over the unmarked sheet of paper on the top of my writing sheaf.

'Not yet, no. I was considering what I might say.'

Her finger continued to explore the objects on my desk. My gut tightened. 'But your wax cradle is hot.'

Fear reached for my throat, threatening to steal my voice, as my mind searched manically for a plausible lie. 'Yes, I was silly. I wrote asking if she was with child, forgetting how tactless it was in the light of her recent miscarriage, so I threw it on the fire.'

She looked at the hearth and then back at me. I could see her suspicion turning like mill cogs. 'You are not known for your tact, are you?'

'It is something I am trying to improve upon.' It was all I could do to resist expelling a huge sigh of relief. 'Even *you* are not perfect, Grandmother.' It was a risky strategy but I felt that a mild insult would provide a distraction and I was right.

'Perhaps you should look to the plank in your own eye before you point out the splinter in mine.' Her voice was clipped. 'To think of the years I have cared for your every need.'

'My every need?' I could feel my anger rising, despite the fact that this was my own manufactured altercation. 'Perhaps it was so, while you remained convinced of becoming the Queen's grandmother. But now you believe me to be a spent force and the Queen is bent on naming my cousin James, I am little more than a prisoner in your house. What about my need for freedom?' I couldn't help my raised voice.

'I have no idea what you mean. You have quite an imagination, Arbella. I advise you to rein it in.' With that she turned and swept towards the door. 'The children are running riot in the long gallery,' she added without looking back at me, 'where I have forbidden them to go. Will you fetch them down.'

I stuffed the letter under my dress, my small triumph blossoming in me, and followed her out.

We separated on the stairs, she going towards her withdrawing room and I mounting towards the staterooms. I could hear Wylkyn and Frannie with some of the other young cousins, out of breath, laughing, the throb of their footsteps beating back and forth. It sounded as if they were playing chase. I longed to join them, to fling myself back into childhood, tuck up my skirts and run, to feel that breathless abandon once more.

The high chamber was empty and its fires were not lit, making it as cold as outside. There had been a new consignment of artefacts from Wingfield and I noticed a glass vessel had been set in pride of place on the table at the centre of the room. It was a thing of great beauty, indescribably delicate, its glass body a great orb that flared out at its opening into edges so fine they were almost invisible.

I remembered clearly, though it was far back in my early childhood, where memories are like dreams, the visit to Grandmother's glassworks. I had watched, spellbound in the hellish heat, as a measure of sand was transformed into a luminous blob of matter, spinning and twirling on a rod before cooling to glass. It was an inexplicable alchemy that something as ordinary as sand could be transformed in such a way. Those glassworks had provided every pane in the vast Hardwick windows.

During our visit, Grandmother was presented with the glass vessel and I was given a perfect crystalline teardrop. I

held it to my eye and the world was changed, its angles softened, objects distorted, magnified, nothing quite as it should
have been. It had seemed a marvel to me, though it was likely
nothing more than a drop that had fallen in the making of
something else, given to a child for amusement. I still have
that drop in my cache of treasures, can even now feel its
smooth outline through the bag.

I reached out my finger to touch the glass vessel but
thought better of it, imagining it shattered over the floor and
Grandmother's fury. A loud crash rang out. I took a moment
to register that the vessel was intact and the sound had come
from the long gallery. Running through, I found the children
standing paralysed, flushed, faces terrified, beside the shattered fragments of an alabaster urn. I stopped. We could all
hear the sound of hurried footsteps making their way up the
stone steps.

'Go, go! Take the back stairs. Quick. I'll say it was my fault.'

They span round and ran to the door but Wylkyn hesitated momentarily, meeting my eye, as if to say he should be
a man and take what was coming to him. I nudged my head
towards the exit, mouthing, 'Go.' He slipped away just as
Grandmother made her entrance, flanked by Dodderidge
and Reason.

'What on earth?' She looked horrified, quite grief-stricken,
as if it was one of the children lying in pieces on the rush
matting.

'I'm afraid my skirts must have brushed it as I was trying
to get a better look at my parents.' I pointed to the pair of
portraits above, knowing that a lie must not be too elaborate as to rouse suspicion, nor be too simple as to seem
implausible.

Grandmother stooped to pick up a shard. 'It was a unique
piece, irreplaceable . . . the finest alabaster.'

Her upset was baffling; it seemed as if she was on the

brink of tears. I did not know it then, that a person can appear to grieve for one thing when it is something else that has caused the sorrow, and not even be aware of it. 'Where are the children?' she asked.

'I sent them down to the nursery some time ago.'

I wanted to step towards her, reach out a comforting hand to her shoulder, but was rooted to the spot.

'Can I never have anything beautiful without it being destroyed? I will not allow you to demolish everything I have built, Arbella.'

I caught a look of confusion that passed between the two men and I was no less puzzled than they by her words, but then was suddenly struck with the thought that perhaps she had discovered my secret plan. It could easily have mired her in disgrace, toppled her empire; we might all have been up to our necks in charges of sedition if things went wrong.

I'd known it before, of course, but it was only then, there before the broken urn, I fully realized that my plan – a princess of the blood marrying without royal assent – could easily be construed as high treason and that the consequences might well be grave and far-reaching.

I imagined Grandmother distancing herself from me, shrugging me off like an unwanted garment as I went to the block. Grandmother would do whatever was necessary. She was a survivor; there had never been any doubt of that.

'When was it you stopped caring for me?' The words spoke themselves without my permission and I wished I could take them back. Dodderidge was making a gesture with his hand, flattening it and lowering it, as if to say, *Don't make it worse.*

'When you disappointed me,' was her answer. As she said it she seemed to forget her distress over the broken urn, investing her voice with its usual firm authority. 'When defiance became your watchword.'

149

'I'm sorry, Grandmother. Truly sorry.' I was not sorry, either for the loss of that urn or for being the source of her disillusionment. Ripples of anger moved through me but I focused my mind on my escape, and was convinced then that she remained in the dark, for had she known of my secret plans she would not have been talking of disappointment and defiance but of betrayal and treason.

'I have lowered my expectations in respect of you,' she said as she made to leave the room, indicating that Reason accompany her. 'See to it this is dealt with, would you, Dodderidge.'

Once she had left, I leaned back against the cold wall and expelled a cloud of breath, closing my eyes to gather myself. Even then I was trying to think of ways to regain Grandmother's approval, refusing to see the futility of such an aim.

'It is likely she's short-tempered from lack of sustenance,' Dodderidge said quietly. 'Once Christmas is here and there is meat on the table she will be in better humour.'

I opened my eyes. 'I doubt it.'

We stood in silence a moment, he looking at his hands. They were fine and long, the kind of hands a musician would envy.

I walked over to the door, closing it. 'Can I trust you?'

Those hands rose towards his face, flapping. 'Do you need to ask? Of everyone under this roof you can trust me the most, My Lady. I have served you for more than twenty years.'

I thought about it then; I couldn't remember a time when Dodderidge was not with the family; I knew him better than I knew any of my uncles. 'I need you to perform a service for me.'

I noticed a spark ignite in him and he stood straight, towering over me, his stoop forgotten. 'Whatever you ask is my command.'

'It is a matter that requires the utmost delicacy and one which might distance you from my grandmother.'

'It is *you* I serve.' He looked so very solemn, like a man on the eve of a battle.

I took the paper from beneath my clothes. My breath quivered. 'I need you to go to the Earl of Hertford at his house in Tottenham. Uncle Henry has promised a good horse to take you there. He says it will be stabled at the sign of the bell in the village tomorrow. You must request a private audience and then explain to Hertford that I am offering my hand in marriage to his grandson Edward Seymour. Impress upon him the importance of his support for this union. Ask that he send Seymour here to Hardwick, although' – my mind was whirring – 'he must come not as himself, but –' I paused to think – 'as a man with land to sell. Grandmother will not be able to resist that.'

Dodderidge was folding and unfolding those long hands, 'What of the risk to you?'

'Never mind that.' I saw the concern written clearly on his face. 'Uncle Henry has everything under control.'

'Royal permission?'

I nodded, not wanting to lie to him but neither wanting to worry him further. 'I'm relying on you. Are you sure you can do this?'

'But . . .' he hesitated and I feared he would change his mind. 'Who will watch out for you here with both Starkey and me away?'

I was touched by his caring and had to force a wave of sadness into submission. Not an hour went by that I did not think of dear Starkey. 'You will not be gone long. I can manage to look after myself. And Aunt Mary is here.'

'I am glad of that . . .' He hesitated. 'But even so . . .'

'Please tell me you will do this.'

'Will it not rouse the earl's suspicion to be approached by

one such as me? I am not of his standing. A mere retainer, an ordinary man . . . It is not correct. He may be insulted.' He was still folding and unfolding his hands. 'Would your uncle not be a more suitable candidate?'

'Uncle Henry is so unpredictable and you – you are uncommonly resourceful, Dodderidge. I know you will find a way to convince him. I am sure anyway that Hertford will be as keen on this idea as I am . . . as we are. After all it will set his family back up where they belong. Remind him of that.'

He took the letter between the tips of his finger and thumb, as if it might burn him, and slid it out of sight into his doublet. I hadn't noticed before that his clothes were quite shabby and threadbare in places.

'Can you borrow another suit of clothes?' I realized what a silly thing it was to say, for no man in a forty-mile radius was likely to be as tall and lean as Dodderidge. I wished I had the means to send him to the tailor in Nottingham on his way south but I had little, and even less since I'd sent all my valuables to Cousin Bessie.

'I have a doublet put away that was made for my wedding. I wonder if it might still fit me.'

'Your wedding? You are not a married man, Dodderidge.'

'I lost my wife when you were still a girl.'

It is easy to forget that those who serve you have lives of their own in which you play no part, and it struck me then that, although Dodderidge knew everything about me, and had served me for years, I knew almost nothing about him. I wanted to ask what had happened, how had she died, had he loved her, yet all I found myself saying was, 'I'm sorry.'

'It was long ago. Time is a great healer.'

The truth of his platitude resonated with me, for the death of my mother, the cause of utter devastation to my seven-year-old self, had lost its potency over time and thoughts of her had become entirely abstracted.

'I'm sure the doublet will do. The earl will certainly be more given to agreement if you —'

'If I look the part.'

'See, we are like an old married couple, finishing each other's sentences.' I said this to lighten the atmosphere, which had become burdened with the weight of the events that would shortly begin to unfold. He looked wistful and it occurred to me that marriage to such a man, a kind man, might make a person very happy.

I rarely thought of happiness; it was not something I had been raised to expect.

A pair of servant lads arrived with brooms and a large carton to clear up the broken urn. 'Take care with the pieces,' I said. 'Perhaps it can be put together.'

I sank to the floor to inspect a large shard, painted with what I realized only then was the apple from the tree of knowledge. 'Goodness! It is the fall of man scattered here.' I held up the fragment for Dodderidge to see and we both began to laugh. 'How Starkey would have loved the irony.'

The lads looked from us to each other, shrugging in bafflement at the sight of the pair of us heaving and snorting with laughter, and I was filled with hope, as if the whole world was conspiring towards the success of my mission.

Clerkenwell

Ami slumps against the table with the miniature of Hunsdon in her hand. The thought that she has lost her son's trust once more is too much to bear. She has become so trapped in her own web of guilt and secrets and half-truths she can barely find the strength to answer the tap at the door. She stands, tucks the offending miniature of Hunsdon out of sight, and calls, 'Just a moment,' before splashing water over her face and wiping it dry on her apron. She will not give Mansfield the satisfaction of seeing her brought to tears.

But it is not Mansfield on the stoop with a bag of soiled linens; it is a young boy and she can tell by the look of him, the square face, the tawny shock of hair, that he is Mansfield's son. He puts down the bag just inside the door and loiters, just as his father does, as if waiting for something.

'Do you want a slice?' she points to the half-finished pie that she and Hal had enjoyed the evening before. It will not keep so she may as well share it.

He nods. She cuts a slice, handing it to him. He mumbles a thank-you, eating silently and quickly, as if he hasn't had a square meal in days.

She watches on, remembering Hal at that age. He couldn't get food into himself fast enough. Thinking of him is a physical pain, skewering down into her. 'Like it?'

He comes up for air, nodding. 'It's . . . it's . . . Ma's pastry is heavy as lead.' He covers his mouth, seeming embarrassed that he's insulted his mother.

'I'm sure she's too busy with all your brothers and sisters to find time for cooking pies.'

'I help her sometimes, but not when Fa's about. He says

it's not work for a lad. That if I've got time on my hands I ought to be chopping wood, not cooking.'

She offers him another slice. 'In the King's kitchens all the cooks are men. You can tell your father that, next time he complains.'

'Is that true?' He looks at her, making no attempt to hide his curiosity. 'How do you know?'

'I have spent some time at court.' She holds out her ugly hands. 'Not that you'd think it now.'

'What, in the King's laundry?' He seems impressed at the idea that the woman who washes his shirts might have also washed the King's.

'No, not the laundry. In the Queen's chambers.'

He makes a face of disbelief.

'I wrote poems for the Queen and some of the great ladies.'

'Poems?' He picks up one of the written papers from the table. 'I wish I could read better.'

'Do you not go to school?'

'I did, but Fa says the schoolmaster is crooked and that my time is better spent learning a trade. "With a skill you'll always have work," that's what he says. Once he took me up the bell tower of St James's. "See all them roofs," he said. "Each and every one of them'll need mending one day."' He pauses, dipping his head to look at the floor. 'But heights frighten me.'

'I don't much like heights either,' she says. It is not particularly true but she wants him to feel better about his confession. She knows well enough that boys don't like to seem weak. 'What's your name?'

'Edwin.'

She writes *Edwin Mansfield* on a piece of scrap paper. 'You can read that, I assume?'

'Of course.' He is a little indignant.

'Well, that is a beginning. Let's play with the letters a bit. What is this?' She writes 'win'. He reads it out loud. 'And if I take the D and put it at the end?'

'Win—d.'

'That's right.'

He looks as pleased, as if he'd invented the wheel, and they continue for a while making words out of the letters in his name until he becomes restless. 'I'd better go. Fa'll be wondering what I'm up to.'

'You better had, then.'

'If I come back, will you show me some more?'

'Certainly, if there's time.' She likes the idea of feeding this hungry young mind, feels it might bring her something meaningful. It reminds her of when she taught Hal his letters. Though when she will find the time, she doesn't know, given she has no time even to read.

Just as he is about to leave he turns back and says, 'If you wrote poems for the Queen, then why are you doing our washing?'

It jolts her in the way only the bald truth can. 'You may well ask.'

He lingers in the doorway waiting for a proper answer. She thinks of her youth. It was far from typical, the spirited life she'd led growing up in a family of musicians; the house always filled with song; the visiting poets and composers and actors; the lively arguments – such freedom she'd had, so unlike other girls. And when that was cut short by the death of her parents so suddenly, to have had the fortune to be taken under the countess's wing, to have had an education and access to a world beyond the reach of most.

Lady Arbella springs suddenly into her mind. How opposite their lives had been and yet they had a profound empathy, a shared love of ideas, of the written word. It makes her feel urgently, despite her dramatic downturn in fortune, the desire to spread her knowledge, to make it all count for something.

'Fate can sometimes take a curious turn. I lost my husband and he had squandered all our money, so now I am a poor widow and I have to earn a shilling where I can.'

'Oh,' he says as he slips out into the street and she is left alone with her guilt.

As she prepares for her day of work she runs through the letter she will write to Hal. She will explain that she didn't want him to feel burdened by the stain of illegitimacy, that she wanted him to have a sense of family, rather than always feeling he belonged elsewhere. She had seen noblemen's bastards at court, noticed how they were always slightly sneered upon and never quite fitted. She didn't want that for Hal. She prays he will understand.

Hardwick

'Dodderidge has been arrested.' Grandmother stood at the centre of the chamber with contempt scratched over her face.

I had to muster all my self-control to keep my poise and show nothing of the mixture of emotions – fear, guilt, dismay – coursing through me, causing the fragile structure of hope that had buoyed me up in the previous weeks to collapse.

'That is terrible news. Of what is he accused? Are you sure? Dodderidge is the most honest man I –' I was burbling, like a person with something to hide, so I staunched my words but could not dispel the image of Dodderidge in his best wedding doublet, crouched terrified in the corner of some filthy cell too small to accommodate his tall shape.

'What is he accused of?' she repeated back to me. 'Why don't *you* tell *me*, Arbella?'

Aunt Mary, standing behind her, looked at me with a finger pressed over her mouth.

'How could I possibly know?' A twinge of pain nipped at my side, below my ribs, not a pain I knew, no ordinary colic. Dodderidge's haunted face imprinted itself on my mind's eye.

'Don't be disingenuous with me. Do you think I don't know when you are lying? It was I who raised you.' Grandmother fingered her pearls. 'You are completely transparent to me.'

I could not stop thinking of Dodderidge festering in a cell on my account – how doubtful he had been about the mission – and the gentle pressure I had exerted on him in the full knowledge he would not refuse me. 'Where is he being held? I hope he has not been hurt.'

'If you cared for his well-being you would not have involved him in your folly.'

'I don't know what you mean.' I knew she could see through my feeble deceit by her look, which penetrated like a shard of glass through flesh.

'You sent him on a mission to the Earl of Hertford with an offer of your hand in marriage to the earl's grandson.' I was wondering how she knew this; I had been so careful, so discreet, but there was a hole in my ship and I could feel myself sinking, cold water moving up my body. That strange pain continued to nip.

'Have you any idea what kind of danger this places at our door?' Grandmother continued to shuffle her pearls. 'Goodness knows, I have tried to make you aware of the threats, tried to protect you from all this, Arbella. Think of Katherine Grey, think of what you risk with your recklessness.' She brought a hand to her forehead. 'And as for poor Dodderidge . . .' Pausing, she stepped forward, so I could see her expression, which wasn't angry, as I expected, but full of distress. 'Well, if he hangs for aiding an attempted treason, his blood will be on *your* hands and we will all be brought to our knees.'

Aunt Mary closed her eyes and the colour dropped from her face.

'Treason.' I repeated, lost for words. My bodice was pressing too tightly against my ribs.

'You know as well as I that with your blood, what you proposed to Hertford is treason.'

The rage that had been welling in me found its sudden release: 'A curse on my blood, then,' I shouted, 'for it is that which means I am kept here a prisoner for fear someone should fix their ambition on to me and threaten Her

Majesty's throne.' I couldn't stop. 'You have never cared for me, only for what I can bring you. Is it not enough that you came from nothing and now own half the county, that you, a nobody, will end your life as the Dowager Countess of Shrewsbury, rather than plain Mistress something-or-other –'

She slapped me sharply across the cheek. 'How dare you speak of me like that . . . I, your kin, your grandmother.' Her voice was a low, controlled rumble. 'I did not have the privilege of birth that you had. I had to work for what is mine and you . . . you would waste your birthright on a disgraced family like the Seymours . . .' Her voice trailed off and I saw in that moment that she was jealous, jealous of her highborn granddaughter. Jealous in the knowledge that, however hard she worked to achieve her position, she would never be what I was. And in spite of that I had become as useless to her in achieving her dreams as gunpowder left in the rain.

'Have you never thought that I am a human being, made of flesh, not simply a receptacle for that Tudor blood you prize so greatly? I believed you cared for me once but –' A sudden stitch split my side. I gasped, collapsing to the floor, feeling the rasp of the rush matting against my cheek.

Grandmother stepped away and went back to agitating those infernal pearls. 'Joan, Mary! Arbella is having a turn. Will you help her to her chamber.'

The pain had me in its grip, making my breathing shallow and in turn making me light-headed. I longed to pass out, to be free from the agony even for a moment, but the stabbing kept oblivion beyond reach. I tried to collect my thoughts. *Breathe, breathe, deeply, evenly.* In my mind I began to count backwards from a hundred. It was a method Starkey taught me once, a way to tolerate the intolerable. *Ninety-nine; ninety-eight; ninety-seven . . .* I was writhing on the floor, suddenly aware of the scent of harvest emanating from the matting, pressing my nose to it for distraction. *Eighty-five; eighty-four . . .* The pain intensified, as if I were clasped in the jaws of a monstrous beast.

'Shhhhh, shhhh, sweeting; be still.' It was Aunt Mary cradling my head in her lap, stroking my hair. 'It will pass.'

Sixty-one; sixty; fifty-nine. I looked at Aunt Mary and up at Grandmother and Joan standing over us like shadows, unable in that moment to remember who they were, feeling panic engulf me like a bore of cold water, loosening me from reason. *Forty-four; forty-three.* Aunt Mary's hands were soft and warm; she slowly unpicked my fingers one by one from where they clutched my side. I felt her fumbling at my laces, slackening them, and her other hand slipped beneath my bodice, slowly, firmly stroking back and forth. *Twenty-two; twenty-one; twenty; nineteen.*

'Fetch a measure of laudanum,' I heard someone say.

I suddenly retched up bile, as if my body was trying to rid itself of a poison. Someone flapped about with a cloth, attempting to mop it up. It was bright yellow as a buttercup, or a lemon, or brimstone. I became aware of a low rhythmic moaning sound that was escaping from deep in my body and I felt Mary rocking me gently back and forth. She was softly humming a tune that was familiar but I couldn't remember where from.

I lost count of my backward numbers, lost all sense of things, lost myself, entirely, possessed by the agony emanating from deep within me. Someone held a spoon to my mouth, pouring liquid in. I felt the cold trickle of it run down my throat. The moaning continued, and the rocking, and Aunt Mary's gentle stroking until eventually the pain began to dull and slowly withdraw, a snake slithering into the undergrowth.

I must have finally fallen unconscious for I came to in my bed with Aunt Mary still at my side. 'You are back,' she said. 'My poor sweeting. How are you?'

My head was swimming pleasantly and the pain had receded to a faint echo. 'Who are all those people?' I asked, looking towards a crowd of faces hovering on the other side of the chamber.

'We are alone. It's the tincture playing with your imagination.'

I looked again and they had gone.

'Dodderidge!' The memories came flooding back and with them the awful realization that everything had gone irretrievably wrong and Dodderidge had paid the price. 'Is there news of him?'

'Why don't you sleep some more and we will talk of it all later. You are in no state —'

'What is this?' I touched a cross that hung on a fine chain from her neck, felt the cold of silver against my fingertip. 'A crucifix?'

'You are imagining things again, sweeting.' It disappeared, or did she tuck it away? 'Why would I wear a crucifix?'

I could not think of a reason why Aunt Mary would wear such a thing. But then again I could not think of a reason for anything, for my mind was flickering with improbable thoughts, landing on each one momentarily before fluttering away, leaving only a vague impression that could not find words to be described.

Somewhere it occurred to me that I might be muddling her with that other Mary, the Queen of Scots. Hadn't *she* said to me once, *Ask Mary Talbot?* My thoughts swirled and drifted, unable to catch hold of anything, my head like butter on a hot day. 'It must be the poppy.' But I'd felt sure of the cool touch of metal against my skin.

An image of Dodderidge alighted. I tried to hold on to it before it flitted off, finding words to attach to it. 'What happened in Tottenham?' The words sounded strange on my tongue.

'You are in no fit state.'

'No.' I heard myself, firm, resolute, clear, quite unlike my buttery head. 'I *must* know. How did Grandmother find out?'

'Hertford was not as amenable to the idea as we'd believed . . .' She hesitated. 'I shouldn't be burdening you with all this now.'

'Tell me!' I said, surprised once again at my firmness. I was using all my willpower to stop myself from drifting away.

'He alerted Cecil at once and placed Dodderidge under lock and key.'

'Cecil.' I tried to focus on what I was hearing. 'So the Queen knows. What has *she* said of it?' I felt the world draw tightly around me.

'She has said nothing.'

'Nothing.' Was 'nothing' good or bad? I could not tell. Did it mean she was truly coming to the end of her days, or . . . my thoughts were wandering again and I could think only of Katherine Grey, that bright-eyed feather of a girl, trapped behind the oval of glass on Grandmother's side table, starving herself to death with grief. 'How do you know this?' I forced my mind to focus.

'Cecil wrote to Mother; I saw the letter. Sir Henry Brouncker has been ordered to question you.'

'To question or interrogate?' As I said that Mary's face was horror-struck. 'I'm just naming it for what it is.' I knew well enough that Cecil's men did not merely question, not when treason was suspected. 'Cecil was once my champion.'

'Not any more. He supports your cousin James's cause now. That much I know. With Cecil behind him, James has become an unstoppable force.'

'But my wedding was to change all that.' I was trying to remember why my wedding would change things, but couldn't grasp any sense of it. 'What will happen to me, Mary?' My voice sounded small, like a child's.

She took my shoulders and looked me directly in the eye. 'It is a setback. That is all. A setback. You shall have your wedding.'

I scrutinized her face for signs that she truly believed what she was telling me, finding nothing there but doubt and apprehension. I sensed my head clearing a little but the price of that was a resurgence of pain, pecking at me, tearing out gobbets of my flesh. 'And Uncle Henry?'

'He has gone to talk to Beauchamp to see what can be salvaged.' I saw the hope ignite in her as she said it.

'Lord Beauchamp?' Her hope did not catch hold in me. If Uncle Henry was prepared to show his hand then things must have been worse than Mary suggested. I tried to imagine them, Hertford the grandfather, Beauchamp the son and Edward the grandson, but couldn't; I didn't know what they looked like. My mind was repeating *the throne or the tower and nothing in between*, like a Greek chorus. 'What is the reach of Beauchamp's influence without his father's backing?'

'We do not know yet, but many won't support a foreigner such as your cousin James wearing the crown. We may have a tentative friendship with Scotland now but most Englishmen will always consider the Scots as the enemy.'

'But Beauchamp cannot muster the nobility as his father can, surely?'

'It is possible.'

My face scrunched up and a groan formed in my throat, as the pain returned in earnest.

'More tincture?'

I nodded, murmuring, 'Just a half-measure.'

I heard the chink of the spoon against the phial.

'We must get you better for Sir Henry Brouncker,' she said, but her words were not making sense.

'Who is that?'

'Never mind, sweeting. Try and sleep.'

'Will you stay with me?'

'I will be here by your side all night.'

'I mean longer, not just the night.'

I heard her hesitation. She cleared her throat. 'Gilbert wants me back in Sheffield.'

'Does Uncle Gilbert know?' My mind was turning to butter once more and I couldn't remember who knew about my secret affairs, whose side everyone was on.

'No, and best he doesn't. I can't stay too long, for it might arouse suspicion.'

I felt my hand grip hers as if I were a drowning woman clinging to a tuft of grass on a riverbank, which made me think of the girl in that play, what was her name? 'The girl who drowned.'

'What did you say?' she asked.

'The girl in Mister Shakespeare's play who drowned herself. You told me about it. You saw the play.'

'You mean Ophelia. Why are you thinking of that?' Her voice was soft. 'It was a sin, to take her own life, even if she was a fiction.' She stopped, stroked my hair away from my face and rearranged my coverlet. 'Don't think of that; turn your mind to happy things. Remember when you were small and Gilbert was teaching you to ride. He mounted your pony to demonstrate something, – I can't remember what – and it bolted.'

Mary was laughing and I had a memory of Uncle Gilbert, vast, like a titan, on Dancer, his feet almost touching the ground but my laughter kept slipping away from me, revealing the image of Ophelia that lay beneath; Ophelia with the face of Jane Grey. She was holding her severed head up above the water to prevent herself from drowning, the gore spilling, making clouds of vivid pink; and then she was not Jane but the Scottish Queen, who evaporated to leave Katherine Grey in her place, fragile, emaciated, slipping slowly beneath the surface.

'Was Katherine Grey a sinner too?' I asked.

'What made you think of her, sweeting?'

'She refused to eat.'

'That is not considered a sin. I believe she had a proper burial. Let's not talk of that; it's the poppy addling you.'

I shook my head sharply to expel those dead girls.

'Stay a couple more days, I beg of you.' I was still gripping Mary's hand.

'I will stay until you are better. Gilbert cannot take offence if I am nursing my sick niece, can he?'

I felt in that moment that if I were to let go of her I would disappear for ever into the vortex of my own mind.

The disease ravaged me, leaving me weak and muddle-headed and anxious for news of Dodderidge, though none seemed forthcoming. I had lost all sense of time but was aware it had been a while since I had left my bedchamber. I was resting and reading a letter from Starkey that must have arrived some weeks before, as he talked of his plans for Christmas, which I knew had been and gone. It had been opened, this time without any attempt to hide the fact. There was nothing in it of interest to anyone but me, only abstract ideas extrapolated from his reading of the ancients. It made me miss keenly our conversations.

Joan entered brusquely with my best silk brocade gown in her arms. 'Your grandmother wants you in the long gallery. Here, put this on.'

I stood holding my arms out obediently, while she whipped the gown over my crumpled petticoats, fastened a scratchy lace ruff about my neck and began bustling about the room, searching for gloves and sleeves.

'Why this rush? Where is Aunt Mary?'

'Your aunt left for Sheffield yesterday, do you not remember?' She had tied my sleeves on and was scraping my hair

166

away from my face, up and over a wad of wool, twisting it and pinning it tightly at the back.

'Of course, Sheffield.' I'd thought my confusion was in abeyance but clearly it was not, for I had no memory of Aunt Mary's departure. I had no memory of anything much, save a shadowy sense that something bad had happened. There was a woman hovering behind Joan, holding something which Joan snatched up sharply and fastened into the tower of hair she'd created.

'Who is that?' I whispered, wondering if the woman behind was really there or was one of the battalion of people that visited my dreams.

'You know Bridget,' she said loudly in reply. 'Your aunt's woman.'

Bridget stepped forward, smiling with reassuring apple cheeks, and I remembered then who she was. 'Do forgive me, Bridget, I haven't been myself lately.'

'No need to apologize, My Lady. Your aunt asked that I stay with you.'

I felt the decoration fall from my hair, catching it as it dropped. It was Grandmother's jewel, set with an emerald the size of a robin's egg.

Joan was on hands and knees, fumbling beneath the bed. 'There must be a pair of suitable shoes somewhere here.'

Bridget whispered, 'If you have need to contact your aunt, I will pass on any –' she stopped as Joan emerged, mouthing the word *letters*.

Something was wrong if I needed to pass letters secretly to Aunt Mary too. My unease proliferated and I wondered whether Bridget had news of Dodderidge.

'I knew they were here somewhere.' Joan shoved some slippers on to my feet. They were too tight. She stood back to appraise me – 'Goodness, you look terrible' – and began pinching some colour into my cheeks. No permission asked to touch my person. I supposed it was no longer deemed necessary.

'The jewel, where's the jewel?'

I held it out. 'It fell.' She took it and began to pin it in my hair again. 'Why am I wearing Grandmother's emerald?'

'I'm just doing as I've been told.' Her mouth was a harsh line, full of pins. 'Now, where are your pearls?' She was searching, opening boxes, looking beneath things.

'I sent them . . .' Realizing what I was about to say, I stopped.

'Sent them where?' She looked like a cat with a glimpse of a mouse, ready to pounce.

'I'm all in a muddle,' I said. 'I haven't seen them.'

There was a moment of suspended silence as she looked at me, pondering on whether I was lying. But then she harrumphed. 'You'll have to do without them, I suppose. There's no time to look.'

'What's the hurry?' I asked again, but as she marched me towards the door she merely replied that Grandmother would tell me.

'Wait!' I shook myself free from her grasp and went to the ewer, pouring some water into the basin.

'There's isn't time for that.' Joan was tugging at my shoulder.

Ignoring her, I sluiced my face with the cold water, feeling instantly better, more myself, and I could sense my wits returning. Bridget passed me a cloth. I rubbed my face dry, feeling icy droplets escaping down the front of my dress.

'I must say, you look better for that,' said Bridget, offering me her smile again, and I remembered her clearly then, how she and Aunt Mary had taken shifts to sit with me through the worst of my illness.

'I *feel* better for it.'

Joan sucked her teeth. 'Ready now?'

I sailed past her, out of the door, through Grandmother's chamber, and marched smartly up the stairs, with hefty Joan in breathless pursuit.

Grandmother was pacing the gallery with Uncle William and Mister Reason. All my painted relatives looked down from the walls.

'At last.' She seemed agitated 'Mister Reason, go down and tell our guest that we can receive him now.'

She took me aside, pulling me by the hand to the centre of the chamber. 'The Queen's agent is here to talk to you.' Her rings bit into my fingers where she held me. 'Now, for pity's sake, don't dig yourself further into this treason, my girl. I did not raise you to be another Katherine Grey. We will all be tarnished if you do not think of some plausible reason for your actions.'

Everything – my thoughts, the room, Grandmother's voice, her face – was distorted and I tried to focus on the splash of icy water, as if the mere thought of it might irrigate my jumbled mind, but couldn't quite put things into the correct order. Fear was gathering like dark clouds and I must have looked gormless, for she took both my shoulders and stopped just short of shaking me, saying, 'Lord preserve us all.'

She began to walk then, linking her elbow through mine, indicating for Uncle William to hold my other arm, pacing as if we were taking our usual daily exercise in the gallery, under the watchful eyes of those ranks of relatives.

We were at the far end when Reason returned with a man who, from that distance, seemed to have few distinctive features, save for the fact that he wore a rather gaudy outfit of raspberry wool, the sort of thing designed to impress, and a tall black hat with a large bouncing feather, framing rather than disguising his receding hairline. He stopped. Reason positioned himself with correct deference a little behind, wearing a frown.

Sir Henry Brouncker, for that is who my visitor was, seemed unable to prevent his gaze from floating about the room, clearly, by his open-mouthed look of wonder, marvelling at the stately proportions and the sheer expanses of glass. Grandmother purred beside me, seeming to forget momentarily her woes, as the place had the desired effect on this royal emissary, who would doubtless spread word of the Dowager Countess of Shrewsbury's splendid abode.

'Sir Henry,' she raised her voice to be heard from the far reaches of the room. 'Come, come.' She beckoned with a gloved hand. I didn't recognize those gloves, they were made of kid and gold lace, threaded with pearls and precious stones. Her dress, too, was scattered with jewels and I understood then why Joan had pinned the emerald pendant into my hair. Grandmother was determined to assert her status on this man in any way she could. She would intimidate him with our splendour. I looked at Uncle William on my other side. He was in embroidered silk and velvet, with an army of gold aiglets, and his gingery moustaches were trimmed and curled as if he was to sit for his portrait. I wondered if Brouncker was beginning to feel his raspberry suit a little less lavish. 'Have you met my son, William Cavendish, and my granddaughter, the Lady Arbella?'

'No indeed, I have not had the pleasure.'

The occasion seemed to be rubbing off on me, for my muddled thoughts began to form an orderly line. I noticed that Grandmother hadn't introduced me as Her Highness as she always used to; my relatives on the walls were bearing witness to this denial. A flutter of fear palpitated in my throat as I watched the man approach, in his blushing suit and stiff ruff framing a formless face that had all the allure of a potato.

I leaned in towards the solid shape of Uncle William to steady myself.

Brouncker's approach seemed to take an age, as if he were rowing himself up against the tide. Grandmother's indomitable hauteur buoyed me and she turned to me with a nod and a smile, which I reciprocated. It was the first affectionate gesture that had passed between us since that fateful letter had arrived, cancelling my visit to court, almost two years before.

'Fret not,' she whispered. 'You are more than a match for this one.' I felt a chip of love for her then, sensing myself no longer in isolation with a disparate scattering of supporters, but at the heart of something great and powerful and unassailable, a family that had united behind me.

Brouncker fell to his knees and held out a letter to Grandmother, making an effusive greeting, noticing her beautiful gloves, his eyes dancing over the brilliants stitched on to them and over her lavish satin sleeves before alighting finally, pupils dilating, on the heavy pearls, big as marbles, falling to her waist. I saw that the letter carried the royal seal and recognized Cecil's precise script.

'Sir Henry.' I projected my hand forward towards the fellow and the ostrich feather in his hat bobbed giddily as he dipped to kiss it. His palm was slightly clammy, his lips dry and unpleasantly rough, but as he stood he smiled and his formless face took on a lively, congenial aspect that was less at odds with his outfit. *Perhaps*, I thought, *this wouldn't be so bad after all.*

Grandmother had opened the letter and was reading. 'So you are here on Her Majesty's business. Well, we knew as much.'

'I am indeed, My Lady. Just a conversation in the hope that the Lady Arbella might be able to shed light on the circumstances with your retainer Dodderidge and his meeting with the Earl of Hertford.'

So it was to be a gentle exchange rather than an interrogation. Grandmother squeezed my hand once more, which spurred me a little.

'I'm afraid I will need to sit,' I said. 'I have been unwell, you see, unable to leave my bed for . . .' I realized I didn't know how long I'd been ill. For all I knew I had lost several months, although I gathered from the chill in the air and the grim sky beyond the window, with the leafless trees silhouetted against it, that spring hadn't arrived without my knowledge.

'Why don't you take a seat, dear?' said Grandmother, as if she always spoke to me with such affection. 'Sir Henry will not think it rude under the circumstances.'

Brouncker was nodding in deferent agreement as Grandmother led me to a throne-like seat at the end of the chamber, beneath the painting of the Queen in a dress that I noticed, only then, was not dissimilar to the one Grandmother was wearing. 'William, would you fetch a seat for Sir Henry.' She pointed to one of the small stools that the children used to sit on. I had forgotten how Grandmother had a formidable instinct for creating an atmosphere of intimidation. I had been on the receiving end of it only too often.

'We shall give you some privacy,' said Grandmother, taking Uncle William's arm and moving slowly off towards the far end of the gallery, like a galleon put to sea.

Brouncker carefully lowered himself on to the stool and the effect was complete: I on a throne and he at my feet.

I caught sight of my shoes. I didn't recognize them. They were very pretty; sparkling with little jewels, and pinched horribly. Brouncker was talking but the rushing of blood in my ears prevented me from hearing. I watched his mouth move, his shining bead eyes flicker. Heat blossomed beneath my dress.

'How was your journey?' I asked as a way to bring myself back. 'Not too arduous, I trust.'

He was talking about the weather but my head started to swim once more.

'Might I be direct, My Lady?' he said eventually.

I looked at those beadlike eyes and slowly nodded, as a knot of trepidation tightened in the pit of my stomach.

'It has been reported that you sought the hand of the Earl of Hertford's grandson.' He was smiling but his tone was not light to match and I imagined his teeth were sharp fangs, like a cat's; fear began to creep from my belly through to the far reaches of my limbs. The word *treason* circled my head.

'Then your information is incorrect, sir.'

'So your man Dodderidge did not visit the earl at his house in Tottenham with a proposal from you?'

That pain had returned, jabbing at me, a crow pecking at carrion. 'You are mistaken.' I managed to speak but felt as if my voice was far, far away and I couldn't help thinking of Dodderidge. My heart stammered as I realized I might have to sacrifice my dear friend. I didn't think I could. 'Dodderidge is visiting his sister, who is ailing.'

'Dodderidge is under lock and key at the Westminster Gatehouse.'

'Now, yes. But I meant he left here to visit –'

'We know he was at Tottenham, he was arrested there,' Brouncker interrupted.

My head was spinning. He was looking at me intently, too intently. 'At Tottenham . . . yes.' I was all a dither. 'Yes – on an errand.'

'For you?' Too intently.

My head was empty.

He was riffling through his pockets and pulled out a creased sheet of paper, unfolding it, flattening it out, presenting it to me as if it were a New Year gift. The crows pecked on, still circling about me. *Treason, treason, treason*, they carked.

I swallowed. The paper was written over. 'What is it?' I began to read. What was it? Had Dodderidge jotted down my instructions? It looked like his hand. Was it a confession? There it was, the plan, each detail explained in ink. 'I did not write this.' The words were dancing on the page. My mouth was dry. *Peck, peck, peck.*

Brouncker said nothing, only looked at me with an expression that was impossible to read.

Then words spewed out of me: 'Dodderidge must have gone to Hertford of his own accord. Perhaps he saw some profit in it. He is a man who will do anything for gain.' A fog of shame gathered over me; I was filthy with it. 'No! I am confused. My illness has muddled me. Dodderidge is a good man. A loyal man.' I tried to retract my betrayal but just as blood cannot be unspilled, words cannot be unspoken.

'Your *loyal* man Dodderidge has named names; your chaplain Starkey is one of them.'

I was back in that moment: Starkey's arms about me, his body pressing up to mine.

'Not him!' It came out as a cry. I had cursed them all, all who championed me. 'I cannot . . . I do not . . . you must be . . .' I rubbed my hand over my side; if I could, I would have ripped my dress from my body. *Treason, treason, treason.*

'My Lady.' Brouncker's face was an inch from mine, as if he could see my soul through the orbs of my eyes. 'You are not being clear.'

'Clear!' I couldn't find words. *Peck, peck, peck.* A groan blew out of my mouth. 'Perhaps . . .' I needed time to collect my thoughts.

'Perhaps?'

'I could give you a written statement . . .' Pain seared through me, impeding my breath; I thought I would faint.

'Air!' I dragged myself out of the throne-chair, taking a step towards the window, then became aware of the floor coming up to meet me with interminable gradualness as if time had slowed; the emerald dropped from my hair with a soft little thud, one shoe freed itself from my foot, whispering as it skidded over the matting, my skirts sighed as I crumpled to the floor.

Brouncker pulled off his raspberry doublet and shoved it beneath my head. It was coarse and itchy. He crouched over me, unsure what to do, fingers hovering, not quite touching.

'Not this again!' I heard Grandmother say. Her voice was teeming with disappointment. I felt privy to everything, the woodworm scuffling in the legs of the old chair beside me, the mice burrowing behind the panelling, the inner workings of Grandmother's mind.

Uncle William got to me first, scooping me up into his arms. 'Light as a cloud,' I heard him whisper. I felt, in that moment, as if I could be invisible; the transparency that Grandmother accused me of could be turned to my advantage; I could disappear at will and reappear elsewhere, like the queen in Uncle Henry's three-card trick.

I could hear Grandmother ordering Reason to get the doctor and then explaining to Brouncker that I had been ailing, that they had feared for my life. I hadn't known that. People don't tell you when they think you are dying, I suppose, unless it is sure and the chaplain is to be fetched.

Uncle William took me to my bedchamber. His solid grip was the only thing that prevented me from drifting off into the air. His face, behind that neat moustache, was stiff with concern. Uncle William could not have been less like his brother Henry; he had none of Henry's abundant charm, was dependable, favoured pragmatism and hard work and the making of money. It was no wonder Grandmother favoured him. He laid me carefully on the bed and pulled a cover up over me, before adding another log to the fire and stirring the embers until it was ablaze.

I drew myself into a ball as the pecking intensified; I began counting backwards again.

'I will fetch one of your women,' he said quietly, leaning over me.

I gripped his wrist saying, 'Not Joan, send the other one, the new one.' I couldn't remember her name. 'Mary's woman.'

'You mean Bridget?'

'Yes, her.' My grip loosened. 'And tell Sir Henry that I will give him a written account of events, as soon as I am capable.'

Once he had gone I was left with those vile birds, my circling harpies, and Grandmother's words: *We feared for her life.* Was I dying? If so, was I afraid? I didn't know.

'Am I done for?' I asked Bridget as she bent over me. She looked flushed, those round cheeks redder than ever, and was wiping damp tendrils of pale hair away from her face. She must have run up the stairs.

'I don't believe you are.' She said it with such confidence I truly believed her. I could hear the now familiar chink and gurgle of the tincture bottle, imagine the relief it would bring. Opening my mouth like a baby bird as she poured it in, I readied myself for blessed oblivion. She tenderly manoeuvred me round and undid my gown, sliding it off and then my bodice, lifting it away as I began to drift. 'We need to produce a measure of water for the physician to inspect. Do you think you are capable?'

I nodded and she slipped a shallow bowl beneath me, carefully, so carefully, as if I were excessively precious, one of Grandmother's alabaster artefacts, or that glass vessel so fine its edges were like air. I felt my water come; it was a mighty release and eased the pain fractionally. She extracted the bowl and, though she tried to hide it, I saw the horror on her face as she inspected its contents.

'What? What is it? Let me see.' I don't know how I found the words in my semi-stupor but there they were.

I could feel her reluctance.

'Show me, Bridget!' I said it like an order and she placed the bowl close to my head. It smelled strong and acrid. I tilted myself to see and was momentarily confused, thinking I had been bled and not been aware of it, for the bowl was full of blood. But it wasn't blood; blood is a dense red and this was more translucent like carnelian, the colour of the Scottish Queen's Agnus Dei. 'Bring me my writing things.'

'I think you should rest.' Bridget set the bowl down and sat beside me.

'I must explain myself to Sir Henry.'

'Not now; later.' She began to sing very softly, a lullaby, the kind wet nurses sing to fractious infants.

'He's gone,' said Grandmother, looming over my bed. I was propped up with pillows and the sheets were spattered with inkblots from my efforts to articulate my account of things. I had done it once and was requested to redo it, for apparently Brouncker could not make sense of what I said. 'This won't be the end of it. When the Queen hears how you have confounded her agent she will be . . . well, I can't imagine she will be anything other than incensed. All this business about a secret lover. I don't know . . .'

'A secret lover?' I couldn't remember exactly what I had written; my head was so muddled with the poppy. I focused my thoughts and a vague impression came to me of having invented another suitor to prove I didn't intend to wed Edward Seymour. It had made complete sense at the time.

'I have sent word to Her Majesty begging lenience,' she continued. 'But she is unwell. This is the last thing she needs.' Grandmother seemed unusually distracted. 'I don't know, Arbella. You'd better find a way to explain yourself or you will be on your way to the Tower – mark my words.' She turned her gaze to the ceiling with a deep sigh.

My mind began to clear of fog: 'I have become a liability, haven't I? Perhaps it would be better for you if I *were* in the Tower and you and Cecil could wash your hands of me entirely.'

'Don't be silly, Arbella.' She looked away as she said it and I knew I'd hit on the truth. The fog lifted further.

'I *am* aware Cecil wants my cousin on the throne.'

'I don't know why you believe that. Cecil merely does the Queen's bidding.' She lowered her voice, smoothed it. 'You've been very confused in your illness. I think you perceive conspiracies where there are none. We are family and Cecil has long been an ally.' She straightened my rumpled coverlet. 'Now, if you would just give me the name of this suitor –'

I spoke firmly over her. 'I'd like Brouncker sent for.' It came to me with brutal clarity then; it was not the Queen who was my enemy, it was Grandmother and Cecil who worked against me. Brouncker was a direct line to the Queen and if I pleaded with him directly, begged genuine forgiveness, neither Cecil nor Grandmother could twist my words to their own ends. 'Now I am well enough I feel ready to make my deposition to the Queen. I will give the identity of my suitor to her, through Brouncker, and it will all be resolved.'

'Dearest.' She held her pearls in a fist by her throat, like a noose. 'Write it all down and I'll see it gets to Her Majesty. There's no need for that dreadful little man to be called back.'

'I *insist* upon his return,' I said.

She took my writing box and set it down on my lap, opening it, pulling out a quill, thrusting it towards me. 'For goodness' sake, just write down his name.' She was only just managing to control her temper. It was plain she couldn't bear thinking things might have occurred without her knowledge.

I took the quill from her and placed it back in the box. 'Nothing will pass my lips until Brouncker is sent for, nothing, not even a sip of water.'

'Don't set your will against mine, young lady, for you will never win.' She stood and swept from the chamber.

'I wouldn't be so sure,' I called out after her. I knew she was no match for me when it came to abnegation. I had been rehearsing my powers of self-denial for years, just as a young man prepares for the battlefield, with daily practice. Propelled by a surge of inner force, I got up from the bed and called Bridget in to help me dress.

'You are up!' she said. 'I'm so glad to see you're feeling better.'

'I'm more than better.'

'There is something –' she began to say but I interrupted her, not taking in the look of concern she wore.

'Has there been a reply from my aunt yet?' I had written, some days before, begging Aunt Mary to return.

'I have it from one of the pages that your letter to her was intercepted. Your grandmother threw it on the fire.' She twisted her apron in her fingers until it was a mess of creases.

'On the fire,' I repeated, not knowing what else to say, thinking of all those burned letters, all the ash building up into a great black edifice of invisible words, thinking too of all those cracked seals, of the correspondence read before it came to me.

'Is there another way to get word to her?'

'There is a fellow in the stables.'

'I'd like her to send help to Dodderidge, at least ensure he is comfortable and not suffering ill treatment.' I wriggled out of my nightgown and raised my arms for a clean shift to go over my head.

'Leave it to me.'

'You have quite a network in this household, Bridget, with the friendly page *and* the stable hand.'

'They are not my friends, My Lady, they are *your* friends. There are more here at Hardwick who support you than you think. There is Mister Chaworth who goes about with your glove tucked into his hat-band.' Bridget began to lace my bodice with quick fingers.

'Mister Chaworth wears my glove in his hat – goodness!' I had always thought Chaworth just another of Grandmother's many retainers. He had certainly never made himself known to me as a supporter. 'What does my grandmother say of it?'

'She doesn't know it is your glove.' Bridget raised her eyebrows and held my petticoats open for me to step into. 'But there is something import—' She tried to speak again and once more I didn't take note and spoke over her:

'I see now why my aunt has left me in your care. Can Mister Chaworth be sent to discover the whereabouts of Brouncker? I have asked my grandmother to call him back but she seems reluctant to do so. If we can at least get him as far as the gates . . . Tell him to say to Brouncker that I will reveal the identity of my suitor, to him alone. That way it will reach the Queen's ears before Grandmother's.'

She was at my front, fastening the hooks of my sleeves, and whispered, 'This suitor is an invention, isn't he?'

I nodded, whispering back, 'But it's turned out to be a good ruse to get the Queen's agent back.'

'But will your grandmother allow Brouncker in?'

'I have a feeling she will.'

Bridget tipped her head as if about to ask what my plan was but seemed to change her mind. 'There is something else.'

'What else?' Her crumpled expression made me instinctively brace myself.

'Something they wanted to keep from you; they thought you too fragile.'

'And do *you* think me too fragile, Bridget?'

She answered me with a question: 'Who is Starkey?'

I shrivelled inside. 'What's happened to Starkey?'

'He was dear to you, then?'

'"*Was*"?' My heart began to flap.

'He took his own life.'

Someone let out a terrible howl, the sound of a man on the rack or a beast at the knackers. It was I who made that ungodly sound. It echoed about the room for an interminable time. 'No,' I said. 'It can't be possible. He was a man of the cloth. A man of God wouldn't . . . You have misunderstood.'

'I'm sorry.' She was looking away from me.

I felt my flailing heart shatter, fragments lacerating my vital organs. First Dodderidge had lost his freedom and then Starkey, dear Starkey, cast himself into eternal damnation, all for me.

'They said he was disappointed at the loss of a position. He hanged himself. I don't know more.' She spoke quietly, shaking her head.

Desolation took hold in me – desolation and remorse, mingling to make a monster. I knew it wasn't Starkey's thwarted prospects that led him to suicide; I knew him too well to believe that – people don't kill themselves over disappointment, least of all Starkey. It was the fact that he had aided me in my unsuccessful treason; however small his part in it was, he would have found a way to render himself culpable. Perhaps he believed he had led me to it.

Brouncker's voice resonated in my head: *Dodderidge has named names; your chaplain Starkey is one of them.* Had the authorities grilled Starkey too? Had he feared revealing something under interrogation? Perhaps he knew more than I thought he did.

He would have rather died than unwittingly betray me; that I knew. He would have meditated on other noble deaths, Cleopatra preferring suicide to dishonour, Socrates choosing hemlock rather than flight – the upholding of justice. *The difficulty, my friends, is not in avoiding death, but in avoiding unrighteousness, for that runs deeper than death.* We had talked often about such things but always hypothetically; I had never believed either of us would have to make that choice.

I imagined him buried in unhallowed ground, condemned for eternity. Remorse swelled in me, clogging my thoughts, and I found myself on my knees, pleading with God to see my dear friend's actions as those of a martyr rather than a sinner, for what he did, he did for me, for my cause. When did he abandon his belief in God's plan?

I knelt there for some time; my face buried in my palms, unable to move, the demon that cursed all who loved it. An image ran through my mind: a river pool strewn with flowers, a body floating just beneath the surface, blurred by ripples, Starkey's waterlogged features just visible. 'No, no, no, no . . .'

'My Lady.' Bridget was at my shoulder.

'I might as well have killed him with my own hands.' I yearned for the release of tears but knew I was incapable. If you are dry and brittle as glass you cannot make tears. I began to feel determination building in me, a desire to render Starkey's death meaningful; if he had lost his belief in God's plan then I would sustain it in his stead.

In my head I was composing a new letter to Uncle Henry.

Clerkenwell

A month has passed since Hal left and a suffocating despair has crept up on Ami. No matter how hard she works – and she works until she can barely stand, until she can barely think – she cannot obliterate her guilt.

She has written to him almost daily, scratching out her pleas, but her letters have all been returned unopened. She has thought of Starkey hanging, his neck snapped by the noose. Though she never knew him and Lady Arbella never spoke of him, his gentle spirit came to life for her in those pages and died there too. In her darkest moments – she can hardly bear to think of it – she has inspected the large beam that runs the width of her chamber, calculated in her head the length of rope she might need. It is only Hal who keeps her from that sin without redemption. She has hurt him enough already.

Lady Arbella's papers sit still unfinished. Ami tries to rediscover that sense of inspiration she'd had a few weeks back, when the story had grabbed her by the throat, but the feeling is lost. She looks at her monstrous hands and can remember Cecil, or Salisbury as he had become by then, taking her fingers, like a nurse inspecting a child's nails, saying, 'It is most *unusual* that a woman would seek to publish – and such subject matter.' He clearly meant that, like the King, he disapproved.

She had wanted to say, 'Not most unusual but *unprecedented* – I am the first,' to throw his disapproval back at him, let him see how proud she was of her achievement, but she'd said nothing.

'I see you have written a poem to the Lady Arbella.' He still held her hands, continuing to inspect them.

'I have written poems to many women,' she'd said, but he wasn't listening.

'Not the hands of a laundress, are they?'

Her breath had faltered. He knew. She was not dismissed from court for offending the King, not really.

Mansfield arrives, interrupting her thoughts, walking in, as usual, without knocking. It is as if he owns her already.

'How's my favourite laundry lass?'

'I'm hardly a lass.' He approaches with a look that makes her feel naked – the wasp is back buzzing incessantly round the jam. 'Truth be told, I'm dog-tired.'

'Well' – he moves up close to her – 'the bedchamber is a mere few steps away.' He smells different, ambergris or something. His constant pestering has worn her down and she has resigned herself to the inevitability of giving him what he wants – perhaps then she will be rid of him.

'It's not like you to go wearing fancy perfumes, Mansfield.' She steps away. 'Are you trying to impress me?' She wonders if she is flirting with him or trying to keep him at bay. *He* certainly thinks it is the former, to judge by the look he's wearing.

It would be so easy to submit to him. She imagines being freed from the back-breaking cycle of washing, the sores on her hands healing, all the time she would have to write and think.

'Maybe.' He grabs her then and kisses her firmly, his mouth suckered on to hers. She allows it, telling herself to let it happen. But she is finding it hard to breathe; the ambergris is cloying, too sweet.

'Get off!' Using all her strength, she pushes him violently away. 'I can't.'

A chair falls as he loses his footing and staggers back over the room, spitting an oath.

'Please,' she says, trying to gather herself together. 'I don't want to make you an adulterer.' This is not what is foremost in her mind at all, but she knows it is the best way to provoke his conscience a little. It has worked in the past with him, at least.

He meets her gaze in sullen silence, looking like a dog that has just been beaten.

'It's not that I don't like you. I just think you have mis-interpreted me,' she witters. 'I would need to feel more.' What is she saying? She finds she can't express herself. 'I know you think, because of my past, that I have loose morals, but I loved Lord Hunsdon. I didn't do it for any-thing but love.'

She realizes how ridiculous it is to talk of love under such circumstances and can see the disbelief scrawled over his face. What could a girl of eighteen possibly have wanted with a man beyond his three-score years? 'Oh, never mind.' A thick silence wells and she fears she has gone too far, but from nowhere an idea flares up in her. 'Your boy, Edwin.'

'What about him?' His eyes narrow. He seems angry or confused, as if she is trying to trick him.

'Would you like me to teach him his letters?'

'What are you getting at?' Suspicion is crawling over him.

'I could teach him to read in lieu of my debt to you.' She can't believe she has not thought of this before, that her edu-cation is a resource she can tap. Suddenly her world, a world that had been shrinking only moments before, seems to expand as if filling with endless possibility.

He looks, with his open-mouthed stare, as if she has sug-gested she roast his offspring for supper.

'And what would any brats of mine want with books?'

'If they can read, well, they will never want for employ-ment. They could go up in the world.'

'So there are no tumbledown houses in London, are there, Widow Lanyer, no roofs to mend?' The sarcasm doesn't suit him. 'There'll be plenty of work for *my* boys until kingdom come.'

'But if they know their letters and numbers they won't be easily fleeced.'

'Are you suggesting that I'm –'

'Of course not. You're nobody's fool.' He relaxes a little, seems to have decided it wasn't an insult. 'But we all want the best for our children, don't we?'

She hopes his silence means he is considering her proposal.

'Letters *and* numbers?' He turns to face her and she knows she has gained the upper hand.

'We could come to an arrangement about the numbers.'

'I have three boys of the right age. The rest are too young, and the girls, I don't want my girls being ruined by book learning.'

Ami wants to snap back a retort but holds her tongue, just says calmly, 'For what I still owe, I will teach your eldest lad his letters and if you want the others taught, and want them to know their numbers too, then perhaps we can reach an arrangement.'

He looks at her and then at the floor, seeming to cogitate. Maybe he is trying to calculate the value of what she is offering; after all, learning cannot be weighed like a bag of nails.

'Knowledge is priceless.' She pauses for her words to sink in. 'So do we have a deal?' She holds out a hand.

His face breaks into a sudden smile and he laughs, saying, 'Well, I must say there are no flies on you, Widow Lanyer,' taking her hand and shaking it firmly. 'It is agreed.' He hesitates then, looking surprisingly sheepish. 'I'm . . . I'm sorry for what . . . you know. It was unforgivable . . .'

'There is little in life that is truly unforgivable, Mister Mansfield. With some things it can be best to pretend they never happened.'

She senses that her magnanimity is making him feel like the smaller person. Forgiveness can be a powerful tool, for it leaves an adversary morally indebted. It was Henry Hunsdon who taught her that.

'You have a heart, Widow Lanyer; I'll say that for you. I'll send the three boys on Monday. The littlest is only six. Is that too young?'

'Not at all. The younger the better.'

She opens the door for him, to find Goodwife Stringer on the stoop with the tabby held by the scruff at arm's length. Ami suspects she has been listening, or trying to.

'Good morning, Mister Mansfield,' she says, tilting her head to one side, with a smile spread over her face. He mumbles a greeting and excuses himself, striding away down the street. The smile turns to a sneer directed at Ami. 'Your cat has been getting at my hens. They've stopped laying.'

Ami takes the tabby, apologizing, holding her tongue rather than suggesting that it might have been the recent thunderstorms that have stopped her hens producing.

'Still alone?' She is craning past Ami to look into the house, casting her eyes about.

'My Hal is still on progress with the court.' She resists the temptation to slam the door in the woman's face.

If she is impressed she hides it well. 'Do you know about Mad Dot?'

'What about her?'

'Found beaten to death.'

'Good Lord!' She thinks of the poor woman searching in perpetuity for her dead children – a kind of hell. No one would wish such a violent end on a person but perhaps it was a release.

'Someone overheard her talking to the devil, you know.'

'Terrible business.' Ami will not be drawn into talk of witchcraft. She knows only too well that her words might end up twisted. Suspicion alights so easily and she is already regarded as an oddity.

Goodwife Stringer begins to walk away but as she does she turns. 'You'd better take care.'

Ami wants to challenge her, ask what she means, but she doesn't want to add fuel to the woman's fire.

Once the door is closed she sits a while, relishing in the thought that there will be no more laundry. She thinks of Hal, feeling for the first time in the last month a sense of calm, realizing that all he needs is time and that the more she pursues him the further out of reach he will put himself.

The day stretches out before her, empty, hours of daylight, so she picks up Lady Arbella's papers, taking up where she left off, allowing the story to get beneath her skin, finding once more, at last, that prickling of anticipation that things obscured will be revealed. She reads voraciously, hoping for answers, stopping only to cut herself a hunk of bread and a slice of cheese, returning to her chair at the window to continue reading as she eats, until the story possesses her and time is of no consequence.

Hardwick

Uncle Henry's reply was swift in coming. Bridget fumbled in the folds of her skirts, pulling it out. It was crumpled and smeared with dirt but I recognized his writing. We were at the back end of the knot garden behind the high yew hedge that obscured the view from the house. I was aware we hadn't much time before Joan, or someone else, was sent out to see what we were up to, out of sight like that.

I had folded my grief up and stored it away, but Starkey whispered to me constantly. *Where are you?* I whispered back. In the orchard beyond, the apple trees were in full March bloom and the optimistic blue of the sky was clear save for the occasional white billow of cloud. That, with the doves *coo-currooing* from the roof of the stables and the hopeful chatter of the finches flitting about the hedge, made spring seem almost within reach.

I unfolded the paper.

Your star is rising, Arbella. We will go ahead without Hertford's support. Beauchamp is in agreement. The Queen is ailing. They say her mouth is so ulcerated she can barely eat or drink. Your time is coming. Seymour and his father are waiting for us . . . I have armed men mustered all around you . . . Come to the gatehouse at midday tomorrow and we will get you away.

I looked at Bridget. 'Tomorrow at noon, I will be spirited away.' I walked on, out of the shadow of the yew. Inside I was effervescing. 'My escape is planned. You can tell our friendly page boy to go to my Uncle Henry with the news that I will see him tomorrow as planned and tell the lad in the stables to make sure Dorcas is ready, saddled up for me by noon.'

'May God go with you, My Lady,' she replied and I turned to see her drawing her finger across her front from left shoulder to right.

My suspicion began to stir. 'Why did you do that?'

'Do what?'

'You were crossing yourself.'

'Why would I do that?'

I began to doubt what I'd seen. I was light-headed from lack of nourishment; I had kept my vow, nothing had passed my lips and with each refusal I felt my power flourish. Brouncker's return had become inconsequential but I continued my stand so as not to arouse Grandmother's suspicion. She knew my will was not so easily broken. 'Of course, why –'

'I was only wrapping my stole more tightly. Do you not feel the chill?' She tucked the ends of her shawl into her girdle. 'There, that's better.' She thrust her hands beneath it with an exaggerated shiver. Of course she was cold; I was layered in furs but she wore only that thin woollen scarf. 'Did you think me a secret Catholic?' She made a laugh, as if such a thing was entirely absurd, and I felt silly for allowing my imagination to run away with me. 'It is no surprise you are on edge, with the news of . . .'

'My escape,' I whispered.

'Exactly.' We walked on back, counting the paces from the gatehouse to the door – the path I would take in the opposite direction the following day when Uncle Henry arrived – eighty-eight steps and he would be waiting at the gates with Dorcas to whisk me away.

Staff supper was being laid out in the great hall, servants scurrying to and fro laden with dishes. As I passed I threw Uncle Henry's letter into the fire, stopping briefly to make sure it caught. I tried to imagine my freedom, able to conceive it only in abstract sensations, wings spread, the wind beneath them, flying up.

I walked on through the hall and up the stone flight of stairs, past the tapestry of Job's dead children, to the private rooms where family supper was about to be served.

'You look better,' remarked Grandmother. 'That walk must have done you good. You have some colour in your cheeks again.'

I pretended to smile at her, as if offering peace. 'I needed some fresh air after being cooped up in my chambers for so long.' There were a thousand things left unspoken beneath our falsely bright exchange.

The new chaplain said grace and we sat. Uncle William offered me bread, which I refused. The chaplain, a bald man with a large nose, was attacking his food, masticating with his mouth open. I looked away. The children were snatching up titbits from each other's plates when their mother wasn't watching. She ate delicately, in small mouthfuls. Uncle William piled his plate and gorged himself, dirtying his moustaches, mopping every last residue of sauce with his bread. Grandmother talked more than ate, making forced conversation about a recent land acquisition and trying to ignore the fact that I was sitting beside her like an exclamation mark, while hunger gnawed silently at me, making me stronger. The dogs looked at me hopefully, through habit, but they eventually slunk down to where the children sat.

'At least have a sip to drink,' said Uncle William.

'Thank you, I won't,' I replied.

Grandmother wore her exasperation openly and I gloated inwardly, feeling my escape almost at the tips of my fingers.

Eager to return to the privacy of my room after supper, I made an excuse and floated away, light as air. Joan tried to follow me but I sent her on an errand. Sitting at my desk, I began to write, scribbling out my thoughts as fast as I could think them, until my hand ached. The act of writing helped me to focus my mind on the preparations for the following day's journey.

Starkey's ghost hovered, for the plan that had begun with the valuables he'd delivered into Cousin Bessie's safekeeping was coming to fruition; I wouldn't allow his death to have been for nothing. I whispered as much to him. He whispered back: *God's plan, it is God's plan.*

A twist of anticipation tightened in me. I would wear the plainest dress I had, to avoid unwanted attention, and would cover myself with a hooded cloak. No one would question such a garment at that time of year. The only concession to sentiment I would take was my small bag of treasures. I tipped the little pouch out, inspecting each item: the bell from Geddon's collar; the tear of glass, which magnified things, made the invisible visible; Uncle Henry's weighted die that only rolled a six; and the Agnus Dei, blessed by the Pope. It glowed in the candlelight as if lit from within.

'What's that?'

I jumped, surprised, and the object fell from my fingers, rolling over the floor.

'Bridget, you gave me a fright, creeping up like that.'

'What is it?' She stooped to pick it up, tossing it as if it were a coin.

'Nothing, just a thing the Scottish Queen gave me when I was a child.' How could this girl, so cavalier with a sacred object, be a secret Catholic? I reprimanded myself inwardly for having allowed my imagination to run away with me earlier in the garden.

'I'd be careful who sees this; it looks like a popish toy.' She held it out to me, meeting my eye. 'No need to worry about me, I won't tell anyone, but please take care.'

I began to list all the things I would need for my journey

when Bridget asked: 'Have you ever wondered what it is like to just be an ordinary woman?' She paused, adding in response to my obvious puzzlement, 'To not be a princess of the blood?'

'Someone asked me once what I would like to be if I were a commoner.' A little current of air riffled the papers on the desk and I knew it was Starkey.

'And what did you say?'

'I said I'd like to be a groom.' I was thinking of being reunited with dear Dorcas the following day, wondering if she'd know me after all these years.

'But you'd need to have been born a boy for that.'

'Exactly,' I replied. 'Why do you ask?'

'Because all women who are not princesses imagine what it would be like to be one.' She laughed then. 'Silly, isn't it? Now, I must make sure you have a few necessaries for tomorrow.' She began to busy herself about the chamber, adding as an afterthought, 'Now that I know what the life of a princess is truly like, I would not wish it on my worst enemy.'

It was another bright day and the sun was almost at its highest point. I stood in the shade of the portico, looking down the path – eighty-eight steps to the gatehouse – listening out for horses. I thought of Uncle Henry's armed men in the woodland around Hardwick, down in the valley, unseen – dozens of them, he'd said. I would knight them all when I was queen. I could hear the clank and clatter of dinner inside. 'If you will not eat you may not sit at my table,' Grandmother had ruled, and I knew I had won. Little did she know how she played into my hands with that punishment. The thought buoyed me up, made me strong. Hunger twisted through my gut – I was never more alive. I wondered what the Queen was feeling with her ulcerated mouth. We were both starving – she to death, I to life.

I heard them, at first a faint thrum, becoming louder, the rumble of hooves and jangle of tack, slowing and coming to a halt at the gates. Through the arch I could see three horses, one was Dorcas, saddled up and riderless. Uncle Henry dismounted; I couldn't see his companion. My anticipation began to buzz as if I'd been colonized by a swarm of bees. Starkey whispered: *Go, go, this is your chance – fly away, Philomel.* I made my way forward. Uncle Henry was talking to one of the guards, gesticulating forcefully; it turned quickly into what appeared to be an altercation. A young man, one of the pages, ran past me towards them and I could only suppose that Grandmother was surveying the scene from her window above.

I walked on, counting my paces: *ten; twelve; fourteen.* I expected my empty body to feel weightless, to float, but on the contrary it was as if my bones had been poured with lead; I could barely put one foot in front of the other. Nevertheless, from somewhere I found the strength to shift myself down that path – *thirty-six; thirty-eight* – past the flower-bed now shaped in an E, with its new plants, fresh and green. E for Elizabeth, S for Shrewsbury – the A for Arbella was there in the lawn still, like a ghost, where the sparse pale turf had not yet quite married with its lush neighbours. I walked on, my heavy, heavy legs pleading with me to stop, telling me it was impossible.

The page had turned and was making his way back to the house, presumably for orders. I didn't mean to, but I looked up then and back – like that couple in the Bible who were turned to salt – to the central window; there she was, a familiar black shape in it, calling me like a lodestar, making me lose my resolve. I stopped the page. 'Tell her I would like to talk to my uncle, at least.' *You don't need her permission any more,* said Starkey, *fly away.* But asking permission was a habit; I was unused to the idea of freedom. The boy ran into the house and had returned to me before I had taken even a dozen excruciating paces: *forty-eight, fifty.* The guards had multiplied and formed a line across the gates.

'Your uncle may enter, but alone.' The boy's face was red. I couldn't tell if it was the result of his running or embarrassment at being the one chosen to play a part in the denial of my freedom. He continued on to relay Grandmother's message to the guards. One of them stepped forward, raising his line of sight to where she was framed in the window. What would she do? Make a gesture like Caesar, the thumb pointing up or down, to dictate whether I would live or die?

I resisted turning this time, kept my eyes on the gates and watched as the line of guards parted to allow my uncle through. I was rooted to the spot, so light-headed my attention began to wander and I imagined the birds were talking to me, warning me; the doves on the roof were purring the word *da-da-dangerrrr.* I could not tell where the menace lay, out there beyond the gates or back behind the glass. *Fly away.*

Uncle Henry looked red-faced and worn, paunchy, older. Thin straggles of grey hair hung from beneath his hat. Of course he was older; I hadn't seen him for a decade. He had never before greeted me without a smile. That day was the first time.

'The bitch has given me half an hour with you,' he spat, taking my arm and helping, almost lifting, me, towards the house. *How strange,* I thought, *that I am such a great weight, bones of lead, yet to him I am light as the finest glass, glass so fine it would shatter in a breath of air.* My mind wouldn't stop perambulating off in different directions, only occasionally alighting on the sensible thought that it was folly to have embarked on such a journey having ingested nothing, nothing at all, in three days. I might have felt cleansed as a saint but I was in no fit state to go travelling about the country.

We passed through the great hall, where forty-odd pairs

of eyes watched us in silence from the dining tables: estate workers, servants, embroiderers, grooms, most of whom I'd known since childhood, all wondering what was happening. Bridget was there; Bridget knew. Uncle Henry rattled with arms, a sword hanging from his belt, a dagger beside it, a pistol tucked into his doublet. We threaded our way through the tangle of passages to the schoolroom, where Starkey's spectre flitted about, like a draught that made my heart billow.

I sat, at last, in the high-backed chair beside the barren grate and listened in a daze to Uncle Henry explaining what would happen. '. . . We can storm the place. I have enough firepower out there. I have only to give my signal and mayhem will be loosed.' His eyes blazed in anticipation.

'People will be hurt,' I muttered, seeing only then the reality of what I had agreed to: that it would be a battle, that people would suffer, may even be killed.

'What did you expect? That you could simply walk out of the gates?' His fist clutched the pommel of his sword.

That is what I, in my naivety, *had* expected: that Grandmother's resolve would be magically overcome simply by the sight, the mere thought even, of Uncle Henry's armed men. But of course Grandmother was not cowed by anything. How could that fact have not occurred to me?

'Don't go faint-hearted on me now, Belle.' There it was, the glittering smile I remembered. 'Think of it. Wed to Seymour, the pair of you will be unassailable.'

'Yes, unassailable,' I said, hearing Starkey: *You were bred to it; it is God's plan for you.*

'That's more like it.' He began pacing the room. 'This is what will happen. You will come to the gate to see me off. I will give the signal and my men will be here, quick as a trice, to deal with the guards. They are waiting . . . ready for a fight.'

'I don't want anyone hurt.'

'Belle!' His voice softened. 'Look at me.'

I looked; his eyes were bloodshot, as if he hadn't slept for days.

'Trust me.'

A noise caused us both to turn towards the door and there was Grandmother standing tall, one hand on the jamb. 'Give me a minute with her, Henry.' It was not a request, it was a command, and he responded like an infant to his nurse. 'You look terrible,' she added as he passed her to wait outside the room.

She closed the door and came to sit beside me, drawing her chair up close. 'It's cold in here.' She took off her fur wrap – that horrible dead creature with rubies for eyes – and put it around my shoulders, touching her knuckles gently to my cheek. 'Frozen.' She leaned back; her chair creaked.

'He can't be trusted. You think you know him but you haven't seen him more than a handful of times in your life. To you he is all magic and laughter. But *I* know him and I know that you are no more than another gamble to him – his greatest stake in a life of risk. He stands to win the highest prize if he can get you on the throne.'

'I was raised for that – *you* raised me for that.'

'You *were* raised for that, but things have changed – things beyond my control.' Her tone was filled with authority, as if she understood everything, and perhaps she did, with her connection to Cecil. But Cecil had betrayed me. 'If Henry doesn't succeed in his great plan, his wager – and he won't, for a gambler always loses in the end – it will be *you*, not him, in the Tower awaiting trial for treason.'

'His plan is a good one. He –'

'Pah! Henry's even less competent than Essex, and look what became of Essex. His scheme is not what you think it is. I know the man he came here with, Stapleton, a renowned papist. He doubtless has a ragged army of disaffected Catholics waiting in the woods. He will have promised them you are open to conversion, dangled you as a Catholic queen to get them on his side, promised them he has papist connections abroad to put you on the throne. It will be deemed a Catholic plot and you will pay the price, my girl.'

From the side of my eye I could see Starkey hanging by the neck from a beam.

'Why, if you risked so much, as you said you did to bring my parents together, will you not help me to wed Edward Seymour? Isn't it the same?'

'You must learn to assess the level of risk in any undertaking. The risk must always be worth the reward – that has been the key to my success.' She paused, sitting forward. 'I will make everything right, Arbella.'

'Why should I trust you more than Uncle Henry?'

She took my hand then. Her skin was cool. 'I may not be the most warm-hearted of women but I have raised you and been fond of you in my way.' She let my hand go. 'You have enough examples. Don't be like those Grey girls, who thought wedlock would set them free. And look what happened to the Scottish Queen.'

Starkey was silenced. Grandmother's pull was proving too great a force for me to resist. In hindsight I have often wondered if it was because I had known nothing other than Grandmother's rule and, even though hers was a loveless regime, it was a familiar one.

I was the dog that would not leave the master who beats him.

'I'm sorry,' I heard myself say.

If I had been the type for tears then it would have been a moment for them, but neither of us was given to excessive expressions of emotion. That bald fact made me see I was more like Grandmother than I'd thought. I had her recalcitrance and determination and perhaps, too, her courage. She was right, I was nothing but the cardboard queen in Uncle Henry's three-card trick: *Follow the lady, where is she, not there no, she is here, I have her.* 'I will ask him to leave.'

She stood and exited without another word.

Uncle Henry was incandescent with rage as he fired off questions at me. 'Why would you listen to that embittered old hag? Hasn't she kept you prisoner here for a decade? Have you lost your nerve? Did you think we could take you without a struggle? Do you think I mustered all those men for nothing?'

I thought he might hit me but, turning his back, he kicked out at the wall instead, leaving a mark on the whitewash and a roar of frustration in the air. Perhaps if I had sensed a fragment of true fondness from my uncle – not just that twinkling smile reserved for those he was about to fleece – the outcome of that day might have been different. It might have been worse but then again it was equally possible that Grandmother was wrong.

He stormed from the room. I watched from the low window as he traversed the garden towards the gate – those eighty-eight paces. My fingers wandered to the bag of treasures hanging from my waist, finding the weighted die. It no longer represented the brilliant mercurial uncle who would magic me away to freedom. It had become a reminder that no one could be trusted.

I took it out; rolled it, willing it to say something other than six but three pairs of tiny eyes stared up at me.

PART II

I must shape my own coat according to my cloth, but it will not be after the fashion of this world, God willing, but fit for me.

Arbella Stuart, Letter to Sir Henry Brouncker,
Ash Wednesday 1603

Travelling south

I was unprepared for the impact the Queen's death would have on me. It was like a blow to the head, leaving me senseless for a time, for the force that had invisibly defined my existence, my entire purpose, was gone. She named James on her deathbed, coerced by Cecil, some said, and as a result I was free, or so I believed.

Had I done nothing, the outcome would have been the same. My struggle to escape; the effort it had taken to force the return of Brouncker; the scheming; the risk – none of it had made any impact. It had given dear, loyal Dodderidge a most terrible ordeal, but the greatest and most futile sacrifice had been the loss of Starkey. Looking back, I have come to understand that some fractures can appear to mend, but leave an invisible fault line, a place of fragility, and Starkey still whispers to me even here, now, beckoning, and I long to go to him.

The violent upheaval that had hung over the country, on tenterhooks in fear of civil war, hadn't occurred; the Catholics, who apparently had such a long-held fervour to see me enthroned, melted away into the crevices of England. England seemed to forget that James was a foreigner, the son of an executed traitor. In the end, it seemed, I was not worth fighting for. I was not male, and after half a century of female rule, England had no more appetite for a woman on the throne. God's plan had died with Starkey.

I was twenty-seven years old and had never truly experienced freedom; I hardly knew what to do with it and, as an animal that has spent its life caged feels safe only within the familiar confines of its prison, I took my first steps tentatively.

That fearless boy-girl who had ridden, flying, bareback all those years ago was not the same hesitant wraith who, reunited at last with Dorcas, took a sedate walk around the home farm. The mare seemed to sense my nervousness in the saddle and plodded obligingly, gentle as a lamb. A person can be broken just as a horse can.

She knew me, even after a decade's absence, whickered and snuffed, blowing hot breath into my collar, as if we had ridden out only the day before. I recognized the groom who led her to me; a man in his middle years, with cropped steel-grey hair. People age, but their eyes don't change.

'Tobias?' I said, remembering our play-fight at the Chatsworth Stand Tower. 'Have you been here all along?'

'I left for a time, My Lady, but returned a few years back. I've been taking good care of this girl for you.' He scratched Dorcas behind the ears. I was wondering if he was our friend in the stables who had been running errands. 'Well, I am most grateful to you, Tobias. Dorcas is very dear to me.'

'Will you be riding her or taking the carriage on your journey south?'

'I'll be riding. Make sure she's well rested, won't you.' It was in that moment that the full realization settled on me, with a strange ambivalence, that I would at last be leaving Hardwick. It had been my whole world for more than a decade and it dawned on me that freedom meant having no home of my own. I would be dependent on the kindness of others, for I had no great means, only that paltry package of jewels in the care of Cousin Bessie. Grandmother had settled almost nothing on me, James refused to release the Lennox lands that were rightfully mine and I was obliged to beg a stipend from the royal coffers. To that end I wrote letters to Cecil, who held the key, pleading that the new king bestow a living on his impecunious royal cousin.

Grandmother came to the door to see me off. It was an

awkward moment and I was glad to have Aunt Mary at my shoulder for moral support. We said goodbye rather formally, as if I'd been a houseguest, and although I hadn't expected an embrace I'd thought perhaps a peck on the cheek might be forthcoming. But we stood, neither wanting to be the one to step forward. Though it was spring and quite warm, she was wearing the white stoat with those infernal eyes, but rather than unsettling me as they always had, they reminded me that I would no longer be scrutinized.

She made an attempt at something that couldn't quite be called a smile and I felt suddenly, strangely rueful about all the trouble I'd caused, when she'd cared for me and protected me in her own way. I would have liked to articulate my gratitude but as I began to speak, so did she.

'I wanted to . . .' She paused and I felt she was going to say something, an apology, an expression of love, or regret. My heart was on the brink of opening and I remembered Starkey saying, *An apology is a powerful force for healing even the greatest of rifts, but most difficult to arrive at.* We looked at each other. She was clutching her pearls. 'You can take the carriage as far as Wrest Park. I have no use for it for a week or two. I'll send one of the boys to bring it back.'

'There's no need; I was planning to ride and we've got the luggage cart.'

I saw a small flutter of disappointment move over her face.

'I see.' The pearls clicked like gaming counters.

'We'd better be off,' said Aunt Mary, 'if we are to make it to Newstead before dark.'

'Yes, you'd better,' said Grandmother, and I turned, numb, to walk those eighty-eight steps to the gatehouse, where the horses were waiting.

It didn't take me long to find my confidence in the saddle and Dorcas responded accordingly, picking up her pace to ride ahead as we used to, once we were on to the soft ground. I began to unfurl. The air smelled crisp and grassy and the trees all sported their brilliant spring coats, new and fresh, giving me a sense of things beginning.

Margaret Byron was at Newstead. I was pleased to be re-united, even if only for a night. She had made me a pair of embroidered sleeves as a gift, her needlework exquisite as ever, and talked unceasingly about her baby, who was with the wet nurse. The only time she mentioned her husband was to say, 'I've given him a son, so he's happy. That was what I was for, after all.' I didn't say it, but I wondered where the passionate Margaret had gone, the girl who was in love with love. Perhaps she had realized that love comes to nothing in the end.

On we travelled towards Wrest Park, where we were to stay a few weeks with Cousin Bessie. My wings unfolded slowly, aching from lack of use. On the first morning I woke before dawn and, for the simple reason that I could, I went to the stables, tacked up Dorcas and rode alone out in the woods in the half-light, breathing in the dank scent rising from the loamy ground. The trees made dark shapes in the vagueness of early morning and the floor was spread with a muted carpet of bluebells.

Dorcas pricked her ears and we stopped to listen to a nightingale – the hopeful herald of summer. It inevitably brought back Ovid's tale of Philomel from all those years before at Hampton Court, but even that miserable memory was outsung by the nightingale's enchanting refrain.

You are truly free, whispered Starkey, *as Philomel was finally free in her feathered coat*. Starkey followed me everywhere, in each current of air, each cracking twig, each unexpected palpitation of my heart. For years my world had been the walled garden at Hardwick, where nature was clipped and carefully arranged, so that dawn wood, silent save for the song of a single bird, was an Eden to me.

Further joy arrived in the shape of a communication from Dodderidge:

I am released without charge and would like to return, if you are willing, to your service.

He mentioned nothing of the hardships he had endured on my behalf. Even I, confined as I had been for most of my life, knew that interrogation could be brutal, especially for one of no particular consequence.

News came thick and fast to Wrest Park, messengers travelling back and forth with the latest on the whereabouts of the King's party. Our evenings were spent mapping my royal cousin's progress south through England towards the capital, all the nobles vying to play host to their new monarch, hoping for a position in the royal household.

From Wrest Park I was to go not to court, because plague kept everyone away from Whitehall, but to Sheen Priory, the residence of the Marchioness of Northampton, a woman I knew barely at all. She had served the old Queen in her youth at the same time as Grandmother. It was an odd kind of freedom really, for letters from Cecil directed my fate, dictating where I would go and when.

It was summer by the time I arrived at Sheen. The going had been light and we'd made good time on the road south, reaching the ferry across the Thames earlier than expected. The house was ancient and rambling, its red brick bathed in sun and its windows framed by creeping greenery. The gardens surrounding it were an unkempt riot of colour. As our boat slid silently alongside the wooden pier I saw a gardener in a wide-brimmed straw hat, bent over a cluster of sweet peas. She was cutting the blooms off with a large pair of shears and tossing them into a basket nearby. It was like a scene from Arcadia and I half expected a shepherd to appear with his flock.

I stepped from the boat and peeled off my travelling gown, filthy from the road, handing it to Bridget.

'Do you think I should change?' I asked her, suddenly awkward, unsure of myself in that unfamiliar setting, realizing how unaccustomed I still was to the world beyond Hardwick.

'Do you think that is her?' Bridget nudged her head in the direction of the hatted woman, who was making her way towards us.

'Don't be silly.' She was teasing me as a way to put me at my ease, I supposed. The woman had taken her hat off and was waving it. I couldn't understand why a gardener would be approaching us, clearly intent on making a greeting. Grandmother would have been mortified had her own staff behaved in such a way.

'I think it *is* her,' said Bridget. 'Look at her air of authority. I'd better make sure the luggage is dealt with.' She turned back towards the barge where the lads were unloading. I wanted to grab her hand, make her stay with me, so I wouldn't have to confront the stranger alone. Despite my years, I felt no older than an infant clinging to its nurse's skirts.

The woman was calling out, 'Wonderful, wonderful to see you have arrived safely.'

She wasn't young, in her fifties perhaps, with the soft plumpness that sometimes comes with age; but she looked magnificent, her complexion translucent white, almost blue, hair the colour of quince jelly, threaded with silver, everything about her awry, her dress loosened so it drooped away from one round, freckled shoulder. I thought of Grandmother, how different she was, not a hair astray, primly laced, nothing out of place, and her abhorrence of freckles.

I began to walk to towards her and when I was near

enough I saw something in her expression, a scrunch between her brows, suspicion perhaps, or concern, I couldn't tell which.

'I trust your journey was not overly arduous, Highness.' She dropped into a curtsy. Despite her unconventional appearance, this was a woman clearly accustomed to the requirements of precedence.

'No, no . . . please,' I stammered. 'There's no need, really.'

'All those years serving the old Queen' – she smiled again, broadly, baring a set of small straight teeth – 'old habits die hard.'

'I am so very grateful to you for your hospitality.'

'Oh, look, here come your horses.' She pointed out towards the river and the ferry lumbering across. I could see Dorcas tossing her head frantically and the groom trying to calm her. 'I can't blame them getting nervous on that contraption. They'd probably rather swim over.'

I was unsure whether she was joking and couldn't think of what to say. I had become so unused to people I didn't know and at Hardwick Grandmother had always provided a buffer between myself and her guests.

Our hostess led me through the gardens, and whereas I'd thought them unkempt at first sight I realized that their wild beauty was governed by an almost invisible organizing principle. The deliberate informality was so unlike the harsh symmetry of Hardwick that I felt once more as if I had stepped into a land of fable. 'It's beautiful,' I said, wishing I had come up with something less banal.

'It is a wonderful bower, isn't it?' That look had returned; as if I were a puzzle she was trying to solve. 'Do you like my ornamental cherry?' She pointed to a sapling, gangly as an adolescent, close to the riverbank, the earth freshly dug at its base. 'I thought it would look rather lovely by the water.'

'Ornamental – it won't bear fruit?'

'Its sole aim in life is to give pleasure.' She stroked its trunk, seeming wholly enamoured with her spindly tree.

'Lovely,' I said, but the idea of planting a fruit tree just to look at, indeed to talk of it as if it had an aim, was incomprehensible to me.

'I expect you would like to change,' she said then. 'I have given you rooms overlooking the river – thought you might like to watch the comings and goings.' Then she put two fingers in her mouth and whistled like a cowherd. A pair of hounds appeared magically from the undergrowth and followed us towards the house. 'Did you bring any pets? These two can be rather territorial but they're harmless enough.'

I found myself telling her about the little dog, Geddon, that had belonged to the Scottish Queen, who had attached himself to me when I was a girl and wouldn't let anyone else near.

'There might be a puppy for you,' she said. 'One of the spaniel bitches is whelping. All the ladies at court have little dogs. They make a frightful mess, chewing the chair legs and pissing on the tapestries.' She laughed and I supposed I looked shocked, for she said, 'You must think me vulgar.'

'Not at all,' I replied. In truth I liked her ease, her light conversation.

'I'm not English, you see, so I can get away with it. My lax behaviour can be put down to eccentric foreign ways – even after decades here and two English husbands I am still Swedish to the core. I think the Queen – the old Queen – liked me the more for it. I was fond of her; but it was easy to be fond of her if you were one of the ones she chose to like. The others . . .' She didn't finish and I remembered Elizabeth – how ferocious she had seemed to me at times, how small and intimidated I had felt beside her.

'I didn't really know her.'

'You were hardly given a chance, kept locked away out of sight all those years. I never could understand that.' She was absently twisting a lock of hair around a finger. 'She was a very jealous woman *au fond*.' I had never heard anyone talk of the Queen as a person beset by ordinary emotions. 'Well,' she continued, 'I hope you will feel at home here. I know what it is like to be in someone else's house. It can be hard to feel at ease.'

'I have never had my own house, so I know nothing else.' I didn't mean to sound embittered, but it came out that way. She had touched a nerve and I felt like poor Dorcas tossing her head.

'I suppose you have not,' she said, glossing over my aggrieved tone. 'But a husband will rectify that.' She gave me a conspiratorial look. 'I suspect the Privy Council are poring over suits from foreign princes at this very minute.'

'If they are, I shall be the last to know.' There it was again, my acerbity, undisguised, the sense I had of myself as a spinster with no purpose and no place in the world.

'Well, that is the price of status, I suppose.' We walked on in silence for a moment. 'I didn't expect you to be . . .' She hesitated. 'To be so . . .' She inspected me, as if seeking clues as to what might be going on beneath my surface. 'I didn't expect you to be so well. I had been under the impression you were –'

'I *was* ailing,' I interrupted, still unable to curb my brusque tone, 'but I'm quite recovered now, thank you. I won't be a burden . . .' I wondered then if she had offered to house me or if I had been billeted with her at the behest of Cecil, near enough to court to keep an eye on, with Richmond a stone's throw away and Whitehall a short trip downriver.

'No, I would never think that. It is an honour for me to house the King's first cousin. You are truly most welcome here.' She smiled, radiating warmth. 'You are still thin from your illness. Never mind; we will fatten you up here. We enjoy our food in this house.'

Fatten me up for what?

The house was dark and it took a few moments for my eyes to accustom themselves to the gloom but there was a fire blazing in the hall, which burnished the panelling with coppery light. There were several people scattered about at the far end, children and grandchildren, I imagined, but the marchioness hustled me through. 'You can meet everyone later. The last thing you need is a crowd to confront when you haven't had a chance even to catch your breath from the journey.'

I was grateful to her for sensing my inhibition.

She led me up an ancient staircase lit with red and blue beams from a stained-glass window. Everything smelled of beeswax polish and the floorboards creaked underfoot as I followed her along a twisting corridor. She swung open a door at the end. 'I have given you Katherine Grey's bedroom.'

'Katherine Grey?'

'Her mother lived here for a time and this was Katherine's chamber.'

I'd long been haunted by sad Katherine Grey and there she was at Sheen, making me wonder momentarily if there was an invisible pattern to fate. 'Did you know her?' I asked.

'Not really, she was older than me, and by the time I was serving the Queen she was . . . well, she was no longer there.' I supposed she meant by 'no longer there' that Katherine Grey was already imprisoned. 'But everyone talked of her. Not in front of the Queen, of course, that was forbidden. I took her to be one of those people who made an impression, for everyone to still be talking about her so long after she'd gone.'

The chamber smelled of camphor and rosemary and the

ancient floorboards listed to one side. The bed was vast and its drapes were embroidered with scenes from the *Odyssey*: Penelope at her loom, suitors climbing in through half-open windows, pushing at the door, kneeling at her feet.

'I will have some fresh flowers sent up,' said the marchioness before leaving me alone with Bridget. Grandmother hadn't approved of cut flowers; they were an affront to nature, she said.

The view from the window looked over the gardens rolling gently towards the river, a wide swathe of sun-touched silver with a pair of swans gliding by as if for show. It was a pretty, contained view, such a contrast to the vast undulating Derbyshire countryside that I'd become used to seeing framed in Grandmother's legendary windows. Bridget busied herself with my things and we talked of Dodderidge, who would be joining us soon. I wondered why he wanted to return to my service, given I was the cause of all his troubles.

'It'll be loyalty, I expect,' said Bridget. 'Is he a loyal type?' I had grown so close to plain-speaking Bridget that I had forgotten she'd never met Dodderidge.

'But people are loyal to a cause rather than an individual, I think.'

'I beg to differ, My Lady. A cause is nothing without a person at its heart.'

'Sometimes you talk like a book of idioms, Bridget.'

'I don't know what you mean, but I shall take it as a compliment.'

There was a small portrait of Katherine Grey watching me from the wall beside the door. Her eyes looked out from beneath arched brows and a high, ruffed collar blossomed up about her ears. Her mouth carried the flick of a smile at its corner, making it hard to believe that this creature, clearly brimming with life, had made such a wretched end for herself. *What were you like? Did you inspire loyalty?*

Did you ever believe you would be queen like your sister? I asked her silently.

'She seems nice, the marchioness,' Bridget said, helping me into a clean shift.

'She does,' I replied. 'I like her. She has no airs. Though she seemed puzzled by me, looked at me strangely. It was as if I was not what she expected.'

'That is because you are *not* what she expected.'

'What do you mean?'

'They all thought you'd be mad as a basket of snakes. Thought it was the reason you didn't get the throne. Everyone expects you to be some kind of slobbering idiot or crazed loon.' She laughed. 'You must have given them a shock, poised and beautiful as you are.'

'Why on earth would they have thought that?'

'It was put about, apparently.'

'Put about by whom?' I asked, disturbed at the idea of people saying such things of me.

'Cecil, I wouldn't doubt,' was her answer. 'He had the most to gain.'

'Where do you find such pieces of information, Bridget?' I was always surprised at her knowledge. For a woman who couldn't read she was exceedingly well informed.

'I listen!' She tapped the side of her nose with a smile. 'You'd be surprised the things people say when they think you are too stupid to understand.'

Later at supper, after I had met the small battalion of family, the marchioness leaned into me and quietly said, 'I truly thought Elizabeth would name you as heir. She often talked of it, and she spoke more frankly to me than to most. I don't know what happened. Everything changed after the business with Essex.'

I wanted to quiz her about it, to plumb her for information, but wasn't quite sure how to form my queries. There was so much I didn't know.

'I'm not sure I would have made a very good queen,' I said. I was thinking of my many conversations with Starkey about what kind of queen I would be, realizing that the myriad hypothetical aspirations I held would have turned to dust in the face of reality – all those ambitious courtiers wanting to make a puppet of me.

'I don't know. We shall see what happens,' she said, closing the conversation by offering me a dish of sweetmeats, telling me her youngest daughter had made the marchpane fruits, pointing to the girl at the other end of the table. I watched them all for a while as I pretended to eat, the easy chit-chat, the bursts of raucous laughter, and wondered how I would ever fit into that new world.

Dodderidge arrived on the following afternoon. I was at the pier to welcome him. He looked gaunt, older, more stooped than ever, and with a haunted look about the eyes, but he smiled as he greeted me, saying, 'Free at last, My Lady.'

'Both of us,' I replied.

We sat on a stone bench in a corner of the garden, where the sun splashed through the foliage, casting warm pools over the ground.

'I should never have asked you to go. I regret terribly the horrors I have visited on you.'

'No!' He turned to me, meeting my gaze. 'I was honoured to be able to serve you. I'm only sorry I failed so . . . so dramatically.'

'None of us could have predicted Hertford's reaction. He had seemed open to the idea at one point, or so my uncle said. But I have learned that Uncle Henry is not what I thought.'

'I had word you were ill,' he said.

'I was, but I am well now.' I could feel Starkey hovering. It was Dodderidge who spoke of him first.

'I'm afraid it was I who implicated Mister Starkey. We had

been in touch, you see. They twisted his name out of me.' He had dropped his face into his palms and his shoulders were quivering slightly.

'What did they do to you?'

'I'd rather not talk of it.'

'Well, you are here now.'

'Yes.' He raised his head and his eyes were not rimmed in red as I expected but blazing with rage.

Sheen

The days passed in a blur of early summer: rides out along the riverbank; a fair in the village that had all the servants in a frenzy of excitement; boat trips to see a nest of new-hatched cygnets; great tournaments of bowls on the lawn; and walks with my new spaniel puppy, Ruff, a bundle of affection. It was a blissful month. But that serenity was to be blasted open with the arrival of a letter.

It bore a seal I didn't recognize and was from Lord Cobham, a man I recalled meeting only once, briefly, at Hardwick, years ago. He was one of Grandmother's godsons, and all I remember of him was a fuss he made about not having been assigned the best bedchamber. 'That's the kind of man he is,' Grandmother had said of it. I never had so much as a conversation with him.

After a paragraph of spectacular fawning, in handwriting so neat it offered no character, he made the suggestion that he and 'other noble and upright men' believed my place on the throne more right than any other. They were 'aggrieved on my behalf'. I should write, he suggested,

to Europe's heads of state, promising peace, religious tolerance and my desire to be led by them in my choice of husband. That way we will remove the impostor . . . England won't stomach a foreigner and he is not yet crowned, so there is a chance . . .

My newfound freedom suddenly crumbled. Nothing was as it seemed. I was no more free than during my incarceration at Hardwick. From there the shape of my future had seemed simple, possible. A year ago I might have been delighted at such a thought, to fight for my throne, to wrest it from the clutches of my cousin, but not now. I had been operating under the illusion that were I simply to escape, all would fall into place; or, as Starkey might have put it: God's plan would have come to fruition. But with the new perspective of my counterfeit liberty it dawned on me that there were invisible malign forces nipping at me as they always had.

This man I didn't even know thought I would trust him to help me get the throne, wanted to raise an army to put me on it and then what? There was only one way that could end. I dropped the missive with a gasp, as if it had burned me.

The marchioness, quick as a hawk, picked it up, inspecting the seal. 'Cobham?' She sneered. 'What does *he* want?'

I found myself pouring out the contents of the letter without a thought for caution.

'Cobham is an imbecile. Can I look at it?' I nodded and she read it with a frown. '"Befriend all the heads of Europe . . . Raise an army to overthrow the Scot . . . As the King is not yet crowned, treason is not a possibility . . ."' She wiped a hand over her forehead, reading on. 'He talks of Ralegh; I might have known Ralegh'd have something to do with it. No place for *him* either in the new regime. Cobham takes idiocy to new heights with this.' She tapped the paper with her index finger.

'What should I do?' I was so thankful to have her, with her level head, to advise me.

'Send it straight to the King and apprise Cecil of its contents. That way you cannot be accused of sedition.' Her voice was firm and reassuring. 'Say you do not entertain such notions. Say it in the strongest manner.' She put an arm round me. 'You're shaking.'

'I . . . I . . .' – I could barely speak – 'I don't know if I can cope with more of this.'

'You're terrified; you poor, dear girl.' She took me in her arms then, holding me tight until I thought I might suffocate. She smelled of dried roses.

I don't know why I trusted her but I did, and I allowed her to lead me into a little room – 'the garden room,' she called it – where she sat me down, summoning one of the maids with a bell and asking for hippocras to be brought. I'd thought it only a drink for celebrations but it was good for calming the nerves, she said. Its thick sweetness clung to my tongue and made my head heavy but I stopped shaking enough to write to the King. I sealed Cobham's letter in with mine and sent it off with one of the marchioness's messengers.

I heard of Cobham's arrest and Ralegh's, among others, soon afterwards, and wondered if they would come for me. Each arrival at the priory, the sound of horses alone, sent my stomach to my throat and made my heart falter, but all that came for me from the palace was a letter, heavy with the royal seal, containing my instructions for the coronation. I was to accompany Queen Anna during the proceedings, *before all other ladies of the court*, it stated.

'You see?' said the marchioness. 'The King is bringing you into the fold. He regards you as close family, first lady after the Queen. You have nothing to fear, dear. Everyone will know that Cobham and Ralegh sought to use you for their own ends.'

'I hope that is true.'

'Once the court has settled, you will be invited to join them, I don't doubt,' she said to me.

'For my whole life I have wanted that, dreamed of it: to take my place at court; but now I am not so sure.' I hesitated, realizing the truth of what I was saying. 'If I had my own house I would wish it to be like yours.'

'You flatter me,' she said. 'But I doubt you will live like

this. You are destined for a palace of one kind or another.'
She laughed, as if I'd been joking.

'You will be a great prize on the marriage market,
although . . .' She let her words trail off, leaving me wondering what had been left unsaid. Perhaps she was going to
articulate something that I had pondered on, that any son of
mine would have a strong claim and might become a focus
for insurgency, were England to turn against their new king.
The lessons of the Greys loomed large and, as I retired that
evening, Katherine watched me from the wall of my bedchamber as a reminder.

On coronation day we travelled to and from Westminster
Abbey by river, for plague was still rife in the capital and the
streets were to be avoided. It rained – a heavy summer rain
that took everyone by surprise and thundered on the canopy
above us in the Queen's barge. Queen Anna, bovine with a
cloud of pale hair and breasts like blue-veined cheese, sat in
anxious silence, twisting her gloves.

Lucy Bedford was beside her, a high-spirited young
woman with a breathless voice and given to bursts of trilling
laughter at the slightest provocation. She sat arm in arm with
the Queen, close as a lover. Her familiarity seemed audacious
to me but Queen Anna didn't appear to mind. Lucy pointed
out things of interest through an opening in the hangings:
'That barge belongs to the Howards; look at the size of it!'
'Isn't the Savoy Palace lovely?' 'Can you see Essex House, it
is where . . .'

Lady Rich, who was next to me, threw her a granite look,
saying firmly, 'I'm sure Queen Anna knows what happened
at Essex House, Lucy.' It was said that Lady Rich was there
on the day of her brother's insurrection, that she held out
when the house was besieged by the Queen's troops. I
remembered Lady Rich for her kindness to me when I'd

been turned on by that pack of women – nearly fifteen years had disappeared since then, stolen from me. Lady Rich had the look of her brother. My infatuation for Essex seemed inexplicable at two years' remove from his death, but then he had barely existed outside my imagination and I had become another person since then.

Queen Anna wasn't listening to Lucy though; she just kept on twisting the gloves in her lap as if trying to squeeze water from them. 'I am not going to take the sacrament.' She sounded like a child stating an intention to refuse a bowl of porridge.

'Please don't vex yourself, Highness. It's all understood. The archbishop has made an arrangement.' It was Jane Drummond who said this in her Scot's burr, smoothing her hand over Queen Anna's ermine-clad shoulder. Jane was dark and handsome and young; they were all young, save for Lady Rich. All those creased harridans who served the old Queen were long gone.

'I suppose you know she's a Catholic,' whispered Lady Rich to me.

'I don't understand . . . I thought . . .'

'I know!' She raised her eyebrows. 'Converted, so all the more fervent! Her husband seems to think it doesn't matter if she's discreet. All the girls want to follow suit – they think it'll bring them favour. Not me, I'm too old for all that.'

I was confused – I had so long been led to believe that Catholics were the enemy – and began to see that there was much I didn't yet understand about the court.

'You won't though, will you?' she continued.

'What, convert? No, of course not,' I said.

'The King intends to implement a new lenience towards Catholics. No more fines for recusants. Probably a good thing, but let's see how long it lasts.'

'And isn't there a treaty planned with the Spaniards?' I'd

heard this talked of round the table at Sheen. It had seemed so implausible; Catholic Spain had been the enemy for as long as I could remember.

'I think Cecil's keen to promote it. *He's* not done so badly for himself – still top dog.' I wanted to ask her about Cecil, she seemed to know so much and I felt so ignorant, but she changed the subject, leaning in even more closely, murmuring, 'She's very obstinate; manages to get her way over most things.' I gathered she had returned to the topic of Queen Anna. 'She refused to travel from Scotland without her beloved "Freddie", who was being raised elsewhere.' In response to my obvious puzzlement she added, 'The Scots send their children away very young, you see. James relented; she got her way, and she got her way too over her faith.'

There were so many questions I wanted to ask but we had arrived at the pier and we all had to help manage Queen Anna's robes, acres of velvet and fur, in the rain. A canvas roof had been slung over the pier but the planks were slick as ice and several women skidded in their kid slippers. We could hear the roar of the crowd and nerves beset me suddenly.

'You go in after the Queen,' said Lady Rich, pushing me forward. It was an honour but I felt self-conscious with all those eyes on me, wondering, given I had never been seen in public before, who on earth I was to hold precedence over all the other women. Or, it struck me like a blow to the gut, were they thinking: *There is the one Cobham and Ralegh would have seen on the throne?* I had to force my mind off the trial. My presence there had been requested by Cecil, in Winchester, where it was to take place in the autumn, though he had assured me my testimony would be *only a formality*. Formality or not, I still felt clammy and nauseous when I thought of it.

Despite the rain, which showed no sign of relenting, drenched crowds lined the route as we made our way to the abbey, but once finally inside we found it was half empty. Most who were meant to be there had been delayed by the weather. Queen Anna looked strained and weighed down by her damp robes and James, who must have arrived only moments before us, was seething with anger, as if he thought God had deliberately sent the downpour to mock him.

I had never seen my cousin before, only portraits. He was smaller in life, rather mean-looking I thought, but perhaps that owed much to his foul mood on the day. The royal children were there, stiff with brocade: the nine-year-old Prince Henry Frederick and his sister, Princess Elizabeth, younger by three years, though not baby Charles. They looked lost and small in the great expanse of the abbey. A woman I supposed to be their nurse thrust them at me and Elizabeth pushed her warm little hand into mine. I looked at the woman, questioning. 'Her Majesty said they were to sit beside you at the front.' In fact their presence made me feel a little more at my ease, as if I now had a role in the whole thing.

The Prince looked at me and smiled. Even at his tender years I could see the startling appeal that was lacking in his father. There was a great fuss about the King's train, which was so copious the guests had to be made to stand back to accommodate it in the aisle. I realized only then that it had been more than forty years since the old Queen was crowned and most there could never have witnessed a coronation before.

Throughout the ceremony the latecomers quietly filtered in and before long the place was hot with life. The smell of damp wool pervaded, mingling with the incense and, even from the front, the archbishop couldn't be heard clearly over the continued thrum of rain. True to her word, Queen Anna didn't take the sacraments, which caused a murmur of disapproval, pews creaking, amongst the ranks of Protestants. The choir were magnificent, like a host of angels. I had never heard the like, was quite transported by the sound, and so, it appeared, was little Princess Elizabeth beside me, closing her eyes to listen.

When it was done with and we'd made our way back to the barge, Queen Anna collapsed into her seat with a sigh, and called me to sit beside her, whispering in her accented English, 'The crown was heavy as a brick and the holy oil smells foul.'

She leaned in so I could sniff her temple; it reeked of something rotten. 'Must've been ancient. They used the last of it on me. When Freddie is crowned I suppose they'll have to make some more. I wonder how that is done. Do you suppose they bring it from Jerusalem? Who will bless it, do you think? The Pope must've blessed this batch a hundred years ago.' She touched a finger to her forehead and then, as if remembering the sanctity of it all, she crossed herself. It was peculiar to see such a gesture made openly.

'I expect it will be blessed by the archbishop,' I said.

'Of course . . . the archbishop.' Then she smiled, revealing a line of pink gum above her teeth. Though I knew she was about my own age, she seemed to me quite childlike with the babble that had replaced her previous anxious silence.

'Will we make a Catholic of you, Arbella?' Queen Anna laughed to make it seem a jest but I suspected she was at least partly serious.

'I think not,' I replied, sounding as firm as was possible without causing offence.

'Have you not heard? I always get my way,' she added flippantly.

I wondered if she was really too dense to realize that, were I even thought open to conversion, the whole house of cards she lived in might have threatened to topple.

The King was due to leave on progress after his coronation, to avoid the plague, but before he left he sent for me. I had hoped I might discover an affinity with my cousin, despite the past; he was a man of learning and I imagined we could perhaps enjoy each other's company. But as I approached I began to feel increasingly anxious that he would bring up the trial. *Only a formality*. I kept repeating Cecil's words in my head but didn't feel particularly reassured.

In order to get to my cousin I had to negotiate my way past Lennox, the Cyclops at the mouth of his cave, and then another group of Scots, lotus-eaters drinking and smoking in the anteroom, who laughed openly as I passed. I feared I had dirt on my face or that Lucy Bedford might have pinned a note to my back in jest. Once in the King's presence, there was the Scylla and Charybdis of Erskine and pretty-boy Hay to be dealt with. They gazed disdainfully, with whirlpool eyes, as I made my way across the chamber, fearing ridicule.

The King appeared rough, pale and slack-skinned with chapped lips and a sparse beard, as if he had been left outside for too long in bad weather. His clothes were surprisingly plain and I noticed a small stain on the front of his doublet.

I addressed him in Latin, assuming such a gesture would warm him to me, but he said, not to me but to Erskine, with one eye directed my way, 'I don't like a woman with Latin, do you? Makes them seem cunning.' His Scots accent made him hard to understand and it took a moment for me to grasp what he had said. When I did, I immediately became light-headed with embarrassment, wishing I was a child and could run from the room. Then, directly, he asked, 'Are you any good with a needle? Queen Anna's a fine needlewoman.'

'Her Majesty is certainly a better needlewoman than I.' I was grateful to find the bland compliment amongst my dithering thoughts.

'I've had one or two marriage proposals for you. I suppose it was inevitable. Nassau is keen.' He seemed to be talking to himself. His tongue made the circuit of his dry lips. 'But if I match you with him it risks upsetting the Spanish and we are so very' – he pinched his thumb and forefinger together for emphasis – 'close to a treaty. I can't put that in jeopardy. The King of Poland's been sniffing about; he's sending an envoy. Wants to have a look at you.'

Erskine muttered something unintelligible and Hay responded with a smirk.

'Queen of Poland?' The King had turned his bloodhound eyes on me, smiling openly so I could see the morsels of food in his teeth. Grandmother's voice wormed its way into my head: *Don't smile, it will make you seem meek.* Smiling certainly didn't make my cousin seem meek, far from it. I couldn't tell if he was making some kind of joke at my expense. 'I suppose I'll have to restore your father's lands to you if you wed. Can't have you going off to Poland penniless, can we?' I still had no idea if he was toying with me. I knew how long Grandmother had negotiated in vain to gain my father's bequest on my behalf. 'You'll be a rich bride, Coz.' He laughed and I remained silent. 'You don't seem very pleased. Do you think me a Scottish miser whose word's no good?'

'No, Highness, indeed I am overwhelmed at the thought of it.' I hoped he couldn't detect the weight of cynicism my voice carried. I couldn't help it. Those lands might have bought me my freedom but he dangled them over me as a makeweight for marriage.

He sucked his teeth. 'You'll have to fatten yourself up before the envoy comes; there's nothing of you. He might mistake you for a boy!' Hay sniggered at that. James reached out a fist and grabbed the top of my bodice. 'See, empty!' The trio of men then burst into laughter and I longed for the floor to swallow me.

'What do you think I should do about it all?' he asked.

Do about what? Did he mean what should he do about my body? I felt their eyes on me, stripping me bare, finding me wanting. My mind churned for something to say. But he carried on. 'Cecil is of the mind that you should stay here where we can see you – not be married abroad. He thinks We wouldn't want any of your pups claiming Our throne.'

I felt a flare of anger towards that snake Cecil, still holding sway over my destiny as he always had, and wanted to ask what exactly he might have meant by that.

'You have two sons to see any pretenders off, Highness,' said Hay with a smug air, as if he'd had something to do with the making of Prince Henry Frederick and baby Charles himself.

'Ah yes, my two boys.'

'Dynasties are built on boys,' Erskine smarmed, locking his gaze on to me and smoothing his beard with the tips of his fingers. I wanted to shout at him, tell him that *I* of all people should know that.

'What do you think?' James's question was directed at me.

Fortunately, I'd quickly realized he had no desire to know my thoughts on anything, least of all on whether I should be married or not.

'I think I should like to be obedient to Your Highness in such matters, and if Cecil is of the mind that I ought to stay here, then I consider it a privilege that Your Highness might also wish it so. I am most grateful for your kindness –'

'It's all very well,' he cut in, 'that Cecil should want you to remain a maid but I ask myself, what is an unmarried woman for?' He paused, allowing his question to hang. 'Unless she is a queen, I suppose.'

A grim feeling overcame me. 'I . . . I don't –'

'Yes, yes,' he said, and with a wave of his hand I was dismissed.

As I backed from the chamber, my mind turned over his question, finding no proper answer: what *was* my purpose? I remembered Margaret Byron's comment about birthing her boy: *That was what I was for.* I was almost at the door, preparing to confront the lotus-eaters once more, when the King called out, 'Do you share my wife's faith?'

I wondered if it was a trap, a trick question, but if it was I didn't know what answer would redeem me. I heard Starkey in my ear: *The truth leads to the light.* 'I do not, Highness.'

'Ha!' he turned to Hay, slapping the younger man's shoulder. 'You owe me ten English shillings.'

It was only as I walked away that I realized there had been no mention of the trial.

I was glad to return to the calm of Sheen while the court left on progress, stalked by the plague, hangers-on dying here and there, it was said, forcing the great train to move on ceaselessly. The King didn't mind, or so the gossip went, as it gave him ample excuse to hunt with his close coterie of Scots. The King's fondness for hunting was forcing the privy councillors to chase him around the shires to attend to the business of running the country.

Catholics began to emerge from the shadows. The first in my orbit was Bridget: 'I can be truthful now, My Lady, and confess to my Catholic faith,' she said. 'I had kept it concealed for fear of ever compromising you.'

I remembered that time in the garden at Hardwick, when I thought she'd crossed herself. How fearful I'd been then. It was unsurprising, given I'd been living under the constant threat of kidnap by Catholics for a decade. With hindsight I thought it a wonder I hadn't completely lost my mind as people had been led to think. But the threat had not diminished with my new circumstances, it had merely changed, become something I understood even less.

'I had my suspicions,' I said to her. 'And what about Aunt Mary?' I thought of that glimpse I'd had once of a dangling crucifix.

'She too,' was Bridget's reply. No wonder people thought I'd be willing to convert.

Aunt Mary and Uncle Gilbert wrote long letters from Sheffield, begging for my news, and I felt thankful, given it seemed I no longer existed for Grandmother, that my aunt and uncle continued to treat me tenderly. I harboured a small uncertainty, however, over Aunt Mary's part in Uncle Henry's foolhardy plan, the extent to which she knew of his aims. But I felt I couldn't ask her, feared she would be irretrievably hurt by my aspersions.

I felt a great affinity with Uncle Gilbert as he, too, had long been on the wrong side of Grandmother's affections – indeed, we were numerous, Grandmother's outcasts. But she, anyway, belonged to a world that had passed. Aside from the fact of our fondness for each other I was aware that the Shrewsburys were powerful allies for me. I had come to learn, being out in the world, that family allegiance was of paramount importance; I had known it, but only then did I fully understand it. I felt protected in the marchioness's tranquil world but, outside of it, I sensed the fragility of my position, only too aware of the impending trial, which, I concluded in my darker moments, could easily be used to get rid of an inconvenient royal cousin who might prove a threat to the throne.

On the way to the trial the coachmen had a wager on whether Ralegh would be executed. It was The Lord High Admiral, Nottingham, who accompanied me. He was an old associate of Grandmother's, a frequent visitor to Hardwick. I remembered noticing as a girl that he'd easily squeezed deference out of Grandmother, so concluded he was a powerful ally. And it seemed he meant to take me under his wing, as he murmured encouragements: 'You must not fret over this, My Lady. *You* are not on trial.'

The journey was arduous, two days in the wind and rain,

and our carriage had to be hauled out from the mud on more than one occasion, with me standing shivering under a tree, shrouded in Nottingham's cloak. As we approached the bishop's palace, where the trial was to take place, we had to push through a hostile crowd which had amassed, shouting against Ralegh, saying he had a Spanish heart and worse, unrepeatable, things. I hadn't realized the extent to which he was loathed; why would I have, in my cocoon?

The carriage drew up right beside the entrance to avoid the rain and the crowds, but my clothes were still damp as clay. The great hall was a cavernous space, teaming with people and echoing with their excited gabbing; they were like a crowd awaiting a bear-baiting. They noticed me enter with Nottingham, who thankfully stuck close by my side, their chatter dulling as they watched me cross the expanse of floor. My gut churned and I feared I would be unable to speak, when I was called upon to do so.

Cecil was there and I could barely muster the words to return his greeting as I was led to a pew. I kept my eyes down. The Attorney General, Coke, in a mountain of robes, eventually called for silence. A hush fell, so quiet that I could hear his chain of office chink as he took his seat. I shook uncontrollably and hoped people would assume it was the cold.

When it was Ralegh's turn to be questioned there were jeers as he strode to the front, seeming unperturbed, as if he were to be rewarded rather than condemned.

'Never forgiven for his part in Essex's downfall,' whispered Nottingham. I hadn't considered until then the reach of Essex's popularity, even more than two years after his death, and perhaps it was more so because he had died a kind of martyr for the Stuarts. I gathered that in the end Essex *had* supported my cousin James's claim, so it was inevitable, I supposed, that his perennial enemy Ralegh would lose favour once James was installed. I felt dangerously ignorant, as if I might unwittingly make a false step at any moment and find the tables turned on me.

The crowd continued to bay outside all morning, and throughout the proceedings I was trying not to think of how I would cope with the kind of tricky interrogation Ralegh was being subjected to by Coke. 'Just tell the truth,' Aunt Mary had advised, but I felt sure Coke would twist my answers and turn on me. I wished to God she were by my side but she'd been ailing and was still convalescing in Sheffield.

Coke continued to badger Ralegh. 'You meant to make Arbella a titular queen,' he insisted repeatedly. Every time my name left the Attorney General's lips he caught me with his eyes and held them on me for longer than was comfortable, as if he knew something I didn't, and I felt further dug into the business. Ralegh cast me as a nonentity in his responses, as if I weren't even sufficiently noble in his eyes to be the Queen on a chessboard. He thought to belittle me but the gallery didn't like it, stomping their feet in protest. Better I were a nonentity, I thought, than the object of men's ambitions.

As the questioning continued, Ralegh, deft as an acrobat, refused to condemn himself, tying Coke in knots and distancing himself from Cobham, whose guilt had already been proven. Coke was no match for Ralegh's quick wits and his exasperation became increasingly apparent. He hooked me with his eyes once more, asking Ralegh, 'Are you suggesting, then, it was Lady Arbella who approached *you* with this proposition?'

I gasped and the jury's eyes turned on me, each of them wearing a look of undisguised bloodlust – they might have been a pack of wolves.

Strangely it was Cecil who jumped to my defence: 'Let us not scandal the innocent by confusion of speech. She is innocent of all these things as I, or any man here . . .'

I felt a wave of nausea break over me, knowing I was about to be called to the stand. But in the end Nottingham insisted upon speaking on my behalf, denouncing Ralegh in the strongest of terms for seeking to draw me into his treason. I was publicly deemed blameless. So Cecil had meant what he said when he had declared it a mere formality.

Ralegh was convicted. Coke's words could barely be heard above the heckling as he was sentenced to be hanged, drawn and quartered and packed off to the Tower with Cobham to await his fate.

The crowds outside were jubilant and the weather suddenly improved, the sun making an appearance for our journey home. But though there seemed an abundance of good will directed my way, I still could not shake off the sense of doom that had settled over me; for surely, I reasoned, there would always be those who sought to use me for their own ends and they would doubtless come disguised in friendship.

Clerkenwell

Ami reads on, completely absorbed, deciphering the tangle of text; she has barely stopped to sleep or eat. The past returns vividly; she remembers it all, the old Queen's passing and the atmosphere of tension, as if England had been a pot on the boil with its lid too tight. The coronation had felt like a great expulsion of breath across the nation. She remembers the relentless rain but no one said it was a bad omen. They were all too relieved to have avoided a conflict at the old Queen's passing. No one so much as mentioned that it might have been Lady Arbella on the throne.

The Countess of Cumberland had invited Ami and her family to watch the procession from the window of her Westminster house. Ami had dedicated a poem to the countess and read it aloud to great delight. It felt like an achievement as she'd been labouring over it for months. But Alphonso had drunk too much of the countess's wine, had fallen asleep, snoring through his wife's recital, leaving her obliged to invent embarrassed excuses for him. Hal had been delighted to see the royal children pass. 'I think I will marry the Princess Elizabeth when I'm grown up,' he'd said, making the whole company laugh. He was nine. It chokes her to think of him now and his relentless silence.

She remembers Ralegh's trial too. Strangely, she'd forgotten it was the Lady Arbella who'd been the focus of his plot. People only talked of Ralegh and what a filthy traitor he was. How loathed he'd become, when a decade earlier he had still been thought a hero. It had shocked her at the time to see how fortune can turn so easily; but now her own fortune has plummeted she understands that it takes only a single small event to send fate utterly awry.

Evening is falling, so she takes a stool on to her stoop to catch the last of the light, reading on like a woman possessed. She can sense that her own story is about to intersect with Lady Arbella's. The idea excites her, makes her wonder how she will be portrayed, whether she will recognize herself. Will she be there substantially, at the heart of the story, or as a ghost in the margins?

Whitehall

The King was kissing Sir Philip Herbert, there in the watching chamber for all to see. I couldn't quite tear my eyes away from the tangle of their wet tongues, didn't know what to think of it. Queen Anna, at my side, seemed to barely notice.

A maid in a diaphanous costume, dressed as a nymph from the masque performed earlier, was spewing in the corner. Her friend, pale and wobbly on her feet, was holding back her cascade of hair; the filmy white layers of her own outfit were stained with red wine, giving the pair of them the appearance of murderer and victim. I wafted the stench of vomit away with my fan and rolled a few needles of rosemary between thumb and finger, bringing them up to my nose. I had heard one of those girls earlier say to the other, *Noli me tangere*, flashing her eyes my way. It seemed I would never shake that off. I glanced at Queen Anna; she showed no sign of flagging.

The marchioness had been right, for I was called to court once the plague had run its course and the King was returned to the capital. It was a bewildering place. Whitehall was a maelstrom of relentless merriment, startlingly opposite to my memories of Elizabeth's sedate court. I felt quite lost and, paradoxically, I longed for a match to take me away, but the King of Poland's suit, which had seemed so distasteful a year before, hadn't been mentioned recently and I had little opportunity to ask the King about my future, for the Queen's household rarely mixed with the King's, except on festive occasions.

I sat at the heart of that sordid scramble, desperate for an excuse to leave for the quiet of my chambers and a book.

As the King's cousin, the first lady of court after the Queen, I had been allotted a suite of rooms. But I was obliged to take my cue from Queen Anna and she was wont to stay until dawn, despite the fact that she was once again pregnant.

My freedom had been short lived and I longed for that brief easy life I'd had at Sheen. I was watched at court, much as I had been at Hardwick. I might have been cleared of any part in Cobham and Ralegh's plot but I was still considered a risk, though it was never mentioned.

Cecil, seated nearby, watched the King and his pretty favourite too, with sharp rodent eyes, but his expression was a study in neutrality. He plucked invisible motes of dust from his clothes, like a hound casually grooming itself, with one eye on the lookout for rabbits. His unruffled surface seemed to me to mask treacherous depths. He may have taken my part at the trial but I felt sure that had more to do with his enmity for Ralegh than support of me, for if he was truly my ally I and not my cousin would have been on the throne. I hadn't forgotten his betrayal.

A servant smothered the nymph's puke with sawdust and brushed it into a bucket as the two drunk girls flopped down on to a cushion in each other's arms like a pair of exhausted puppies. The musicians had played relentlessly for hours; I wondered how their fingers were not blistered. Their sound was becoming tiresome, to me at least, but apparently not to Queen Anna, who was tapping her feet and clapping along with each new tune.

'What's your opinion of . . . ?' she asked, leaving her words deliberately hanging.

I wasn't sure whom she meant but, following her line of sight, I realized she was talking of the boy who was still sprawled across her husband. He was smooth and sinuous with undulating golden hair. His outfit was . . . what was it?

Some kind of exotic thing, draped and swagged, that seemed meant to echo the ancient world but was more likely a reason for him to leave those shapely legs uncovered. A masque, and there were many, seemed to me a barely concealed excuse to go about in public half dressed. 'I don't know . . . ' I was lost for words, watching that embrace.

'He's very pretty. I wonder if he's a poet. He comes from a family of poets. We were at Wilton last year and you couldn't move for sonneteers.' She laughed that light little laugh of hers and rubbed her belly with the flat of her hand, as if to remind herself it contained a baby.

The Queen seemed to me like water, always finding the easiest passage through and, when not twinkling or babbling, placid as a pond. I never had the opportunity to witness that legendary obstinacy of hers but I suppose even the most stagnant of pools is occasionally turbulent.

'Sir Philip's mother is a fine poet,' I said.

'What do you think of women poets? I like them. There is a tenderness to their work.' She had a propensity to ask a question and then answer it herself, which gave the impression that she spoke for the sake of it rather than anything else. 'Do you know the work of Aemilia Lanyer? I don't suppose you do. She is not well known – sometimes comes to court in the Countess of Cumberland's party.'

'I don't think I do,' I answered, but the name chimed faintly from the past. '*I* have tried my hand at writing verse.'

She looked at me closely. 'You have the disposition for it. I don't think I'd have the concentration. We must organize a reading.'

'Oh no – not yet; nothing is finished . . . only scribblings.' I wished I hadn't mentioned my writing, for it was so private, so intimate – a baring of the soul – and I couldn't imagine showing it to anyone.

'The King doesn't approve. Thinks women shouldn't bend themselves to intellectual things. What do you think? You like intellectual things. I suppose it depends on one's education, doesn't it.'

'I believe, as Socrates did, that women should be educated in the same manner as men.' I was thinking, of course, of Starkey. 'I was raised in an environment that fostered –'

'They share a love of hunting.' It took me a moment to understand that she had stopped listening to me and had returned to the subject of the beautiful young man.

'Do you think that means they share a love of killing?' I asked her. 'Or simply the exhilaration of the chase?'

'I don't know what you mean.' She appeared perplexed.

'Is it cruelty they have in common?' I had heard my cousin had a cruel streak but had not yet witnessed it – not then – unless you can count the unkindness of that erotic display under the nose of his wife.

She tilted her head to one side and seemed to be pondering deeply. 'Are you any good at trumps, Arbella? Can someone bring me a pack of cards?'

Reading back, I fear I have given the impression that I held her in disdain for her shallowness, but in fact that was not the case. I grew rather fond of uncomplicated Queen Anna. As she often liked to point out: 'None of the others is like us. They are not born royal.' I didn't like to remind her that our experience could not have been more different: she a king's daughter raised at the Danish court, married at fifteen to a Scottish monarch then becoming Queen Consort of England too. And I . . . well, I was little more than an aging spinster, approaching thirty, unused to court, awkward amongst people, whose royal blood had become a drawback. But she was kind, extended the hand of friendship, and in a place where one's enemies came in all guises she seemed too transparent for duplicity. 'Only *we* understand the duty that comes with high birth.'

'Is duty the price of privilege, do you suppose?' I asked.

If ever I talked even remotely philosophically she would take on a look of profound puzzlement before changing the subject: 'Shall we have a round of spillikins?' 'Let's play blind man's buff.' 'What do you think of my new gown?' It made me mourn Starkey greatly. *What would he have thought of all this,* I wondered. He would have been quietly amused as I recounted the events of each day in Queen Anna's chambers.

I had Dodderidge and Bridget with me, loyal to the core, but no one could fill the gaping void left by Starkey. During sleepless nights a voice sometimes insinuated itself into my head: *You killed him. There is a price for that.* It frightened me, that voice, for it spoke the truth.

The cards were brought and Queen Anna played with an intense glee, scoring each point with a flash of the eyes. 'I'd have thought you'd be a more challenging opponent, given you are so clever.'

'Your skill confounds me, Highness.' She liked that, responded with a broad smile. I had begun to learn the little quirks of court: flattery and self-deprecation, but it all seemed so silly to me, and however much I played their game I remained something of a misfit, though I was respected in a remote way by most of the Queen's women, for my status alone, I suspected. I sometimes watched the way they all transported themselves, the easy intimacy of their friendships, the ways in which they would touch each other, a head rested on a shoulder, an arm hooked through an elbow, fingers intertwined. It was anathema to me, who flinched if someone touched my sleeve unexpectedly.

'The King intends to make you godmother.' She rubbed her belly once more. I could sense Cecil was keeping one ear on our conversation.

'Did you hear?' I turned to him pointedly. 'I am to stand godmother.'

He muttered a few words about being delighted for me and made an excuse to move away. It was a minute victory.

There was a small mountain of crystallized fruits nearby. Queen Anna helped herself, offering one to me.

'No, I don't think I will.'

'I'll have two then – eating for two!' She stuffed a second into her mouth.

I never failed to achieve an inner welling of power in those small acts of self-denial and felt lean and efficient in the face of Queen Anna's corpulence.

'I am greatly honoured to be chosen as godmother.' It was true, I *was* honoured, but a phrase I'd once heard somewhere popped into my head: *Always the godmother never the mother*, and a wave of longing surprised me.

'Your position warrants it,' she said brightly, her mouth still full, but all I could see was her pity for the oldest maid at court. The powerful feeling slid away, leaving me bereft.

My dress was uncomfortable; it was made of itchy material with metallic threads that chafed my skin. At least it covered me, unlike some, which were audaciously transparent, leaving nothing to the imagination. I had begged leave to sit out of the masque, couldn't bear the idea of all those eyes on me, but had reluctantly agreed to wear a costume. So my hair was garlanded with wilting flowers and my feet were strapped into blistering sandals with thongs twisting up my legs like ivy. I felt ridiculous, like the elderly aunt dressed up for everyone's amusement.

My scratchy outfit had once belonged to Queen Elizabeth. Queen Anna had sanctioned the pillaging of the old Queen's wardrobe, something that had caused much excitement when the consignment of garments had been delivered and dumped in a great glittering pile in the middle of the floor.

Most of the women had thrown themselves on it, grabbing, tugging, shaking each other off, squealing, like a pack of hounds at the kill.

Queen Anna watched on, laughing at the spectacle, eventually announcing over the hubbub that *she* would assign the dresses. One was handed to me; it was heavy as a sack of stones and embroidered exquisitely with flowers on a bed of gold cloth. I was obliged to take it to the Queen's tailor to have it redesigned and looked on in horror as his shears cut through the precious fabric. It was refashioned to show my ankles but I wouldn't allow him to cut the bodice away at the breast, as most of the other women had. The tailor's response to that refusal was a pitying look.

He charged twenty pounds for his work that I could ill afford and I had had to borrow Aunt Mary's jewels to supplement my own, those same jewels that had brought upon Starkey's demise – to me they seemed cursed but I had no others to wear. They had once seemed so splendid, such treasures to shore me up from uncertainty, but they paled in the light of all the other women's startling arrays of brilliants, as if they wore all the wealth of their families scattered over their bodies.

The Queen wore her hair high and pinned with a constellation of diamonds that sparkled in the candlelight as she bobbed her head in conversation with Lucy Bedford, whose dress was also encrusted in precious stones. Lady Rich wore twenty thousand pounds' worth of jewels, or so Jane Drummond had told me. Even with Aunt Mary's borrowings I couldn't compete, and I longed to deck myself in Grandmother's magnificent pearls, but Grandmother and I were no longer even on letter-exchanging terms. I had written several times but received nothing in return.

Being at court was an expensive business; my meagre settlement went no way to achieve the splendour appropriate to my position, and once my retainers were paid there was little left for lavish couture. The blasted masque dress with its gold thread rubbing me raw would only be worn the once. I lived in a constant state of deficit, calling on favours and the good will of relatives and capitalizing on the hopes of those who thought I might be able to reach the King's ear on their behalf. The truth was, though the King occasionally granted me an audience, he had no interest in what I had to say and usually packed me off back to the women's chambers with indecent haste.

'Are your ears burning?' said Queen Anna, breaking out of a huddle with Lucy Bedford. 'I'm sure they are; Lucy and I have been discussing suitable husbands for you.'

'Oh dear,' I said. I don't know why. She meant well and had no idea how inadequate she made me feel. Despite the fact I had begun to regard marriage as my sole means to escape from my penury and set up my own household, if I thought too deeply on it – on the proximity of a stranger, of a strange body, the invasion of pregnancy – I was filled with dread. 'I don't think Cecil wants to see me wed.'

'It's not up to him, is it?' I wanted to point out that it probably was up to him, given my marriage was a state matter. 'And you can't remain a maid. That would be . . . ' she paused. 'Well, it would be unthinkable.'

There was a hiatus in the music and Queen Anna announced finally that she had a mind to retire. The thought of being released from the discomfort of my dress propelled me through the spaces of Whitehall towards my rooms. I encountered Cecil, approaching me in the long gallery, which was unsettling, as I'd felt sure he'd still been in the hall when I'd left. He always gave the sense of being in more than one place at a time.

'Ah, Lady Arbella, I am glad to encounter you alone; there was something I wanted to discuss . . . ' he paused and cleared his throat slightly, 'of a personal nature.' He moved into one of the window alcoves, waiting for me to follow.

My first thought was to make an excuse, as my rooms beckoned, but curiosity got the better of me. 'Of a personal nature?'

'Yes.' He lowered his voice. 'I intend to impress upon His Majesty the need to increase your allowance. I cannot promise you a particular outcome but I think we can persuade him to squeeze a little more from the coffers for his cousin.'

'I am grateful to you.' *But why,* I wanted to ask, *do you seek to help me?* Perhaps he thought I'd be of use to him one day.

As if reading my mind he replied, 'I have always taken your part, since the old Queen's days. You know that, don't you? I have always been fond of your dear grandmother and, quite naturally, that fondness extends to you.'

I nodded, dipping my head as if to obediently lap up his endearments but was thinking: *You have no inkling that I used to read all your correspondence with Grandmother, that I know of your betrayal.*

'Have you settled in well – into the Queen's household?' He tugged his sleeves smartly to smooth out the wrinkles.

'Quite well.'

'Perhaps, then, you might be of the mind to put word my way if you find anything amiss.'

Is he canvassing for me to spy on the Queen's women for him, I thought. That would explain his apparent favour. 'I don't know that I have the observant qualities required for espionage –'

'Goodness me,' he interrupted, 'you didn't think . . . I merely suggested that you report to me any problems you encounter, so, as an old family friend, I might come to your aid.' Like Grandmother, he never smiled, but he tilted his head a little and offered me a benign expression.

'Ah . . . well, thank you.' I bade him goodnight and went on my way to my rooms, wondering what our conversation had really been about and wishing I'd had the courage to ask him outright, if it was indeed he who was standing in the way of any potential marriage plans.

Oxford

'My Freddie will make a wonderful king one day,' Queen Anna whispered to me. We were listening to Prince Henry Frederick give a speech of thanks to his hosts at Magdalen College, where he was being admitted as a member – the reason for the court's invasion of Oxford.

'I believe he will.' I had become quite used to telling people what they wished to hear, for that was the way at court, but in that case my reply was honest. I watched the boy, wondering if his mother secretly wished he shared her faith but the heir to the throne, even at the tender age of eleven, was resolutely Protestant. I had had the opportunity on a number of occasions to make the acquaintance of my young cousin and found him delightful company. He had a love of poetry that his father thought frivolous and was a generous, active boy, keen on the martial arts, often to be seen fencing in the palace courtyard.

The words he spoke on that occasion, eloquent and littered with classical references, must have been penned by another but he invested them with nuance, as a seasoned orator might have. Standing straight, he looked out to his audience with a directness of gaze that made each of us feel addressed personally, emphasizing his words with his hands as if he were playing an invisible harp. Not once did he refer to the paper he held. Henry Frederick had a presence far beyond his years. His companions paled beside him. When I think of the Prince now I wonder why I wasn't beset with envy, for after all he was everything I might have been: a boy, the heir. I did occasionally imagine being him, inhabiting his body – physically we were not unalike, both lean and angular with kinship stitched through our looks; had we swapped clothes I might have passed for him in a dim light.

'That is Will Seymour,' said Aunt Mary, pointing to the group of young men around the Prince, 'the brother of . . . you know.'

'Which is he?'

'With the pheasant feather.'

I looked, but at least four wore pheasant feathers – there was a fashion for them that year – and though I was curious about the Seymours, I didn't want to seem overly interested, even to Aunt Mary. 'They all look the same to me.' That made her laugh but I didn't know why. 'And what about Edward,' I added, suddenly curious to see the man I might have wed, 'is *he* there?'

'I can't see him. He married, you know. Anne Sackville. I think Hertford pushed him into it quickly to avoid any further –' she stopped.

'Any further trouble with me.'

She nodded. 'I'm sorry.'

'Why should I care? He was not mine to lose. I never even saw a picture of him.' Though I had barely thought of Edward Seymour since I arrived at court, I had the sense of another door closing and I was reminded that even after two years in the royal entourage a suitable match for me had not materialized.

Once the speeches were done with, we milled about, waiting to dine, and I discussed with Aunt Mary how I might find a way back into Grandmother's favour. I had been given leave to visit Hardwick in the spring of that year and had been coolly received. If truth be told I had found myself missing the calm of my old home. It was an irony, I was aware, but the madness of court was relentless and I was wearing thin with it.

When I'd arrived at Hardwick, the dogs I had fed under

the table for all those years had given me a rumbustious welcome at the door, jumping up at my skirts, eager eyes filled with delight to encounter their old benefactor. They'd followed me up the staircase to Grandmother's withdrawing room. Nothing had changed, as if time stood still there. Mister Reason reading by the window, a brace of cousins playing cards, the chaplain warming himself by the fire talking quietly to Joan, a couple of women concentrating on a length of embroidery by the window. Grandmother was needlessly criticizing their stitching and one of the women, I could see, was on the brink of tears.

'I find it strange that you should be so eager to return when you spent such great effort to be gone from here,' was her opening gambit to me. To be honest, I'd missed her. They say that prisoners can grow fond of their jailers and perhaps that was it, but she *was* my grandmother and we had been in each other's company daily for many years; the habits of a lifetime are hard to break. She appeared very elderly, which shocked me, for she had always given the impression of being hard and fast, unchangeable, like a range of mountains or an ancient cathedral. She had been unwell too, and had a hacking cough.

'The King has promised me a patent of nobility to bestow on whom I choose.' My cousin had indulged me a little. I supposed Cecil was behind it, coming good on his word, for my allowance had been marginally increased too. It helped pay my household and kept my wardrobe fit for court. Aside from Cecil's influence, I wondered if those favours were because, at some profound level, my cousin felt a modicum of guilt for having taken my throne. Of course that was fantasy on my part, he can never once have questioned his right to be king.

'A patent of nobility. For a barony, I sup—' Her words were choked by a fit of coughing.

'I intend to offer it to Uncle William.' I passed her a cup of spiced wine, which she sipped slowly as the fit abated.

'Good,' was her answer. There was nothing in her expression that demonstrated pleasure towards me, though I scrutinized her for signs. 'Baron Cavendish of Hardwick.'

'It has a nice ring, doesn't it?' I felt like the rejected puppy trying to gain a shred of affection from its owner.

'Glad to see you are making your presence at court count.'

I had stayed only a few days, thankfully not in my old bedchamber but in one of the grand state bedrooms upstairs, where the wind whipped and rattled at the windowpanes, keeping me awake through the nights. I left Hardwick exhausted and didn't relish the idea of returning.

Dinner was announced, and the Prince's party filed past. Aunt Mary fiddled with her crucifix. I couldn't accustom myself to the new Catholic tolerance and always felt the need to tell her to tuck it away out of sight in her bodice for fear it might put her in harm's way. 'I don't know,' she said, continuing the conversation about Grandmother. 'I think once you are out of her fold there is no returning. Think of Henry.'

'I suppose you are right.' I didn't much want to think of Uncle Henry, had tried to avoid him as far as I could, since that thwarted escape when he had shown his true colours. 'And how is Grandmother with Gilbert these days?' I added.

'She maintains he still owes her money. Whether he does or not, he cannot pay, our expenses are far too great. And she doesn't need it. She's richer than all of us put together.' I could see from her expression that I'd opened an old sore. 'It's time for Mass.' She seemed glad of a new topic. 'I wish you'd join us.'

Queen Anna held Mass in her chambers, which all the Catholic ladies attended – seemingly more of them by the day.

'You know me,' I said.

She whispered, 'We'll make a true believer of you yet.' She said it all the time. It was meant as a joke, or so I thought then.

She was making to go but a question was pressing at me: 'Mary . . .'

'What is it? You look perturbed.'

'It's just. I don't know. You and Bridget . . .' My words were tangling up. 'To what extent were you . . . were you . . .'

'What's the matter?'

'What part did you play in Uncle Henry's plan to wed me off . . . the Catholic business . . . you know?'

'Sweeting!' Her eyes looked tender and I let her take my hand, which she stroked softly. 'Know this, dearest one; I sought to help you wed only so you would be free. The rest was my brother's wild scheme. I would *never* choose to endanger you. Not *you*, you are close as a daughter to me.' Those eyes had begun to well up and I regretted mentioning it.

'I'm sorry,' I said. 'I should never have harboured even the smallest doubt.'

'No, I'm glad you said something.' She dabbed at her face with a handkerchief. 'It's no wonder you don't know who to trust, since so many seem to want to use you for their own ends.'

'You must go, or you will miss the service.'

She tucked her handkerchief away in her sleeve, made an attempt to tame her wild hair and primped her ruff that had begun to wilt. 'Oh dear, I am a mess.' I noticed, too, that there was a gem absent from her necklace, like a missing tooth, but said nothing, not wanting to perturb her further. She pinched some colour into her cheeks. 'There, I shall have to do.'

As she left she said, 'Bless you, dear Belle.'

The rest of us went to the service at Christ Church, where we had to listen to the bishop's interminable sermon. It was an indictment of Eve, or 'the wicked temptress of Eden', as he called her, seeming not to want to defile himself by uttering her name.

I drifted, wondering what had become of the King of Poland's suit. In my mind the idea of marriage offered something to fantasize about, a hope to cling to, much in the manner I'd clung, with wilful ignorance, to the possibility of Essex as a saviour in my girlhood.

'. . . she lured man into temptation, too weak to resist temptation herself . . .' droned the bishop.

I had overheard Lucy Bedford say of me, 'She is without mate and without estate, poor thing.' I couldn't bear the idea of having become a figure of pity. The Polish suit had not been mentioned again, or not to me at least. I had begun to fear that my cousin meant to use me as a diplomatic pawn, just as the old Queen had, and that I would be obliged to live my days out, an invisible woman in the purgatory of court.

'. . . the fall of man, the pain of death, all the wickedness in the world can be laid at her door . . .'

I thought about those months spent with the marchioness, that glimpse of a happy life. In truth, I was envious of her in her easy world, for I was beginning to discover that I was not the sort to fit easily anywhere.

Later, in the women's rooms, I sat apart, watching. The Queen and Lucy Bedford were playing cat's cradle, giggling as the string tied itself into a web of knots, forcing them to abandon their game. The Queen absently stroked the younger woman's hair; it was a commonplace act but still I couldn't accustom myself to the physical intimacy of the women at court. Jane Drummond had, the previous week, hung an arm around my shoulder. I sat, paralysed, as if that arm were a blade so sharp any false movement would cut me. I took to sitting on my hands so as not to invite the holding of them.

I sat a little aside, as usual, and an unfamiliar woman

approached who appeared to be attached to the Countess of Cumberland's party. Her dress was plain, in contrast to the embellished luxury of most amongst us, but she was smartly turned out and I supposed her one of the countess's gentlewomen. She was not young but had an unusual kind of beauty, sculpted and dark, that transcended age and made me stare at her as she spoke. There was something familiar about her but I couldn't think what it was. She greeted me with deference – 'I have long been an admirer of yours, My Lady,' head dipped reverentially – though omitting to tell me her name.

I assumed it was her hope that I would make a plea on her behalf to the King; it was usually the reason people sought to befriend me. I sound bitter. I *was* bitter, for my life, just when I thought it would dilate gloriously, had shrunk like a fruit left in the sun. I'd believed there was freedom awaiting me beyond the walls of Hardwick, but I'd been wrong.

Where have I seen you before? I asked myself. The woman was gazing at me expectantly, as if I might come out with something interesting, but I could only think to ask her, 'What did you make of the bishop's sermon?'

'You do not want to know, My Lady.'

I hadn't the inclination to be drawn into a verbal game of courtly cat and mouse: *Oh no you don't; oh but I do; I couldn't possibly say* . . . But she interrupted my thoughts.

'I could have torn the bishop's head off.' She made a wrenching action with her hand. 'All that nonsense about "the wicked temptress". I refuse to believe that Eve was solely responsible for the fall of man.'

I looked round to be sure we were not being listened to. 'You would rewrite the Scriptures?'

'No, not at all. It is a matter of interpretation.'

She had a fervour about her that garnered my fascination. I felt stimulated to be having such a conversation instead of the usual banalities exchanged in the Queen's rooms, the asinine games and the talk of romance. 'Go on.'

'I have given it all much thought.' As she spoke she gesticulated earnestly. 'Adam should have had the power to resist Eve and the serpent. It was *he* who was created first, *he* who had the greater affinity with his Maker, so why then did he listen to Eve and not to God?'

'Are you saying that to believe in Eve as the perpetrator of man's fall renders woman as the dominant sex?'

'Exactly!' Her dark eyes were shining. 'And clearly that is not so. Look who takes charge in the world.'

The zeal she exuded was contagious; it buzzed about my head. 'So Eve is innocent?' I sounded doubtful.

'Not quite, we are none of us without sin, but more innocent than man.' She grabbed my sleeve then, saying, 'I *knew* you would understand. No one else does.' I must have looked horrified, staring at her hand, for she snatched it back sharply. 'I beg your forgiveness, My Lady. You must think me presumptuous. I became carried away. I should not have clutched at you like that.' She wore a look of authentic distress.

Then it came flooding back to me down the years, the girl reciting Ovid's tale of Philomel and my horror, not at the chopping off of Philomel's tongue but because my neighbour had grabbed my arm much as this woman had just done.

'Who are you?' I said.

'I am Mistress Lanyer.'

'The poet?' I remembered Queen Anna talking of her.

She nodded. 'I'm so terribly sorry —'

'No, no,' I interjected. 'How were you to know that I turn to stone at the touch of a stranger?'

'You make yourself sound like a character from Ovid.'

'It *was* you, reading from Ovid . . . years ago . . . I interrupted, had to leave.'

She smiled widely, showing her even teeth. 'You remember.'

'And you are a poet now?'

'I am. Of sorts.' She seemed suddenly self-conscious, her voice shrinking. 'I try to shape my thoughts and scribble them down. I was lucky enough to have more of an education than I might have had.' She pulled a fold of paper from her sleeve and handed it to me. 'It's a poem I wrote for you. I hope you don't think it an imposition.'

I read it silently. It was short, a mere two verses and not particularly good, not when you have heard the alchemical verse of Donne with its intricate rhythms and singular figures, words that combine to touch profoundly and haunt the passages of your mind for ever. Donne it may not have been, but I liked her spirit; for a woman such as her to take up a pen showed mettle.

'This,' I said, reading a line out loud, '"Rare Phoenix, whose fair feathers are your own." This is me.' I was thinking of something I had written myself in those dark days at Hardwick: *I must shape my own coat according to my cloth, but it will not be after the fashion of this world, God willing, but fit for me.*

I felt somehow penetrated, as if she had looked inside my soul, and was deeply touched by that mediocre little poem, which still lies in my bag of treasures. 'I am most grateful to you, Mistress Lanyer.' My thanks seemed woefully inadequate, given the effect those few words had had on me. 'I should like . . .' I clammed up and a silence fell. 'I have written a little poetry myself and wonder if I might send you some for your opinion.' And then I wanted to take the words back, for how could I show my work to this woman I barely knew, when my whole inner world was bared in it?

'It would be a great honour, My Lady. It is difficult to share one's work, like going naked.' She looked at me cautiously, as if I might find the expression vulgar.

But I nodded saying, 'Exactly so.'

'If I may, I too, would like to send you something I've been attempting. It is a vindication of Eve – the ideas I've been talking of. But it is very rough – quite unformed.'

I felt an instant like-mindedness, as if we were stars that belonged in the same constellation; it was a feeling reminiscent of my friendship with Starkey. I found myself wondering if Mistress Lanyer too could be capable of suicide and was horrified by the way my thoughts had turned. Of course not, I reassured myself, not the fiery smiling woman before me: *I could have torn the bishop's head off.*

'I should like very much to see your work.'

I imagined us; two women with a common aim to express ourselves in words, and had a sense of belonging to something meaningful, however tenuous. I thought of those I had been fond of aside from family: Starkey, Bridget, Dodderidge, they were all my servants in one way or another, all in my pay, and had no choice but to care for me.

'I have always thought of you as greatly misunderstood,' she added.

Before I had the chance to ask her what she meant, she was hustled along by the countess, who wanted her for an errand.

'You really have no right to approach the Lady Arbella, like that.' She spoke loud enough for me to hear.

'No, no, it's quite all right,' I said, but they were already bustling off down the corridor.

Denmark House

Sometimes an event occurs that throws the world off-kilter to such an extent that it is possible for everyone to recall with crystal clarity the time and place they first heard of it.

It happened in the month I reached thirty. I remember being with Queen Anna at Denmark House. Her privy chamber had a view across the gardens to the Thames and the light that day, from a low November sun, cast long shadows, rendering everything unfamiliar. It tumbled in through the window, gilding the women scattered about the room, but the places it didn't reach were impenetrably dark. Ruff was sleeping at my feet, twitching in a dream. Just behind me Lady Rich was talking quietly to Jane Drummond about what she planned to wear for the opening of Parliament on the following day.

I wasn't really listening as I was writing feverishly, attempting to compose a few verses to send to Mistress Lanyer. We had been in frequent correspondence in the weeks since our encounter at Oxford, an exchange that was intensely stimulating and had invested me with a newfound optimism and purpose.

I think now about Mistress Lanyer, here where I have ended up, unfolding the ragged leaf on which she wrote that poem, reading her faded words, and emotion jostles me.

The tranquillity in the privy chamber was disturbed with the sudden arrival of a messenger rushing in at the head of a consignment of guards. His hands were shaking slightly as he removed his cap and got on his knees before the Queen. He was pale and slick with perspiration – it was clear to all of us that he was not delivering any ordinary correspondence.

His fear was contagious; all the women in the chamber stopped what they were doing. A cluster of girls at the window clutched at each other; Lady Rich flicked her gaze about, alert as a cat; Jane Drummond began to bite her nails; and the colour fell away from the Queen's cheeks. Only Lucy Bedford seemed oblivious.

'It's your go,' she said brightly, pointing to the chessboard. Lady Rich stretched out a hand and touched her arm with a small shake of the head.

'Speak,' the Queen said to the fellow.

'Your Highness, I hope you will forgive me, for it is not good news that I bring.'

'I will not blame the messenger, if that is what concerns you.'

I was wondering if the King was dead, as I supposed others were, for what else, save an invasion, could have given the fellow such a grave aspect.

I got up without thinking and, tucking Ruff into the crook of my elbow, crossed the chamber to stand behind the Queen. She looked back at me with a brief smile, as if to say she was glad of my support. I began to calculate what the King's death might mean for me personally. I suspected I would fare better once Prince Henry Frederick was on the throne, for we had built up an affinity in my time at court. He professed to be fond of his 'dear English coz' and said to me once, 'When I have it in my power I will settle an estate on you, Coz, so you will have a place that is yours. It seems to me that is what you lack.' He didn't think me a threat as his father did.

But, though astute beyond his years, the Prince was still a mere boy of eleven and perhaps all in that chamber on that day were wondering what might become of England with a boy-king on the throne.

'A truly heinous plot has been uncovered. Catholic

insurrection on a grand scale' – the Queen expelled a small involuntary wince as he said this – 'with violent intention.'

Lucy Bedford gasped.

Queen Anna crossed herself. I judged the gesture inappropriate, given the circumstances.

'I have come with orders from the Earl of Salisbury to ensure your safety.' He nudged his head back towards the guards lined up behind him. Had I not known the circumstances it would have appeared to be an arrest.

'Salisbury?' said the Queen, as if unsure whom he meant, which was unsurprising given that Cecil had only recently had that title bestowed on him. 'Oh, you mean Cecil. And what of my sons and the King?' She rubbed her belly, as if thinking of her children had reminded her of the one she was incubating.

'The King and the Princes are well guarded.'

'And the Princess Elizabeth?'

'I beg you do not fret about the Princess's safety.' He could not look at her as he said this. I supposed he had no idea about the child's well-being, given she was far away in the Midlands. The man was clearly out of his depth.

Queen Anna turned to me, stricken. 'I should never have sanctioned her being raised in such a distant place. It is a barbaric custom to separate children from their mothers. In Denmark it would never happen. Coombe Abbey; I barely even know where it is.'

'It is next to Coventry,' said someone.

I heard Lady Rich whisper to Jane Drummond, 'I'd wager Catesby's behind this business.'

The Queen's distress was eroding her composure and I thought for a moment she might begin to weep; but she was made of sterner stuff than I thought and regained her self-possession to ask the fellow, 'What do you propose to do with us here?'

'An investigation is taking place and I am instructed to ensure that no one enters or leaves Denmark House, until all is safe.'

'So we are prisoners?' Queen Anna wore a slight sardonic smile at the corner of her mouth, as she watched the fellow squirm, but her worry was apparent in the way she picked at the lace edging on her glove until it came right away.

She must have been wondering, as I was, why this unknown young man had been put in charge of her security. But then if the emergency was as bad as it seemed all the others must have been needed elsewhere. That thought turned me cold.

'No, madam . . . it is to ensure your safety . . . it is a time of cri—

'Fret not,' she interrupted, causing his face to redden. 'We will do your bidding, but tell me, what is the threat, exactly?'

'I am not party to that information, Your Highness. I know only that it is grave and that I have been charged with ensuring your safety.' He paused but the Queen said nothing, only picked up the little knight from the chessboard and worried at it with her fingers. 'Your Highness, I also have instructions to protect the Lady Arbella and was told I would find her with you.'

He looked around and clearly had no idea which of the women in the room I was.

I wanted to ask what he meant by 'protect'; was it for my safety or something else? Had I been cast into another conspiracy without my knowledge? The fragile optimism I had felt only minutes before began to fragment and the peaceful vista of my future seemed, in the space of a few minutes, thrown into turbulence.

One of the Queen's dogs had begun to yap repeatedly.

'Will someone get that animal under control,' snapped Lady Rich. A maid picked the puppy up and walked to the far end of the chamber.

'The Lady Arbella; what danger is *she* in?' Queen Anna patted the seat beside her for me to take – a gesture of unity.

'I only follow orders, Your Highness.'

'For how long do you anticipate the danger will last?' asked the Queen quite nonchalantly, as if inquiring about the length of a play or an evening's entertainment. She seemed to have curbed her earlier distress, or had found a way to hide it well, at least.

'I regret to say that all is unclear at this stage.'

'Well, you'd better get on with your business. Tell your men to be as discreet as possible. I don't want the young girls alarmed.' I was thinking it was far too late for that, for all the girls looked terrified.

He glanced briefly my way before instructing the armed men to disperse about the room.

I wondered if he could see my fear or if I hid it as well as the Queen.

'I see at least a dozen men at the gates,' said Lady Rich from the window. 'Are they yours?'

'All the entrances and exits are sealed,' he replied.

Lady Rich seemed, of all of us, in her element. I remembered hearing of her famous courage when she'd withstood the siege at Essex House and felt glad she was amongst our number that day.

Queen Anna had begun to pray, moving her lips in silence and clicking the beads of her rosary between her fingers. When she was done she leaned towards my ear, saying, 'This will change everything.' She stopped a moment then added, 'If we get through it.'

Dread crept into me; I didn't want to think about not getting through it. 'It will doubtless make life difficult for some.' I didn't say that it would be particularly so for her because of her faith. She didn't need reminding. 'Now we have our treaty with Spain the English Catholics – I mean those who –'

'Disaffection breeds discontent.' She'd interrupted me before I had a chance to explain that I didn't include her with those English Catholics, that I meant the fanatics, but I supposed she knew it. 'Tolerance would never have been enough for the zealous.'

'Without their dream of a Spanish invasion, it was inevitable they'd eventually try and take things into their own hands.' I hadn't really considered it until then, the level of Catholic alienation. None of us had, except perhaps Cecil, who considered everything always; he made it his business.

She looked at me then, with disarming directness. 'I know you think me shallow but I am not.' She spoke quietly so as not to be overheard. I thought about contradicting her out of politeness, but stopped myself, for it was true, I *did* think her shallow, though I didn't dislike her for it. 'It is like this: if I am seen to be frothy-headed then I am no threat to anyone. It keeps me safe.'

'And your faith? If you wish to be safe then surely . . .'

'I did not choose my faith. My faith chose me.'

I saw her differently on that day, still and straight and pale as a statue, she appeared utterly resilient and self-assured, so unlike me with my rigid exterior, a thin shell concealing a friable inner world.

'And faith, in a woman,' she continued. 'Ha! They always believe you will change with the wind. Have you not suffered from that impression yourself?'

I supposed she meant those who didn't know me believing I could be moulded into a Catholic queen at their bidding.

'Yes,' she added, 'we women are always assumed to be inconstant.'

The following morning, in the wake of a fitful night, news began to seep out. There was to be no opening of Parliament, we were told – a piece of information that sent speculation spinning out of control. Letters arrived and whispers began to move like a toxic gas through the corridors of Denmark House, replacing our previous dread with an invisible undercurrent of disquiet. Even the imperturbable Queen Anna seemed uneasy, for the truth of what had been uncovered was unimaginable in its potential for devastation. It made our tranquil world a dangerous place.

A man had been apprehended in the undercroft of Westminster Hall with enough gunpowder to explode the entire building. Each account gave a differing number of barrels: 30; 37; 65; 100; more . . . The quantity didn't matter, what mattered was that it was enough to have blown us all to high heaven – Parliament, the King, the Prince, all of England's nobles including us women under guard in the privy chamber at Denmark House, who only the day before had been blithely wondering what jewels they would wear for the opening ceremony. We would all have been there – each and every one of us.

That the violence had been thwarted somehow didn't make it less distressing. The fact that such an undreamed-of scheme had existed, been plotted out, for months, for years perhaps, meant that the threat of such a thing would hang over us in perpetuity. Our innocence was lost. The narrowly averted catastrophe was too great, too terrifying to envision, and we all sat around like wraiths in a state of shock, waiting for the next piece of information.

It emerged that the apprehended man was one John Johnson, but he was holding out, refusing to name his co-conspirators.

'He must lack imagination,' remarked Lady Rich, 'to have not come up with a more convincing alias. No wonder he has been caught.' True to her reputation, Lady Rich appeared untouched by the fear that had infected us all with the jitters, had us jumping at the slightest sound. 'Once he's been racked we shall discover his real identity, I wouldn't doubt.'

My own apprehension continued to simmer and I couldn't help but think back to Cobham and Ralegh's plot, wondering if that nameless man would blurt out *my* name on the rack and it would emerge I had unwittingly been placed at the heart of a treason once more. It was not something I dared articulate, not there in the Queen's chambers, where trust was such a rare commodity.

Lady Rich was right; in the end it came out that the fellow who had been apprehended and was being interrogated in the Tower was named Fawkes. He'd held out for a few days, but there was not a man alive that could stay silent for ever in that place. She was right about Catesby, too, and names of the plotters emerged one by one: a Tresham; a Digby; a pair of Wrights; a Percy.

'Which Percy?' one of the younger maids had cried. 'I beg you, tell me it is not George.' Her eyes churned in distress and her friends had to hold her up. It later transpired that it was a Thomas Percy, which induced a prolonged discussion about which Thomas Percy.

I imagined those men being hunted down, hounds sniffing out their trail, and hauled from priest holes or shot dead making their escape. The word 'treason' was on everyone's lips and the atmosphere was subdued as we awaited each new thread of information. I read my volume of Plato, seeking comfort in its pages, remembering those long-ago conversations about Socrates with dear Starkey. It was an irony, I supposed, that those discussions had all focused on my eventual rise to the throne – what unassailable belief we had had then.

I noticed that all the rosaries and crucifixes had been spirited away at some point – into pockets, under dresses – and there was no Mass on that first day, or not one I was aware of. Conversations were whispered and everyone had their theory. I wondered if any of them knew more than they were letting on.

Queen Anna whiled away the hours quietly playing rounds of primero with Lucy Bedford and Jane Drummond. In the late afternoon another letter arrived, Lucy Bedford the recipient. It was from her husband, who was out hunting down the plotters. No one sought to question how, given the gates were sealed, so many letters were finding their way into Denmark House.

As her eyes scanned the page, her face screwed up and she stepped towards Queen Anna, cupping her hand to say something privately.

The Queen covered her eyes, murmuring, 'Oh God,' and slumped in her chair, as if the air had gone out of her.

'What is it?' I wanted to clasp Queen Anna's shoulder reassuringly but felt unsure about how such a gesture might be received and watched Lucy take her hand and hold it in both of her own, wishing I could muster that same kind of spontaneous affection.

'You'd better tell them, Lucy,' said the Queen, unable to conceal the crack in her voice.

Lucy Bedford stood straight, as if addressing an audience at a playhouse. 'My husband has heard that the Princess Elizabeth has been taken into hiding in Coventry. She is safe.' She squeezed the Queen's hand once more and the Queen dropped her head into the crook of Lucy's arm. 'But the conspirators planned to kidnap her and make her a Catholic puppet queen.'

'The poor child's only nine,' said Lady Rich.

Puppet queen – the term seemed so innocent, so filled with charm. It made me think of that miniature queen in my fat baby hand back in the long gallery at Hardwick. The poor girl, blighted by her blood; I understood what she might be feeling. I remembered Elizabeth, pretty and delicate, slipping her warm little paw into mine at the coronation two years before, and the way she had been transported by the choir.

As that first day wore on great crowds began to amass outside St Clement Danes for a service of thanksgiving for the lives saved on that day. We gathered at the north windows that gave a good view of the Strand, where the crowd continued to grow. None of us mentioned that it was our lives that had been spared; it was too close to the bone.

As evening fell, torches were lit and the celebratory atmosphere outside became progressively rowdy. A group gathered at the gates of Denmark House; it was hard to know if they were hostile or not. Though none of us actually said it, we were all thinking that the Queen's faith might have made her a target for aggression. When a few began to shout and bang at the gates, it was Lady Rich who suggested Queen Anna send the guards down to distribute coins to the crowd. The gesture seemed to satisfy the mob as it dispersed, moving on to join in the building of a vast bonfire in front of the church.

Once the fire was lit, it caught fast; great tongues of flame licked the darkness and sparks popped like stars. It cast a glow over everything, making the scene below seem, with the increasingly frenzied mood of the horde, like an image of hell. I was enthralled, and even when I retired to bed very late, though I was exhausted, I continued to watch from the window. From my bedchamber I could see that a constellation of beacons had been lit all over London and out into the surrounding hills, far into the distance. Each subsequent year those fires have been lit to signify our deliverance from darkness.

The Powder Treason, as it became known, changed everything. The mere idea of such an atrocity, though it never actually occurred, existed as a reality, a canker in the English mind, and its repetition or something like it, became a constant possibility hanging over us all.

The King's position had loosened a little, like a bad tooth, and, Catholic or not, my body with its rich filling of royal blood, just like the Grey girls before me, just like the Queen of Scots, once more represented a threat.

PART III

This letter gives me a tongue; and were I not allowed
to write, I should be dumb.

Ovid, *Epistulae ex Ponto*

Clerkenwell

Ami is weeping silently; she has barely slept in days and papers are spread all about her bed. She is bereft, as there is no more to read, and where she hoped for answers she found only more questions. The narrative had become increasingly abstruse towards the end and she has searched for any fragments that she might have missed. Just a line to say she is forgiven would be enough. But there is nothing.

Ami had been there in the story, and then disappeared. It had been a strange revelation to find her likeness in those pages. To see oneself through another's eyes is to see a stranger. It touches her to know of the impression she had made on Lady Arbella at their first meeting, that she had been recognized as a kindred spirit even then. She counts back. It was eleven years ago, how time has been swallowed up. Hal was a mere boy and she was making a reputation then as a fledgling poet.

Ami remembers the moment clearly, when she had spontaneously grabbed Lady Arbella's arm, driven by an incontinent zeal for her own ideas. Lady Arbella's reaction had been so inexplicably abrupt that Ami had almost made her excuses and backed away. But she'd seen a glimpse of something indefinable, a well of unexplored passion, curiosity, verve, behind that infuriatingly opaque exterior, and she felt compelled to discover more at any cost.

Her reputation for aloofness was unsurprising, her rank alone, her royal blood, set her apart and she had nothing of Queen Anna's ease with people. Ami's heart wilts at the thought of the little girl whom no one was allowed to touch. It was no wonder she'd always seemed so brittle and odd, but it was her difference that had drawn Ami's interest. After all, misunderstood women are her particular preoccupation. But Lady Arbella's writings, that intimate expression of her inner world, have allowed Ami to understand the depth of her friend's awkwardness, the profound loneliness and the teetering on the brink of self-destruction that came with it.

She remembers well the letter that had arrived a few days after their first meeting, in which Lady Arbella had sent a few lines of verse. Ami hadn't quite known what to make of them, there was an unruliness to her style, too many ideas fighting to be heard, as if there was something she wanted to say but couldn't articulate.

She'd asked if she might see more of Ami's poetry. Alphonso had seen the letter and said, 'I don't want this to be an excuse for more time spent at court. You are my wife; you should be here at home with me. It's enough that you are expected to pay homage to that countess.'

She had tried to be understanding of the man who'd accepted her carrying another's child but in subtle ways he'd always made her feel like soiled goods. Perhaps he feared she'd find another nobleman at court and make him a cuckold. She wasn't for a moment deluded into thinking Alphonso's jealousy sprang from genuine feeling; it was his pride that was at stake. She had hidden Lady Arbella's letter and the others, when their correspondence became frequent. On reflection, it was that secrecy that gave the tone of their friendship something, in Ami's mind at least, of the excitement of a love affair, though their discussions rarely traversed the boundaries of poetry and philosophy and ideas.

She wipes her tears away on the bedclothes, and is lifted by the thought that there will be no more washing to do and that tomorrow Mansfield's boys will come for their lessons. The church bells begin to ring; it is Sunday and she must make herself ready for worship. She thinks about Hal, somewhere with the royal progress, saying his prayers in an unfamiliar chapel, and longs for a letter. Give him time, she tells herself, it has only been a few days.

The tabby jumps on to the bed with a mew and begins nuzzling at her hand.

'You're right, puss; it's time I got up.' She sweeps back the covers, scattering the papers. 'Goodness, if Goodwife Stringer knew I was talking to you she'd be sure I was communing with the dark forces.' That woman has been getting beneath her skin.

She dresses. It is a lonely business; there always used to be someone about to help her lace her gown but she refuses to wallow in self-pity and, going downstairs, wraps up a parcel of vittles for poor Mad Dot, who will doubtless be loitering about outside church. Now there is true loneliness, she thinks, when she remembers, with a jolt of horror, Goodwife Stringer telling her the other day of Mad Dot's murder. That brutal event circulates her mind as she walks to church, a reminder that death can visit suddenly, giving her a sense of urgency to make things right with Hal. But their estrangement is his choice, not hers, and all her attempts to communicate have gone unanswered.

Once the service is over Ami sits a while with her eyes closed, praying to be reunited with her son, only getting up to go when the place is almost empty. Outside the day is bright and there is a fresh breeze pushing white clouds over the sky and blowing away the stench from the town ditch. A group of local women has gathered as usual and their children are running about nearby, whooping and yelping at having been released from the tedium of the sermon.

Ami spots Goodwife Stringer holding forth loudly and tries to make herself as inconspicuous as possible as she passes.

'The countess will not be hanged, though she should,' she hears. They must be discussing the Somerset trial. The gossips seem to be constantly picking over the bones of the affair.

'She confessed her guilt; one rule for the nobles, another for us,' exclaims an elderly woman. 'The things that go on at court these days.'

'The Turner woman hung for it, so why not the countess, since they were in it together?' says another.

'We ought to ask Widow Lanyer.' Ami's heart sinks when Goodwife Stringer beckons her over. 'You have court connections, don't you? What do you make of it all?'

'My connections are all in the past. I no longer have friends at court.' It is clear that Goodwife Stringer is spoiling for trouble.

'That's as may be, but you must have an opinion on it.' Ami's prying neighbour casts a look round the other women for approval. 'Do you think the Countess of Somerset used sorcery to do away with that Overbury fellow?'

Ami wonders how the discussion took a sudden turn from equality of justice to the dark arts and suspects that Goodwife Stringer has another aim in questioning her. 'I'm afraid I wouldn't know.'

'Really?' says one of the women. 'I heard different.'

'Well, you heard wrong. Now, I must bid you good day.' She makes to leave but Goodwife Stringer takes her arm, insisting on walking with her as if they are friends.

'I feel obliged' – she speaks in a low voice – 'to warn you.' They are linked at the elbows, close enough for Ami to smell the onions on her breath.

'Warn me of what?' She senses she is stepping into hazardous territory.

'Some people are saying you have bewitched Mister Mansfield.'

'But that –'

She interrupts: 'He *is* often at your house. And . . . well, it is being put about that you are unable to pay your debts.'

Ami cannot tell if she is accused of being a witch or a whore and feels her hackles rising.

'Dill and Birdy say you weren't at the backfield Thursday, Friday *or* yesterday,' she continues. 'I felt I had to defend you.'

You defend *me*? Ami wanted to shout in the pause that ensued.

'I told them you must have come into some money. Is that right?'

'No, no, you've got it all wrong. You've all got it wrong.' Ami's heart begins to beat rapidly. 'I am going to be teaching the Mansfield children. There is nothing more to it than that.'

'Ah, teaching the children.' From her tone, Goodwife Stringer clearly doesn't believe a word of it.

'Yes, I start tomorrow.' Her voice comes out high-pitched and unnatural, as if it is a lie.

'I felt sure there was a simple explanation.' The goodwife smiles, revealing a row of snaggled teeth, before adding, 'But you can't stop ignorant gossip. Some people can't see any difference between a person who writes poems and a person who writes spells.'

Ami is not in the slightest bit reassured as she peels off to her house where the tabby is waiting in the window.

'That cat's very attached to you,' the goodwife calls over from her own stoop.

'It's just a mouser,' Ami replies, regretting it instantly as her terse tone has made her seem on the defensive.

Once inside she bolts the door and stands, leaning against it, until her heartbeat subsides, before pouring herself a cup of strong beer and drinking it back in one go, putting the morning's events to the back of her mind. They are just silly mistaken chinwags, and she has done nothing wrong.

She looks around at the papers scattered everywhere,

collecting them up. A few lines catch her eye: *I think now about Mistress Lanyer, here where I have ended up, unfolding the ragged leaf on which she wrote that poem, reading her faded words, and emotion jostles me.*

Emotion jostles me. What does she mean? It is the sole reference she has been able to find that gives a clue to Lady Arbella's feelings, in the period after Ami had wronged her. She flings the paper aside; despair begins to creep up. She had believed with such conviction that somehow these words on the page would offer up something definitive, even perhaps an absolution, but all she has is: *emotion jostles me.* It is infuriatingly opaque, could mean anything: hatred; regret; rage; anguish; love.

The moment of understanding comes to her in a sudden rush; a sense that there is a way to make amends. Her fascination with this story is because in some way it is her story too, and all women's – and so it must be heard. Ami has been many things – mistress, wife, mother, laundress and tomorrow she will be a schoolmistress – but she is above all a writer and that gives her the power to breathe life into her friend's story.

Ami had thought there was no *Tragedy of Philomel*, that it had been lost, or never written; but now she sees that this – this jumbled collection of fragments – is that story, only told in an unexpected way. It is the story of a woman silenced and with her pen Ami will give her a voice.

Now she feels it, that lost inspiration gushing back into her as if life is being breathed into something half a decade dead. She rummages in her writing box for a quill, paring its worn end to a point and slicing it across at a perfect angle, before removing the lid from the inkpot, dipping her pen into the thick dregs and smoothing out a blank sheet of paper on the table. At last she begins to write:

At the mercy of her glittering fate
In a glass embrace, a girl must wait . . .

Hardwick

Grandmother's final illness was my first opportunity in almost three years to escape the claustrophobia of court. Since the Powder Treason, suspicion reigned, and my freedom had once more been curtailed. I was watched closely, as were many in the Queen's household, particularly the Catholics. But I couldn't be refused a visit to my dying grandmother, though Cecil insisted on an accompaniment of guards for my protection – I knew well enough what that meant.

The winter going was hard on the Great North Road and we made slow progress with the ice, which was invisible and lethal in places. That February the weather was so cold the Thames had frozen solid and there had been a frost fair on the ice that even a hog roast hadn't melted.

Somewhere near Nottingham Dodderidge persuaded me to dismount Dorcas and join the women in the carriage where there were clay warmers for our hands and feet. Margaret Byron, who was recently widowed and had returned to my service, was talking tearfully to Bridget about her son. He had been sent to the household of a relative and Bridget was soothing her, saying that it would give him a chance to become a man, that he'd go soft if he stayed with his mother for ever. It didn't seem to assuage poor Margaret's chagrin and made me think myself glad to never have had to suffer that loss. Perhaps I had resigned myself then – an old maid of thirty-two – to the impossibility of marriage and motherhood. It had always filled me with a kind of horror, anyway, the thought of something taking shape within my body – something over which I had no control.

I passed the time reading through my correspondence

with Mistress Lanyer. Her excitement sprang out of the pages; her defence of Eve was taking shape, she said. *I have pages and pages of verse and it begins to make sense,* she wrote, *inspiration springs from my fingertips as if from some divine source.* I was a little envious, for though I had found peace in my writing and a sense of optimism and purpose, I was making no progress with the *Tragedy of Philomel*.

The tragedy had been her idea. 'I think it particularly apt for you,' she'd said of it once. 'It is dark, I know, but it is ultimately a tale about a silenced woman overcoming misfortune and using her resourcefulness to make herself heard.'

'I think of it more as a story about seeking freedom – the nightingale flying away to the forest,' I'd replied. It is clear to me now, the way each of us interpreted the tale in the light of our own preoccupations.

'But the nightingale is singing, telling her story. It is the song of her silence. So perhaps it is not a tragedy in the conventional sense but a tale of hope.'

'And escape,' I'd added.

I hadn't been able to write more than a few muddled pages; the story simply wouldn't emerge; there was no inspiration springing from *my* fingertips. I was a little jealous, I think.

A red-eyed and dishevelled Aunt Mary greeted me at the Hardwick gates, those same gates by which I had sought to escape, five years before.

'She's gone,' my aunt said. 'I'm so very sorry.'

She scooped me into a stifling embrace, holding it for what seemed an age, not seeming to want to let me go, and for once didn't comment on my thinness. A dark figure appeared in the window upstairs, giving me a jolt. I pointed up with a small gasp.

'It's only Henry,' she told me and I realized my imagination was playing tricks with me, for it was clearly Uncle Henry with his broad shoulders and balding head. I hadn't ever seen him upstairs at Hardwick, he'd been banished long before we moved there.

She led the way inside. The house was bitterly cold, all its polished surfaces unforgiving, and ghosts flitted, weaving in and out of the hangings, whispering in corners. I stood by the fire, rubbing my frozen hands together, but the warmth didn't seem capable of penetrating the chill of six days on the road.

'Would you like to go up now, or wait until later?' Aunt Mary asked.

'I don't know.' A paralysis came over me.

'Come and join the family, anyway. We are all in her withdrawing chamber. She's up at the top.'

'She'd like that,' I said, and not kindly. I could feel bitterness abrading me, dulling my sheen.

She began to lead the way through the familiar rooms and up the wide stone steps. 'You don't have to see her just yet. She'll still be there later.' A wild laugh burst from her, transforming into a wet sorrowful grimace. 'I don't know whether I'm coming or going.'

A line of gloomy Cavendish uncles awaited me: Henry, William, Charles, and Gilbert Shrewsbury – there had been no love lost there. He was probably glad the old debt to Grandmother, the bone of contention, would never have to be paid. Uncle Henry seemed more angry than sad, everything about him clenched and brooding. There was Aunt Frances, whom I hadn't seen for years, looking old, her face blotched with grief. Several cousins: Frances's brood, Lizzie, Grace and Robin Pierpont, a trio of virtual strangers, and Uncle William's offspring, whom I knew well, as they'd lived at Hardwick for years. They clustered round their mother, Wylkyn with, shockingly, a full beard and little Frannie, little no more, looking just like her father. Cousin Bessie gave me a crumpled smile; at last a face that hadn't changed. I began to thaw but a headache emerged from nowhere, pounding at my temples.

'Here,' said Cousin Bessie, pressing into my hands a cup of warm spiced wine, which I took gratefully and drank back quickly, glad of the fuzziness it brought. Aunt Mary stayed by my side and I wondered which of us needed the other more. The house was encroaching on me. Uncle Henry came over and sat at my side. His face was a map of red veins, his nose bulbous. There was nothing left of the flamboyant uncle seducing us all with his magic and tricks – all except Grandmother.

'She cut us out completely, you and me,' he said. I could see the resentment written into him and for a moment saw him as others might: a man who felt he was owed a splendid life, thwarted, eaten away with disappointment.

'She was good to her word, then,' was my reply. I had not expected anything.

'And William is relishing his barony. Baron Cavendish of Hardwick.'

It was old news; William had been given his honour nearly three years before and I wondered if Henry had brought it up because he felt I should have offered it to him. He was the oldest, after all. But I'd only done it to please Grandmother. It hadn't worked.

'He looks well,' I said, and then wondered if Henry would take that as a slight too, but I didn't really care what Henry thought any more.

Aunt Mary refilled my cup and we sat in silence. I cradled the hot wine for comfort, sipping occasionally. Henry was thrumming his fingers on the table until Mary put her hand over his to still him. Food was passed round.

'You must have something after your journey,' said Mary, when I refused it.

'We stopped to eat only an hour ago,' I said, glad that Dodderidge wasn't present to witness my lie. My hunger was keeping me from being swallowed up by the past.

'I think I'm ready to see her,' I said eventually to my aunt. 'Will you come with me?'

We left the family and climbed on up the stairs. I had become used to the splendour of the royal palaces in the last six years but still that staircase, ending on a landing flooded with light from two of Grandmother's vast windows, took my breath away. I remained intimidated by the grandeur; that had been the intention of the design, to strike awe into the hearts of visitors.

We stopped a moment outside the door. I felt the old apprehension that had always gripped me when I was about to confront her. The door creaked open. There were hangings to block out the light and I couldn't stop myself from wondering how they had found panels big enough and how they had managed to put them up. Lamps burned in sconces all around the chamber, giving everything a fiery glow, making it seem like a scene from a play – the witches of *Macbeth* or *Doctor Faustus*'s hell.

She was in the middle on a bed. Joan was kneeling beside her, weeping, but stood when I approached and crouched in a curtsy before leaving the room. She had grown very stout. I wondered if she too was remembering all her little cruelties. I felt Starkey there with me, holding my hand, and mustered the courage to look at Grandmother then; surprised to see she had taken on an air of benevolence in death that she never showed in life. Her skin was papery and her hands neatly folded over her chest; her eyes were shut and sunken into shadowy sockets.

I didn't feel anything and hated myself for that. It might have been better to heave with tears, go mad with grief, like the others. But I didn't know how. I wanted to touch her, curious to know what a corpse felt like, but it didn't seem right; I feared I might disrupt her calm. She wore her pearls. Someone, Joan probably, had carefully pinned them so they sat correctly. A wicked thought popped into my head that Uncle Henry would have swiped them, given half a chance. Perhaps that was one of the reasons for Joan's vigil.

'I know she didn't leave you anything,' said Mary, 'but you must take something while you are here. There's no need to mention it to the others.' I could see the tears on her face glistening. I blinked several times but still couldn't muster any of my own.

'I don't know,' I said but then had an image of myself wearing those pearls at court. How impressed they would all be; even Queen Anna would think them splendid. Perhaps they would help me fit in. 'I don't know.'

'Sleep on it,' said Mary. 'No need to decide just yet. But you should have something to remember her by.'

That night I dreamed of Grandmother. She was standing over my bed as she often had when I was ailing, as I had stood over her earlier that day; her face was set like a wax figure, the eyes blank, and I felt fear catch hold in me like a spark in tinder.

'He hanged himself,' she hissed, decanting those pearls from one cupped hand to the other, the clattering becoming louder and louder, unbearably loud. 'You might as well have tied the noose yourself.'

I screamed but no sound came, though the effort must have woken me. I lay drenched in cold sweat, slowly drawing myself out of the dream, putting a hand back to touch the smooth solid wood of the bedhead as if it might anchor me, realizing that there was a storm outside and the terrible cacophony was only the rain against the window.

I understood then how foolish I had been to wish for those pearls. It is one thing to want to remember and quite another to not be able to forget. An image came to me, of the goblet that had been presented to her at the glassworks all that time ago, before our fondness had been eroded by circumstance. I remembered my wonder on first seeing it, so fine at the edges it was almost like air; it would be silent enough and invisible enough to bear.

But even that goblet had been a mistake. It had survived in the same spot at Hardwick for two decades. But I had not considered that the peripatetic nature of my new life was not compatible with an object so fragile. It was moved from palace to palace in a carton packed with straw, and I was constantly anxious for its welfare, daring only occasionally to remove it from its packing to make sure it remained intact. I wondered how long it would survive.

Clerkenwell

The boys are quietly working on their numbers; the youngest, Peter, has been coughing all morning and Ami is worried he's sickening for something. The weather is fine so the door is open to let in the day and the new window hangings ruffle prettily in the breeze.

She opens her hands out on the table in front of her. In six weeks they have healed with only a single stubborn callus to remind her of her days on the backfield. Her arrangement with Mansfield has been a success and at last she has a little money to spare, and time to write in the evenings when her pupils have gone home. The verses pour out of her, she has filled pages and pages with them, as if the inspiration from all that time when she was unable to write had gathered in a reservoir and only now found its release.

Edwin Mansfield and his two brothers have all proved bright and eager to learn. Two other local boys had started with her last week, through Mansfield's recommendation. They crowd round the table in her small downstairs room, hunched silently over the work she sets. It makes for a good feeling, the sense that she is contributing something good to the world in helping these few boys. She has a soft spot for little Peter; he had asked why he needed to learn to read when he first arrived.

'Because without reading you only have half a life,' she'd said, watching his puzzled face. 'Reading will open doors for you to new worlds.' He had looked at her in wonder then.

'Like the men who sail to the Americas?'

'Yes, something like that.'

It turned out that Peter had a voracious appetite for learning, spurred on by a curiosity that led him to question everything. He reminded her of Hal as a small boy, not because they were in any way physically alike, but because Hal too had a thirst for knowledge.

Nothing could touch the deep sense of loss she felt at Hal's silence but her writing has gone some way to filling the void and hope finally came yesterday in the shape of a letter, curt and brief, a mere three lines to say he was being offered a paid position and that on Sunday he would be home. She could see his anger in the pressure he'd applied to the quill, making deep indentations in the paper, but it was a good sign nonetheless that he was going to come and see her, though he had given no indication of how long he would stay. His visit, however short, would at least offer her the opportunity to explain things to him, to show him the letters his father wrote to her, to give him a sense of who Henry Hunsdon was.

Edwin asks Ami to explain a principle of geometry, coming to sit next to her while she draws out a diagram. As they are discussing it she notices a young woman half hidden behind the open door, who ducks away when their eyes meet.

'Leave us be, Joyce!' shouts Edwin. 'You've no business here.'

'It's your sister?' Ami asks.

'Yes, she won't stop bleating about wanting to learn her letters.' He makes a scowl.

Ami can see the girl's head now at the window, an explosion of straw-coloured curls barely tamed by a linen coif and the same square face of her brothers and father.

'Let her come in,' says Ami. 'It can't hurt for her to see what goes on here. It's almost time to break, anyway.'

'Fa won't like it.' Edwin shrugs and little Peter jumps up to grab his sister's hand to pull her inside.

The girl stands at a loss in the cramped room and Ami makes the boys shuffle down on the bench to accommodate her. Edwin sighs pointedly.

'So you are Joyce Mansfield?' Ami says.

'I am.' Her timidity makes her seem younger than she is, but now she can see her properly Ami estimates she must be oldest of the Mansfield siblings and it disappoints her that Edwin should treat her with such disdain.

'And you'd like to learn to read?'

'I truly would,' Joyce whispers.

'I know what Fa'll have to say about that,' says Edwin, and just as Ami is about to respond, little Peter begins to cough again. This time it is the distinctive hacking bark of croup. Joyce is on her feet in an instant and rubbing his back.

'Take him home, why don't you,' says Edwin.

'I don't want to go home,' rasps Peter. 'I'm perfectly fine.'

'Why don't you go up and lie on the bed for a while,' suggests Ami, reaching for the pot of lavender honey she keeps on a high shelf. She remembers nursing Hal through the croup, how small he had seemed in the big bed. The memory stings more than it should, like a paper cut. She spoons out a measure of honey, giving it to the little boy to soothe his throat.

'That's an unusual jar,' says Joyce, running a finger over a line of indecipherable writing carved into the pottery surface.

'It is, isn't it? I found it here when I moved to the house. It serves me well as a honey pot.'

Ami sends the others out to eat their dinner on the stoop and takes Peter's hot little hand, leading him up to the bedchamber. Joyce follows them to help, folding back the covers and closing the shutters.

'He seems feverish,' says Ami, noting the bright patches of red on his cheeks.

'The baby's been ailing. He must have caught it off her,' says Joyce. 'Shall I fetch a damp cloth for his forehead?'

Ami explains where she will find the ewer of water and the clean cloths and asks her to tell one of her brothers to run home and warn their mother. She inspects the child's body for signs of a rash, finding nothing sinister, but his skin is burning.

'I'm fine.' His voice is feeble.

'You're not,' she says. 'But if you rest, you shall be in a day or so. Close your eyes.' She begins to sing a lullaby, one she used to sing to Hal as an infant. Joyce returns and sits on his other side, folding the cool cloth over his head, and before long he has drifted off so Ami tiptoes out, leaving the girl with her brother.

Downstairs, Edwin has returned, puffed out from running. 'Ma asks if he can stay here for the meantime and Fa'll come and get him later. She can't leave the baby, see.'

Ami settles the boys back down to their lessons and through the afternoon they can hear Peter hacking upstairs until Mansfield arrives.

'I hear the little lad's afflicted.'

'He's up in bed,' Ami says. 'His sister's minding him.'

Mansfield's manner with her has completely transformed; it is almost as if he sees her as an equal, as if the evidence of her learning has somehow divested her of her dubious reputation, taken a little of the woman out of her. He remains at a respectful distance and no longer silently appraises her body.

'Sorry to have burdened you with his care but my missus has her hands full with the baby.' He looks awkward, as if he doesn't like to feel indebted.

'It's been no trouble. Joyce has done it all, really. Listen, why doesn't he stay for a couple of days?'

'I couldn't . . .'

'I have room for him here and with your wife so busy . . .'

'Well . . .'

'Perhaps Joyce could stay and care for him. I assume she's already had the croup. It'll take the weight off Mistress Mansfield.'

He seems hesitant, so Ami says, 'Look, I'd *like* to do it.'

She's fond of little Peter but she has another motive, wants an excuse to have Joyce under her roof for a few days. If the girl's so keen to learn to read then what better opportunity to get her started? She hasn't forgotten Mansfield's words about not wanting his daughters ruined by book learning, suspects his newfound respect for her education might not extend to his own girls. But she can't bear to think of Joyce missing out on an education for no better reason than that she was born female. So when he reluctantly agrees, she reins in her enthusiasm for fear of arousing his suspicion.

That evening, when Peter is settled, they leave him with a little bell beside the bed in case he should wake. Joyce's delight is palpable when Ami suggests that she begin learning to read.

'Oh yes!' she exclaims. 'I didn't dare so much as to dream of such a thing.'

'But don't mention it; not even to your brothers. I'm not sure your father would understand. He fears learning will spoil you.'

'I won't say a thing. I know what Fa's like. 'Spect he'll come round in the end though. He's softer than he lets on.'

They sit at the table and Ami begins to explain the way each letter makes a sound and how the sounds join up to make words. Joyce is a quick learner and is soon concentrating on copying out simple phrases while Ami gets on with her own writing.

Distracting thoughts swirl about her head. She had noticed a certain hostility in the marketplace recently and it is niggling at her. The pie-woman was odd, wouldn't look her in the eye, and said she'd sold out when Ami could clearly see several pies in a basket behind the stall. She has also been aware of people whispering and glancing her way, but she puts her worries to the back of her mind, trying to dismiss them as unfounded, telling herself that she's allowing her imagination to run away with her. Turning her thoughts to her writing, she cogitates on the extent to which Lady Arbella was misunderstood by the Queen's women and how she might convey it. People can so easily misread a person's actions.

They'd thought Lady Arbella such a ruthless wit when truly it was nothing but her desire to express things exactly as she saw them – she couldn't have been more oblivious. Once Ami had witnessed a pair of the Queen's women sidling up to her; one was dressed head to toe in embroidered satin, so new you could almost smell the tailor's chalk on it.

'How do you find my new outfit?' she'd asked, opening her arms out and swaying from side to side to best display the hang of her skirts.

Lady Arbella had looked her up and down for some time before saying, 'It looks much like your old one.'

A snort of laughter had escaped from the woman's companion, leaving her looking, in her splendid dress, as if she'd been slapped.

'Why is she laughing?' Lady Arbella had whispered.

'She thinks you witty,' Ami had replied.

'I merely say things as I see them. The dress is identical to the one she usually wears, only in a different fabric.'

'But nobody speaks the truth in this place. That is what makes it funny.'

Lady Arbella had seemed utterly baffled. It was in those seemingly insignificant moments that Ami began to understand her acquaintance as someone who did not fit easily, even in the rarefied world of the court where she naturally belonged.

'What is it you are working on?' asks Joyce, drawing Ami away from the past and back to her small room.

'I'm telling someone's story. Well, rather, they have told their own story and I am shaping it into verse.'

Joyce is silent for several moments and then says, 'What an incredible thing, to think of a whole life in words.' Her face is filled with wonder as if she's just witnessed an eclipse or some other inexplicable happening. 'It's a kind of magic, that marks on a page can say so much.'

The following day two more of her pupils have fallen ill, so they are a depleted group, with just the two older Mansfield boys doing their lessons. But by the end of the week little Peter is well enough to return home and convalesce, leaving Joyce despondent at the thought of not being able to continue her lessons.

'We shall think of something,' Ami says. 'And my door is always open to you, if you can find a reason to get away in the evenings.'

She settles back into her writing once Joyce has gone. Now the inspiration is flowing it is hard for her to remember what it was like when she was unable to write. Thoughts of Lady Arbella flap about her mind. The story has begun to possess her in a disturbing way she hadn't expected and exacerbates, rather than diminishes, her guilt. She returns to the pages, shuffling through them, re-reading sections, believing she might find the answers she knows are not there. *Emotion jostles me.* 'Tell me what you mean,' she whispers, but there is no answer, only the rumbling purr of the cat.

Verse slides from her pen, weaving itself into shape until it becomes too dark to continue and she notices that the fire has burnt right down. She throws a log on the hearth, watching the bark catch and flare up, crackling, sending brightness into the room. Taking a taper, she touches it to the flames and goes to the box of candles, finding only a single one left, when she is sure there had been at least half a dozen. The unnerving thought that someone has been in her house, rummaging through her things, strikes her suddenly.

She looks around, suspicious now, and everything seems to have been moved slightly, her papers disordered, the kitchen utensils untidied, the instruments on the high shelf out of place. She climbs on a stool with the candle to see if the patterns of dust will reveal anything but there is no dust to speak of. Perhaps her mind is playing tricks on her.

She sits back down to continue her work but unease prods, distracting her, so she goes to bed, lying awake in the dark, thinking of Hal's visit on Sunday. But she worries, remembering the curt tone of his letter, and lying in the pitch black she feels the weight of her inadequacies as a mother and as a friend and neither can she shake off that feeling that a trespasser has been in her house.

Richmond Palace

From upstairs at Richmond there was a clear view of the roof of Sheen and, thinking of the glorious solitude of the riverside walk, I had the idea to head that way in the hope of surprising the marchioness with a visit. I initially considered riding there on Dorcas, but was concerned I might attract too much attention, so a walk it would be. Since the business of the Powder Treason none of us went anywhere unaccompanied. It was for our safety, or so we were told – it was a familiar refrain.

I said in the Queen's privy chamber that I'd walk with Bridget and no questions were asked so I slipped through the back corridors, where it was less likely I'd arouse suspicion. Richmond Palace had been planned with little logic and I lost my bearings almost instantly, taking a wrong turn and ending up exiting by an unfamiliar door that led out to the ponds where some lads were fishing.

I stood and watched them for a while as they scooped their nets through the water, lifting them out, wriggling and dripping with their silvery cargo. A large flat stone served as the place of execution and the means: a sharp thwack on the head with a baton – a brutal dispatch for something so bursting with life. Those fish would be served up at supper, dry and spongy, sticking to the roof of my mouth, leaving a stench on my fingers.

Despite my distaste, I found myself fascinated by the violence and was trying to build an idea about the scene into something I could commit to paper. The wriggling fish, stilled with a stroke, made me think of Philomel's tongue – it was a metaphor I felt sure I could employ in one way or another. After some time I became aware of a young man standing a short distance from me. I didn't recognize him; court was filled with men such as he, beautifully dressed in white stockings and tailored worsted with a jaunty hat and a lace collar.

'It is a pitiless scene,' he said.

I was surprised, as I believed men, particularly young ones, to be immune to violence, but I didn't reply, just nodded, and Ruff became agitated, impatient for his walk, so I moved on. He made a little bow and removed that jaunty hat with an overblown flourish that forced me to smother a smile as I walked away towards the river.

Coming out from the shadow of the building, the beauty of the gardens struck me; it was one of those days in early spring that seems newly minted, everything bright and budding and full of promise, the air alive with birdsong. I let Ruff run loose, stopping a moment as I arrived at the riverbank to watch the water slide lazily by. A small boat floated past, its pilot supine, his cap over his face, his dog a sentry at the bow. Seeing Ruff on the bank set him off barking. Ruff responded, making mayhem of tranquillity. The racket didn't raise the oarsman and I wondered momentarily if he might be dead, but he flicked a hand to swipe away some invisible irritation as he glided on past us.

I thought of Bridget, how distressed she would be if she knew I had wandered off unaccompanied. She lived in fear of 'unexpected events', or that was how she usually put it. She had become suspicious, hiding the rosary that she once wore proudly like a badge, and worried about small things, checking behind the hangings for eavesdroppers and treating any unfamiliar servant who entered my rooms with caution.

Spreading my arms, I took a deep breath; the water smelled clean at Richmond, so unlike the fetid stench of the Thames at Whitehall, where the dense press of the city and its waste spilled over into the flow. I once saw a dead body, bloated, floating face down; I gazed at it, quite forlorn, until it drifted out of sight. The thought made me shiver and I wondered if there were hidden eyes on me, there on the riverbank, making sure I was not stepping out of line. If I allowed myself to ponder too deeply on it, I would have understood, as I do now, that my blood had cursed me to live out my days under secret scrutiny – there was no escape.

Despite the glorious day, and the sight of a mother duck parading her string of ducklings across my path, my mood sank to melancholy as I envisaged time stretching unbearably away into the future. Grandmother had lived for eighty years. The thought was heavy, like a stone lodged in my gut.

Another boat passed, the oarsman waving and calling out a greeting, saying something about the fine weather. I waved back. There was a woman with him, clutching a posy of wild blooms; I supposed them to be lovers, feeling inexplicable jealousy coming from nowhere to prod at me. It gave me the idea to pick flowers for the marchioness and I stooped to tear up some narcissi that were growing in the verge, tying them carefully with a long strand of grass, knowing she would appreciate the simplicity.

On arriving at Sheen I was greeted first by the ornamental cherry. That gangly sapling, just planted on my last visit, had grown into a spreading tree, twenty feet tall with a sturdy trunk and in full glorious blossom. Rather than cheering me with its beauty, it taunted me, reminding me of my six years in limbo. The whispered slur *without mate and without estate* was ever present in my mind, but having reached my middle thirties, my hope of a mate was dwindling. In a sombre mood, I entered the garden from the side gate and saw the house was shuttered, appeared to be asleep. I knocked on the door and waited, pressing my ear up to the rough wooden panel to see if I could hear movement inside. Eventually the old steward arrived to tell me the family was at Longford until Easter.

As I walked away my mood sank further; all the joy seemed to have been siphoned out of the air. The narcissi, so delightful only minutes before, seemed dejected and out of their natural setting. I threw them into the water, watching them separate, drift and catch the current, their yellow faces bobbing and whirling away.

They brought Ophelia to mind, sinking surrounded by flowers. When the play was performed at Whitehall that scene had provoked some tears among the ladies; perhaps they felt an affinity with the poor girl. Jane Drummond had offered me her handkerchief, not realizing that my sniffing was caused by a rheum rather than grief. I could not see why anyone would weep over a pretended death yet cheer at an execution but few shared my logic.

My feet felt heavy and my side began to burn, making me regret my sortie alone, as I had not long recovered from a bout of illness. Since I'd first been struck down at Hardwick it was as if the malady had never quite left, only hibernated, occasionally making itself known again. Aunt Mary had thankfully been in London and was able to care for me while the sickness twisted its path through my body, that familiar pain wrenching the sense out of me once more, those infernal harpies circling and pecking. The physicians nodded and mumbled with each other, confounded by my wine-coloured water, prescribing remedies nonetheless, and as I dragged myself back towards the palace I began to fear a relapse, feeling foolish for having gone out alone in my weakened condition.

My destination seemed ever more distant as I plodded forward; I stopped to rest on a bench. The chill of the stone seeped through the layers of my skirts and into my bones.

Ruff was nowhere to be seen. I called him half-heartedly, making a feeble whistle to no avail. Just as I was considering whether to return to Sheen in search of him, a figure appeared from nowhere with the dog tucked under his arm. He was in silhouette with the sun behind, but I recognized the outline of his jaunty hat.

'I found this little fellow digging a hole in the knot garden and rescued him before the gardener struck him with his spade.'

Once he was closer I saw that his white stockings were stamped with muddy paw prints.

'Your hose,' I said, holding out my hands to take the dog. 'I'm so sorry.'

'They will wash. What's a pair of stockings when a life's at stake? That gardener meant business.' He placed Ruff on to the bench beside me.

'Well, I am in your debt. That was a kind thing to do.'

'I would've required a heart of stone not to intervene.' He smiled widely, revealing a pair of prominent eye teeth that gave him an impish look. 'But you seem pale. Are you ailing?'

'I am just a little tired. I was unwell recently and the walk was too much. It was silly of me.' I hated my own feebleness, wanted to feel strong and capable, but all my stores of strength were depleted. I found myself shivering.

'You're cold,' he said, removing his cape and wrapping it about my shoulders. It smelled strongly of woodsmoke, as if he had stood downwind of a bonfire. 'There. Do you mind if I sit beside you?'

His boldness was tempered by the fact that neither of us knew who the other was, though I supposed he must have been one of Prince Henry Frederick's companions for he was young, only just a man, really. Had he known my position, he would never have asked such a thing.

He removed his hat, at least, and ran a hand through his

thick pale hair, smoothing it away from his eyes, which were sad and grey and quite at odds with that mischievous smile. His skin appeared so smooth I had to resist the urge to stretch out a hand and run my fingers over it just to find out what it felt like, and it occurred to me that he might be one of the beautiful fey boys that the King enjoyed for company.

'It is a lovely spot here,' he said.

I wanted to ask his name but knew that if I did I would have to reveal my own identity and force formality on us, when I was enjoying the simplicity of ordinariness.

A robin hopped on to the end of the bench; a bulbous body on legs so fine it seemed a miracle it could support its own weight. I raised a finger to my lips to shush but the movement sent it flitting away to hide in a nearby bush, where it hopped in and out in a nervous dance. The river glided by silently.

'It *is* tranquil.' I found myself speaking at a whisper.

'I come here for the peace,' he said. 'It is so busy in the Prince's rooms, too many people, too much going on.'

So you are just like me, I thought.

'What are you reading?' I asked, noticing a book in his hand.

'Nothing adventurous. Just Plato. I find . . .' He seemed to seek for something to say, running his fingers over the tooled leather binding. 'I find Plato comforting,' he dropped his voice, 'often more so than the New Testament.'

'I wouldn't say that in public. You might be misunderstood.' I berated myself inwardly for sounding so brusque when I'd meant to agree with him. But of course he'd made me think of Starkey.

A shadow of sadness must have passed over my face, for he said, 'I'm sorry; I have upset you.'

'No, no, it's just that I was reminded of a dear friend. He also had a fondness for Plato.'

A hush fell over us – Starkey hovered – and I wondered, had I married very young and he were, say eighteen, to my thirty-three, if I might have had a son like this young man. He held me with those sad eyes, but I couldn't meet his gaze, feeling unexpectedly awkward.

'I'd better go back. They will be sending out a search party.' There it was again, my ugly unbidden sarcasm.

'Let me accompany you. You have not been well, you –'

'No!' My abruptness was deliberate then. All I wanted was to be away from this young man, with his slender hands and his love of Plato. 'I am perfectly recovered now.' I stood and walked off without a word, the dog following on obediently. Our encounter had been so anonymous it seemed apt to end it without fuss. Though I wanted to, I resisted looking back to have a final glimpse, to see whether he was watching me leave.

Queen Anna had gone from the privy chamber by the time I returned and there were only a few stragglers remaining. I was glad of it and went directly to my own rooms, where the reassuring scent of clean laundry pervaded. Bridget was folding sheets and Margaret was mending linens in the corner. Ruff ran in before me, snuffling round their skirts, wagging his tail.

'Thank heavens,' said Bridget. 'I've been beside myself with worry. I thought you might have been . . .' She crossed herself, then said, 'I shouldn't do that, should I? Can't help it, though.'

'What's the matter, Bridget?'

'She found a hole behind the hangings. A listening hole.' Margaret pointed to the wall behind the bed.

'I didn't want to tell you,' said Bridget. 'Didn't want you worried. Anyway I bunged it with linen.' She pulled back the hanging, revealing a small hole stuffed with cloth.

'I expect it's not been used in years.' I tried to keep my

voice light. 'And if anyone were listening they wouldn't have much of interest to hear, would they?'

'No, I suppose not.' Bridget was looking at me strangely. 'What's that you're wearing?'

I only realized then that I had forgotten to return the young man's cloak.

Bridget took it from me, inspecting it. 'Fine fabric, well made, smells of woodsmoke,' she said as if looking for clues in the wake of a murder. 'Where on earth did it come from? If I didn't know you better, I'd think you'd been trysting.'

Margaret looked over, unable to disguise her curiosity.

'It's nothing sinister. I was cold and a kind young man offered it to me.'

'So much for solitude.' Bridget smirked, mumbling, 'A kind young man!'

'For heaven's sake, Bridget.'

'I suppose he has a name so we can give it back to him?'

I shook my head. 'He must have one but I don't know it.'

'You'll set tongues wagging, taking the clothes off a man without even so much as knowing his name.' She raised her eyebrows and exchanged a look of mock outrage with Margaret.

'*You* can deliver it back to the Prince's chambers if you like. That's where he came from. And you can cast your eye over all the fellows there while you're about it.'

She laughed out loud then. 'They're too young for me by a decade, the Prince's gentlemen.'

'Yes, he was very young. That's true.'

She set the garment aside and continued with her folding, the spyhole apparently forgotten for the time being, chatting about Dodderidge, who was worried about his lame mare.

'I hope it's nothing serious. He loves that horse,' I said, but truly I was hoping it wasn't serious because if it was I would have to find a way to replace the creature. Dodderidge couldn't manage without a mount, not with all the toing and froing he did on my behalf.

'And Mistress Lanyer sent word.' Bridget said this through pursed lips.

I suspected Bridget didn't like Mistress Lanyer because she was neither a noblewoman nor a servant, nor even a foreigner. It might have been better if she'd been a Catholic, but she wasn't that either. Bridget liked things that fitted into their proper category and Mistress Lanyer didn't. That was precisely why I *did* like her, though I wished she were more often at court. Her husband evidently preferred to keep her for himself.

'What did she say?'

'She is coming to Richmond.' Bridget rolled her eyes slightly. 'We'd better get you ready. You can't go to prayers dressed like that and . . .'

She and Margaret bustled about finding various garments, which they helped me into, finally fastening my best lace ruff around my neck. All I longed to do was sit quietly with a book by the fire, dog on my lap, but questions would be asked if I wasn't seen at prayers. People might have thought I was hearing Mass with the Queen and it wouldn't have done to complicate things unnecessarily. I thought back to the days before the Powder Treason when so many of her ladies would join her for Mass, returning suffused with the faint exotic smell of incense and just-blown-out candles.

I quietly took my place in the chapel, dropping to my knees, automatically uttering the familiar responses to the chaplain's prayers. I was not really thinking of God, for my mind kept alighting on the young man from earlier, clutching his volume of Plato. I didn't know what it was that touched me about him, but something had; perhaps it was his sad eyes, and I wondered if it was some kind of latent maternal instinct that had been provoked.

I remembered holding the newborn Princess Mary at the font, my little goddaughter who'd barely survived a year. That infant didn't prick even the slightest motherly feeling in me, only awkwardness at the snuffling, mewling bundle that made me relieved to hand her back to the nurse. I reasoned that a woman of my age might well feel wistful about being childless for an older child rather than a baby. But though he was young, it was impossible to think of him as a child; he was a man.

Evensong was followed by supper and a play. The Prince attended, with a small entourage, but my young man (in my mind I had somehow laid claim to him) was not amongst them. I felt a little dip of disappointment; I had no idea why. There were interminable rounds of music and dancing, and just when it all seemed to be ending Queen Anna suggested a game of rise pig and go, so I was obliged stay while every-one drove themselves into a frenzy of shrieking, chasing each other about the watching chamber.

I was fit to collapse by the time I got back to my own rooms. In the anteroom Dodderidge was playing chess in thoughtful concentration with Mister Crompton, a doe-eyed, crooked-mouthed young man who kept my accounts me-ticulously and had joined my household on Aunt Mary's recommendation.

'I hope you're not losing, Dodderidge,' I said.

'Alas, I am being Cromptoned.' It was an expression we had coined, as Crompton had an uncommon talent for the game and none of us had yet beaten him, nor were we likely to. He had a way of meeting one's gaze, his beguiling eyes filled with apology as he inevitably uttered, 'Check mate!'

Neither Bridget nor Margaret were in my bedchamber so I undid as much of my clothing as I could without help, unpinning my sleeves, contorting myself to loosen the laces of my bodice and lifting off that infernal scratchy ruff, before taking a seat by the hearth and picking up my book as I had longed to do all evening. I noticed that the cloak still lay where it had been left earlier and found myself pressing it to my face so I could breathe in its woody scent.

The latch clicked; I dropped the garment sharply.

'You're back,' Bridget said. 'You look exhausted. I hope you're not falling ill again. What's that doing on the floor?'

I felt myself begin to blush as if I had something shameful to hide but she didn't see because she was stooping to pick up the cloak. She hung it from the back of the door, mumbling to herself that she wasn't to forget to return it the following morning. 'Poor fellow will catch his death if he has to join the hunting party without it.'

I affected nonchalance and had begun to comb my hair out when Bridget passed me a letter, saying, 'I wonder, would you be so kind as to read this for me, My Lady?'

'If you'd only let me teach you your letters –'

'It's no good. I don't have the aptitude.' This was always her response and I wondered who had drummed that belief into her.

'Your brother is to wed,' I said, skimming the page. 'The girl is called Alice Riffle.' I heard Bridget make a small noise, the kind people make on seeing a basket of kittens. 'Do *you* never think to marry?' I asked.

'My father would never manage enough of a dowry to wed me to a gentleman and I'd rather be here serving you than be the wife of a tradesman. To be honest, My Lady, I'm not particularly the marrying kind.'

'Well, that makes a pair of us, then.'

'Oh, I don't know about that. You are much in demand with all those foreign princes.'

'For goodness' sake, Bridget, that was ages ago. There has not been a bite on my line for years. I'm too old for all that.'

'Queen Mary was older than you when she wed Felipe of Spain.'

I wanted to say, *And look what became of her*, for she died miserably and in want of a child, but didn't, as Bridget often referred fondly to Queen Mary. I supposed because she was the last Catholic to rule England, though it was long before Bridget was born or even thought of. What I remembered most about Queen Mary was Grandmother telling me of the two hundred and eighty souls who burned on her command for refusing the Catholic faith.

'The King and Cecil are minded to keep me an old maid,' I replied, to which she huffed and bent down to pull out the truckle bed before blowing out the candles.

True to her word, Mistress Lanyer arrived the following day. I found her pacing back and forth nervously in a corner of the great hall. She had a scrap of paper in her hand and seemed to be learning something from it, as she was mouthing words with her eyes shut and occasionally referring back to the paper as she paced. When she saw me passing by she dropped into a deep curtsy, as if I were the Queen.

'There's really no need for that. This is not a formal occasion.' No matter how much I encouraged it she wouldn't give up her deference. It seemed to me out of place, given she was more than my equal in intellect, but we saw one another too rarely to easily discard the reserve of acquaintances.

She smiled widely as she rose to her feet. I was always struck by her looks – which came from her Italian father, she said – the fine wires of raven hair escaping from her cap and eyes so dark her pupils were lost in them. She seemed, beside us washed-out purebreds, as if she'd been left longer in the barrel when her die was cast. Her fingers were stained with ink as mine were; she took my hand and held it up next to hers to compare, laughing as they matched exactly, the same tear-shaped mark on the middle finger of our right hands.

'You'd better not forget your gloves, if you are to see the King,' I said. 'You know how he hates a woman who fancies herself a clerk.'

She raised her eyes comically. 'I won't be seeing the King.' She might have said, *Thank God*, then but didn't, just paused before adding, 'I am to present a poem to the Queen. And the Prince has asked to see me. Apparently he is interested in my work.' She couldn't conceal her excitement; it was there in the way she was worrying at the sheet of paper.

'So you found someone to make the introduction.' I felt a little flat, wishing it had been I. She had mentioned to me, the last time I'd seen her, that she was seeking a way to get her work to the Prince. He was making a reputation for patronizing poets and artists and it would have been easy for me to mention her to him. It simply hadn't occurred to me; all I'd thought of had been a wish that I had the funds to be her patron myself. I'd recognized in that moment that I was raised to expect things to be done for me but not the other way round. It made me feel thoughtless – a bad friend, but what did I know of ordinary friendship?

'Yes, it was Will Seymour who spoke on my behalf.'

'Seymour,' I said. 'You know the Seymours?'

'Not really, but my cousin is a musician in Hertford's household. He said he would try and pull some strings for me. Will Seymour is one of the Prince's gentlemen, you see.'

'He is also the brother of the man I was once to wed.'

'Goodness, of course.' She placed her hand over her mouth as if she had said something terrible. 'I'm sorry, My Lady. You can't want to have all that brought to mind.'

'It's long ago, now. Ancient history.' I realized that the whole of England must have been gossiping about it back then. It made me feel as if someone had walked in on me while I was naked. I knew well enough the virulence with which news spread when it concerned the misdemeanours of the nobility but I had never thought to apply it to my own case.

Tactful as ever, she tapped her paper, changing the subject: 'I must be word perfect for the Queen.'

Mistress Lanyer had an appealing straightforwardness about her, a natural way of behaving around others, a thoughtfulness, an ability to ascertain what they might be feeling. It was an innate sense of how to put others at their ease that I wished I could emulate. Other people, those I was not used to, caused me to feel sharp, making impossible even a pretence of cordiality.

'Will you stay long?'

'Sadly, no, My Lady,' she said. 'I am on my way to Cookham, to the Countess of Cumberland.'

I wanted to tell her I longed for my own house so I could be hostess to her and we could write great treatises together on the virtues of female poets, but it seemed pointless to wish for the impossible when I couldn't even afford a new horse for my steward.

My disappointment must have shown for she said, 'I know. It's a shame, isn't it?'

Mistress Lanyer's poem was a success with Queen Anna who unpinned a pearl from her hair and folded it into the poet's hand, saying, 'We shall have to ask you to write a masque for us to perform, don't you think?' She turned to Jane Drummond. Jane nodded in agreement. 'What shall we ask you to do?' Her eyes were back on Mistress Lanyer, who was about to reply when Queen Anna said, 'Cleopatra!'

'An Egyptian theme,' said Jane. 'I can imagine it already.'

I was thinking it would give them an excuse to parade

about half undressed whilst Mistress Lanyer was trying to explain that she only wrote poems, not dramas. But her voice was drowned in the din of the women, who had been joined by Lucy Bedford – just back from birthing her fourth – discussing the imagined Egyptian masque.

As soon as the opportunity arose, Mistress Lanyer sidled away to return to me. 'Don't worry,' I said. 'It will all be forgotten by morning and she will be commissioning Mister Johnson to write a masque on the bare-breasted Indians of the New World, or something like it.'

Mistress Lanyer laughed. 'You are quite the wit, My Lady.' She laughed so very easily and I could never understand whether she was laughing at me or with me. I certainly hadn't intended to be witty; I was merely stating what I believed to be the facts. The Queen's ladies liked nothing more than an excuse to put their bodies on display.

'Oh look, here they come!' Mistress Lanyer stood up suddenly and turned towards the door. A hush fell over the chamber and everyone got to their feet as the Prince and his party made their way towards the Queen.

The Prince nodded to me as he passed. Our shared love of literature had made us close; he had the warmth of his mother and none of the brusqueness of his father and I believed Queen Anna was right when she said, as she often did, that 'her Freddie' would make a perfect king. He was imbued with a rare appeal that seduced strangers unwittingly, and when he went out in public the cheers were deafening, more so than the muted applause directed at his father. It made me wonder what the King thought of that, if it made him feel unstable on his throne. We could never have imagined then that the Prince had only three more years to live.

There was dancing. With so many young men to partner them the excitement of the maids was palpable. I watched them all, casting bright eyes over each other, whispering, tinkling with laughter, high colour in their cheeks, as they tripped about the chamber to the music. Had I been brought up in such an atmosphere, I wondered if I might have been different, warmer, less abrupt, easier to befriend. We are all the products of our past, as Aunt Mary liked to say. The atmosphere at Hardwick certainly didn't foster merriment and if there was dancing, some ancient earl had usually been foisted on me, for none of the younger men was ever of high enough rank for it to be deemed correct. I had only real-ized once out in the world that correctness was Grandmother's preoccupation and nobody, not even the King, cared as much as she had about rank.

At some point in the evening Mistress Lanyer was taken to be presented to the Prince, suddenly losing her composure, hands fluttering nervously as she tidied her hair and straight-ened her clothes.

'You look perfect,' I said. 'Besides, he is only a fifteen-year-old boy, not so dissimilar to your own son, I expect.'

She puffed out a breath. 'You're right. He's just a boy. I don't know why I get myself into such a state.'

'He's a sweet lad,' I added. 'And he loves poetry, so you have nothing to convince him of. Try and forget he's the heir to the throne.'

She offered me a wan smile as she was led away, and before I realized what was happening someone had planted them-selves in the seat she had vacated. It was the beautiful young man from the previous day, proffering a smile, displaying those impish eye teeth.

'I believe you have something of mine,' he said.

I was confused, didn't know what he meant, and the strangely intimate tone in which it was said suggested, absurdly, that he might be about to tell me I had stolen his heart. The very idea horrified me. I concluded that he'd probably discovered who I was and thought me a good candidate to press the King for some favour on his behalf.

'I think not,' came my prim reply. If he thought he was going to get round me with flirtation and flattery he was mistaken.

Someone squeezed on to the bench on my other side, necessitating that I shift in his direction. I became conscious of the minuscule channel of air between us. It seemed to pulsate with . . . with . . . I didn't know what. But whatever it was, it was unsettling me.

'I lent you my cloak.'

'Oh, of course. Yes, I will have it returned. My maid was meant to do so but she must have forgotten . . .' I was rambling with excuses and feeling daft for having misinterpreted his approach, which was entirely benign after all.

He rested an elbow on one of his knees and sank his chin on to his hand, looking back and up at me from under a ruffled brow. His affable air made me wonder how it was possible that I had mistaken him for the usual predatory courtier. He was nothing more than a well-mannered young man. But even so I felt uncomfortably hot in his proximity and wished he would go.

'There's no need to trouble your maid. If you tell me where to find your rooms I will fetch it myself. It actually belongs to my older brother and he'll be furious if I don't return it to him.' He made an exaggerated scowl. 'My brother can be such a brute. Older brothers always have it their way. It must be different for you, with no siblings.'

So he does know who I am, I thought, feeling suddenly at a disadvantage, and a small bubble of indignation began to inflate in me, for if he knew who I was then he had been quite cavalier in approaching me with so little deference. But had I not enjoyed being approached in such a way? I had tied myself in a muddle and began to wonder how it could be that everyone knew who I was, when I barely knew myself. I should have asked him his name then, but all I said was, 'Yes, only children *are* different.'

'None of the squabbles . . .' He paused, and took on a serious air, looking down at his hands, opening his fingers out, and I noticed that someone had taken great care with the paring of his nails. 'Well, being a younger son makes you wonder what exactly you are for' – his tone had become bitter – 'except to shore your family up against . . .' He didn't finish and a hush dropped over us.

I knew what it was like to wonder what you are for, but I didn't say so, and without thinking I gave him an explanation as to how to find my rooms in the maze of Richmond Palace. Then, as quickly as he had come, he was gone, with a bow, into the melee.

Mistress Lanyer returned elated, babbling about her presentation to the Prince. 'He was so congenial, so clever. You wouldn't imagine he was that young.' He had commissioned some verse from her, she said, finally adding, 'I had the impression yesterday that you didn't know Will Seymour.'

'What do you mean? I don't. Why, is he here?'

'You were just talking to him, My Lady.'

'That young man . . .' My words dried up and I had the sensation of something malicious grabbing at my guts.

'Yes, that is Will Seymour, he who made my introduction to the Prince.'

'What is he like?' It must have seemed an odd thing to ask, given I had just been speaking with him, but I found I had a sudden overwhelming desire to know. After all, that young man might have once been my brother-in-law.

'He's a quiet type, nothing like his father; Lord Beauchamp is an incorrigible wag.'

The term made me think of Uncle Henry, but then I was

reminded of how he was when I last saw him at Hardwick, cloaked in stony resentment – *there* was an older brother who didn't have it all his way.

'He's bookish,' she continued.

'He is young,' I said, curious to know his age but not wanting to ask directly.

'Twenty-one.'

So not young enough to be my son, I thought, confused by a tangle of unfamiliar emotions, not understanding the meaning of what I was feeling.

She continued: 'Did you hear that the grandfather managed to prove the legitimacy of his marriage to Katherine Grey?'

'Hertford's marriage; but that was years ago.'

'Forty-eight years, to be precise. You'd think he'd have given up after all that time but apparently the priest who married them reappeared and was able to testify.' She paused, as if thinking very hard about it. 'So those Seymours are almost as royal as you, My Lady.'

'How delightful for them.' I felt my mouth shape itself into a sneer and then regretted it, saying, 'I'm sorry, I don't know what's the matter with me.' All at once I felt overheated, as if I were sickening.

'Is something wrong?' she asked. 'You look flushed.' She put a hand to my forehead. 'There's no fever.' I wanted her not to touch me, to leave me be.

'Would you make my excuses to the Queen?' I stood. Will Seymour caught my eye from across the room. I looked away sharply. 'I probably ought to lie down.'

'I'll come with you.' She got to her feet.

'No, don't. This is an important evening for you and you must make the most of it; don't curtail your enjoyment on my account. My women will be in my rooms.' I took her hand and squeezed it, as others had done to me a thousand times. But to me it was a gesture so unnatural I half expected her to flinch, or snatch her hand away.

But she merely squeezed back. 'I hope to see you tomorrow before I leave, My Lady.'

Dodderidge waylaid me en route to the stables as I passed through the gallery.

'How is she?' I asked of his mare. I could feel impatience prodding at me, wanting to return to my rooms. I refused to acknowledge to myself that it was the hope of Will Seymour coming to collect his cloak that was drawing me, like a bright lure tied to a fish hook.

'The groom's been giving her poultices but her poor knee is still swollen up like a pig's bladder.'

'I'm sorry. I know how much you care for her. You must use Dorcas until she is better. Though go easy on her, she's an old girl now.'

He was profuse in his thanks and worried about what I would do for a mount when we left for Oatlands at the end of the week; I told him I would beg the use of one of Queen Anna's horses, as my mind began to ponder on whom I might be able to approach for funds. Uncle William perhaps, since he hadn't recompensed me for his barony and titles were being traded for several thousand pounds. But Uncle William was notoriously tight-fisted. Grandmother had offered me a gold cup in return for that title. It was Dodderidge who had gone to the brokers in Cheapside with it; the money it raised was gone in a month.

'You'd better get to the stables,' I said, my impatience getting the better of me.

As I walked towards my rooms I began to conceive another begging letter to the King. My resentment simmered, for all he had to do was release my father's lands; then my debts would be paid and my burden on the crown relieved. I would have the means to set up my own house and beg leave from court. In the aftermath of Grandmother's death, when it became clear that, as I'd thought, there would be nothing from her estate for me, I had baldly petitioned the King in person for the reinstatement of my patrimony.

He'd said, 'On your marriage, Coz. Those lands will be your dowry.'

But there was no marriage – not even talk of suitors any more. I'd watched all the women at court leave to marry and return, only to leave again to birth their babies, everything moving on while I stayed in one place, my body growing old without my permission, just the tick of the clock and my writing for company. I imagined the King, once I had left his chambers, laughing with his men at my expense until their sides split.

The hearth was blazing in my rooms – the fuel thankfully came from the palace budget and not my own – and Bridget was sitting with her feet in a basin of steaming ochre liquid while Margaret Byron stood behind, combing her hair out with lavender oil.

'I can feel a rheum coming on and the mustard will draw it out,' Bridget said by way of an explanation. 'I got the remedy from the Queen's doctor's page's brother, so it must be a good one.' She stepped out of the basin and began to dry her feet. 'Oh and that fellow came for his cloak. And . . .' She began talking about the chandler, that she was not happy with the quality of candles we had been sent, occasionally saying, 'Isn't that right, Margaret?' upon which Margaret would agree, but I wasn't listening. I was subsumed with disappointment, the result of having allowed my mind to entertain some absurd romantic fantasy involving a man I barely knew, and felt a fool for it.

I wanted to ask if he had left any message but feared such a question might reveal too much of what I was feeling. What was I feeling? My mind twisted and turned, ending with the thought that two days hence I would be leaving for Oatlands with the Queen and he, Will Seymour, would probably be back at St James's with the Prince's party.

Once in my nightgown I drew the bed curtains tightly round me and sank back in the dark, listening to Bridget settling herself into the creaking truckle, blowing her nose loudly and yawning. Heaven only knew when I might encounter Will Seymour again. I hustled that thought from my mind – the ridiculous yearning of a spinster for a man far too young. I imagined the humiliation were anyone to find out that I, the court oddity who recoiled at the touch of even those I knew well, had entertained thoughts of such a fellow.

Rising early to bid goodbye to Mistress Lanyer, I found her in the stable yard, bristling with optimism about the Prince's commission; she couldn't wait to make a start on it. Her bright mood only served to intensify my own sense of emptiness and I wished she could stay longer, but her movements, as much as mine, were dependent on the wishes of others.

Crompton interrupted us, handing me a letter.

'Don't mind me, My Lady; read it,' said Mistress Lanyer. 'It might be important.'

I didn't recognize the handwriting and the seal was smudged beyond recognition, intentionally perhaps. Mistress Lanyer busied herself with some items of luggage and I walked a few steps away to read.

Plato said love is a good poet but I have grappled through the hours of darkness to render my thoughts in verse. However, the muse has resisted alighting, so I find myself reduced to my own clumsy prose.

When you read this I will be gone. I leave for St James's at dawn, but it is unthinkable that I leave without at least an attempt to explain myself.

I am aware that I have been coy about revealing my identity but this is because I am the younger brother of a man to whom you were once promised and I feared you might reject me on that count alone, given the trouble visited upon you as a result of that betrothal. By the time I gathered who you were I had already fallen under your spell, anonymously woven as we sat together alone on that riverside bench two days ago.

'What's the matter? Is it bad news?' I realized only when Mistress Lanyer asked this that I must have seemed distressed. But I was not; I was overcome with a force of feeling I had no idea how to contain. I thought of our encounter by the river, analysing whether my behaviour there had provoked this. We had barely said anything, certainly nothing that might have encouraged this young man to believe I had cast a spell over him. But neither could I deny the feelings, equally inexplicable, which were seething in me – a physical sensation akin to some kind of sickness.

'No, not bad news, just . . .'

I know a mere younger son can hardly pretend to be a match for a princess of the blood, but I can only hope that you might allow me to, metaphorically speaking, wear your favour and be your friend. If you find my audacity intolerable and do not reciprocate the budding feelings that I can only hope are opening in you as they are in me, then please cast me back into the obscurity whence I came and I will not exist for you.

Your humble servant, W. S.

AD 1609 on the fourteenth day of the month of May

Mistress Lanyer looked at me askance. 'As long as it is not bad news. But what is it, My Lady?'

I wanted to confide in her, believed I could trust her, but felt so very unsure about everything, quite shaken up as if I'd been in an accident, and asked inexplicably, 'Are you my friend?'

'My Lady, I would never presume to call myself your friend, but you have my firm loyalty and love,' was her response.

Her formality stung. I wanted to contradict her and say, *No, you are my friend*, but couldn't quite find the way to put it, saying instead, 'Look, here is Lady Cumberland's groom, with the horses.' I pointed to the far side of the yard where the fellow had his back to us and was hitching a pair of geldings to a litter.

Somehow the letter fluttered out of my grip. Mistress Lanyer stooped to pick it up. 'No!' I said with some force. But she had already seen something.

'W. S.!'

'Give it to me!' I barked, holding my hand out, feeling panic rise through me.

She handed it over. 'I only saw the initials, My Lady, nothing else. You can be assured of my silence.' She drew her ink-smudged middle finger over her lips. 'He is a good man.'

'It's not what you think,' I snapped. 'He's not a man, he's a boy.'

She smiled, with a very slight raise of the eyebrows, and said very quietly, 'When I was eighteen and became Henry Hunsdon's mistress, I was a woman, not a girl,' and turned to walk towards the litter.

Clerkenwell

Ami waits for Hal. A cony, his favourite, is roasting on the fire. It is a long time since she cooked something like this. She has baked bread, too, with fine-ground flour that is more expensive than she can really afford. She tries to settle into her work but her mind wanders. She writes a line and scrawls it out, writes another but cannot make it scan; she is too distracted by the thought of Hal's visit.

In writing Lady Arbella's story things are beginning to emerge, things that begin to make sense. That day in the stable yard at Richmond had been the last time they'd seen each other; when Will Seymour arrived in Lady Arbella's life everything had changed. She of all people deserved a little love, and though she talked rarely of her grandmother's death Ami can see now that it had created a void that was crying out to be filled.

'It's inexplicable,' Lady Arbella had said once. 'I still feel her tugging at my strings from beyond the grave.'

And Will was a good person, not like most of those self-serving peacocks who hung around court. Ami had truly believed he would bring her happiness; that was why she sought to help them. The memory of her failure wells up. *Don't think of that*, she reprimands, knowing remorse will overwhelm her if she does.

She opens the pot on the fire to baste the cony, filling the room with a mouthwatering aroma of roasting meat and thyme. The cat sidles over with a hopeful meow. Spooning the juices over the meat, she remembers the way Lady Arbella always refused food when it was offered to her, so discreetly: 'Oh thank you but I have just had one . . .' 'That is most kind but I am so very full from dinner . . .' Ami never saw her eat heartily, but it hadn't occurred to her then that abstinence could be an act of defiance, the way she took control of her existence. There was an essential paradox that fascinated her, in that while self-denial made Lady Arbella feel powerful it divested her body of force. She takes up her quill and scribbles *separation of body and self* in the margin.

Birdsong distracts her from her thoughts . . . no, not birdsong but whistling, out in the street. It is Hal, already standing in the doorway. He has the beginnings of a beard, a new suit, a fine one in mockado, and a starched ruff, none of which Ami has seen before.

'Goodness, you look quite the courtier,' she says. He allows her to kiss him on the cheek and she dares to think she might be forgiven. He smells of the aromatic fragrances that men like to wear at court.

'I smell something delicious,' he says. 'Not cony?' He goes to the pot and lifts the lid. 'You didn't, Ma.' His eyes are wide and smiling.

'You've got a position,' Ami says. She hadn't imagined it like this. She thought he'd be prickly and distant and angry.

'I know! Isn't it exciting?'

'With whom?'

'Lord Villiers's musicians. A wage, proper quarters and everything.' His bright enthusiasm is infectious and she is happy, truly happy for him, though it will take him away from her more often.

'Villiers, isn't he the new favourite?'

'That's right and it's said he'll be the Earl of Buckingham before long. And what about Somerset and that wife of his being convicted for murder? One day the favourite, the next facing the block!'

'You're as bad as the gossips round here,' she teases. 'They barely talk of anything else.' She pauses, remembering the young girl who became the Countess of Somerset, how sweet and bright she had seemed. Court must have corrupted her. 'You will be careful?'

'Don't worry, Ma, I'm taking care not to make any enemies. I know that court is a slippery place.'

'Of course you do,' she says, realizing her misgivings are unfounded in his case; her boy has his head screwed on straight. 'You're on your way now, my darling. There'll be no stopping you.'

'Look . . .' they both say simultaneously.

'You first,' he nods.

She takes a breath. 'I know I have written as much, but I wanted to say it to your face, tell you how deeply I regret keeping the truth from you. I was wrong. I couldn't find the right time to tell you.'

'No, Ma!' He holds up a hand. She notices his fine lace cuffs and he must see her looking for he says, 'A gift!' He pinches the lace between his fingers. 'But I want you to know that I understand. You were trying to protect me, so I didn't have to live with the shame.'

A wave of relief washes through her and they fall into an embrace.

'He was a remarkable man, your father, and . . .' She can't quite find a way to say it. 'And you were . . . you were made in love.'

'I know, Ma. I just needed a bit of time. Anyway, I'm starving. Is that cony cooked yet?'

She watches him as he lifts the heavy pot from the fire and can't quite believe he is the product of her own body. They sit at the table eating their feast and Ami asks him, 'What changed your mind?'

'I met someone at court who used to know you. He told me how exceptional you were as a poet and what a wonderful friend you had been to him. I confided in him and he opened my eyes.' He takes a rolled napkin from his pocket and unfurls it, producing a fork. He must see her surprise as he says, 'Everyone's using them.'

'Who is it, this new friend of yours?' She carves up the rabbit, flesh falling easily from the bone.

'Will Seymour.'

'Will Seymour is back?' She is stunned as if he has slapped her. 'He talked *kindly* of me?' Her mind is whirring, the past resurfacing, remembering Will Seymour's rage when he had shouted at her: *If this fails, I will never forgive you.* His anger was frightening. *How can he think kindly of me?*

'He sends you his best.' Hal is munching on a forkful of meat, dipping his bread in the juice. 'Delicious . . . Says he'd like to visit sometime; has things to talk to you about . . . refused to be drawn on it . . . all very mysterious . . .' Hal stops, fork in air. 'What's the matter, Ma?'

'Nothing, just that I'm surprised to hear from him. You can tell him, when you next see him, that I'd be very glad of a visit.' She is keen to change the subject, wonders if she would really be glad of a visit, for it will surely rake up her guilt. 'Would you like to see some of the letters your father sent me? I thought they might help you understand a little about who he was.'

'I *would* like that, yes. May I take them back to court with me? I have to return tomorrow but I'll be back next Sunday.' She nods with a smile. 'I found out he was the old Queen's first cousin.' His eyes bulge in amusement. 'Who'd've thought it – I'm from royal stock! There are people at court who seek my favour. They think me someone worth knowing.' He laughs as if it is the funniest thing he has ever heard, and perhaps it is. Ami laughs with him as he cuts himself another slice of bread and passes one to her. 'So what's been going on in Clerkenwell since I've been gone? I can see you've been writing.'

'I have, yes, and I've been teaching some local children.'

'Teaching – I'd wager you're very good at it.' He reminisces about when she first taught *him* to read, trying to remember the name of the primer they used, delighted when she gets the very book down from the shelf. 'And what else, what gossip?'

'Goodwife Stringer has been a nuisance.' She doesn't want to worry him with the full extent of her disquiet concerning the neighbour: the threats veiled in friendship, all the talk of witchcraft. 'Won't leave me alone.'

'I shouldn't worry about that old stoat, she's always got her nose in everyone else's business.'

At that moment there is a knock at the door and Ami is so sure it is Goodwife Stringer that when she opens it to find Joyce she is quite shocked.

'I was hoping I might make some more progress with my learning,' she says. 'But you've got company.'

'This is my son.' Ami steps aside so Hal can be seen. 'Hal, this is Joyce Mansfield, one of my pupils.'

Hal stands up and seems to puff himself out a little as young men do in the presence of a pretty girl. He makes a little bow and Joyce looks embarrassed.

'I won't disturb you. I'll come back another time.' She has turned and trotted off before Ami can invite her to join them.

Hal continues telling his stories from court and Ami silently gives thanks for his return, but thoughts of Will Seymour fill her head, making her guilt flourish like mould on a damp wall. She can feel her past wrongdoings pressing up against her, suffocatingly close, and the idea of a confrontation is filling her with unease. She would like to tell Hal that on second thoughts a visit is not such a good idea but that would only arouse his suspicion, and that is the last thing she wants now she and her son have declared peace.

Greenwich and the north

I had never taken such pleasure in cake, never quite understood the extreme gratification that can be derived from the assault of delicate flavours, almond, vanilla, frangipane. What had once seemed sickeningly cloying had become a glorious indulgence.

'Would you like mine?' asked Jane Drummond. 'It's too sweet for me.'

I snatched the confection from her, barely noticing the look she exchanged with Lucy Bedford.

'You seem different,' Queen Anna said.

'Are you in love?' asked Lucy Bedford.

'Don't be ridiculous,' I replied, but it was clear that some fundamental transformation had occurred in me that had aroused their curiosity. I suspected that love might be the affliction that held me in its thrall. I had so little experience; even in my middle thirties I was barely more sophisticated when it came to the heart than I had been on encountering Essex as a thirteen-year-old and finding myself infatuated.

I turned to the poets in an attempt to gain a greater understanding, discovering, in the verses of Sidney and Petrarch, that love was a longing for that which is unavailable. This seemed a realistic characterization of the emotion that was ploughing up my heart. It was complicated only by the fact that the usual pattern of such things, taking poetry as the standard, dictated that it was the man who longed and the woman who was longed for. This appeared reversed in the case of myself and Will Seymour. At the very least our longing was mutual, or so I inferred from his frequent letters.

I licked my lips to gather the stray granules of sugar and asked Jane if she might help me undo my lacing a little at the back, where it was too tight. I had become aware of a subtle filling out of my flesh, a new softness in my body, and found, rather than being alarmed by it, I welcomed it.

'There, is that better?' she asked as she loosened my ties.

'Much, thank you.' She was looking at me strangely.

I'd struggled to comprehend how it could be that such apparently profound emotions could be conjured from nothing. I supposed I'd thought myself incapable of love, and perhaps those women had been of the same mind. But I was beginning to understand that it was a species of recognition; I realized that Will Seymour had echoes of dear Starkey and concluded that this was the genesis of the feelings that had taken hold in me. For if I had ever loved anyone, it had been Starkey, though only the distance of near on a decade would allow me to understand such a thing.

'All those letters toing and froing,' said Lucy.

It had not gone unnoticed that I was receiving a greater volume of correspondence than usual. I licked my finger to harvest the remaining cake crumbs from the platter.

'I heard it mentioned that the Prince of Moldavia has been making inquiries about you,' said the Queen.

'I know nothing of that, Your Highness,' I replied airily. 'I've never heard of the Prince of Moldavia; indeed, I've never heard of Moldavia. Where is it?'

'It's next to Poland and very small,' said Lucy Bedford, who somehow always seemed to know such things.

'That's certainly a step down from the King of Poland,' I remarked, causing a burst of laughter, 'though I doubt anything will come of it. Besides, it is nothing but rumour.' As long as they had the Prince of Moldavia in mind, they would never guess the truth.

*

It was not until high summer that the opportunity arose for another encounter between Will Seymour and myself. Circumstances and duty had kept us apart but in late July the court convened at Greenwich and it was there that we managed, through complicated choreography, to find a moment alone together.

Though the idea of marriage had not actually been articulated in any of Will's letters, it seemed clear to me that the intention of our meeting was that we might promise ourselves to each other. *There is something I must tell you in person*, he had written. So as I made my way to our rendezvous, a small boathouse set back from the river, tucked out of the way in the cover of a few trees, I found myself pondering on what it would mean to give this man my hand.

Despite his royal blood, as a younger son Will Seymour was dynastically insignificant, or so I had convinced myself, and was thus a perfect choice for me. I would not be wedding beneath my station but neither would our union constitute a threat to the throne. Besides, with Prince Henry Frederick and little Charles – feeble in body but male nevertheless – the royal dynasty was rooted. I imagined us setting up a home away from court, living in easy tranquillity like the marchioness, enabled by my father's bequest, which would come to me on my marriage. Freedom seemed, at last, within reach.

He was already there, waiting in the dark, greeting me with, 'My love!' Inside it smelled dank, like wet clothes, and I was suddenly daunted. It seemed such an unsuitable location to mark a betrothal. I could sense Starkey drifting somewhere in the air and feared perhaps he wouldn't approve. My eyes accustomed themselves slowly to the gloom. We stood opposite one another in silence, neither of us knowing quite what to do next. A tender feeling welled up in me. It felt like a betrayal; I silently asked Starkey's forgiveness.

'Shall we sit?' he said.

There was a form to one side, reduced almost to lace by woodworm. We lowered ourselves on to it. The silence billowed. I followed the patterns in the wood with my finger. Without warning, he moved to take my hand and I flinched, sliding away along the bench, that old habit raising its head when I least expected it.

'That was a liberty, I'm sorry,' he said. His voice was a little hoarse and I remembered him mentioning bronchitis in a recent letter.

'No. It is that I am unused to such . . .' I didn't know what to call it – an assignation, a tryst? I had to resist the urge to run from that place. I heard Starkey whisper: *Carpe diem*, so faint it was no more than a riffle of air.

Girding myself, I seized his hand, holding it tight.

He expelled a small gasp.

I didn't dare look at him. His hand was warm and alive, like an animal. The past came cascading back to me; that embrace, Starkey's body pressed against mine. I pulled him to his feet and grabbed him tight round the torso, feeling his firm arms encircle me too. He was tall and I was surprised by his strength, his muscularity, not like that other embrace at all. Burrowing in his neck, bloodhound-like, I captured his scent.

'My love, my dearest love,' he breathed.

All at once I was engulfed by a delinquent appetite far beyond my control and pushed my body hard up to him, pressing my mouth over his, as if I were a man, wishing I could rip away my cumbersome dress the better to get at him. I didn't know the foreign creature inhabiting me, driving me closer and closer still to that other being. I wanted to ingest him, like the snakes – curiosities Uncle Henry once told me of – that swallow their prey whole and take on the shape of their victim. I was no longer cold and unyielding, I was soft, expansive, fleshy. I would subsume Will Seymour into my body and become him; we would be indivisible one from the other, unrecognizable as separate entities, a single great monster of desire.

Grandmother's voice surprised me: *Desire is a demon.*

He broke the embrace, peeling himself away. 'There is something I must say.'

'No! Let me say it.' I wanted to be the one to ask, to be the one to take charge of this exchange.

'A confession.'

'A confession?' I was bewildered. What was it? He was already promised? 'So confess.' Unclasped for mere seconds, I already felt a boundless craving, as if a vital part of me had been extracted.

He sat with a sigh, clutched his hands on his lap and looked at them like a small boy in disgrace. 'It was my father who wanted me to approach you.'

'What do you mean?' I stepped back, shaking off his embrace.

'He put me up to it . . . to seduce you . . . to make you love me.'

'So when we met on the river . . .' I became rigid and began to shatter slowly, sharp shards of me breaking away.

'It was contrived.'

Smithereens scattered the dirt floor.

'Even the Plato?'

'Yes, even that. I was told you had a fondness for Plato.'

'So who are you, then?' My voice creaked with suppressed rage, as bits of me continued to break away.

'I am the man who loves you, in spite of —'

'In spite of the fact that you plotted to seduce me? Then what? Wed me so your family could have a shot at the throne they've always coveted?' I couldn't stop once I had started. 'You Seymours are all the same. Your grandfather wed Katherine Grey for her Tudor blood, to make an heir for England,

and look what became of her. *She* was the one who paid the price.' I was slamming my fists into my thighs. 'It would have been a long shot with you, a younger son,' I spat, 'a *nobody*. What did you think would be done with the three Stuart heirs, one of whom you serve? You are the Prince's gentleman. The Prince is a dear cousin of mine. You thought what? That I would birth you a boy and your father would do what? Wait ten years and raise an army to overthrow my cousins? A long shot indeed –'

'Please stop,' he said, his voice trembling. His beauty, those sad grey eyes, made me ache. 'I beg of you, stop.'

I was silent. I had used up all my words.

'I hadn't expected to fall in love.' He sounded clogged with distress.

'Love!' I snapped. 'So much store is set in love when it better belongs in the imagination of rattle-brained girls.' It was Grandmother speaking. 'Love is no motive for anything.'

He looked as if I'd hit him. 'You must believe me when I say I love you. I think of nothing but you. You have become my entire world. I am riven with guilt. Oh God, I regret . . .'

'*You* regret! It is *I* who have the monopoly on regret.'

I ran from the shed, pieces of me crunching underfoot.

'Please!' he cried. 'Let me show you I am true.'

'What a fool you have been,' I muttered as I fled through the Greenwich gardens, 'a little idiot, a stupid, stupid, stupid little fool.'

The sun was brilliant, the sky clear blue, roses giving out their fragrance, birdsong in the air; the day was mocking me with its loveliness. I stopped, collapsing to the ground, my skirts ballooning out around me. I couldn't return to the palace. Everyone would see the stain on me; they would see I had taken a bite of that apple, that a monster had been raised from my depths. I sank my face into my hands to blot out the day.

'Lady Arbella, what is it?' I recognized Jane Drummond's doeskin slippers. She was not alone but the advance guard of a troupe of Queen Anna's women taking the air. A small dog jumped into my lap, licking my hands, wriggling. I thought of Ruff in my chamber, longing for his uncomplicated affection. I would have crawled back to that sanctuary had it not been for Jane standing over me, and the others who had stopped a few yards away and were whispering behind their hands. 'Has the sun caused a fever? Are you ailing?'

'I don't know what came over me.' My voice was feeble, a deathbed croak, barely audible.

'We must get you to your rooms and summon a physician.' Jane rattled out orders to the girls: 'Fetch a couple of pages to help; don't just stand there looking thick-headed; one of you bring her something to drink; someone send for the doctor.'

She sat on the grass beside me, placed a cool palm on my forehead then began to waft her fan over my face. 'Don't fret, help is on its way.' She spoke to me as if I were an infant, and part of me wished I were, that I could wind my life back and live it differently, in a world where my father and mother hadn't died. I wanted to weep and moan and shriek and rock with grief, like the mourners in the Bible, but I was dry-eyed and silent and imagined turning to dust and being taken by the breeze, disappearing into the air, becoming nothing.

It was Queen Anna who suggested I take a respite from court. 'A month or two away will do you the world of good.'

Permission was sought and given and I found myself riding north once more with my household. It was a freedom of sorts, and travelling in August was a good deal more pleasant than in February the previous year, when I had last made that journey.

Dorcas, no longer so sprightly, lolloped along, flicking her tail against the flies, and I had tied a muslin cloth over my face, protection from the dust but also to mask the inner devastation which I feared was etched into my features. With several mounted guards, we were quite a band. Dodderidge rode at my side on his beloved mare, who had recovered well from her injury; Margaret, Crompton, my doctor, Mound-ford, and a number of others joined us on horseback, while Bridget and my aging laundress travelled in the cart that lumbered in our wake, piled high with our various possessions. I wished for the company of Mistress Lanyer, for my writing had dried up to nothing and she might have inspired me. The *Tragedy of Philomel* was little more than a few scribbled pages. But she was obliged to keep house for her husband.

As we passed through the towns and villages – St Albans, Dunstable, Northampton – people came out of their houses to watch us pass as if we were a royal progress. I suppose to them we were – the King's first cousin and her entourage – and we must have seemed a splendid sight. No one could have told that I was penniless and that the journey was funded by debt.

I had left a letter with Cecil outlining my financial needs, pleading with him to persuade the King to increase my allowance and appease my creditors. If I could raise even a small amount, I might have the means to set up house somewhere and retire quietly. But I knew it was a dream, I wouldn't be allowed to leave court as an unmarried woman – prey for pretenders – and besides, I could never have raised the funds to support even a modest household.

We had an itinerary of visits, people and places from my past and some I hardly knew who were friends of the family, or friends of friends: Lady Cheney at Toddington; Sir William Skipwith at Prestwood; Lady Bowes at Walton Hall; Uncle Henry at Chatsworth and on to Buxton for the waters; Aunt Mary and Uncle Gilbert at Sheffield; Cousin Bessie at

Wrest Park on the way home. I don't know who had arranged it all (Aunt Mary, I supposed), but I simply went where I was bid and behaved as I should; I smiled and made conversation and complimented my hosts as if there was nothing wrong at all, as if I had not turned to dust.

We arrived at Chatsworth on the seventeenth of September. Uncle Henry had grown fat and still harboured his glowering resentment but I decided to turn my remaining residue of charm on him. There was no sense in holding on to old grudges. In his way he had sought to free me, to put me on the throne where I thought I belonged, even if he had hoped to better himself in the process. The house was dilapidated, the roof was leaking in places and ivy had found its way into my bedchamber through a window that wouldn't quite shut. It was growing up the hangings and winding about the plasterwork and was rather lovely in its own way, bringing the outside in, though seemed also to be the harbinger of ruin for that once splendid house.

The place was groaning with guests, both our party and several others I didn't know. From my ivy-invaded window I watched a game of bowls take place below among a group of young men, swigging periodically from a great ewer containing God only knew what. They became increasingly rowdy and began to throw down wagers, then two of them got into a scuffle over something. I wondered if they were some of the men whom Uncle Henry had once hidden in the woods around Hardwick, ready to spirit me away to my marriage, but shut down that thought before it led to others of my previous intended's brother, whom I couldn't bear to name even silently in my head.

God knows how Uncle Henry could afford to feed us all but the boards were heaving come suppertime: a suckling pig, a side of venison, several geese and other birds, a vast eel pie and another fishy concoction. I didn't eat but pretended as I used to, with Ruff profiting beneath the table. Even cake had lost its allure and my soft fleshiness had soon melted away.

A ruddy-faced man was presented to me but in the hubbub I missed his name. He was dressed in satin the colour of egg yolk and wore a fistful of expensive rings. He spoke with his mouth full and I couldn't hear what he was saying, only fragments. 'Shame we didn't manage to pull it off . . . what a coup it would have been . . . splendid, splendid . . .' I nodded. He wiped his mouth with a large napkin and went at his teeth with an ivory toothpick, making my stomach lurch. 'Do you hear horses?'

I nodded again, 'I believe so.'

'That'll be my boy . . .'

I made an excuse – 'I'm in want of repose after my journey' – and left the company to squirrel away in my bedchamber with Bridget and Margaret. Soon after, Dodderidge and Crompton came to bid us goodnight.

'Couldn't get away,' said Dodderidge. 'Goodness, I don't know how you managed to escape Lord Beauchamp. He monopolized you for the entire evening.'

'Lord Beauchamp?' I didn't understand.

'You were talking to him all night,' interjected Crompton. 'He sat beside you at supper.'

'That was Beauchamp?'

'The very same.'

I lowered myself on to the bed, light-headed.

The two men left and Bridget was cleaning hair from a comb at the window. 'The birds'll like it for their nests,' she was saying. 'Now, what needs doing? I'd better go and rinse these so they'll be dry in the morning. They're filthy from the road. Would you give me a hand, Margaret?' The two women gathered up a few of the fine linens. 'Will you be all right here alone for a few minutes?'

My head was churning. What was it Beauchamp had said as the horses approached? *That'll be my boy* . . . Which boy? The one I'd been betrothed to or the other one; the one who had crushed my heart? *My father put me up to it*, his words were seared into me. Questions circled. Had I stumbled upon a wasps' nest? Was this yet another plan concocted by my Uncle Henry? Which brother had arrived?

Something incomprehensible was happening to me, over which I had no control: a quake, a longing opening up like a vast mouth, that rapacious appetite awakened. I feared that if I set eyes on Will Seymour, despite everything, my resolve would crumble. Yet paradoxically I found myself hoping, against my better judgement, that it *was* he who'd clattered into the yard during supper.

I went to the window but darkness had fallen and no one was about, just a couple of men guarding the gates haloed in the dim glow of their lamps. I imagined him downstairs at the table in the seat I had vacated. Would he know that I had been there only minutes before, had I left a scent like a bitch in season? Grandmother made herself known: *Desire is a demon; it will possess you, my girl, if you don't take pains to resist it.* I feared it was too late for that.

I tried to remind myself of my powers of self-denial, the strength I could draw on, and bring some of that to bear upon my situation. I had to get away, away from the danger. We would pack up and leave under cover of darkness. But the roads were teeming with thieves and brigands; we would have been dead by dawn. I forced myself to think of God, but it was no good. Will Seymour had set up camp in me and there was nothing else; even Starkey had been pushed to the side.

Bridget and Margaret came bounding back full of talk from the kitchens. Bridget was flushed and shiny and seemed a little drunk. 'They're a rough lot in your uncle's employ.'

'I hope no one has upset you, Bridget.'

'Don't worry on my part, My Lady. I can look after myself. The cook was grumbling about a party arriving late and having to produce more food when the meal had been cleared. He got into a row with Mister Seymour's man over it.'

'Mister Seymour – which one?' I forgot to hide my eagerness.

Bridget inspected me with a quizzical look. 'Don't vex yourself, it's not the one you were promised to, it's one of the other ones. What're their names? You know.'

'I can't remember.' My voice was too firm, like that of a child who hasn't yet learned to fib effectively; I was remembering there was a third brother, Francis, who was younger, but Bridget was on to the next topic and didn't notice my discomfort.

'You should see the state of the kitchens.'

'It is Will Seymour,' said Margaret. 'I heard someone say it.'

A wave of nausea broke over me.

I found a sheet of paper and scrawled a note: *Meet me at the Stand Tower. It is on the hill to the south-west of the house. At first light. A.* I folded it, sealed it and said to Bridget, 'Will you see that Mister Seymour gets this. Give it to his man.'

She was regarding me with that look again. 'It's only a query about Mistress Lanyer's poem for the Prince. You should curb your curiosity before it kills you.' This time the fib was convincing.

Dawn diluted the darkness. First a single bird sang out then another in reply and soon the chorus was in full voice. I had slept fitfully, unable to quell the clamour in my mind and that great inner mouth demanding to be fed. Sliding out of bed, I dressed quietly so as not to wake Bridget and Margaret. It didn't seem to matter that my laces weren't properly tied; the usual trussed-up feeling seemed incompatible with my mood. I threw on a hooded cloak and tucked Ruff under my arm as an excuse, should anyone wonder what I was doing out alone at dawn.

I could hear the kitchen staff beginning to wake as I passed, and once outside I slunk by the bakehouse where they were already hard at work. My senses were assaulted by the smell of fresh bread; I snatched a sweet roll from a tray left outside to cool and sank my teeth into its soft body, stuffing it in, unable to control my greed, wanting more as soon as it was gone, filching a second.

I crept on past the stables and through the orchard, allowing Ruff to run ahead, and began to climb the hill. There was not much cover; just the occasional tree, and I hoped I wasn't being watched from the house. I had worn my slippers for stealth but they were wet through with dew within minutes, as was the hem of my dress, which flapped cold against my ankles. But I barely noticed the discomfort, nor was I aware of the ache in my thighs from climbing the steep path. I could have walked uphill the length of England that morning.

It hadn't occurred to me that the tower might have been locked. The keyhole was cobwebby and it looked as if the building hadn't been used in a decade. A memory struck me of that door, freshly sanded, leaning against the wall, waiting to be fitted, and that dead bird falling like a stone. Now the same door was rotten in places and there was a hole at the bottom large enough to admit rats or even foxes. The latch was rusted but I jerked it out of its slot and, holding it up, heaved my shoulder against the door. Nothing budged, so I admitted defeat and sat on the steps watching the path.

He came on horseback through the woods to the rear; to avoid being seen from the house, he said of it later. I stood as he dismounted, something flailing in my stomach, and

Ruff rushed to greet him, dancing about his feet. He seemed taller than I'd remembered, altogether bigger, not a boy at all but a man.

I began to speak as he did and we both stopped, looking at each other across a gulf of awkwardness.

'The tower's locked,' I said, finally.

'I thought my heart would break these last weeks.' His face was crumpled.

I wanted to dismiss it, say something glib like *It sounds as though you've been reading too much poetry*, to lighten the atmosphere. But I couldn't.

'Are you able to forgive me?'

I didn't know how to respond; all the words that came to mind seemed trite in the face of my overwhelming urge to feel his body against mine. 'Come,' I said, leading the way round to the back of the building.

As I touched him with my ungloved hand, the mere graze of fingers, flesh on flesh, I felt the full force of my lust, understanding only then how it can transform a person until they become unrecognizable even to their own self. It was a blessed relief not to be me, but to be some animal version of me, something dormant for millennia reawakened. Was that the demon Grandmother spoke of? We fell to the ground in a scramble, mouth to mouth, limpets suckered to one another. Then we lay in the grass, I with my head on his chest, he stroking my hair.

'My father told me you'd be here at Chatsworth. I couldn't stay away but I said I wanted no part in any new plot involving you. We fought over it last night. He was drunk. I hit him, bloodied his nose.'

'You hit him?' I was secretly glad and hoped Beauchamp's nose had bled all over his egg-yolk satin. 'Does he know you are here with me now?'

'No and he won't know. This is between you and me.'

I sat up and looked him in the face. 'I don't care about anyone else or what they think.' I had an image of the future spread out before me. In it we were wed and I had come into my father's lands – I was a woman of means. We had a house of pale stone, with modest windows and wild gardens where grew a flowering cherry. 'I will marry you when the time is right.'

A smile broke over his face. 'I'm supposed to be the one to propose.'

'Well, I am not any ordinary woman who waits to be asked.' I was smiling too, yet still heard Grandmother's old refrain: *it will make you seem meek*, even heard the faint clicking of her pearls. She'd been wrong.

We fell back into our embrace.

I pulled away. 'So what is your answer?' I said it to tease him, surprised by my uncharacteristic levity.

'It was not a question. I didn't know I had a choice.'

'You don't!'

We kissed again.

'But this must be kept secret for the time being.' It occurred to me that I would have to reach some kind of agreement with the King. 'We wouldn't want to ruffle any feathers.' A stream of thought passed through my head. Any threat I might have posed once had faded to inconsequence. A darker truth prodded at me, but I cast it off.

'The King's permission. Will he give it?'

'I fancy he will.' I refused to entertain the possibility that he wouldn't. 'More than anyone, he believes wholeheartedly in the institution of marriage.'

'So do I,' said William, 'and more so with permission. I don't want my children born in the Tower, as my father was.'

That pulled me up, made me feel wrong to have had unkind thoughts of Beauchamp when he had been born into such misfortune. 'Can he remember his mother?'

'He rarely talks of her but once he told me he had a memory of being wrenched from her. She was screaming, begging for them not to be separated.'

I pressed my mouth over his to silence him. I had sensed my freedom just in front of me, so near if I reached out I might have felt it against my fingertips; but his story made it seem further away, indistinct.

'I once came up here as a child with one of the grooms, dressed in a pair of breeches I'd pilfered from the laundry, and rode bareback like a demon.' He looked at me, his curiosity apparent. 'They all wanted me to be a boy, you see, and so did I.'

'You are perfect as you are,' he said.

I realize now that of all the people who have ever come close to me, he was the only one who never made a comment about my thinness or implied that my body was unwomanly. I'd been called whip thin, garcon manqué, straight up-and-down, but no one had called me 'perfect' before.

We lay in silence for a while. I listened to the throb of his heart through his clothes, evidence that he was a living thing – my living thing. Part of me broke off and watched that woman in the grass at ease, entwined, opening herself to such close scrutiny, wondering what had possessed her, feeling something resembling contempt for her lack of control.

The sun had crept up and was dappling us with bright spots of light through the trees, meaning our moment of ordinary bliss would have to be brought to an end.

The idea of separation was unbearable; I wanted to shrink him and slip him inside my clothes to wear beside my heart. The watching part of me was scornful, derided such a desire, reminded me that this man with his Tudor blood, like mine, represented a transaction – a play for power. But I was not listening to that part of me and, determined to have a relic to keep, took my penknife from my purse.

'What are you doing?' There was a minuscule flash of alarm in his eyes that I liked. It made me feel he was in my power.

'Trust me.'

I held a whorl of his sand-coloured hair between my fingers and sliced it off at the roots.

His hand clasped the place. 'Thief!'

'There are wise women who can make a man love a woman for ever, if they have a lock of his hair.' I laughed.

'You have no need of a spell for that.' He laughed too. 'I am already enchanted.'

The following few days at Chatsworth passed without event; William and I affected a façade of polite distance, finding moments of intimacy when backs were turned, a brief touch of hands, a stolen kiss in a dark chamber, a whispered promise, always accompanied by the part of me that watched, ready for things to go awry.

We were wrenched apart when my party left to take the waters at Buxton, though Doctor Moundford said I appeared to have regained my health miraculously without them. I was never better; it was the sense of a future I suppose, the possibility of freedom, and the knowledge that there was a person in the world who loved me for myself and not for my blood. The other me argued that the two were inseparable but I didn't listen.

On from Buxton we visited Aunt Mary and Uncle Gilbert at Sheffield Castle, welcomed by the pealing of bells. I noticed there that most of the household was attending Catholic Mass, with the whole chapel taken over for it. Bridget went about with her rosary attached to her girdle for all to see, her fingers permanently agitating at it. I attended ordinary prayers with Uncle Gilbert and a smattering of servants in one of the small chambers.

'Do you not fear to attract the wrong kind of attention?' I asked Aunt Mary of her Catholic Mass.

'Nobody really cares any more what we do up here. At court I am more discreet, of course. But even the Queen is less cowed about her faith these days. Time is a great healer; it's been four years.'

We were sitting in the window of one of the turret chambers and a shaft of light fell over her face, illuminating the lines, reminding me of her age. There was a carefree air about Aunt Mary that belied her years, but she was already in her middle fifties then.

'Since the Powder Treason – four years already?' I had the sudden sense that my life too was almost used up; though the thought of William, somewhere loving me, anchored time. But the other me felt, suddenly, hopelessly, far too old at thirty-three for a man who was thirteen years my junior. Had I become one of those lascivious older women, an object of ridicule, sung of in lewd ballads, who preys on young men? The thought horrified me. It was not like that, I reasoned. But I had witnessed the way my desire, when ignited, became monstrous, how it controlled me. Perhaps Grandmother had been right.

Aunt Mary pulled off her cap and set it aside, scratching her head. Her hair was almost entirely grey. 'When will I persuade *you* to join us at Mass?' She threw me a wry smile. I knew she didn't require an answer but she always had to ask, I suppose, just in case I'd had a change of heart.

'We all believe in the same God. That's what matters to me,' I replied, but I was remembering something the Scottish Queen said to me: *The Catholic faith is the true faith; it is the only path that leads to the Kingdom of Heaven*, and I was thinking of the Agnus Dei, cached away amongst my treasures, questioning whether I kept it in memory of my executed aunt or because somewhere deep within me I believed in its intrinsic sacredness.

'It's not quite the same.' She abruptly changed the topic. 'How are you finding Hugh Crompton?'

'An absolute blessing! He's painstaking with my accounts.' I began to thank her for the introduction and then, suddenly curious, asked, 'He's not a Catholic too, is he?'

She said, not as far as she knew.

Aunt Mary came with me to Wingfield, where the air was thick with ghosts. After which we travelled south, the hills eventually giving way to flatness as we approached Wrest Park. My mind revolved constantly around my future with Will and I allowed myself to imagine our shared life, designing its shape in my mind – an ordinary life. The even Bedfordshire landscape had a certain appeal; what it lacked in drama and surprises, it gained in steadiness and simplicity. It would be logical, I thought, to settle near Bessie, my closest cousin, on the route from Sheffield to London where Aunt Mary would often be passing.

Autumn was taking hold by the time we arrived at Wrest Park, the leaves crisping and falling, the air newly chilled. Everybody remarked on how well I looked. The trip had done me the world of good, they'd said. Little did they know. I relished in my secret.

Cousin Bessie had grown plump. She'd been lonely, she told me, confiding that though she'd had several pregnancies none had come to fruition. I saw that even the most perfect-seeming life has its hidden misery. She asked for gossip from my travels and from the Queen's chambers. I fear I fell woefully short in relaying such stories but Bessie seemed satisfied with my company alone; perhaps she was lonely.

I asked her, in passing, if she knew of any houses nearby which might be suitable for me. My question felt weighted, no matter how light my tone. We were back to back, chopping the dead heads from the rose bushes in the ladies' bower. It was a place that reminded me of the gardens at Sheen, quite wild and overgrown, a contrast from the order of the formal planting at the front of the house, the yews clipped into complicated shapes, the trees espaliered into submission, an echo of the Hardwick gardens.

'A house?' said Bessie, turning to face me, a dead rose held aloft. 'Do you have the means to buy a house?' Bessie, being one of the relatives I owed, was only too aware of my financial woes.

'Things might be about to change,' I said.

'You intend to wed and gain your inheritance!' She was shrill with suppressed excitement, eyes wide and greedy for information.

'No!' I could feel the flush on my face.

'You do!'

'Don't be silly, Bessie.'

'It's the Prince of Moldavia, isn't it? I heard a rumour he was seeking your hand. Does the King know? Do you have his authority?' She threw her hands up. 'A wedding, how lovely it will be.'

'Bessie, you're getting carried away.' I didn't exactly want to deny it, for it seemed a convenient way, if the gossips fixed on the idea of the Prince of Moldavia, to ensure the attention remained away from Will Seymour. So, if I am entirely honest, I allowed her to believe erroneously.

Once back at court I discovered that my petitions prior to leaving had not fallen on fallow ground. My allowance was to be increased and a donation of plate had been made to me that would go to pay off some of my debts. But no soon as I had relieved myself of one debt, I had accrued another, for life at court continued to be an expense I could ill afford. But my frustrations were kept at bay with the thought of finally coming into my patrimony and at long last I had the sense of a tangible future.

Will and I were rarely able to meet privately, though he had taken up residence in one of the Seymour houses in Canon Row and on a handful of occasions I had the chance to slip away to visit him there, where we would lie in each other's arms, fully clothed, talking. I had to bring to bear all my powers of resistance to keep my wakened monster of desire in check, for Will insisted we wait until it was right in the eyes of God. It made me understand that his powers of self-discipline, though differently focused, were equal to mine. I often found myself seeking the areas of similarity in our characters to ward off my concerns about the gaping gulf in our years.

'Does it matter to you that I am old?' I asked him once. We were lying flat on the big tester bed at Canon Row, curtains tightly drawn around us and just the light of a single lamp to penetrate the dark of our private universe.

'You are not old, Belle,' he said.

'But older.'

'Not to me. *You* cannot be measured in years. Perhaps it is I who am too young. Not wise enough.'

The truth was that when we were together those thirteen years dwindled to nothing. I often wondered if it was I who lacked maturity – certainly I lacked experience – or if he was older than his years; perhaps it was a little of both.

We fell to silence and he seemed deep in thought, inaccessible to me in a way that felt unbearable. I wanted admission to every secret recess of him, even whilst knowing such a desire was futile. 'What are you thinking?'

'This is the bed where my father was conceived,' was his reply.

'Here?' I could feel her watching me from behind her oval of glass.

'They were wed in the next room.'

'I have felt haunted by Katherine Grey,' I said. 'Wherever I go, she has left an imprint. I feel sometimes that she has woven herself through my life. My grandmother kept her picture beside her bed and that of Jane. She used to say it was there to remind her that even the best-laid plans can go awry.'

Silence fell once more; I looked up at the canopy, embroidered with birds, and imagined Katherine Grey lying in the arms of her husband, gazing up at the same scene half a century before.

I suppose it was inevitable, given the way gossip spreads, that I would eventually be hauled before the King to explain myself. I knew that talk of the Prince of Moldavia's suit was running rife around Whitehall. Fate was playing into my hands and I sensed myself invincible then.

The King looked unwell; the skin on his face was raised and flaky, his eyes sunken and there was food in his beard that none of his bevy of slickly groomed men, who purported to adore him, had thought to comb out. A number of privy councillors had gathered; most appeared as if they'd rather be elsewhere. They pitied me, I saw it in their averted faces; they had no clue of my secret optimism.

Cecil busied himself by lining his papers on the table, though they were already straight. Northampton pared his fingernails with a penknife; Uncle Gilbert, who looked strained, was drawing swirls in the margins of a book – he had warned me of this hearing; it was only Nottingham who offered an encouraging smile.

'Salisbury,' said the King, nodding in the direction of Cecil. 'Start the proceedings, would you.'

Cecil stood, adjusting his cuffs so the frills lay evenly, and cleared his throat with a small cough. 'My Lady, we are grateful that you considered attending –'

'Get on with it, Salisbury,' snapped the King. 'It's not as if she had any choice in the matter.'

'My Lady, it has come to our notice that you have engaged in discussions with a foreign prince concerning your betrothal.' Cecil continued to avoid my eye and I wondered, as I often had, if it disturbed him that he had betrayed me all those years ago. Perhaps he didn't think of it as a betrayal; he didn't seem the type to be inconvenienced by remorse, but I considered whether he ever thought of how things might have been had *I* been the one to sit on the throne instead of my cousin.

'My Lord of Salisbury.' I directed my gaze full on him, buoyed up by the knowledge that I was a step ahead of them all. 'Who might this person be, with whom I am supposed to have engaged in marriage negotiations?'

The King's breath was loud and wheezy.

'It is the Prince of Moldavia. He seems to believe you have come to an agreement.'

'The Prince of *where*?' I said, raising a titter from some of the councillors.

'Moldavia,' interjected the King. 'Have you been talking to his people?'

'I have not, Your Majesty, and nor would I. If this *so-called* prince' – I could tell from the King's expression that, in spite of himself, he liked my scathing tone – 'believes himself party to an arrangement with me, then he is sorely mistaken.'

'The Venetian ambassador is of the mind –'

Nottingham interrupted Cecil: 'The Venetian ambassador bases all his knowledge on hearsay.' A ripple of agreement ran round the table and Uncle Gilbert gave me a small nod. I could not have planned it better.

'Were I seeking a husband abroad, which I am not,' I said, investing my voice with an imperious edge, not unlike that of Grandmother when she had the bit between her teeth, 'one could hardly blame me, given my present situation. How is it so often described? "Without mate and without estate." Yes, I believe that's what is whispered about me. You must have heard it, My Lord.' I looked at Cecil, who mumbled something unintelligible. 'It would seem reasonable, then, would it not, that, given no arrangements are being made on my behalf, I might wish to seek a mate and an estate.'

'Cousin,' said the King, 'under no circumstances will I countenance a foreign bridegroom for you.' His anger was visible in the flash of his eyes and the stiff set of his mouth. 'If you seek such a match, you will feel the full force of my displeasure.' He cleared his throat. 'The law is clear: a princess of the blood cannot wed without royal agreement. You do *not* have my agreement.' He pulled out a large handkerchief and dabbed it over his face. 'I take it you understand?'

'I do, Your Majesty. But I must say I have a strong inclination to wed.' His anger couldn't touch me, for I had my response ready and I knew well enough his low opinion of women. 'Wisdom dictates that is unadvisable for a woman to remain a maid. A woman needs a husband to . . .' I paused for effect. 'To curb her.'

I noticed a ruffle of approbation pass through the councillors and Uncle Gilbert looked as if he might cheer. It made me think of something Mistress Lanyer had said once: *All men are of the mind that a woman left unmarried will tilt the world off its axis.*

'Indeed it is true, My Lady,' said Cecil, looking towards the King to see if he had overstepped the mark by responding first.

I knew I had won before my cousin spoke.

He lifted both hands in exasperation. 'Take a husband in England, a loyal British subject, and let's hear no more of it.' He stopped to wipe his handkerchief over his forehead again. 'And not a Catholic.'

'Of my own choice, Your Majesty?' I noticed the recording clerk had stopped writing.

I could sense a tension in the room and supposed they felt uncomfortable at the idea of a maid making her own choice of husband just as a widow might. It wasn't the usual way of things. Mistress Lanyer would have liked it.

'Yes, yes.' The King had clearly had enough and was impatient to leave.

'In that case you have my solemn and heartfelt promise that I will not seek to wed a foreigner, Your Majesty.' Victory was throbbing through me.

He got to his feet to leave the chamber with the councillors following suit. The clerk began to pack up his things. I locked a firm look on him. 'You heard His Majesty,' I said quietly. 'Why did you not record his last statement?' He looked about for support from one of the men but they were all making for the door. I stood over him, rather more close than was comfortable, and he reluctantly opened his ledger, beginning to scribble.

Nottingham and Uncle Gilbert offered to walk with me to my chambers, but Cecil interrupted, 'I should like that privilege, if the Lady Arbella will have me.'

Nottingham looked over for a sign of my assent. I nodded, thanking him and my uncle for their kindness, curious as to Cecil's motive behind this false gesture of amity.

We walked in silence for some time until eventually he spoke. 'I sincerely hope you will make a sensible choice of husband, My Lady.'

'What do you mean by that?'

'He shuffled his hands, dipping his head in faux obsequy. 'Marriage is for this life and the next. It is wise to be sure you choose someone . . .' He paused, appearing to be seeking the correct word. 'Suitable.'

'Suitable, you say?' I wondered if he suspected something,

he had spies everywhere, after all, but reasoned that if it were the case then surely he would have raised it before the Privy Council. 'I believe *you* once sought my hand.' I knew he would not want to be reminded of the failed bid he'd made to Grandmother for me once, as it was a minor humiliation, I supposed, and might have made him recall that he had none of his titles then and was overreaching himself. Such a thing would have mattered to him. 'Do you think you'd have been a *suitable* companion for me in this life and the next, My Lord?'

'Things are different.'

'Yes, you have gone up in the world,' I said, presuming him to be implying it was I who had gone down.

But when he replied, 'And you will always be a princess of the blood, My Lady,' it became clear what he was getting at.

'Which makes my choice of husband state business.'

'Yes, indeed!' He was straightening his cuffs again and I saw clearly that he couldn't bear the fact that I had been given, incontrovertibly, the right to make such a choice. 'I feel sure you will choose wisely and avoid any' – he paused to clear his throat – 'any covert papists.' The suggestion of a threat slid through to his surface and I perceived something of what had given him his reputation for ruthlessness. Essex at his trial, the rumour went, had said of him something to the effect that he was a wolf in sheep's clothing.

'A papist! Perish the thought.' I laughed, enjoying the fact that he was so far off the mark. 'The King forbade it.'

'Your aunt, Lady Shrewsbury, attends Mass quite regularly, I'm told.'

'As does the Queen,' I said. 'My aunt makes no secret of it.'

'No,' was all he said in response and we fell into silence once more until he added, 'You may not believe it but I do have your best interests at heart.'

I didn't answer him. His attempts to intimidate me were falling on deaf ears, for my mind was taken up with the thought that Will and I were free to wed and with the King's blessing, whether Cecil liked it or not. As I allowed that thought to percolate I felt light and free and entirely unburdened.

My mood must have shown for Cecil said, 'You seem most content, My Lady. Perhaps you have someone in mind already.'

It was not quite a question, though I sensed he would have liked an answer, and I realized I was at liberty to tell him, to tell the whole world if I cared to. But I preferred to keep it to myself, simply smiled with a slight shrug.

As his hunched figure receded down the corridor I was filled with a sense of my own potency. I had triumphed over them all; my future was in my own hands and I would have my husband with his Tudor blood, like mine.

Clerkenwell

Hal is back again for a few days' leave and those weeks of silence, so distressing to Ami, have become vague and distant. He is repeatedly playing a scale on his pipe, each note pitch-perfect.

He stops a moment, pipe hovering, to say, 'I'm proud, you know – to have a mother like you . . . a teacher, a writer.'

'You couldn't be as proud of me as I am of you.' There is little to compare with the joyous feeling that has come with seeing her boy set on a path to fulfilling his dreams. It makes her think of Lady Arbella, who had so many false starts on that road. How greatly she lacked a mother, with everyone around her trying to shape her for their own benefit. Ami had known so little of the obstacles her friend had encountered at every turn. It is rare to truly know another; there is so much of a person kept hidden in the secret pockets of the self.

She has been writing fervently, trying to capture the ebb and flow of that life in verse, feeling profoundly, as if she is living it herself, the heartbreaking disappointments and then the moments of victory, pouring elation into her. She has re-read Lady Arbella's account, back and forth, over and over, until, as if from a process of distillation, the verse floods out of her.

> In a battle of wits, her tongue is a sword,
> As she reclaims her future, word by word,

'Oh, I forgot,' Hal says, jolting her from her thoughts. He gets up to fetch something wrapped in a cloth from amongst his belongings, presenting it to her. 'One of those pies you like so much. We can have it later for supper.'

She can't help thinking of the pie-woman who refused her service last time she went to market. It had made her uneasy and she suspects Goodwife Stringer has been spreading nefarious rumours about her, labelling her a whore, or worse. She hasn't had the courage to return to market since, so Joyce has been running errands for her instead. She had made an excuse to herself that she was too busy but suddenly she feels the full force of her concerns.

'What is it; what's wrong, Ma?' Hal grips her arm.

'Nothing, absolutely nothing, really . . .'

'Tell me what it is.'

'It's nothing, just that Stringer woman. She's been making trouble.'

'Not more trouble; What sort this time? She always was a meddlesome piece of –' he stops short of the oath.

'I think she suspects me of casting spells, or something.' As Ami explains, she finds she can't quite articulate the havoc Goodwife Stringer has wrought in her, with all her pretend advice and sham friendliness; it seems quite benign in the recounting.

'It sounds as if you've let your imagination run away with you.' He smiles and seems so unconcerned that she finds herself quite reassured, puts it down to living alone. Perhaps the pie-woman was just distracted on that occasion; perhaps it was nothing to do with Ami at all. 'She's just a busybody.'

The tabby jumps on to the table and begins sniffing at the pie. Hal picks her up, saying, 'Wouldn't you just like some of that, puss? Well, it's not for you,' before dropping her back to the floor and cutting himself a slice of bread from the loaf Ami made for his arrival.

Ami finds herself laughing. 'Glad you talk to the cat too. I'd begun to fear Goodwife Stringer would overhear me chatting like that and believe I was conversing with a demon.'

'I don't know a soul that doesn't talk to their animals. They can't all be communing with the devil.' Hal is laughing too now and all those fears that had been building up disperse.

'Where's the honey?' he asks as he slathers butter thickly on the bread. The sunlight falls over the sculpted contours of his face. Ami watches him, transfixed. Only a mother can be this fascinated by the ordinary actions of her offspring. She reflects too that a month ago there would have been no butter and that makes for an additional satisfaction.

'Top shelf,' she says, standing to reach up for it; but it is not there. 'That's odd.' She is trying to remember when she last used it – when little Peter was sick, she thinks.

'I expect one of the children put it somewhere. Never mind. This bread and butter is so good it doesn't need it.'

She has the fleeting sense once again that someone has been in her house unbidden, but dismisses the thought. Hal is right; it's probably only one of the children.

'Here, have some.' He hands her a slice, which she takes, sinking her teeth into its yielding surface. 'You always did make the best bread.'

They eat in silence for a while, enjoying the peace.

'I forgot to tell you, Will Seymour says he'll visit next month. He's away at present.'

'Next month!' The memory of his blast of rage forces itself on her once more and her guilt catches like a spark in tinder. She wants to tell Hal to make some kind of excuse, to put Will Seymour off. But, like the extraction of a rotten tooth, she knows this confrontation is one she cannot avoid. She reassures herself with the fact that Will Seymour has been kind about her, that he instigated Hal's return and at least he will be able to tell her what provoked such a change of heart.

She will have the opportunity to ask his forgiveness – that is a reassuring thought. It is possible, even, that he will be able to shed some light on the absences in his wife's story.

She has trawled the papers for clues but has continued to find only silence. It is *her* forgiveness Ami craves, with the same species of hopeless yearning that a lover has for the unobtainable beloved in a sonnet.

They hear someone calling her name outside. Hal is on his feet, unbolting and opening up the door with Ami behind him.

'Joyce.' She is glad to see the girl, had wanted Hal to make her acquaintance properly. 'Come in. We were about to eat. Have you eaten?'

Joyce makes a tentative step over the threshold. She is looking at her hands, which are clenched.

Hal makes a little bow: 'A pleasure to see you again, Miss Mansfield.'

Ami smiles inwardly, watching Hal's feathers fluff up.

'It's Peter!'

Only then does Ami realize that something is not right, Joyce is too pale and has a haunted look about her.

'What is it, love?' She puts an arm around the girl but finds her stiff and unyielding.

'The Lord's taken him.'

'But . . .' Ami can't make sense of it. 'He was all better.'

'He took a turn and . . .' She cannot seem to get the words out. It doesn't matter anyway, how he died, just the hard fact of it.

'Oh no, poor dear boy. Poor, poor you.' Silent tears course down the girl's face. Ami takes her in her arms.

'Ma sent me to tell you. She said she knows how fond you are . . .' Her voice cracks. 'How fond you were of him.'

Ami is thinking of that eager little boy, a sponge for knowledge. What a cruel world it is that would cut off his life before it has even begun. 'And the baby? The baby was sick too, wasn't she?'

'The baby's fine. It's just P-P–' It is as if she can't bear to say his name.

'I think we should walk you home.' Ami, without letting go of Joyce, pulls a wrap down from the hook and nods to Hal to come with them.

The family is at prayer when they arrive and Mistress Mansfield quietly invites them to join in. Her eyes are red and swollen. Ami has only seen her at church, they have never spoken, but she is warm as an old friend. Ami shrivels inwardly on thinking that she even considered, however desperate the circumstances, sleeping with this woman's husband.

'I know you did so much for him,' she is saying. 'He spoke of you all the time.'

She leads the way into a chamber and there he is in his box. Ami can feel her tears welling at the sight of that coffin, so impossibly small it might be a carton of oysters. His face is grey and pinched and he is wearing his best suit of clothes. She can hardly bear to look, ransacks her mind for an explanation, but some things simply can't be explained.

Whitehall

As I arrived in the Queen's chambers a sudden hush fell. I knew, by the weight of the silence, that the truncated topic of discussion had been about Will Seymour and me. Since my triumph before the Privy Council two months before, I had become indiscreet, feeling it mattered little if people knew we were courting. The gossip was inevitable, particularly given I was thought such an unlikely candidate for romance, and of course our difference in age provoked, if not quite scandal, then a good deal of curiosity.

But I still harboured a secret; what wasn't known was that since Candlemas, ten days past, we had been formally betrothed. Will Seymour came to my chambers, got on his knee, and before witnesses – Dodderidge; Bridget; Crompton; Margaret; and a Seymour cousin, Mister Rodney – promised himself to me and I to him. It would be disingenuous to say that I was not aware of the political implications of such a match; but in that moment my mind was not set on politics; it was set on liberty.

It is true, the watchful part of me was well aware that one can never know which way the wheel of fortune will swing when it comes to the crown. So perhaps, as I made my promise, I held a minuscule hope for a turn of that wheel, even if only for the royal child we might eventually have produced, but we never talked of such a thing. Was it implicit in our actions? I cannot say and nor can I speak for Will, though he did whisper, 'Sometimes I wish you were not of royal blood, so you would know I wed you without aspirations.'

'You do not think my blood defines me, then?' I'd asked.

He didn't answer. There was no answer to that. 'But your youth makes you seek ideals.'

'I'm not so young that I do not know my own mind.'

I did not point out that age could bring with it *less* clarity of mind. What was clear, however, was that ambition was not foremost in either of our thoughts on that day, for everything was pushed to one side by that engrossing desire, which had us in its clutches. I cannot remember the circumstances that melted our witnesses away, leaving the pair of us, my finger adorned with a pointed diamond, alone in a chamber with a bed. All clear memory has been clouded by the intensity of feelings as our two bodies collided, laces hastily loosened, clothes pulled up and aside. Giving way to my bestial nature, I could never have imagined the blissful sensations to be found therein, increased and stirred by the fact that we teetered at the edge of sin. There was a moment when William faltered, saying, 'Ought we not wait until we are truly wed?'

'A betrothal is good enough in the eyes of God,' I breathed. There would be no waiting. You cannot postpone the tide.

'Come and sit here with me, Lady Arbella,' said Lucy Bedford, shuffling along the bench to make space. 'Tell me, are you looking forward to tomorrow's masque?' She must have seen my hesitation, for she added, 'We see so little of you these days.'

'You know how I like a quiet life and my books.'

'Not an entirely quiet life! No more *noli me tangere*, from what I hear,' said Jane Drummond, causing the Queen to laugh and say she was glad to see I'd been enjoying myself for a change. Her smile seemed entirely genuine. There was no guile with Queen Anna; that was part of her charm and perhaps also the reason her husband was so disenchanted with her. He may not have appreciated an educated woman but a woman with a sharper wit might have turned his attention away, occasionally, from his beautiful boys.

I was drawn into a game of cards, wagering pennies I could ill afford, though the bright beacon of my imminent inheritance had made me more relaxed about such things. The four of us played several rounds of primero. Quick, deft Lucy Bedford won each game.

'Another round,' said the Queen. 'So I can gain back my losses. Your turn to deal, Arbella.' She passed me the cards. I began to peel off my gloves to better shuffle them. 'Is that a new ring?' She had hold of my hand and was inspecting my finger. 'A diamond. A good one too.'

'It looks like a betrothal ring,' said Jane Drummond. As the words left her mouth the three of them fell silent, all gawping my way. I cursed the hot blush that meant I was going to have to give them an explanation.

'Are you betrothed?' asked Lucy. 'To Will Seymour?'

From the side of my eye I thought I saw Jane Drummond swipe an index finger across her throat but when I turned her way she had both hands folded in her lap.

'A little romance is harmless enough, but a *betrothal . . .'*

'I have permission.' They were all aware of this but I felt I needed to remind them because doubt was printed all over their faces. 'Any British subject.'

'But *Seymour,'* said Lucy. 'He's so young.'

'I don't think it's his youth that causes concern.' Jane looked at the Queen for confirmation of this.

'I think you both rather suited, with your shared love of books. And you have seemed so well of late.' Queen Anna was twisting her pearls round a finger, which reminded me of Grandmother, despite the kindness of her words. I felt myself wither slightly. 'I hope the King is of the same mind.' She looked at me with something akin to pity. 'He knows, I presume.'

'I have not sought to hide the fact.' My face began to burn again, for that was not entirely true. Perhaps I ought to have given notice of my betrothal.

'And Salisbury?' interjected Jane. 'What does *he* think?'

'He has long been my champion. I have his blessing.' I don't know why I continued to lie when they all suspected Cecil was no great friend to me, unless it was convenient to him. Perhaps I believed that in the saying of it, it might somehow be rendered true. 'We intend to live a quiet life away from court.'

'Away from court!' exclaimed Lucy Bedford, as if I'd said we were to go to the frozen wastelands of the north.

'We are not all as ebullient as you,' said Jane Drummond. 'I think that sounds like a good idea.' But I saw her swap a brief look of concern with Queen Anna.

I began to feel unbalanced, as if the floor were listing like the deck of a ship in bad weather. I drew my gloves back on, hiding the evidence, and began to deal, fumbling with shrouded fingers. 'Lay down your wagers,' I said. My voice was thin.

There was movement at the door and one of the King's ushers entered with a couple of pages in tow. The Queen sighed, as if she'd been disturbed in the middle of important business. 'Yes?'

'I have a message of summons for the Lady Arbella.'

The company of women fell silent once more; a group of girls across the room dropped their needlework and began to gape. The rustle of fabric as Lucy Bedford covered her mouth with a hand seemed loud as thunder.

'Go with her, Jane,' said Queen Anna.

I stood. 'That won't be necessary.' I sounded curt and didn't mean to. I was grateful for her kindness but my prevailing thought was my need to appear impervious to what I was about to face.

Will was kneeling before the King when we arrived and various privy councillors were gathered. Prince Henry sat under the canopy of state beside his father and offered me a discreet half-smile as I joined Will on my knees. There was no smile from the King; his expression was more one of irritation. I thought perhaps he was still unwell, for his skin had a yellow tinge to it and the whites of his eyes were bloodshot.

I glanced towards Will, whose gaze was fixed on the floor. It struck me that we had the appearance of a bride and groom before a chaplain. His anxiety betrayed itself in the way he clenched and unclenched his jaw, making a pulse visible in his cheek. I wanted to touch him, to feel his flesh under my fingers, to tell him that I was strong enough for both of us. He couldn't bring himself to look at me.

'Perhaps you would like to explain to me why I have heard rumours that the pair of you are betrothed.' The King held me hard with his eyes. Cecil was watching Will closely and I wondered if he thought him the softer target.

'I would never seek –' began Will, but I spoke over him.

'I had Your Majesty's permission. Any loyal British subject.' The floor was listing again and I sensed nausea pressing at my gut. 'And without my inheritance . . .' I paused, took a breath. 'It is normal that I should seek a husband of similar standing.'

'Of *similar* standing, perhaps. Cousin, you are a woman of learning.' He said it with a look of distaste. 'But you seem to lack common sense in choosing to match yourself with a man of *royal* lineage.'

I found myself dumb, unable to find a defence.

'I smell foul intentions,' said Cecil. The group of councillors shuffled, Uncle Gilbert was struggling to hide his anger towards Cecil and I thought I saw the Prince throw a brief sharp look his way too. So the chamber was divided, clearly.

Will began again. 'I would never wilfully seek to disobey Your Majesty's wishes. I was of the mind that being nothing more than a younger son with little influence, there would be no impediment. It was I who intruded upon the Lady Arbella on Candlemas Day, with nothing in my thoughts but to raise my own fortunes by attachment to a lady of great virtue and honour. It was all my own doing, my own ambition. The Lady Arbella has done nothing, agreed to nothing. There is no betrothal, merely a statement of intention that can easily be undone.'

I wanted to shout at him, shake him, make him tell the truth, no matter the consequences. But I remained speechless, bewildered that he could so easily undo all we had by its denial. Was he trying to protect me? Was it out of fear for himself, I wondered, or for love for me?

'You say you *intruded* upon her on Candlemas,' said Cecil. 'And on what prior occasions?'

'That was the first time.' Will's reply was so steady, so emphatic. I hadn't imagined he could be so accomplished in perjury. But then again, it was *essentially* true; it had been the first time he intruded upon me – upon my body in a literal sense.

'And since?' It was Cecil again. He flicked sharply at some invisible fleck on his shoulder. Someone in the room was cracking their knuckles.

'Twice only, at Fleet Street and at Canon Row.'

I battled against a surge of impressions, the smell of our bodies together, the fleshly sensations, forcing them out of my head.

The King shifted in his seat with a groan. He met my eyes momentarily with a venomous look. I supposed he didn't like to be wrong, for he knew as well as I that he had given his permission for my betrothal, and most of the men who stood in that chamber had been witnesses to the fact.

A sudden shaft of sun pierced the February cloud, spilling through the window over my future husband and me. It would have been impossible not to see the pair of us haloed in glorious light. I wanted to cry out: *See, even God approves.* All at once I felt girded, determined to leave the chamber with specific and public consent for my intended marriage. Before I had the chance to form my appeal, Will began to speak.

'There is neither promise of marriage contract nor any other engagement whatsoever between the Lady and myself, nor was there any marriage intended' – I began to collapse inside. He was abandoning me – 'unless Your Majesty's gracious favour and approbation might have been gained therein. It was always our intention to obtain such approval before proceeding to any conclusion. I am Your Majesty's loyal and humble servant and beg your gracious pardon.' He stopped. I glanced over at him. The shaft of sun had gone and he was cast in shadow with a scrunch of fear between those sad grey eyes. His forebears were weighing heavily on him, I supposed, Katherine Grey haunting me once more. I knew what would happen next, knew well enough that with my cousin it was vital to stand one's ground and Will hadn't.

I opened my mouth to speak – an attempt to salvage some hope – but the King spoke first: 'And you, Cousin?'

I knew full well he wasn't asking for my opinion but was waiting for me to also beg forgiveness. I couldn't bear to do so when I felt I had done no wrong. His impatience registered in the tap of his fingernail on the arm of his chair. *Tap, tap, tap.* 'If Your Majesty is of the mind that I have erred, then I too –'

'No,' he interjected. 'A *full* admission of wrongdoing.'

Prince Henry flashed his father a weighted look and I had the momentary fantasy of a time in the future with that boy on the throne – he would give me my freedom, my inheritance, my marriage; I had no doubt of it.

I mumbled something to the effect that I was at fault, grovelled a little.

'That's more like it.' The King smiled freely, seemed genuinely pleased. 'If it was lack of funds that forced you into such a hasty match then we shall ensure something is done about that, won't we, Salisbury?' He turned to Cecil, who nodded in assent. 'Give it time, Cousin. There need be no great rush to the altar.'

I wanted to ask what he meant by that, whether it was a concession to postponement.

He continued, 'We understand that you do not want to wed beneath your station. A little time, that is all.'

A mote of hope settled in me. He held out his hand, I shuffled forward, stooping to plant a kiss on it and he ran his fingers over my cheek. His exhausted yellow eyes revealed a softness, kindness even. 'It's settled, then.' My gaze briefly met Prince Henry's and he made an almost imperceptible nod.

'You may take your leave,' stated Cecil. The ray of sun had shifted on to him, rendering the dense black of his velvet doublet denser still, making his chain of office gleam. I could tell he believed me defeated but *he* hadn't seen that indulgent look in the King's eyes.

Will and I stood and reversed a few steps before turning, as if in a dance. The door swung open and the guards let us pass. Will didn't say a word, not even out of earshot. He looked crushed. I wanted to take his shoulders and rattle him until he found his fight; I wanted to grab him and pull him into a corner, force myself on him.

We stopped at the top of the stairs. 'So,' I said. 'What now?'

'I can't.' He still wouldn't look me in the eye. My heart was being tugged at painfully as if caught on a nail.

'You can't what? Did you not hear him when he said, "a little time"?'

'You've misunderstood his meaning, Belle.'

'No! You are wrong. You didn't see the look in his eye.' But as I said it I began to question whether I had imagined that look, imagined the sympathy in my cousin's tone.

'I can't do as my grandfather did. Look what happened to Katherine Grey. I will not let the same thing happen to you.'

'I am *not* Katherine Grey. I am different; this is different. The King has two male heirs, two sons of his body; Elizabeth had none. It's not the same.'

'My family has lived in the wilderness for three generations . . .' His eyes were glossy with distress. 'I can't.'

'Have you forgotten your father was *desperate* to get us to the altar, at any cost?'

'But my grandfather –'

'Since when were you in Hertford's pocket?' I touched his hand but he pulled it away, a brutal gesture.

'I will not jeopardize your safety.' He sounded strong then, and stalwart.

He waited several moments for my response.

'Go, then,' is what I said.

What was I supposed to do, get on my knees and beg as women do in plays? Weep and wail, prostrate myself, threaten to take my own life?

Despair taunted me as I watched him descend the steps in silence. When he had turned the corner at the bottom, I whispered, 'But I love you,' understanding only then the preposterousness of such an emotion. Love was God's great joke on humanity, a means to reduce us to lunacy, chasing our own tails in its name.

It was that Seymour cousin, Mister Rodney, who came to my rooms later that evening, begging to see me. I refused him, told Dodderidge to say I was suffering from a headache, which I was – flares of pain and zigzags of light dancing before my eyes which necessitated lying in the dark.

'He comes with a message from Seymour,' said Dodder-idge. 'Insists that he has been instructed to deliver it in person directly to you.'

I jumped on the possibility that William had had a change of heart and felt a twinge of optimism.

I heard Rodney enter. 'Do you mind the dark?' I said, assuming Dodderidge had explained.

I pulled myself up but the throbbing in my head intensi-fied. Dodderidge, as if reading my mind, placed a large pillow behind me, which I sank back into, closing my eyes and pressing my fingers to my temples. 'Show me the letter, then.' I imagined Will's familiar handwriting: *I regret my earlier harsh-ness, dearest one . . .*

'It is not a letter, as such, but something to read out to you.' My optimism began to eke away.

'Would you like me to leave?' asked Dodderidge.

'For God's sake, no.'

I heard Rodney's footsteps traverse the chamber, the rus-tle of paper, and opened my eyes to see his dark outline tight by the window against a chink of light, where he had opened a crack in the hangings to read.

He cleared his throat and began – *Mister William Seymour has tasked me with conveying his thoughts . . .* I could take in only fragments: *prejudicial to your contentment . . . extremely dangerous to his safety . . . he humbly desires your ladyship to desist from your intended resolution concerning him.*

There was nothing familiar about the tone, nothing I rec-ognized of Will. 'These are not his words. This is Hertford. Tell me I am right, Mister Rodney.'

'I fear, My Lady, you are not. I watched Mister Seymour write them himself.' He sounded apologetic and I under-stood that the task he had been set was distasteful to him. There was pity in his voice. I didn't want pity. 'May I con-tinue?' he asked.

I wanted to say I had heard enough but I suppose I held a forlorn hope that there might be some note of tenderness in his message. The sliver of brightness from the window seared into my head, like a hot knife. I shut my eyes once more but the flicker of light and jabbing pain persisted. 'Go on.'

He resolves on his part to no longer trouble you with this matter and has no doubt that your ladyship will find someone more fitting to your station – I wanted to put my fingers in my ears and hum to shut him out – *whilst he will seek a meaner match.*

'More fitting to my station,' I whispered, not intending to say it out loud. 'I wonder who that would be, given my station is so elevated.' I was grateful for Dodderidge's reassuring presence but nothing, no one, could prevent my inner collapse.

Mister Rodney carefully folded up the paper, slid it out of sight in his doublet and stood waiting for my response. 'You may go,' I said. My voice was small.

'Is there nothing you wish me to convey to Mister Seymour, My Lady?' There it was again, the pity, making me prickle with anger.

'No,' I said, but then just as Rodney was at the door I added, 'Tell him that as long as he is Hertford's mouthpiece, his words fall on deaf ears.'

When he was gone I took my betrothal ring from my finger and gave it to Dodderidge. 'Take this to Cheapside and see what it fetches.'

Three months crept by with interminable sloth and it had become increasingly hard to wear a public face of forced jollity, when my inner world was in smithereens. I had expected the sense of loss to lessen in time but my devastation, rather than diminishing, seemed to burgeon as the days went by and all I had to shore myself up were the hunger pangs that I had once more befriended.

My health was suffering and I carried round an almost permanent feeling of nausea and faintness. Bridget was concerned. She tried to hide it but it was etched all over her and much to her frustration I refused to let her call for Doctor Moundford. She had started to pilfer cuts of white meat and manchet bread from the Queen's kitchens and pitchers of light broth, which she would try to persuade me to sip in small spoonfuls. I could bear none of it.

'Your costume for the masque has arrived,' said Bridget as I returned from a wearisome afternoon in the Queen's chambers. My heart guttered at the thought of parading myself before the entire court wearing the hideous garment lying on the bed. Every surface of it was cluttered with embroidery, rattling with pearls and shells and fingers of coral, layered with gossamer flounces, tailed with floating ribbons. It had cost what I paid Bridget for a year's service. 'You'd better try it on,' she added. 'In case it needs altering.'

'If only I could find a way to avoid participating.' I imagined all the eyes of the court on me, boring into me, mocking the King's spinster cousin in her gaudy outfit. *Mutton dressed as lamb*, they would whisper behind their hands, *Without mate and without estate.*

'It will only be for an hour, My Lady.' Bridget began to help me out of my clothes.

'It's never only an hour. There will be an eternity of feasting and dancing in its wake.'

'Could you claim illness?' She held up the costume for me to step into and began to fasten the skirts. 'It would not be a lie.'

'I must be there for the Prince's sake.' On the previous day Henry had been invested as Prince of Wales, the first in a hundred years. The crowds had been jubilant but the King had found it hard to hide his displeasure at his son's popularity. I'd

362

seen it in the tight set of his mouth. There had been a scuffle with some Catholic recusants after the ceremony – the old fear had returned a few weeks prior when a papist assassinated the French king, causing an invisible vapour of paranoia to seep once more through the corridors of England's royal palaces. But the masque was to be in the Prince's honour and to please that dear boy I would wear my costume, however ridiculous it made me.

'I don't understand,' Bridget said, behind me. 'This thing will not do up.' She was tugging the panels of my bodice. 'I gave the tailor your measurements, he can't have got it so wrong.'

'He must have muddled them with those of someone else.'

All of a sudden she gasped; I turned. She had both hands clapped over her face, only a pair of eyes, round with shock, peeping out above.

'What is it?'

'Mary, Mother of God.' She crossed herself and then repeated it, as if to be sure, and slumped on to the corner of the bed.

'Be careful,' I whispered. 'You don't want to advertise your faith at present. You never know who might have an ear to the door.'

'But, My Lady, you have missed your courses.'

'I don't know why that is of consequence.' I wriggled out of the costume, annoyed by her excessive response to a badly cut dress. 'I rarely bleed. You are well aware of that.'

'But the nausea and now this . . .' She pointed to me, standing there in nothing but my shift. 'How could I have been so daft; I should have realized . . .'

'You think I'm . . .' A little snort of derisive laughter escaped from my mouth. I'd always suspected the conception of children might be difficult for someone like me. I didn't bleed like other women, my body was different, sharp and formless, a hostile place to incubate an infant.

But slowly, as the first cup of wine brings a feeling of giddiness only after the second has been drunk, I began to see the truth of what she was thinking. All at once I became aware of my body, heavy through my feet into the floor as if the boards might bend under its weight, my breasts aching and swollen, my belly no longer that familiar convex landscape with its jutting escarpments but gently undulating. 'Oh God.' Harshly and silently I berated myself for my wilful ignorance and sunk down beside her on the bed. 'What will I do?'

'You must wed.'

Panic began to buffet me. I lay back and tried to fix my gaze on the button into which the bed canopy was gathered at its centre, as if it would hold me steady. 'If only –' I began but stopped. If only what? If only I had been a different person, had a different life, was not raised behind glass, was not that wooden puppet in the hands of a dead queen.

I could not regret giving myself to him, for those were some of the few moments in my life that rang true. I stared at the button, seeking an answer. 'The King said, "give it time". What do you think he meant by that?' I don't know what use I thought asking her would be, for I already knew he hadn't meant three months when he'd said 'time'. Indeed, what he probably hoped for was that with time my intentions would turn to another. He was not to know that I had already given myself to Will, all of me, body and soul, that I had let loose my bestial other, that it was too late. The watching part of me said: *I told you so.*

'I suppose that means he is not entirely against it.'

'Yes, Bridget!' I sat bolt upright. 'That's right – not entirely against it.' I reached over her for my writing box, took out a sheet of paper and uncorked the ink. Its vinegar whiff sent my stomach into a roll. I straightened the quill tip, dipped it and scrawled a note: *Come to me at once. It is a matter of the utmost importance, a matter that will change the course of both our lives.*

'Find Crompton or Dodderidge and ask that they deliver this in person to Mister Seymour.'

Bridget bustled off on her mission. I went to the window, opened it and took several deep breaths to calm my queasiness, surprised to see that everything was as normal out there when my whole world was in chaos. A man in a crumpled hat pulled a handcart piled with dung, a milkmaid balanced two buckets on a yoke, a party of young men, courtiers judging by their clothes, ambled by, stopping to watch the milkmaid pass. She blew a frond of hair away from her face out of the side of her mouth. One of the boys whistled. She walked on. The boy began to follow her, his friends geeing him up. She turned, milk swilling over the lip of her bucket, leaving a dark patch in the dust. 'Leave me be.'

'Just a kiss,' he said.

'My pa'll butter his knife in you.'

The boys laughed and walked away.

As I waited I was surprised to be visited by a tentative sense of hope. I could not be denied my marriage; it was God's will. If an infant had been planted in the hostile regions of my body then God's will was at work and my cousin would recognize such a blessing. Surely, he was more concerned with the fear of Catholic plots, of assassinations, than of his spinster cousin getting wed.

I thought of the infant sprouting deep inside, a miraculous thing – *a royal thing*, whispered the watching part of me. I understood fully then the power generated by two bloodlines commingling, and the danger of it, like saltpetre and flame. It was as if my life was opening up, offering a vista of my future and the future of the seed germinating in the core of my body. I imagined telling Will, the joy blossoming over his face, feeling his arms about me, his whisper in my ear, *My darling, Belle, I could never love you more than I do in this moment.*

I was beset, suddenly, by an all-consuming hunger. Bridget had left me a plate of bread and cheese. I fell on it, stuffing great mouthfuls into my maw, washing it down with small beer, swigged back straight from the pitcher, munching, chomping, relishing the tang of the cheese, my taste buds enflamed then soothed by the plain yeasty calm of the bread. The plate clanged to the floor, scattering remains, which I gathered on my hands and knees, ramming them into my mouth until every last crumb was gone. I was brought so low, I might have licked the matting and still hankered for more, looking in the anteroom to see if there were any leftovers waiting to be cleared away, ransacking the place, finding only a few sugar comfits forgotten in the bottom of a paper cone. They stuck to my teeth, cloyed in my mouth, filling my senses with a glorious sweetness.

I collapsed into a chair and succumbed once more to the familiar roiling nausea, which came in waves, regretting my rash episode of gluttony as each one crashed against me. I closed my eyes, taking slow, deep breaths.

The latch jerked me out of my torpor. And there he was, entering the room wearing the look, in his sad grey eyes, of a condemned man. I heaved myself out of the chair, wanting to meet him on a level.

'I shouldn't be here,' he said. His voice was hoarse. 'What is it?' He was trying to sound firm but I sensed the tenderness beneath his surface and knew I would not have to dig far to get to it.

'God has made up His mind for us.' I smiled and put my hand on his sleeve. He didn't pull back, but nor did he quite reciprocate, just stood still, not meeting my eyes, his inner conflict apparent in the rigidity of his jaw and the slight tremor I felt beneath my touch.

'What do you mean?'

'I mean we have made an infant – you and I.'

It seemed to take a moment to settle in. His eyes widened as if something had startled him, then he dropped like a dead weight into the chair and sank his face into his hands, murmuring, 'Oh Christ!'

'Look at me!' I snapped. 'Where are your guts?' He looked up and I slapped him smartly across the cheek.

He held his palm to his face in shock and then took my hands and pulled me down on to his lap. 'I'm so filled with shame. I wanted to defy them all and . . . but . . . I was afraid.'

'Shhh.' I stroked his hair and rested my head on his shoulder. 'It takes courage to admit one's fear.' I had heard someone say that once. 'It doesn't matter, for now we don't have a choice.'

'I thought I would die of longing for you.'

We were wed on the twenty-first day of June in my chambers at Greenwich Palace, making our vows in front of half a dozen witnesses – not a soul would be able to deny our nuptials and deem our offspring illegitimate.

The following morning I began to bleed.

Will believed he had dislodged our baby in the consummation of our marriage; no matter how I tried to convince him that no fault lay at his door, I was unable to pull him from his sorrow. For myself, I could not find a way to grieve for such an abstraction, a thing so small and invisible, nothing more than a clot, a thing that had served its purpose in bringing us together, a thing God had chosen to take back.

'There will be more infants,' I told him, and whispered stories of how our life would be, the children we would have, the home we would live in, how the gardens would grow and which books would adorn the shelves of our library. 'We have each other.' And slowly my husband emerged. His love for me made mine seem paltry but I loved him in my own way; I still do, very much.

Tap, tap, tap. The renovations continue beneath my rooms. My head swirls. I put my quill down on the desk; I have amassed a stack of written paper and wonder if anyone will ever be able to decipher my scrawl, blocks of it half scratched through, crossed out and written over, up into the margins, asterisks and arrows here and there for guidance. Am I the only one with the key that unlocks my inky marks?

Bridget is sewing quietly at the other window. I see her glances flick my way. She is concerned about me. I have lived with her long enough to interpret those looks. But of course it is not Bridget; Bridget is no longer with me. Perhaps I might stop telling my story at this point. It seems fitting for it to end in marriage – unless it is a tragedy, of course. What did Aristotle say about it?

I listen for Starkey but his whisper is very faint. Does he say, *Happy endings satisfy ignorance?* I don't know what he means. Beyond the window, on the lip of the opposite roof, a squabbling flock of pigeons has gathered. My hand is cramped from writing. I hold it up, fingers spread, smutted with ink. My wedding ring is loose; I have a sudden fear that it might slide off my finger unnoticed and fall between a crack in the boards. I take it off, kiss it and cache it away in my bag of treasures.

When I look back on that time at Canon Row, the spell they call the honeymoon, the cocooned time before our marriage became public, I think of it as my moment in Paradise.

Clerkenwell

Ami's thoughts keep returning to Lady Arbella's baby that never was. Had she not been carrying that child, it seems clear that the marriage would never have been. Was it God's intervention? she wonders. But there is so much she cannot find a way to understand about the mysterious actions of God – little Peter's death, for example.

The vicar had rolled out the usual excuses at the funeral; how it is a great fortune to be called on by the Lord so young, to be one of the chosen few. Ami had her doubts about that, just as she had her doubts about God's intervention in Lady Arbella's marriage, given the ultimate outcome of that event. The usual precedent for such stories of misery is the trials of Job, but Ami refuses to see Lady Arbella's relentless adversity as a test of faith; it seems to her too convenient an explanation.

It occurs to her that such thoughts, not exactly doubts, but a questioning of the Scriptures certainly, would make her even more the subject of market gossip were they voiced aloud. Her mind swirls around ideas of how to depict the absence of that infant. She reads the scrawled fragment once more, the text spiked with unexpressed sadness: *an abstraction, a thing so small and invisible, nothing more than a clot.*

She writes a few lines of verse but screws the paper up, tossing it aside, standing and picking up her wrap, with the intention of taking some air to clear her head. But as she opens the door Goodwife Stringer is upon her, pushing her with some force back inside.

The woman shuts the door and stands, feet apart, back to it, looking at Ami with what can only be described as disgust.

'What in heaven's name are you doing?' says Ami, her outrage simmering.

'There are one or two things you need to explain.'

Only then does Ami notice that several other people are outside, looking in through the window like ghouls.

Goodwife Stringer's arms are folded firmly over her bosom.

'I don't have to explain anything at all to you,' she says, wishing to God that Hal was still about, but she supposes that Goodwife Stringer has waited for his departure to make this confrontation. She stands her ground, despite the fear filtering up her body.

'As a friend . . .' The woman's voice is smooth with insincerity. 'I feel I have to warn you.'

'Warn me about what?'

'The Mansfield boy that died. They are saying it was the work of the devil.'

'For pity's sake! Who is saying such a thing? The poor child was sick.'

'What's this?' Goodwife Stringer is inexplicably crouching to pick something up from the floor and Ami realizes, with a jolt of dread, that it is the scribbled verse about the miscarried baby, which could so easily be open to misinterpretation.

In silence the woman opens up the paper, casting her gaze over it.

Ami's heart thuds.

'What does it say?' she asks, and Ami realizes with a gush of relief that of course she can't read well enough to decipher it.

'It is only a rather poor piece of verse.'

Goodwife Stringer lets the sheet float back to the floor. 'And how do you explain this?' She rummages in her apron and pulls something out.

'My honey jar!' Ami exclaims. 'What are you doing with that?'

'Do you think me a cretin? This is no honey jar.'

'Of course it is.' Ami is in a tangle of confusion. She can hear the people outside murmuring. She prays for Hal's return but he won't be back until late, for he has a performance tonight.

'You dosed the boy with this.'

'Yes, to soothe his throat. He was suffering from the croup.'

Ami steps forward to take the jar and it slips from her fingers falling, breaking open, golden honey seeping out over the dirt floor. They both stand in silence, looking at the mess, until Goodwife Stringer says, 'You know as well as I that it's a witch bottle.'

'What in heaven's name is a witch bottle?'

'They said you would deny it but everyone knows you have bewitched Mister Mansfield and seen to it that the boy died because of what he knew of your wickedness.'

'This is utter madness.' Her mind is flailing as she realizes that the force of imagination can make invented things appear real, and if enough people believe it then it will be so. Goodness knows, as a writer, she should be aware of that. She can't help remembering the poor woman hanged as a witch a few weeks ago, how all the locals had been thrilled by the occasion, and is suddenly cold to the bone.

She looks up to see Edwin Mansfield standing in the open door and others behind him, neighbours, people she recognizes from the market. Panic begins to take hold.

'Edwin,' her voice is pathetic, pleading. 'Tell her she is wrong.'

But Edwin turns tail and is gone.

They came for Will first. There were two of them, whom I knew vaguely from court. They were polite, as if it was a social visit. Will offered them French wine from his cellar, which they accepted. We sat around the table and Rodney poured it out into the glass drinking vessels. He'd had to wipe the dust from them, so rarely were they used. They were all smiling and making light conversation but I was aware of the number of henchmen outside, more than would be normal for anything but an arrest.

'Why have you come?' I asked, not caring if my baldness was rude.

'The Privy Council would like a word with . . .' – he looked back and forth between Will and me – 'your *husband*.'

Will stood, saying, 'Let's go, then,' seeming, thankfully, uncowed by what he was to face.

Rodney helped him on with his boots and cape and they were gone, their wine barely touched. From the window I watched them mount their horses and leave. I stayed there pressing my skin against the cold glass, hoping against hope to discover that some mistake had been made. I waited for several hours, just me and my watching self, refusing to move until Bridget prised me away and into the bedchamber.

I lay awake all night, with each sound: horses passing, the rumble of a cart, the bark of a dog, giving rise to hope and leaving grim disappointment in its wake. I lit a candle and unfolded the square of parchment containing that lock of stolen hair, bringing it to my nose in an attempt to capture the ghost of his scent. Time crept until eventually the cock started to crow and the servants began to bustle about, a boy was whistling in the yard and the cook was banging pots below.

Just as I was dressed they came for me. I didn't make any pretence, just got my things, asked Crompton to tell the groom to ready Dorcas and Dodderidge to take care of Ruff. How simple a dog's life is. If I had the chance to come back I would choose to come as a dog.

I don't remember the route we took, can barely remember being up before the Privy Council, only that they wanted to know why Will had denied we were wed.

'I can only suppose he was afraid,' I told them, and gave specific details about the ceremony: who witnessed it, which chaplain married us and held out my hand so they could all hum and hah over the ring. The King seethed as I defended my husband and both Nottingham and Uncle Gilbert looked desperate with concern. I knew there was nothing they could do to help me.

The King said: 'Mister Seymour will have plenty of time to ponder on whether it was a wise decision to defy Us now he is in the Tower.'

I flinched inside but would let nothing show on my exterior, just fixed my gaze on my glowering cousin to show I was not afraid. I noticed on the faces of the Council that none agreed with the King's harsh response to my marriage. Even Cecil looked apologetic and dipped his head sympathetically as he told me: 'You are to be taken into the custody of Sir Thomas Parry, at Lambeth.'

'Not the Tower for me, then?' My tone was glib. It didn't suit the occasion and several of the Council looked at me with pity. I remembered hearing that when Katherine Grey was in the Tower, and Hertford held there too, they contrived to spend time together, must have bribed the guards, and conceived a second infant there. I supposed my cousin was ensuring such a thing did not occur again. It seemed my life was unfolding in a similar pattern to that ghost of mine whether I wanted it or not.

It was only then, thinking of Katherine Grey and the baby she had birthed in the Tower who was the father of my husband, that I thought of that sprout of a child Will and I had made and truly mourned it. All at once my emotions were coming at me like musket fire and I felt a shortness of breath as if the floor might be suddenly pulled out from under me. I wanted to tell them that we had wed for that infant but couldn't bring the words to the surface.

Cecil approached as I was being led out. 'I'm sorry,' he said. I wanted to ask if he was sorry for everything: the betrayal that took my throne from me and gave it to another, for his duplicity, or just for failing to persuade the King to offer me lenience on that day.

'Your apology is worth little if you cannot shore it up with action,' I said with Grandmother's voice. He seemed downcast. Perhaps he felt guilty; I hoped so.

It was Nottingham who took my arm and guided me down the privy steps to the pier. 'I'm so very sad it has come to this, my dear. The King had made his mind up. There was nothing I could do.' He helped me into Sir Thomas Parry's awaiting barge.

Nottingham looked old; he *was* old, I supposed, he had already seemed ancient when he'd taken me under his wing at the trial in Winchester seven years before. Seven years in the purgatory of court.

Uncle Gilbert rushed down to the pier just as I was embarking. 'I will petition him,' he said, breathless from running. 'I'll get word to your aunt too. We will do everything we can.'

I looked out into the water, watching the oars slap and suck, thinking of William downriver in the Tower, imagining what might happen if I slid into the depths, whether my clothes would be heavy enough, clogged with wet, to drag me under. If it had been winter I might have gone quickly, my body paralysed with cold; but it was July and balmy, the oarsmen were singing and people waved, doffing their caps to see Sir Thomas's barge go by.

My first thought on arriving at Sir Thomas's Lambeth house was to get word to Will. I knew that Mistress Lanyer used a laundry maid who was occasionally employed at the Tower in some capacity; she had mentioned her once as being a magician with ink spots on linen. With this in mind I hoped she might be able to find a way to get my letter through without arousing suspicion, for any letter sent by the usual channels would be sure to be read. Of all the people I knew, I believed Mistress Lanyer had sufficient mettle; moreover, she was not part of the court, no one would think to question her.

I wrote a short missive to Will, telling him where I was and insisting that he did not lose faith.

> . . . *I will appeal to my cousin and you must do so also. Hold hope that we will be reunited before long.*
> *Your ever-loving wife, Arbella Seymour.*

A little splinter of defiance burrowed its way into me on writing my name thus. I folded my letter inside a note of explanation for Mistress Lanyer and asked Crompton to deliver it to her in Bishopsgate.

'You seem more buoyant than I might have expected, given the circumstances,' he said.

'My cousin only wants to make an example of me. That is all.' I said it, and it was what I believed, but there was that other part of me, a darker self, the self without hope, who had imagined being swallowed into the wet jaws of the Thames only an hour before.

My letter found its way to Will, for there was a reply in my hands even before Bridget and Margaret had unpacked our things.

Thank the Lord to have news of you, my dear sweet wife, and to know that you have not sunk into despair. Your word has invested my desolation with a glimmer of light.

Do not worry yourself on my account, for I am not under close guard. I have pleasant rooms, Rodney is with me and I have the run of the courtyard gardens and frequent visits from my brother Francis.

I shall petition His Majesty on both our parts, appeal to his belief in the holy institution of marriage. You may well be right in saying he only intends to make an example of us and will give us our liberty if we show sufficient humility and remorse. We must have patience, my love.

I live only for the moment that I can be in your sweet company once more. Your faithful and ever-loving husband, in this life and the next, W. S.

AD 1610 on the ninth day of the month of July

Summer gave way to autumn and my hands became cramped with writing letters of appeal. It was as if the forward trajectory of my existence was to ever be frustrated, with time folding back on itself, back to the Hardwick of 1603 and my pleas to Elizabeth, begging her clemency. The King's pity was not forthcoming and Queen Anna, though she privately supported me, regretted that she could not disobey her husband. But I held on to the last vestiges of my hope.

Other letters passed up and down the Thames, from the Tower to Lambeth, which were surely passed over by Cecil's eyes. They contained the banal details of our health with exclamations of affection between husband and wife and little more. But they served to conceal another correspondence, secret missives, sent with the help of Mistress Lanyer, in which we plotted our escape.

Will would contrive to substitute himself with another. He would receive a visit from his brother Francis, whom I had never met. They would swap clothes; he would slip out in plain sight and take a barge to Lambeth, where we would spend the night together. I drew a plan of the house marking the best route to my rooms and told him the shifts of the gatekeepers, which ones liked to doze off after a shared flagon of ale. I was not tightly guarded. Everybody knew that, like my husband, I was too easily recognized to make an attempt at escape. It was all mere fantasy, a fiction with which we buoyed our spirits, but it was a dangerous fiction and those letters were to be burned on reading.

The days became short, the hours of light truncated and the lonely nights stretched out unbearably. I lay awake, acutely aware of the passage of time, my life passing unused, as if I were a splendid suit of clothes never worn, left to fade and become food for moths. I sat often at the window, fur-wrapped against the winter chill, watching the moonlight on the river and the dark silhouettes of the boats slipping by, like barks on the Styx. I talked to my ghosts, to the Scottish Queen and dear Starkey and Katherine Grey. *How was it*, I would ask them, *in the moment you met your end? Were you afraid?*

On one such night I saw a small craft slip up to the bank that abutted the gardens, not to the pier but another place hidden in the rushes. I heard a whistle then a response, a slight rustling, the faint crunch of steps. I felt my breath catch in my throat, as my imagination grasped at things – the whisper and click of a door below – and then nothing, just the usual night sounds, the creak of the old house breathing and the distant shouts of the rivermen. The door to my chamber sighed and there was Bridget, confusing me, as I'd thought her asleep in the truckle bed, lighting a candle from the embers of the fire. Will was with her.

'I thought I'd surprise you.'

I stood and reached out my hand, expecting it to pass right through him, but it met with the woollen surface of his cape and then with the warm ungloved flesh of his fingers.

'How?' I whispered.

'Francis is asleep in the Tower. It was easy . . . almost too easy.'

'Your brother Francis?'

He nodded. 'We are uncommonly alike.'

My first thought, even before thoughts of love, was of escape. 'Let's flee now. Take a boat upriver . . .' But as I said it I realized that there was nowhere to go in England where we would not be found, unless we were to live out our days in a priest hole.

'Come, Belle. We must not lose hope of the King's mercy. You said it yourself: in time he will give us our freedom.'

'But if we need to, it is good to know –' I stopped myself, as if saying it might curse things.

'Good to know, yes. But we will not need to.'

I was then beset with a pressing concern. 'But you will have to return. How will you get back in without causing suspicion?'

'Vex not, Belle' – I was unaccustomed to being the one who needed reassurance and it occurred to me that Will's imprisonment had made a man of him. 'It is all planned. Mistress Lanyer, what a woman she has turned out to be – such resourcefulness. She will meet me in the morning and we will go in together with the laundry cart. I will pose as my brother Francis and she will be a woman come to bring me fresh linens. The laundry is the means by which your letters come to me.'

'What if –' I began, but he silenced me with a kiss.

Every night I yearned for his return but he didn't come. The risk was too great and if we were to ever gain clemency from my cousin we had to be seen to be compliant.

I knew before the month was up that we had made another infant. I recognized the symptoms that I had so wilfully ignored on the previous occasion. I ate ravenously, so much so that Lady Parry began to comment.

'Goodness, anyone would think you were eating for two,' she said at the dinner table one day. 'You shall have to curb that appetite once advent is upon us.' She was a twitchy, bird-like woman who, I could tell, didn't like the warmth with which her husband treated me. Hers was a frosty demeanour that paid correct respect to my status but little else. She picked at her own food in a manner I recognized, eating almost nothing yet giving the opposite impression.

I noticed Dodderidge's eyes shift about the chamber and wondered what he knew, whether Bridget had told him something, and felt a prickle of panic. Had the fellow who mans the jakes seen Bridget emptying out the pans of morning vomit? Had Lady Parry's seamstress noticed the inserts Margaret had sewn into my dresses?

My gluttony had been noticed; it was only a matter of time before everything else became apparent. It struck me then, something I had refused to entertain, that the end result of my condition would force some kind of change upon the King. But what that change would be was impossible to know. I didn't dare write to Will with news of it, for fear of the letter falling into the wrong hands. What could he have done anyway, save fall to despair?

As time went by, and the curious looks of the Parry household became hard to disregard, the impossible nature of my situation began to crystallize, casting shadows of doubt where there had been such a sense of optimism only weeks before. I stopped eating, rediscovering my own discipline, as if I could overcome my condition that way. It created a strange competition with Lady Parry.

'Here, My Lady,' she would say, passing a great dish of sweetmeats my way. 'These are most delicious.'

'No, no. You first, I insist,' was my reply, in the full knowledge that etiquette dictated she do my bidding. I watched her take one and nibble at its surface. If you'd seen her expression you'd have thought it poison, not sugar.

'Delicious,' she said through tight-drawn lips. 'Will *you* take one?' She held the dish towards me.

I looked at the confections, coloured like an array of summer fruits, impossibly pretty. 'I think I won't.' Her distress was my triumph – surely no one could compete with me when it came to the resistance of temptation.

It was a desperate attempt to arrest my body's disobedience, its unbidden swelling, its new unwanted plumpness, and in my lucid moments, which became increasingly few and far between, I understood that I was treading on the very lip of my sanity. It alarmed me greatly when I thought that only death would see me out of my situation – that thought lurked permanently in the shadows.

With hindsight it was inevitable that my harpies would return at a time of such great fear and vexation. And so they did, with their ruthless pecking and the excruciating pain, the delirium and the fever and my waters red as wine. Bridget called for Doctor Moundford, administering the familiar tincture while awaiting his arrival. She was as well acquainted with those harpies as I and knew the only respite from them lay in that cordial which loosed me entirely from reality.

By the time I was sent up before the King to account for the rumours that I was carrying an infant, I no longer was. Though I only knew it was so because Bridget told me. When

I began to bleed, she said that I was so loosed from my sanity I couldn't tell the difference between my waters and the blood.

That second loss confirmed my belief that my body was not well designed to harbour an infant safely. *Was it too cold*, I asked myself, *too sharp, in there?* I barely felt the pain of it then – perhaps I was afraid to give vent to my weakness even to myself – but now the anguish over those lost babies is manifested in a profound and unrelenting wretchedness.

Tap, tap, tap. Perhaps it is my babies knocking.

'So, Cousin,' said the King, 'what can you say about all this talk?'

I could barely hold myself upright and begged for a support. Someone dragged over a prayer stand. I knelt and imagined for a brief moment that I was before God.

'I am not with child,' I said, knowing only that I was free from the sin of a lie, unable to make sense of anything else. The Privy Council appeared as a host of angels and I believed myself delivered from life; but then I found I was back in the barge with the bitter winter wind cutting through my coat and the ice-cold water flicking from the oars on to my face, pulling me out of my dreams.

Clerkenwell

Silence wells, thick and sticky as the honey that creeps from the broken jar. The tabby sniffs at it, taking a tentative lick. Goodwife Stringer raises her eyebrows as if to say: *There is my proof.*

Ami's mouth is dry, her tongue swollen, and even if she knew what to say in her defence she isn't sure she would physically be able to speak. Whatever she did say wouldn't be believed; that is clear as day. There is no space for the truth in this small room that is becoming ever smaller, the walls closing in.

She wonders where Edwin Mansfield ran off to – to fetch the vicar or the constable? Her imagination casts her into scenes of being lynched by the crowd of ghouls outside.

She waits for the woman to make her move, wondering what had ignited her suspicion in the first place, rummaging around for reasons, when she knows full well that conclusions can be drawn on the most spurious of excuses. Was it the fact that she defended Eve in her poetry, poetry that Goodwife Stringer has never even read? Was it her perceived morality based on her past, or the simple fact that she was different from the other women in the parish, that she was educated and so they couldn't place her tidily in their scheme of things? She is one of life's misfits, like Lady Arbella.

The gathering outside mumbles on like some kind of Greek chorus.

All at once a great rage ripens in her, handing back her voice. 'What do you intend to do with me, Goodwife Stringer?'

'It will be for the magistrate to decide.'

'And you will be content, I suppose, when you have seen an entirely innocent woman on the gibbet for sorcery. When it comes to Judgement Day –'

'Don't talk to me of Judgement Day,' she barks and Ami can see she has hit a weak spot, for the woman is flustered, reddening and breathing uneasily. But it is only a moment before her composure is restored.

A figure appears in the doorway. It is Joyce; Edwin is with her, hand in hand and following behind are Mansfield and his wife, babe in arms and the other children, like a clutch of ducklings in their wake.

They all crowd in.

'How I am glad to see you, Mister Mansfield.' Goodwife Stringer is simpering, impressed by this man who started as poor as the rest of them, yet has become wealthy by his own hard graft.

Mansfield is an example to them all. *Not like me*, thinks Ami, who has slid down in the other direction.

'This woman has brought terrible misfortune on you and your family,' she continues, 'and I am glad to tell you that justice will be meted out on her.'

'Misfortune, you say?' Mansfield takes a step towards Ami, who shrinks back. He takes hold of her upper arm. *I am done for*, she says to herself, preparing to submit to whatever horrors she is about to face.

There is the ghost of a smile on Goodwife Stringer's lips.

'It's true misfortune *has* visited our family, in the death of our little lad. But it's not in the shape of Widow Lanyer, who's done nothing but help us.'

Mistress Mansfield speaks up now; she is a small woman but has dignity and poise and projects her voice clearly through the room. 'She cared for our boy but God chose to take him back.' She also comes to Ami's side and, hitching the baby on to her hip, takes her hand.

'She's bewitched you all.' Goodwife Stringer appears genuinely distressed and turns to the people in the window. '*You* can see it, can't you?' she says to the gathering. 'They've all been enchanted.'

But the crowd looks away, clearly uncomfortable, and one utters, 'I'd say you're mistaken.'

'Widow Lanyer is teaching our children their letters,' says Mistress Mansfield. 'She's a woman of education, a published poet, yet humble enough to take in laundry, break her back earning an honest crust. And *you* would seek to condemn her. Shame on you!' She stands to her full if inconsiderable height, pushing her chin up. 'I'll tell you this: my husband sought to seduce her – yes, he confessed as much to me on bended knee, full of shame – and Widow Lanyer sent him packing. If *that* is what you call enchantment, then it's you whose mind is skewed.'

'My wife speaks the truth,' says Mansfield. 'I was weak, which I deeply regret, and I truly apologize to both these good women here.'

Beyond the window there is a murmur of approval.

'But that is a witch bottle.' Goodwife Stringer points at the broken vessel. 'See the spells written on it . . .' She sounds less sure of herself.

'How d'you know? You can't read,' comes a voice from outside.

'It's just a jar she found in the house when she moved here.' It is Joyce piping up. 'Filled with honey. Look.' She crouches down to dip her finger in the remains of the jar, bringing it to her mouth.

'I'd say you've nothing but rumour and supposition to go on,' says Mansfield. 'It is busybodies such as you who bring shame on our parish.'

Someone laughs outside. It is the pie-woman from the market. 'Gone too far this time, ain't you.' There is a general muttering of agreement amongst the gathering. 'I reckon the magistrate'll have *you* up for making trouble, put you in a scold's bridle, that'll stop your tongue.'

Goodwife Stringer visibly crumples, losing her shape. 'I'm sorry,' she murmurs into her collar, unable to meet any of their eyes. 'It seems I was mistaken.'

Later Ami finds a pie has been left for her on the window sill and with it a basket of fruit and a jug of ale. Joyce reappears at the door.

'Come and sup with me, dear,' Ami suggests. 'The pie won't keep in this weather, it's far too much for me alone and Hal will have eaten already.'

Joyce bursts out with, 'Fa's come round! He says I can learn my letters but he won't pay for it, says I'll have to offer to help you around the house or something instead. He's shelling out enough for the boys, he said.'

'Oh, Joyce, this is wonderful news. I'm sure I can find some things for you to do. It won't be long before you're proficient enough to help me with the little ones.'

'Do you mean it?' She is beaming as if she's just learned she's to marry the heir to the throne rather than skivvy for a tutor.

'Of course I mean it. Now help me get that pie on the hearth to heat.'

'I'd like to learn some Latin,' says Joyce, beginning to lay the table, hiding her face behind her hair as if she's embarrassed to admit such a thing.

'Anything is possible,' says Ami, 'if you set your mind on it.'

It makes her think of Will Seymour, who swore he'd never be able to forgive her but seems to have done so. Has he really, though? She will know soon enough.

To Barnet

'The Bishop of Durham,' I said. 'Durham House is only a short way across the river. I'm sure I can see it from my window.' I felt lighter.

The little of importance I had learned from my most recent audience with the King was that I was to be moved from Parry's care. I had envisaged a journey, a rustication, and had worried about travelling when I was still so unwell, not to mention the idea of a physical distance opening up between Will and myself, to thwart my fantasies of a joint escape. So over the river to Durham House felt like a reprieve.

Parry, his head tilted in pity or something like it, replied: 'No, My Lady, the bishop is to take you to Durham in the north.'

Rain thrummed at the windows and a shutter banged. 'The *city* of Durham?' It was twice as far as Hardwick; that was all I knew of the place. You couldn't be further from London and still remain in England.

'The rumours of your, your' – he looked uncomfortable and was stuttering slightly – '. . . your previous . . . um'– mumbling now: 'condition' I think he said, 'makes His Majesty feel it would be cir-circumspect to ensure you do not have further opportunity to see your, your husband.'

What do you *know?* I thought, holding on to the shreds of lucidity. *Has someone here made you aware of that night visit? Did you pass it on? Or was it your wife?*

'Condition? There was no "previous condition".' My lie was unfaltering. 'I have been unwell, that is all. I remain so.' I stopped. Parry looked rueful and I felt a little sorry for him, being set a task that he clearly found repugnant. 'I can't think why His Majesty is so afraid that I might make an infant with my husband, when I am kept here and he in the Tower.'

'It is a case of mitigation.' Parry seemed not to know what to do with me. He pulled a ring on and off his finger repeatedly. He would be glad to see me gone, I felt sure, if only to relieve himself of the responsibility.

'Besides, I don't know why he thinks an infant of mine such a danger to his throne when he has three heirs of his own body.'

'I suspect it is since the French King was assassinated last year.' The ring fell to the floor. He stooped to gather it. 'He fears plots.'

'But Durham?' The distance of the entire country would certainly be an effective barrier to conception, but I also knew there would be no return. I would go there and be forgotten. It would be as if I were dead.

I remembered the Scottish Queen and her years traipsing between my stepfather's houses in the north as Elizabeth's prisoner. Had Elizabeth hoped *she* would be forgotten? I felt the air about me thin, had difficulty breathing.

'I question the legality of my being held indefinitely without trial. I have not been accused of a crime; I have not committed a crime.'

'I'm sorry, My Lady,' he said, heaving out a sigh. 'I'm sorry to have had to be part of this.'

'So you agree, then, Parry, that it is not legal?'

He looked at me, shrugging minutely, and said quietly, as if afraid to be overheard, 'You might write to the Lord Chief Justice.'

'I will. I will demand to be tried and, as I am entirely innocent; they will be obliged to free me.' I was already composing the letter in my head. 'My husband too. It is right, is it not, that we are innocent?'

He closed his eyes and lowered his head before lifting it

again slowly, which I took to be a gesture of agreement. 'I have instructed your servants to make you ready to leave next week. Hopefully the weather will be better. The bishop will accompany you on your journey north.'

'And a consignment of guards, I don't doubt.' I didn't seek to hide my scorn. 'In case there is an army of Catholic insurgents waiting to convert me and make me their puppet queen.' I felt trapped in a life that travelled in circles, always arriving at the same point, ad infinitum.

'Yes . . . I mean, no. You will be accompanied, yes, but for your safety.' He seemed embarrassed, slowly shaking his head, and put the ring back on his finger. He was a decent man at heart; perhaps he didn't agree with my banishment. 'But you may take your immediate household, your maids, your steward, your doctor.'

My first thought, before writing to the Lord Chief Justice, was to get word to Will, and once Parry had left I penned a letter explaining the plans that had been made for me.

. . . But I will endeavour to thwart them, so await my word, for I will NOT go to Durham – not if I have the power to prevent it.

I sounded more optimistic than I felt.

I am insisting upon a trial, for we have done no wrong. It is not within the law to hold us without a formal accusation. Make yourself ready, my love. Your wife, Arbella Seymour
On the twenty-eighth day of February – AD 1611

As the days passed and nothing came from the Lord Chief Justice I began to sink back into despair. Crompton and Dodderidge tried to distract me with chess. Crompton let me win, thinking it would please me, but I was furious, in a manner that was out of all proportion.

'If *I* win it will be on my own merit,' I shouted, swiping at the chess pieces with my forearm so they spilled over the floor. 'I am not a child to be indulged!'

Crompton's apology was effusive and authentic, provoking my shame. How could he have known his misplaced gesture would infantilize me, render me voiceless. I felt my only means to make myself heard was to continue scrawling out letters. I wrote in desperation to anyone I could think of who might be able to help me but my pleas in the best part went unanswered.

Uncle Gilbert's efforts to petition the King were equally ineffectual. A letter from Aunt Mary – a small ray of hope – arrived via Crompton, in a packet of embroidery silks:

If it comes to it, we will get you away – and your husband. You must do everything you can to make your progress slow once you are on the road. I am raising funds; I have already sold some of the Scottish Queen's fine needlework, which fetched an exorbitant price – all the Derbyshire papists regard such things as relics and if those few bits of needlework can serve you they are well dispensed of. Do not write to Gilbert of this, indeed tell no one, not even your close household, not for the moment. Your loving aunt, Mary Shrewsbury.
   March, the second day, in the year of Our Lord 1611

My illness, which had been slowly receding, made a resurgence as the date of our departure neared. Doctor Moundford and Bridget became increasingly concerned for my welfare, tutting and muttering at the foot of my bed like a pair of magpies. But in my lucid moments I insisted upon continuing to scribble out pleas, which Dodderidge transformed into a legible state in his neat secretary hand. The act of writing, however futile, felt somehow life sustaining.

The idea of Durham had become in my mind akin to the idea of death – the two places, each as abstract as the other, were pressed up together so tightly that not a sliver of light was discernible between them.

The Bishop of Durham arrived just after dawn. On first seeing him from the window of my bedchamber I had thought him to be dressed in purple robes, the full regalia, but I must have been delirious because I saw, as I approached him across the hall, that he wore black travelling garb. He had a small face that was lost in an ample beard and sharp eyes that gave little away. His manner was not exactly terse but it was tidily clipped and had nothing of Parry's undeniable warmth.

My appeals to have my case heard in court had fallen on deaf, or at least reluctant, ears, for still no reply from the Lord Chief Justice had materialized. There was nothing to do but commence the journey north with the fading hope that something might change. My ever-diminishing prospects lay with Aunt Mary. I waited in my chambers longing for the arrival of a messenger or something at least that might delay our departure. Nothing came, but I clung to my hope.

I entered the hall, barely able to walk unaided, propped up on Doctor Moundford's arm, my pain dulled by an assortment of tinctures. The bishop's annoyance at having been kept waiting was palpable, despite his attempt to hide it beneath a mask of formality. Neither could he disguise his shock on seeing me; it was there in the slight intake of breath and the widening of those sharp eyes. Until then I hadn't considered how my illness might have ravaged me, I hadn't thought to inspect myself in a mirror, but realized I must have appeared horribly gaunt and I could feel the film of cold perspiration over my face and the flush of fever beneath it.

After our greetings were made he said, 'There is a litter awaiting you at the Westminster pier, My Lady, furnished with cushions and well curtained from the wind. I was informed that you might be too unwell to ride.'

The mere thought of rattling about in the back of the litter increased my feelings of dread. But I wouldn't allow that vague spark of hope to be doused. I thought of Will, down-river. What was he thinking; was he too was quietly negotiating ideas of escape?

Once over the river I was dismayed to discover that the bishop intended to travel in the litter with me.

'I should like my women to join us,' I said, perturbed at the thought of being alone with him in an enclosed space.

'I really don't think –' I could see I had upset his carefully aligned plans with this request. 'I must insist –'

He was trying to speak but I continued. 'I'm not entirely sure it is appropriate that I should travel unchaperoned. I know you are a man of God but . . .' I left my words hanging and watched as somewhere beneath his voluminous beard he pursed his mouth and I assumed he was weighing up whether it was a battle worth fighting. I wondered if he was having regrets about assenting to the task he had been set in becoming my jailer, though it was likely he'd had no choice in the matter.

After a long pause he said through gritted teeth, 'As you wish, My Lady.'

It was just as well Bridget was there, for we had barely reached London's northern outskirts when the motion of the coach had become too much for me and were it not for her swift intervention, shouting for the driver to halt, I might have spewed all over the bishop's sumptuous black travelling habit.

This happened several times, with Doctor Moundford insisting on each occasion that we stop for half an hour for him to administer to me, until the bishop's patience was demonstrably threadbare.

'I really don't think she is well enough to be making such a journey,' muttered Margaret to Bridget more than once. Though I was feeling abysmal I recognized, through the miasma of my nausea and the excruciating pain in my side and head, that some advantage might be gained from my poor condition, for at the rate we were progressing, a decade would pass before we arrived in Durham.

Darkness began to close in long before we reached Barnet, where it had been arranged that we would spend the night. We had only travelled as far as Highgate and a decision was made that we should stay there, so lodgings were hastily secured. I was unable even to walk myself to the door and the bishop, clearly exasperated paced up and down as Doctor Moundford carried me upstairs to a bedchamber, where a maid was hurriedly changing the linens and another was laying the fire. They both turned and gawped, dropping hastily into curtsies. Someone must have told them the King's cousin was arriving, though judging by their expressions they had not expected such a miserable creature.

Memories of my time at Highgate are vague but I was aware of the bishop and Doctor Moundford in a heated altercation beside my bed as to whether I was in a fit state to travel. The bishop crumbled under Moundford's insistence but after some days, in which, shattered with pain I drifted in and out of awareness, the bishop came to me and announced that our journey was to recommence on the King's order.

'It'll risk her life,' said Bridget under her breath. The bishop must have heard, for he looked momentarily stricken, revealing at last a glimpse of conscience.

I had to be carried back to the litter for another excruciating journey. Six miles took the best part of a day and we didn't arrive at the Barnet inn until early evening. Bridget and Margaret, horrified by the flea-infested pallets, insisted on all the bedding being changed and so the innkeeper's wife, a loose-faced woman with a large bosom, hadn't a shred of good will towards us.

The following day Moundford firmly refused to let me travel further and at some point one of the royal physicians arrived with orders from the King to ascertain whether I was fit to continue the journey. I remember clearly the look of horrified fascination on the doctor's face as he inspected my waters – his brow furrowed, his head shaking slowly from side to side.

The doctor's report must have convinced my doubting cousin, for I was allowed a month at Barnet to recover my health and a house was commandeered for our use. We were all thankful to leave the infested inn but it meant another agonizing leg of the journey, though happily only of a mile's duration. The bishop left us there, to go on to Durham and prepare for my arrival, or so he said, kissing my hand and smiling. It was the first smile I'd seen from him. I supposed he was greatly relieved to be passing the responsibility for me on to another for the time being.

That other was Sir James Croft, an affable man who was to prove quite well disposed to me. I received him in the bed-chamber, where I lay propped up on a heap of pillows, drifting in and out of consciousness, with my guardian angels Moundford and Bridget standing one at each bedpost. Margaret sat quietly sewing in the corner and Crompton and Dodderidge hovered by the window, beyond which a cherry was in full blossom, wavering in the breeze, torturing me with memories of happier days at Sheen.

My recovery was slow but steady, though we kept news of my revival within my close circle. Crompton procured, as if by magic, letters from Aunt Mary. Arrangements were being made to get me to the Continent with my husband. In addition to the Scottish Queen's needlework, she had sold some jewellery but needed still more funds and had to raise them without Uncle Gilbert's knowledge. His position on the Privy Council might compromise him, she said, and force him to reveal our plan. She asked whether I had anything of value that might be sold. I had little: a few jewels, mostly paste and inferior metals, some rather second-rate pearls, but then I remembered the glass vessel I had chosen from Grandmother's things.

Dodderidge brought me the casket in which it had lived for the three years it had been in my possession. He untied the binding and lifted the lid. It was the straw packing, I suppose, that smelled suddenly of Hardwick, those acres of matting that had infused the house with the permanent scent of late summer. I was back there, with that old cloistered feeling, the sense that I was waiting for my life to begin somewhere beyond those vast, cold windows.

'Oh dear!' said Dodderidge, bringing me back to the bedchamber and its view of the tormenting cherry tree.

I peered in to find amongst the straw only a few slivers of glass. It seemed impossible that a thing so large could have been reduced to such a sparse quantity of matter. Its form was imprinted on my memory, the great balloon of a belly, nothing but air encased in a thin skin of crystal, balanced on a delicate shoe and tapering to the top then flaring out into that almost invisible lip. But of course its beauty lay in its fragility, the fact that it was made of almost nothing. I picked up one of the shards.

'Take care,' said Dodderidge.

I was imagining running it up the soft part of my inner arm where the blue filigree veins sit close to the surface, wondering how it would feel. Would the blood gush out of me? My heart jabbered and my breath grew short; I was held in suspension like a sight hound with his eye on something in the undergrowth. *You could take your life back, make it yours,* whispered the part of me that watched.

There is no honour in taking your life through hopelessness, whispered Starkey; *it is not sufficient reason. You have done nothing wrong.*

'Here, let me . . .' Dodderidge gently prised the fragment of glass from my fingers.

I met his gaze firmly. 'You don't think I was . . .'

'What a shame' – he was changing the subject, ever tactful – 'it was a valuable piece, would have fetched a fair amount. There are always your pearls, My Lady.'

I asked him to bring them to me. Holding them, running them through my fingers, reminded me inevitably of Grandmother's great clattering strings. Mine were paltry in comparison; some small as seeds and threaded on knotted silk to make them stretch further.

'We wouldn't get much but it would be better than nothing.'

In the end it wasn't necessary to sell my miserable pearls as Aunt Mary sent word that a windfall had come her way. She refused to mention by what means.

Clerkenwell

Ami is reading back through Lady Arbella's papers again. The words press close about her: *I trusted her.* Not trust but trusted; the past tense seems to speak volumes, makes her feel choked. There is another invisible narrative between its lines: her own side of the story. She remembers so well slipping letters for Will Seymour in between the folds of his clean linens. She remembers the fear she felt, but also the exhilaration, carrying the basket through the gates of the Tower for the first time.

Will Seymour has sent word of his visit. He is coming in a few days. She wonders what he will think of her two small rooms with a dirt floor; the thought continues to nag that, despite what Hal has said, he is still angry. A little knot of apprehension has tied itself in her gut. Perhaps she would rather he were angry; perhaps she thinks she deserves it.

Even in the Tower Will had been surprisingly bright and full of verve, when she had delivered the letters. He was determined to find a way to be with his new wife and talked about her in the most tender of terms. Ami had been so very glad that Lady Arbella had found such a devoted man. They all truly believed then that it was only a matter of time before the couple would be free. People talked about them, of course they did, it was a scandal to set the tongues wagging. Most believed the King should simply let them be, they thought him cruel.

Ami had found Will Seymour transformed from the callow youth who'd made her introduction to the Prince. He had filled out, was muscular and tall, with an air of authority.

396

Lady Arbella was right in saying his incarceration had made a man of him.

It was surprisingly straightforward getting him in and out of the Tower. He wasn't kept as a close prisoner; that would have been an impossible challenge. He had the freedom of the Tower environs with just a curfew at dusk, and even that was laxly observed. The guards all played cards with the prisoners, making wagers, drinking beer, and you'd have been forgiven for thinking them all comrades together.

Between them they – Will, Francis, Mister Rodney and she – worked out the easiest way to ensure that William could visit his wife without mishap. She knew the exact times of all the daily deliveries. The firewood cart came first, the laundry cart a little later, after the butcher, mornings and evenings, regular as clockwork. The lieutenant insisted on the laundry being delivered all at once to diminish the comings and goings, despite the fact that most of the prisoners had their own laundresses. They all had to gather at the gates and wait for the cart to go in together.

It all felt like a bit of a game. She remembers Will, in his brother's clothes, turning up heavy-lidded from lack of sleep and haloed in contentment, after his visit with his wife. They walked back in together and not a question was asked. It had been just the same when he'd left on the previous evening.

It is strange to write herself into her verse. But there she is emerging from her own pen. She cannot shy from the truth of her part in it all. It is a confession of sorts.

Hal comes crashing in wearing a broad grin.

'Where have you been out so early?' she asks.

'Oh, here and there.'

'Anyone'd think you had a secret sweetheart with all your here-ing and there-ing lately.'

'Don't be silly.' Hal settles down to fitting a new reed on

his pipe and Ami begins to clear up her papers before her pupils arrive, contented in this calm little bubble of family.

'Listen, Ma, I've been thinking,' Hal says a few minutes later, 'why don't you open a school?' But Ami's mind is elsewhere, caught up in other thoughts.

'Ma, are you listening? Did you hear what I said?'

'I'm sorry, my love, I was . . .' She pulls herself back from the vortex of the past.

'I said, why don't you open a school? You've already turned away half a dozen new pupils in the time I've been home. If you had more space –'

'A school?' she interrupts, 'Oh, I don't know.' In her head she begins to run through all the reasons why it is not a good idea: an expensive lease; the responsibility; the fear of more debt.

'It makes perfect sense.' He pauses to look at her directly. 'Give me one good reason why not.' He brings his pipe to his mouth and blows, testing the new reed.

'I'm too old.'

'Ma! Firstly, you are not too old, you're forty-six and seem a decade younger. Plus your age is in your favour; you have accrued wisdom; that's a good thing in a teacher, isn't it?'

'Things are manageable as they are, Hal. I'm earning enough and so are you.'

'You could get away from that woman.' He leans his head in the direction of Goodwife Stringer's house and raises his eyebrows.

The idea suddenly sounds more tempting, though Goodwife Stringer has been conspicuously scarce lately. 'I suppose I could look into it.'

'I have a confession to make.' He's grinning now, that look he used to give her as a small boy, when he wanted something.

'Oh yes?'

'I made a few inquiries and there's a building near St Giles-in-the-Fields that might suit you.'

'St Giles, north of Convent Gardens?'

He is nodding. 'Close enough for your present pupils to walk there and far enough to get away from that busybody.' He points a finger at the far wall.

'But I'll never raise the money for the lease.'

'Surely Father . . .' He hesitates. '*Your husband*, left enough —'

'It's not quite like that.'

'What do you mean?' He is sitting stock-still, pipe aloft, awaiting an explanation.

'Alphonso left us without a penny. He lost everything and more.' The minute the words are said she wishes she could retract them. The instrument slips from his fingers and falls to the floor with a clatter. He doesn't pick it up.

'Why didn't you tell me?' His expression moves from aghast to angry, making the threat of tears suddenly prick at her eyes. She cannot bear another estrangement from her boy, just when all was so well. 'Another lie!' he adds bitterly, dropping his elbows to his knees and slumping his chin on to a fist.

'I didn't want you to worry; didn't want you to not go to court out of duty to me.'

He stands abruptly and picks up the pipe, putting it on to the shelf, not looking at her. 'How can I trust anything you say?' He then begins to put on his boots and coat.

'Don't go,' she pleads. 'Let me explain.' She gets up and grabs his sleeve but he shakes her off.

'I understand! You didn't want me to worry. You seem to think I'm still a child and not capable of dealing with the realities of life.'

She lets him go. There is no point in trying to get between him and his anger, and her pupils will be here soon anyway.

*

Once the children have gone for the day she goes out to see if she can find Hal, fearing he might have returned to court, but she reasons, surely not without all his things, without his instruments, without at least a goodbye.

She searches through the market where the stallholders are packing up. Out in the backfield she can see Dill, Birdy and the others folding the day's linens. Her hands are completely healed now. Suddenly Salisbury is in her head: *Not the hands of a laundress, are they?* A new uneasiness falls over her and she finds herself suddenly caught up with imagining some disaster has befallen her boy, convinced it is God's punishment for her past failings. She circles round, towards the vast shape of the church, bathed in golden evening light, its spire soaring up.

Her uneasiness is unfounded for there Hal is, sitting in a splash of sun on the church steps – with Joyce. They are deep in conversation, the kind of intense attention to one another that forgets about the existence of all else. Ami feels a frisson of joy at the sight of them and slips away unseen, not wanting to interfere in something that seems so intimate.

Not long after she gets back home, Hal returns. There had been a momentary storm, sudden glowering clouds, pelting rain, thunder, and he arrives soaked to the skin. 'I needed a bit of time,' he says.

'I know, sweetheart. I know. Listen,' she says, taking both his hands, 'I am so sorry, sorry I kept so much from you, treated you as if you were still a child.' She hesitates, watching water drops glisten and fall from the dark tendrils of hair around his face, before adding, 'Sometimes it can be difficult for a mother to see when her child has grown up – difficult to let go.'

'It's all right, Ma; I understand, I really do – needed a bit of time to think, that's all.' He smiles that wonderful lightning-bright smile and Ami's agitated heart settles.

'I've been thinking of ways to raise the money for the

lease,' he continues, stepping away from her to shake the water out of his hair like a dog. 'I might be able to get a loan from someone at court. Villiers perhaps, even.'

'You want to be careful of what he might ask in return,' she replies, teasing slightly. 'Villiers likes a beautiful boy.'

Hal laughs. 'Really, Ma!'

'Goodness, how silly I have been,' she exclaims as a thought alights. 'Wait!' She rushes to the stairs, climbing them two at a time.

'What is it?' calls Hal, following her up.

When he enters she is crouched down by the bed lifting one of the floorboards. Amongst the dust and mouse droppings she finds the small package where she left it. She unfolds the old linen wrapping and holds out her open palm to him. In it is a stone the size and colour of a raspberry, set with three suspended pearls.

'Been keeping it for a rainy day.'

His fingers hover over it.

'Take it, it won't bite,' she says. He carefully picks the jewel up and holds it to the light. He turns back to her, puzzled. 'The Queen gave it to me. A consolation of sorts when I was dismissed from court.' She pauses, taking a breath. 'There's something else I haven't told you.'

He is silent, and looks away from her abruptly.

'It is only partly true that I was sent away for offending the King with my verse. Lord Salisbury – he was the one with all the influence in those days. Salisbury learned that I'd aided a prisoner escape the Tower.'

'Ma!' He looks horrified. 'Who?'

'It was Will Seymour – an innocent man who should never have been held.'

Hal's look transforms to one of wonder. 'But I've heard of the story of Seymour's escape; it is well known.' He meets her gaze. 'It was *you* who helped him?'

'Not me alone, of course.'

His shoulders begin to shake and he brings his hands to cover his face. He is laughing, 'Well I never . . .'

Relief floods through her; sharing her secret is a burden halved. Sometime she will tell him what really happened that day, but this is not the moment. She takes the jewel from his hand and slips it into his pocket.

'Take it to Cheapside tomorrow; see what you can get for it. *You* won't be fleeced if they know you work for Villiers. You're the one with friends in high places these days.'

Barnet

The days crawled by at the house in Barnet and, as I began to recover, my compulsion to write returned. I penned letters of thanks to the King for my month of respite, letters to Cecil, letters to Aunt Mary. Margaret and Bridget began to work on an embroidered woodland scene, so complex and detailed we swore they would never finish it. Still none of us managed to beat the deceptively doe-eyed Crompton at chess, though Doctor Moundford came close once.

Sir James was proving a lenient jailer; he joined us often in the evenings and as the end of the month neared he recognized that my recovery was fragile – I still could not walk the length of my bedchamber – so he went, with Moundford, to petition the King in person. As a result the journey north was postponed a further month. I took this to be a sign that the King was relenting, for he also allowed me a visit from Aunt Mary.

The blossom outside my window had all dropped by the time she arrived, dishevelled from the road, with mismatched gloves and birds'-nest hair. 'My poor dear sweeting,' she said as she sank beside me on the bed. 'You are so pale. Is Doctor Moundford taking good care of you? Are you eating properly?'

'Moundford is a wonder,' I replied. 'If it weren't for him and Bridget, I might not be here.'

'And Crompton, is he serving you well?'

'I don't know what I did without him. He's so discreet and painstaking with my accounts.'

'Yes. He's certainly very good with money.'

She seemed to be saying something else but I didn't quite

know what. Crompton did make my meagre income stretch, it was true. I was waiting for her good news from court; news that the King was mellowing, that Will and I would be released to live as husband and wife. Just the thought of it caused my heart to dilate. 'So the King?' I began. 'Will our penance soon be over?'

'I'm afraid not.'

'But I thought –' My expanding heart began to shrivel.

'No.' She looked at me and took my hands, speaking very quietly. 'The only answer is to get you both away to the Continent. I have begun to make arrangements.'

Strangely, through my desperation I felt a faint thrill. After all, I was not one to meekly wait for a pardon. All the talk of escape and raising funds had seemed only abstract until that moment. 'Is it possible?'

'Your husband is not closely watched. He has walked out of the gates before, I understand.'

I nodded.

'Anyway, Crompton has all that in hand. Now we must discuss *your* escape.'

'No,' I stopped her, 'I need to know everything. Firstly, what has Crompton got to do with all this?'

'He'd better explain for himself,' she said, before leaving the chamber to fetch him. Left alone, my head swirled with the thought of my freedom and I felt myself unfurl, my resolve reviving.

They returned together. Crompton pulled up a stool and began to explain the plan that he had concocted in respect of my husband's escape. 'I am having a black beard and wig made,' he said, 'and an ordinary suit of clothes. He will follow out the linen cart. Your Mistress Lanyer has proved most willing to help with this. She will take the suit in and accompany him out in plain sight. No one will be the wiser until it is too late.'

He cast those beguiling eyes over me and I wanted to ask him how such an angelic appearance could hide such a devious nature. Aunt Mary looked on, wearing an air of pride as if he were her own invention – perhaps he was, it was she who had placed him in my household.

'Mistress Lanyer's own laundress sometimes takes in washing from the Tower, so it will be easy to substitute herself with some excuse or other, as she has done before.'

'I don't want her put in any danger. It won't be –'

'Of course,' said Aunt Mary. 'Don't worry, sweeting, everything will be watertight.'

'Who will provide the decoy?' I asked. 'Last time it was his brother Francis. They are very alike I'm told.'

'Your husband is not keen to involve his brother.'

I wanted to ask how he knew all this about my husband; when he'd had time to visit him without my knowledge. But instead I directed my question at Aunt Mary. 'How long have you been concocting plans for me?' I was more curious than displeased. I truly believed Aunt Mary had only my welfare at heart.

'It is always vital to have a contingency in place.' I didn't quite know what she meant by that but Crompton had begun to talk again and the moment to ask for something more specific had passed.

'Your husband will feign a toothache to explain his absence about the place. His servant will make his master's malady generally known but *he* will believe that your husband is leaving only to spend a conjugal visit before your journey north.' He paused, opening his hand like a conjurer performing a disappearing trick. 'The smaller crime will hide the larger.'

'I don't understand,' I said. 'Why complicate things further?'

'Ah, My Lady of Shrewsbury asked the very same thing.' He turned to Aunt Mary for acknowledgement of this. 'You see, if suspicion is aroused or word somehow gets to the Lieutenant of the Tower and your husband's servant is questioned and, God forbid, a story squeezed from him, well,' he opened both palms to the heavens like a chaplain making a point in a sermon, 'a search will not be sent out. They will likely opt to await his morning return. Meanwhile, you will both be well on your way to France.'

Questions nagged at me but before I had a chance to work out what to ask first, Aunt Mary said, 'And you too will walk straight out of these gates. Sir James in turn will believe you are going to visit your husband in the Tower for the night on the eve of your departure to Durham.'

'What a pleasing symmetry of deceit,' I said, filled with incredulity. 'Sir James is a lenient jailer, but I don't think . . .' I began to realize that I knew little about anything. I had been so ill I could barely make sense of myself, let alone those around me. It was no wonder I had no awareness of Crompton's secret dealings.

'Sir James will be easily bribed,' said my aunt bluntly.

'I happen to know he is deeply in debt,' added Crompton. 'He's a gambler.'

'And he has a soft side. Bridget tells me he's a great romantic. He won't be able to resist reuniting a husband and wife for the night.'

Bridget, too? Was there anyone in my household who had not been party to this? 'Where will the funds come from?'

'You know I have raised a sum,' said Aunt Mary.

'Yes, but . . .' I was thinking of all the expenses that would be incurred. 'Bribes, boats will have to be paid for, horses, we must be able to pay our way in France . . .'

Crompton interrupted me: 'Three thousand – two hundred of that for bribes. I think two thousand eight hundred will be sufficient.'

'Good grief, wherever did you raise such a sum?' It was

the vast amount that made me believe that the whole thing might be more than a fantasy.

'You don't need to know,' said my aunt in a manner that clearly stated she would not be drawn on the topic.

The plan was growing in my mind, allowing me to access a reservoir of hope. 'But –'

'But what?' Aunt Mary's face was suddenly stern.

'I don't want Dodderidge involved in this. He suffered enough on my behalf the last time.' Bringing up that thwarted first attempt at escape all those years before made me feel suddenly heavy.

'You have my word,' she said, the stern expression melting away.

'And,' I added, 'the source of funding apart, I will not be kept in the dark about any of this.'

Crompton wore a half-smile and Aunt Mary nodded her agreement.

'I will remain abed.' I felt the plot twine itself around me, filling me with ideas, driven by the thought of being together again with my husband. The power of my desire would see me through this, I knew. 'As long as reports go back to court of my fragile condition there is less danger of being ordered north before we are ready. Also' – this had dawned on me from nowhere – 'when I leave this house I will wear a man's garb beneath my clothes.' I saw Crompton's eyebrows lift slightly. 'Once on the road I will be to all intents and purposes, a fellow, so if we are stopped it will be of no consequence.' I was remembering that time as a child when I had ridden bareback in breeches and felt a sense of everything being part of a pattern too great to understand as a whole, as if that childhood transgression had been a preparation for this. 'Will it be you accompanying me, Crompton?'

'Probably. Bridget too, I'd think, and Margaret. But all the finer details have yet to be carefully drawn up.'

He looked so utterly free of guile but a question rose to my surface. Bridget's involvement I understood, and Aunt Mary's and Margaret's, and to an extent Mistress Lanyer's, but this young man was an enigma. 'Why are you helping me, Crompton, when it is such a great risk?'

Without missing a beat he replied, 'I can't bear to see an innocent person imprisoned.' It seemed tenuous as an excuse but, given what I knew of his character, the obsessive adherence to logic that made him an unbeatable adversary at chess, it made a certain sense that he would not want to see something out of its proper place. 'And also I swore loyalty to you when I entered your household. I stand by that.'

Aunt Mary was smiling; I smiled too. *It will make you seem meek.* I smiled more widely and the list of Grandmother's rules to live by faded, drifting off into the air, leaving me feeling, if still feeble in body, then robust in spirit.

To Calais

It was Hugh Crompton's spare suit of clothes I wore beneath my dress as I walked out of the house in East Barnet on an early June afternoon, accompanied by one of the grooms. I bade goodbye to Dodderidge at the door, leaving Ruff in his care, promising to send word as soon as we were settled.

'You *will* take care, My Lady,' he said, his voice stumbling slightly. His eyes were filmy with age and his hair was all but gone.

'I'll send word as soon as we're settled, so you can join us.' He seemed unable to speak. 'I'm so grateful –' I began, realizing the inadequacy of those words in return for a lifetime of service.

'No need . . . I . . . I . . .' His long fingers hovered.

I took hold of them and pressed them to my heart saying, 'God bless you,' and we walked to the door together in silence.

It was a mile and a half's trudge to the inn where Crompton was waiting for us and, having spent the best part of three months in my bedchamber, I felt the effort greatly. But I gained strength from the thought that in a few short hours I would be safely away at an abbey in northern France with my husband, imagining the moment of seeing him in the Blackwall Inn that was our rendezvous. The idea of freedom had become so abstract it was impossible to conjure in my mind but I felt its imminence in the way one can sense a change in the weather.

If I was afraid I had no sense of it as we walked wordlessly along the grassy Barnet lanes, serenaded by birdsong and the bleating of lambs. The sensation of the breeches against my legs as I strode along invested me with a sense of potential, as if the world was mine for the taking.

Crompton was in the lane outside the inn and guided me into the deserted stables, shutting the door behind us, leaving the lad on watch outside. The smell of dung and horse reassured me – it was an honest stench. Dorcas greeted me in her usual way, nudging my shoulder, inviting me to scratch the mound behind her ears. Her muzzle was flecked with grey but she wore her age lightly and must have sensed my exhilaration, for she began to shake her head, raring to be off. 'Soon,' I whispered, 'soon, girl.'

'Here,' I said to Crompton, removing my cloak and turning my back. 'Unlace me if you would.' He didn't mention his awkwardness at performing such an intimate task but he held his breath as he untied me and then swiftly stepped away to make busy in a large bag in the corner, from which he pulled a spare rapier and belt.

My dress slid away leaving me in my doublet and hose, or more accurately Crompton's doublet and hose. I held out my hand to take the sword, buckling it about my waist, enjoying disproportionately the weight of it and the metallic rattle it made as I moved. He then passed me a wig of mousy curls, which I fitted on over my own hair. Dorcas watched on curiously. 'How's that?' I asked.

'Just.' He carefully tucked a stray lock of my hair beneath the wig and handed me a black hat to put over the lot.

'Will I pass?' I drew the rapier and thrust it into a hay bale, striding forward.

'You might carry yourself in a more masculine fashion, My Lady.'

I laughed then. 'You cannot call me that.'

'No, I suppose not.' Amusement flicked across his mouth. 'What, then?'

'Charles.' I didn't hesitate to give him my father's given name. 'Call me Charles Bell.'

'So, Mister Bell,' he said, suppressing a smirk, 'watch me and then do as I do.' He walked several paces along the stalls, legs apart, shoulders swaying, elbows slightly bent and hands half fisted.

I did as he did, finding my swagger as I moved, learning it as one might a dance.

'That's more like it, Mister Bell,' he said. 'We'd better be off. It is twelve miles to Blackwall, where the others will be waiting.' He and the groom led the horses out.

I rolled up my dress and stuffed it into one of the saddle-bags, tightening the girth strap, adjusting my stirrups, and led Dorcas out to the mounting block, stopping as I was about to swing myself up, grabbing Crompton's sleeve. 'Tell me this is true, that I am not dreaming.'

He turned those doe-eyes on me saying, 'It *is* true. You will be with your husband and away by nightfall.'

I felt a great surge of elation, a profound sense of something beginning, as a mother must feel at the birth of a baby.

It was inevitable that, as soon as I was mounted, astride, I would be catapulted back to the only other time I had ridden in such a manner, dressed in a man's breeches. The life I had only ever been able to understand as moving in circles, arriving relentlessly back at the same point, stretched out, became a spiral, moving on and up, revisiting the past differently each time, with a sense of progress at last. Dorcas responded to this new me with a flick of her tail and moved into a trot.

'I am Charles, Charles Bell,' I whispered over and over to myself, rising in the stirrups rather than being bucked up and down sitting to the side. How comfortable it was, moving, as if Dorcas and I were a single animal, through the lanes, lush and verdant and smelling of recent rain. Out on the heathland she lifted her head and without any girding, found a residue of strength in her old body, powering forward away from the others like a three-year-old. I tried to hold her back but she was having none of it and we were subsumed together by an overwhelming sense of velocity, our combined pleasure effervescing as an unstoppable force: a comet shooting over the sky, an arrow fired from a bow, a bird soaring, a lead bullet whistling towards its fate.

'I am Charles Bell.' My mind ran through the stages of Will's escape. He would be already dressed in his black wig and beard and the ordinary suit of clothes; word would be out that he had been laid low with a toothache; Mistress Lanyer was probably with him already, helping him dress; Mister Rodney would be in place nearby, with horses. I was already on the boat, could feel its rocking motion under my feet, and a laugh fluttered in me at the thought of how Will and I might appear embracing, both disguised as we were, like the King and one of his young men.

After an hour's hard riding we came over the crest of a hill and there was the Thames, an unrolled bolt of silver cloth, with a cluster of ships gathered about the little port at Blackwall. To the south, at the place where the river looped round, was the dolls'-house shape of Greenwich Palace containing the miniature King with his tiny court, all oblivious to the covert happenings a mile downriver.

Bridget was out in the yard at the inn to greet us. The place smelled of fish and water and escape. I slid down from Dorcas, feeling a wave of tired elation as my feet hit the ground. I handed the reins to the groom with instructions for her care. I kissed her velvet muzzle with its flecks of grey and whispered, 'See you soon, girl.' I refused to consider the possibility that we might not be reunited.

'He's not here yet,' Bridget said. She had the knuckle of her index finger between her teeth.

'Will?' A void began to open up in me.

'He's late.'

'He'll come, I'm sure.' But my certainty was far from robust and Bridget knew me well enough to see that. Neither could she hide her worry; it was there in the constant glances towards the road and the chewing of her fingernails. It was unlike Bridget to be so perturbed. But still, despite the hollow feeling, I could sense him pulling towards me like the tides, as if we were drawing together by the power of our combined wills.

The inn was dingy with low ceilings and mean windows stained dark from grime and tobacco smoke. Someone was playing a pipe in the corner, tapping his foot. Men were milling about; the oarsmen, I was told. They looked hardy enough to row us all the way downriver, through the night, to where our brig was waiting in the estuary.

The waterman introduced himself, calling me 'sir', scraping his cap from his shiny pate. This was a netherworld in which no questions were asked. But I was secretly pleased that I had passed so easily for a man at close quarters even if it was dark as midnight inside that inn. Crompton spread a map on the trestle and pointed out exactly where we were headed. I ran my finger along the curves of river bobbing with rudely sketched boats, to where it opened out, past Gravesend and Tilbury on, far, far on, beyond the village of Leigh, further still to where the river opened its jaws wide. Someone had drawn a crude sea-monster, a galleon and little triangular waves. Crompton pointed to a cross in ink. 'There is our brig.' That elation boiled up in me again.

'We must be mindful of the tides. We can wait an hour, an hour and a half at most. We'll be rowing all through the dark hours as it is,' said the waterman.

'He'll be here.' I had never felt more sure; I could feel him approaching.

Bridget led the way up to a chamber where Margaret was waiting. She smiled at me, tilting her head, looking up from under her lashes.

Bridget began to laugh. 'You thought she was a fellow. It's our Lady Arbella under that hat.'

Margaret reddened, mumbling a denial.

'Always did have an eye for the fellows,' I said, laughing, remembering that young girl who was so easily swayed by romance as I lay down on the bed with its greasy upholstery and listened out for the sound of horses arriving in the yard below.

'Take a little rest, My Lady,' said Bridget. 'We have a long night ahead.'

I was too excited to sleep. Each sound outside had me up from the bed and at the window. 'He is coming by land, is he? And not by water.'

'By land, I think.'

The window on the other side gave on to the little port, a few ships out in the deep water, a curve of pebbles with a few upturned craft and a pier where two small boats were tied. One was stacked with luggage; I recognized my trunks and one, in a distinctive red tooled leather, I knew to be Will's. I remembered it from those three blissful weeks at Canon Row. How distant that time seemed now, but I still had the memory of his hands on my body, it had become part of me. 'Everything has been thought of,' I said.

'That's your aunt,' said Margaret, 'and Bridget and Crompton.'

I felt shored up by all these people, prepared to do so much for me.

There was a kerfuffle in the yard, hooves on the cobbles. 'They're here,' cried Bridget.

'Better get ready.' I crossed the chamber to the window. There was a party below, men dismounting but no one I recognized. I remembered Will would be in disguise too, in his black wig. My breath fluttered and caught in my throat. One had black hair; he looked up. 'No,' I said, my heart dropping. 'It's not them.'

I remained at the window and watched the sky begin to take on the pinkish hue of evening. Crompton came up. 'We can't wait much longer, My Lady.'

'Half an hour, just half an hour.'

His face looked strained, his mouth drawn. He looked as I felt.

The half-hour was gone in an instant.

'He'll come on later,' said Bridget.

'Of course he will,' I replied. I was keeping the hollow feeling at bay, but only just.

The stairs creaked as we descended. Crompton was paying the innkeeper and all the men were gone, out and into the boats, I supposed. None of us said it but we must all have been entertaining the possibility that Will had been caught and wondering whether there was a search out for us already.

No, I reasoned silently; if he had been caught he would say he intended upon a conjugal visit at Barnet, he would slip the lieutenant a gold piece and all would be back as it was. That is what I told myself, refusing to see that such a scenario would mean I was striking out alone.

We left a man to wait for Will and made for our boat. The oarsmen were sullen and grumbled quietly about the late hour as we embarked. There was a flock of seagulls carking and swooping around a heap of waste nearby. One perched on the pier, close to us. It was vast, with a vicious hooked yellow beak and a swivelling eye, like a white devil. We cast off and moved out into the river and the men began to sing as they found their rhythm. Once in the fast-flowing middle channel I felt the wind, sharp on my skin, flicking the ties of my cloak against my face.

'He'll be just behind us,' said Crompton.

If the men wondered what I was doing, a fellow sitting in a huddle with the maids at the back, they said nothing. I turned to watch the sunset, a glorious palette of pink and orange splayed out over the sky. My neck became cricked I gazed for so long, watching out for the sight of Will approaching. Each distant speck became a boat. The men rowed in silence, their song having petered out, so the slapping rhythm of the oars and the heave of breath were the only sounds; even the wind had dropped on the silent river. Before long it was too dark to watch for boats. The waterman lit the little lamp at the bow and it was soon the only spot of light in the gloom, that and the gibbous moon that occasionally peered out through a crack in the cloud.

In the dark Starkey began to whisper, but his voice was indistinct and the rocking motion of the boat must have sent me to sleep, despite the flapping in the pit of my stomach, for I woke to find us docking at Tilbury and Crompton in a whispered altercation with the waterman.

'We must push on,' he was saying.

'My men have been pushing on all night. They need to rest a while, have a drink.'

'Let them have their drink,' I said, surprising the two men who'd assumed me still asleep. I hoped that a short delay might give Will the opportunity to catch us up, or if not him then a messenger with news. Surely Mistress Lanyer would have sent word if there had been a hitch. All my instincts told me he was out and in my wake, I felt him nearing. I know now that my instinct was true.

There was a rowdy crowd outside the tavern by the docks. It sounded like a cockfight or something similar. 'I will stay aboard with my women,' I added. 'You go with the men to make sure they don't desert, or drink themselves into a stupor,' I said to Crompton.

'No need to fear for that. I've kept back their fee.'

'You think of everything, don't you?'

'I had to offer them double to continue. But happily I had something set aside for contingency.'

'You see, everything!' It made me realize once more the complicated choreography involved in my flight and I was thankful I had such competence on my side. 'I am grateful to you. To you all. I will reward you for your loyalty when . . .' I stopped. The part of me that watched was whispering in my ear of the uncertainty of my future, how I would be eternally dependent on the hospitality of family and friends on the Continent. When *would* I reward them? *There is an ulterior motive to their loyalty*, said that part of me, *a darker aim to see you crowned, or if not you then a child of yours.* I tried not to hear, to listen to Starkey instead, urging me on, but the voice of my pessimism was loud. *Is it your hope or theirs?*

Tap, tap, tap. I continue to scrutinize myself for the answer to that and truly don't know whether I was a woman seeking escape and freedom to live with her husband, or a woman with an altogether greater ambition. Both, perhaps; after all, a person cannot veer from the trajectory set at birth, can they? So many questions – I wonder if it is ever possible to know what someone, even oneself, truly thinks or believes; it is so easy to hide the truth in a dark corner of the heart.

Margaret was shivering, so I pulled my cloak around her and Bridget followed Crompton off the boat, returning a few minutes later with a jug of toddy and something to eat. I hesitated when she held out the food but took it when she said, 'I'm not putting up with any of your not-eating nonsense, My Lady. You need your strength and we don't know when we will have our next meal.'

There was no messenger, no sign of Will, by the time

417

the men returned laughing and singing, their spirits thankfully up again. We continued on for what seemed an interminable time, the little boat clinging to the coast, weaving to avoid sandbanks and sea grass, occasionally having to turn back to find a deeper channel through. The men's high spirits were short-lived and they became restless. Had we not been in the wilderness, without the remotest sign of a village or even a house, they might well have deserted us.

The darkness was fading as I began to smell the sea, a wild, briny scent that reignited my optimism. Birdsong began to fill the air, not the familiar finches and pigeons but the strange cries of seabirds, birds I'd never seen before, with stilt legs and elongated beaks. The waterman began to point them out, naming them: the gannets, gulls and the waders, a colony of shags, a lone heron, a pair of egrets, a sudden flight of red-beaked terns twisting in unison up and up, opening the sleek span of their wings, flipping together, black heads disappearing, silvery plumage rendered invisible against the palest grey of dawn.

The sight of masts in the distance meant we were at Leigh, the final port in the estuary. I pictured it on the map, beside the scribbled sea-monster. There was some discussion with the waterman, provoked by another threat of mutiny from his men, but Crompton, still with no apparent agitation, managed eventually to persuade the men to continue, with the promise of a greatly increased reward. We moved on, out into the expanse of empty water; I had never laid eyes on the sea and the paintings I had seen of it failed to capture the sheer, flat, endless, muted, nothingness, the almost imperceptible edge where sky and water touched. I wondered how we would ever find our waiting boat, if it were still waiting, but eventually, an hour's hard pull on, we saw the single mast and a flag bearing a yellow cross, our pre-arranged sign, dancing hopefully in the wind.

We drew up next to the anchored brig and a ladder was unrolled down the side. I unfolded my aching body and began to climb up that wavering rope ladder. My wig became caught, flapping manically and, clinging on with one hand, I pulled it away from my head, throwing it into the water below. My own hair flew up in the wind, freeing itself from its ties. One of the men tried to hook the wig with an oar but it had floated too far out. They must have all been wondering who was this woman dressed as a man whose escape they had rowed through the night to assist.

I climbed on up and at the top a pair of arms helped me up on to the deck.

'*À votre service,*' said the ship's captain, a rotund, smiling man in satin who looked more like a Parisian blade than a seasoned smuggler. His eyes lingered a moment on my breeches and boots and then on my wild tangle of hair. '*Je m'appelle Capitaine Corvé. Soyez la bienvenu à bord mon modeste, petit vaisseau...*' He continued on, not seeming to care whether he was being listened to or not, as Bridget and Margaret were heaved up to join me, followed by our luggage, winched up on ropes, and then eventually, having settled up with the waterman, Crompton swung himself up and over on to the deck.

I went aft, looking back up the estuary, hoping beyond hope for a sign of William; there was nothing but endless water, grey and empty save for the strange birds and distant banks of sand. As I watched, the drab seascape transformed, lit beautifully in the golden light of sunrise, and in it the two small dark shapes of our departing rowboats.

In that moment of contemplation, beckoned by the watery expanse, I forced myself to face the possibility that I might have to head for the Continent without Will. But his fist was gripped about my heart and, try as I might, I couldn't prise those fingers open. *Your plan was bound to fail,* said that part of me. Our luggage was being stowed and Corvé was shouting commands to the deckhands. It was only moments before he would order the anchor to be lifted. I prayed for time to slow and give Will a chance to catch us up but there was a leak in my resolve and despair was flooding through it.

Margaret must have sensed my distress, for she came alongside me and placed her arm about my shoulders. I didn't flinch.

'Do you think he's been arrested?' I couldn't bear to think of my Will having the truth forced out of him.

'Of course not!' She didn't believe it for she had tears running down her face and I wished, in that moment, more than anything, for a similar release.

Crompton stepped up, saying, 'As we were late arriving we have to wait for the tide to turn. It will be at least two hours before we can weigh anchor.'

'Two hours?' A seed of hope planted itself in me, sprouting, blossoming. 'Two more hours.'

'Why don't you go below and settle in? There is a cabin prepared down there, a bed. You could try and sleep a little.' His voice was steady but his fingers betrayed him, tapping nervously.

Bridget and Margaret slept but I waited on deck, sensing the jitters building. Corvé pulled out a perspective glass from his doublet with a flourish, eyeing us all to see if we were impressed with his toy, and I was reminded for an instant of Uncle Henry. He scanned the horizon to no avail.

A little later Crompton asked for a man to be sent up the mast to look out. It dawned on me then that they weren't seeking only my husband, but also those who might be in pursuit. Back in Barnet the household would be waking and my absence noted. I prayed Sir James would assume my imminent return, but eventually the truth would emerge, if it hadn't already. An indelible image fixed itself in my mind's eye of Will being escorted to the Privy Council by a consignment of guards.

Crompton began to pace up and down the deck.

My gut twisted.

The wind whipped up, the brig rocked and bucked and a dark bank of boiling cloud became visible on the distant horizon.

'Let's pray that storm holds off,' Crompton said, just as Corvé gave the order to weigh anchor. 'Thank heavens,' he muttered.

The boat was a sudden hive of activity as men climbed the masts to loose the sails and others pulled up the great chain, which fell clattering to the deck, followed, eventually, by the anchor, tangled with dripping weed. The sails smacked as they unfurled, ballooning out, and the brig began to shift, rapidly picking up speed.

'We are away!' Crompton, forgetting himself, slapped me on the back as if I were a comrade, but I couldn't find a way to share his joy. I was rent in two, for the price of my freedom was the loss of my love.

The wind whipped my hair, snapping it about my face; an icy spray of brine smacked sharply over my skin and I held out my arms, letting my cloak fly out behind me, imagining wings to lift me up and away from my despair.

Bishopsgate

Ami was ready. The basket, with the suit and black wig folded out of sight beneath the linens, waited beside the back door. Alphonso was dead to the world upstairs in the bedchamber, and would be for some time if the drunken state of him on the previous night was any measure. Hal was sleeping too and she'd told the maid she had an early errand and to get him up and off to school without her.

She hadn't been able to eat, was far too het up, and paced the hall back and forth as she waited for the bell to ring out for matins. Then she would leave, giving her enough time to get to the Tower before the laundry cart went through the gates. It was a drill she'd practised before. On the previous occasions she had enjoyed the subterfuge but on that day the stakes were higher.

She thought about Lady Arbella leaving from Barnet and imagined her reunited with Will Seymour at some place or other in Blackwall. Mister Crompton had been deliberately opaque about the plans. 'If you only know what you need to know there will be less risk if you are . . .' He looked at her. His eyes were appealing and gentle but his character was razor-sharp. He'd thought of everything, it seemed. He didn't finish what he was saying but she knew he meant if she were hauled before the Privy Council to account for what happened.

She caught herself biting her nails, took a breath to calm her nerves and ran through the drill in her head. A banging started up, someone at the back door, desperate to gain entry, making her heart jump into her throat. Opening it she found a boy in a big apron covered in ink – the printer's apprentice,

422

she was sure; he was puffing and wiping sweat off his face with his sleeve. He must have run all the way from Adling Hill.

'Mistress Lanyer.' He bent over, trying to catch his breath.

'What is it?' She was confused, for this boy, as far as she knew, had nothing to do with their plans.

'Mister Simmes needs you at the print works. He says it is urgent.'

'Tell him I'll be there this afternoon.' Relief washed through her. For a moment she'd thought things had gone awry.

'He says he must see you this morning. There is a line he cannot read in one of your poems and the edition is meant to go out today.'

'Then it must go out tomorrow. Run along and tell him I'll be there later.' She rummaged in her purse for a ha-penny to give him.

'I've been told to say that if it isn't done today it will be another three months before he'll be able to get to it. He has a pile of other work, see, and all of it's urgent.'

Her mind churned over possible remedies. Her book had been with Valentine Simmes since October. It was June already and the bookseller Mister Bonian was supposed to have it the following week in his shop. He'd been pestering her, had orders he said. She had waited a decade for this – the publishing of her book, the culmination of a tortuous cre-ative path and an answer to all those who doubted she'd do it. Only Lady Arbella never doubted her. Her husband thought her an aberration for wanting to publish a book.

'If you tell me which line I will write it clearly for you to take back to him. That should do it.' She was glad to have found a resolution, for the matins bell had started up. She hurriedly got out her writing things. 'Come on, I've no time to waste. I have to be somewhere.'

'I'm afraid I don't know which line it is. You really do need to return with me.'

There was no choice. She was calculating the time it would take to get to Adling Hill and then on to the Tower and thought it feasible. 'Come on then.' She threw on her cape, picked up the basket and was out into the back alley before the bells had stopped ringing. The boy trailed her as she marched at speed down Bishopsgate and across to Moorgate then dropped down towards St Paul's. If she kept her pace up there would be plenty of time.

Valentine Simmes was in the door of his print works as she arrived, hot and in need of a drink. The place smelled oily with printers' ink and the great beast of a press sat in the middle of the space.

She stopped his apology in its steps: 'I am in a terrible rush, Mister Simmes, so if you could be quick with your query.' The boy offered her a cup of small beer, which she swallowed back in one.

'It is here in line eight hundred and three.' Simmes had the place marked in the manuscript, opening it to show her. 'Do you see there is a blot? I cannot make out if it says "prove" or "reprove".'

'Oh, it's "prove". It wouldn't make sense as "reprove".' She tried to hide her annoyance at being dragged all the way there for something any idiot could have worked out for himself.

'I thought as much,' he said, 'but wanted to be absolutely sure, for if it was wrong the sense would have been altered entirely and once in print, well, it is there for ever.'

She was suddenly grateful, thinking of her words immortalized, grateful for his meticulousness.

'You must be very proud. It is a remarkable work . . . true subtlety of thought there. Greatly original.'

Her heart expanded. 'Goodness, I don't know about that.'

424

She was being disingenuous for she knew her work was better than most.

'Your Description of Cookham. The emotion you convey, the sense of loss, is profound.' He shuffled through a stack of papers, taking an age, finding a sheet from which he began to read aloud:

Farewell (sweet Cookham) where I first obtained
Grace from that Grace where perfect Grace remained . . .

She was enjoying hearing her own words, was quite entranced, felt proud of her achievement and as he recited on, she quite forgot the time.

. . . Those pretty Birds that wonted were to sing,
Now neither sing, nor chirp, nor use their wing,
But with their tender feet on some bare spray,
Warble forth sorrow, and their own dismay.
Fair Philomel leaves her mournful ditty,
Drowned in dead sleep, yet can procure no pity . . .

She raised her hand to stop him. The mention of Philomel had reminded her, with a jolt, of her urgent mission. 'Now I really must be off, Mister Simmes.'

She was out again and running along behind Baynard's Castle and on past Angel Lane and the bridge, where there was a bustle of people to be negotiated. A stitch, sharp as a blade, prodded her side and her lungs were fit to burst, forcing her to stop a moment to catch her breath. Newly girded, she continued on past St Magnus the Martyr and the fish market, attracting strange looks from passers-by, red-faced and staggering as she was, carrying her great basket of linens. But she didn't care, for St Dunstan's was to her left and she could see the entrance to the Tower and the laundry cart outside. Running faster now, she saw the great gates opening and the cart crossing the bridge over the moat, could hear the rumble of the slats as it passed, could smell the rank stench of the water. And it was over and beyond the gates, which were closing. She ran on stopping only as the gates shut firmly, just as she reached them. Dropping the basket, she beat at the great broad planks with her fists, crying out for someone to open up until tears of frustration subsumed her.

Her head began to spin as the full realization of what had happened, of what she had done, came to her. The whole plan, organized to perfection by Mister Crompton, would collapse because one small cog had failed to make its turn. She thought of Will Seymour waiting for her within, counting on her, and not only him, but Lady Arbella also, who was at that moment galloping to Blackwall to rendezvous with her husband.

Ami had wanted nothing more than to play her part in bringing them together, to give them the happiness they deserved. Lady Arbella had been dished out such a mean ration of joy in her life and Ami had believed she might make a difference, but she had failed them both. It was sheer vanity that had caused her delay. If she hadn't stopped to listen to Valentine Simmes reciting her words, indulging herself in hubris, she would have made it to the gates on time.

Shame gushed into her as she slumped on a nearby wall, unable to face the potential consequences of her irresponsibility. But she refused to give up all hope. There was nothing else for it; she would have to return and go in with the late laundry cart. She would have to run down to Mister Rodney who was waiting with the horses in the yard behind the Guildhall and warn him of the delay.

Self-reproach formed into a sharp stone in her gut as she waited, through that June day, for the late cart and by the time she saw it lumbering along Tower Hill towards her she was sick with nerves.

'It's you today, is it?' said the driver with a wink. 'T'other one's got a face as long as a yard of tripe.'

'She's a good laundress,' said Ami, taking on her role, tempering her refined accent to meld in with his. 'Can get ink spots out of anything.' He was talking about Margey, who sometimes did laundry for her as well as the Tower's inmates, and to whom she had several times paid a shilling for her silence to take her place with the Tower cart.

Once inside she made her way to Will Seymour's rooms, up the steps beside the water gate. He pulled her in and slammed the door.

'What in hell's name kept you! You do see that if this whole thing falls apart the blame will be at your door.' He was taking great care not to raise his voice but couldn't disguise his rage. His protruding eye teeth, usually an attractive quirk, made him seem demonic, but her shame was greater than her fear.

'I'm so sorry, so very sorry. But it's not too late.' She unpacked his suit and the wig, helping him into them. They might have laughed had the circumstances been different, for the black beard was like some kind of animal and the suit cheap, ill-fitting. While he finished dressing, she pulled all the dirty linens off the bed and stuffed them into the basket.

Then they walked slowly down the steps and out on to the cobbles – a laundress and a bearded labourer – past a pair of guards, feeling their scrutiny, and towards the gates to wait for the cart to be loaded. The guards were talking. Blood rushed through her ears. One of them peeled away from his companion and ambled towards them. Her heart hammered. Did he suspect something? She didn't dare look over at Will.

The guard walked right up to her, looking her over, fat and wheezing in the heat, peeping into the basket in her arms. She held her breath. He plucked at some of the linens.

'What's a' – hot flowers of sweat blossomed in her armpits – 'beauty like you doing laundry for such sinful inmates as inhabit this place?'

'Got to keep the wolf from the door, aint I?' Her voice was mercifully free from tremors.

He smiled. 'Well, don't work them lovely hands to the bone, will you?'

She found a smile for him and then, thankfully, the cart was loaded and they were ready to saunter out in plain sight.

As the gates closed behind them she whispered to Will, 'Keep on going, round to the right towards the yard behind the Guildhall, where Mister Rodney is waiting.'

He turned before he left, and hissed, through that ridiculous beard, 'If this fails, I will never forgive you.' She still remembers the venom in his eyes, as toxic as her shame.

'I will never forgive myself,' she muttered to his departing back.

The following morning early a messenger came from Mister Rodney with a note that said: *Fortune is with us. The package is well on its way to France.*

Ami lights the lamp and sits herself down to read what she's written, picturing Lady Arbella exultant on the foredeck of that French brig, a figurehead, in breeches, splashed with brine, her cloak billowing out behind her. Somewhere deep in the far reaches of her mind her heroine knows that Will too is on his way to France, can picture him on the deck of his own boat, looking out at the same expanse of water.

Ami wonders if this is not a fitting place to end her story – a place of promise, of triumph, of lovers on the brink of union. She wrestles with the idea.

She remembers theatrical denouements she has watched: the bloodbaths of tragedy, actors dripping in red matter, audiences open-mouthed in horror; the same players, on the

following night, spinning across the stage, dancing in celebration of a wedding, the crowd weeping with joy.

She can imagine Lady Arbella up there with them, the balcony of the stage serving as the prow of her ship, a fellow
crouched below wafting a breeze her way to make her garments flutter. The audience wills her on. They have witnessed
in the previous scene her husband's escape from the Tower;
they can already picture the fate-crossed lovers reunited,
their eyes are welling with happy tears.

'Onward to France, and liberty,' she cries, thrusting her
fist into the air, 'where my dear husband waits for me.'

But is omission not as good as a lie? Was it not her aim to
make a misunderstood woman understood, to give a voice to
her silence, to hold up a mirror to a life? The imagination is
a strong current that can pull you under. Goodwife Stringer
has demonstrated lately the way an erroneous belief can lead
a person to a place where truth is obliterated.

She takes up her pen and continues.

> The breeze boils up, the sails excite,
> Stuttering forth to where lovers unite.

At sea

'Calais!' I cried. I had watched the distant vague mass slowly transform, taking on the shape of pointed turrets and high walls. We were making excruciatingly slow progress, our boat struggling and zig-zagging against the wind.

I held out my hand. 'Look, Margaret, I am shaking.' But Margaret was spewing over the side, again. 'We will be on dry land soon.'

She turned a green face to me and attempted a smile. I should have been near dead with exhaustion but some kind of invisible force kept me going. Bridget had slept, like a corpse, for the entire journey; even Crompton had dozed for an hour, upright in a chair, head lolling, mouth open. Margaret had lain moaning, with her face pressed to the lip of a bucket until I prised her up, out of the putrid air below and on to the deck.

I noticed a heated conversation taking place between Corvé and his boatswain, who was pointing towards the stern. I followed his finger and saw the unmistakable shape of a boat in our wake. Light-headed with elation, I joined them, leaning out for a better view, unable to tear my gaze away from that small dark form. Where we were struggling in our cumbersome vessel with the wind against us, they were sleek and compact and bearing down swiftly. I could just make out the several pairs of oarsmen explaining their speed.

'Will!' I shouted. 'I knew he'd make it.'

Crompton was at my side, grabbing my shoulders, facing me, grinning. 'Thank God!'

His eyes glimmered. 'Are you crying, Crompton?'

'No, of course not! It's the wind.'

A laugh burst out of me and, forgetting myself entirely, I snatched the perspective instrument from Corvé's hand, placing it to my eye.

A small circle of sea appeared through the lens, a gull bobbing on its surface in magical detail. I moved the instrument back and forth, finally catching the craft in my sight, seeing clearly then the eight pairs of oarsmen and a number of men at the rear, one standing, looking back at me through an identical device. I scanned their faces, looking for Will, reminding myself he was disguised.

'Was it a *black* beard?' I asked Crompton.

'Yes, yes, a big black beard and a matching wig.'

I scanned the faces once more.

'What is it?' asked Crompton. 'What's the matter?'

I passed him the instrument so he could see for himself that Will was not on board, only a small pack of heavily armed men and behind them, fluttering prettily in the breeze, was the King's banner.

Crompton blanched, drawing an arm across his forehead and, turning to Corvé, asked how many men crewed the brig.

Corvé held up both hands, fingers spread, indicating ten, then began to bark orders at his men to angle the boat, get some wind behind the mainsail, speed us up, outrun them, but we all knew it was futile. The weather was against us and their sleek craft was moving through the water at speed. We didn't need the perspective instrument now to count their numbers, with the eight pairs of rowers and ten others, they were twenty-six strong.

The lads had opened a chest and were pulling out pikes and swords, distributing them around. Corvé produced a pair of pistols from somewhere, tossing one over to Crompton, who began to load it.

The boat was bearing down on us, almost within range.

'Get down!' Crompton pushed me to the deck as a musket fired, the bullet thudding into the side of our boat.

Margaret screamed.

I crawled to the bow and grabbed hold of her, pulling her with me behind a large coil of rope. Margaret was shaking and moaning and I shouted down to Bridget to help me get her below decks.

Corvé fired into the air, a deafening warning shot, and crouched to reload. Crompton held his aim, waiting. The boatswain was barking out orders to the men to take their places. I looked around at them; they all seemed barely out of boyhood. One close to me had a peach-like complexion and round cheeks that made my heart lurch.

Dragging Margaret, I crawled across the floor towards the hold, where Bridget was waiting, white-faced.

Another shot was fired. Another bullet whistled and thumped into the side of our brig. We slid behind the mast. Margaret was shaking violently and whimpering but her fear made me strong, we couldn't both fall to pieces. The musket fire began to come in volleys, a hellish cacophony, the scent of gunpowder filling the air; it was the smell of fireworks and celebrations.

A boy, struck on the arm, collapsed down beside us, clutching his wound. It was the smooth-faced lad, terror stitched through him. 'I'm not ready to die,' he cried. 'I want my mam!'

A new volley of shots hailed on us as I unpeeled his fingers and inspected the injury, a black hole, smelling of burnt flesh, oozing bright blood. The bullet had passed clean through and even with my limited knowledge I knew that to be a good thing. 'You'll be all right,' I said and, seeing the doubt on him, added, 'really. Today's not your day to go.' It crossed my mind that it might be mine and, as if on cue, a bullet clipped the mast an inch from my temple and ricocheted up, tearing through the mainsail, causing Margaret to scream again, a great, blood-curdling terrified wail.

'Stop,' I said, taking both her upper arms firmly, 'just stop. Rip me off a length of your petticoat, the cleanest part, to serve as a bandage.'

She wriggled out of her undergarment and began to tear off a strip, seeming a little calmer with a task to focus on.

Another volley of shots cracked, smoke billowed, men shouted, as I wrapped the bandage tightly round the boy's upper arm. 'Make a sling from your scarf,' I instructed Margaret who was grey with fear.

Through thick grey smoke I saw a rope fly high through the air. On its end was a hook, which lodged itself under the lip of the brig.

'They're boarding,' shouted Crompton. 'We can pick them off as they climb.'

Corvé staggered, tripping over something, sending his gun skittering over the deck towards me. I picked it up, sensing the power of life and death in its weight.

I stood.

Corvé was gesticulating wildly, indicating I should toss the arm back to him, and behind him a rank of deckhands gathered brandishing a motley assortment of weapons.

I saw them for what they were, a few petrified boys, not even men, who thought they were simply sailing to France. They would be maimed, killed, for what? So that some woman they didn't know could have a taste of freedom. The smoke was making my eyes smart; I wiped them with my sleeve and, tucking the gun into my breeches, bellowed, 'HOLD YOUR FIRE!'

I walked forward, out of the shadow of the mast.

'You'll get yourself killed,' screamed Margaret, tugging at my leg. I shook her off.

There was a lull in the fire as the men began to climb the ropes. Crompton had his aim. I ran, swiping my arm at him, feeling strength I didn't know I had come from nowhere.

'Don't fire!' I cried.

'Are you mad?' he screamed.

I pointed my pistol his way, shouting, 'Drop your gun!'

'Steady.' I saw real panic in him as he took a small step towards me.

'Leave it,' I said firmly in Grandmother's voice, as if commanding a dog. 'If we try to repel them it'll be a bloodbath. Do you truly want this on your conscience? I will not risk innocent lives being lost on my account.'

He slumped and dropped his face into his hands, reminding me of the moment I'd first told Will I was carrying his child.

I grabbed Margaret's undergarment and walked through the smoke towards the side of the brig, arm up, the flag of white petticoat dancing from my fist signalling my surrender.

St Giles-in-the-Fields

Hal holds open the door, 'Close your eyes, Ma!' He takes her arm and guides her inside. 'Now you can open them.'

It is a spacious chamber with a brick hearth and windows set high on both sides. There is space enough, she estimates, for five rows of four desks. She can see them there already, a pupil at each, girls as well as boys, studying quietly. In her mind she can smell the ink and hear the soft scrape of chalk on slate. She is walking up and down occasionally, offering advice or standing at the front, all eyes on her, conjugating a verb in Latin.

'And through here,' Hal calls her from a doorway at the far end. She follows him through into a smaller room bathed in light. There in her mind's eye she sees Joyce sitting cross-legged on the floor with a circle of little ones, singing a numbers song.

She had suggested to Joyce a few days earlier, that she come and help her in the school.

'A school? A proper school?' she'd exclaimed.

'It was Hal's idea.' She watched the girl light up on hearing Hal's name. 'He's found me a building near St Giles.'

'Near St Giles,' she repeated, as if she couldn't find words of her own, then said more quietly, 'and you want *me* to help you with it?'

'I hope you will say yes.'

'If Fa allows it, then I'd love nothing more.' Joyce turned away then, so her face wasn't visible. 'Is he spoken for?'

'Who?' Ami was momentarily confused. 'What, Hal? Goodness, no.'

'Ah,' said the girl, looking up again, trying to conceal a smile.

Ami had wanted to ask Hal about Joyce, after seeing them together that day, but at the same time didn't want to interfere.

She watches him pace the room counting, measuring its length.

'This couldn't be more perfect,' she says.

'And there are three large rooms upstairs too.'

It seems too good to be true. 'And the lease?'

'It's a fair price.' He begins to list the costs but she interjects.

'Tell him I'll take it.' Through the window she can see the agent loitering in the meadow out front.

'I reckon I can haggle it down a little. The place does need a lick of whitewash.'

'I'm sure you can, with your talents for negotiation.' She brings a hand to his shoulder. 'Given the amount you levered out of that Cheapside jeweller for my trinket.'

'He said it was the finest stone he'd seen in a month of Sundays. I didn't exactly need to squeeze it from him. His eyes were popping out of his head.'

'There will be plenty to set everything up, in any case, and a fair sum left over.' She is struck, and not for the first time, by the worth of that raspberry-sized piece of matter that had lived so long beneath her floorboards. It is a good feeling to have prospects, a woman of her age, a widow, with a nest egg, and there is enough even to settle Alphonso's old debts.

Outside, a deal is agreed, she shakes hands with the agent. It is a new start.

'Life is a series of beginnings and endings,' she says to Hal as they walk away, back towards Clerkenwell. 'It's funny,' she adds. 'All along I had the means to settle my debts, yet didn't realize it. Had I known the true value of that jewel —'

Hal interrupts her, saying, 'Perhaps it was meant to be.

You might never have come to teaching if you hadn't needed to earn your living.'

'I suppose not.' She wonders when he became so wise.

'How's your writing coming along, Ma? Are you nearly done with it?'

'I'm not entirely sure,' she replies.

She cannot find a way to explain that the truth is untidy, how the story has begun to crumble beneath her fingers. She has been struggling to order it into a legible form. Arbella's account had, towards the end, become even more convoluted and fragmented; like a dreamscape it had lost its coherence, become a string of impressions and feelings – and memories.

The Tower of London

Tap, tap, tap. I try to write but my hand struggles to hold the quill just as my mind refuses to hold my thoughts. Most of what I write is illegible and the rest is smeared by my sleeve.

I tip out my bag of treasures, rolling the die that always lands on a six – three pairs of black eyes, set in ivory, watching me. I unfold the paper containing my husband's hair, bringing my nose to it. His scent is gone. Nestling in my palm is the tear of glass to represent all the tears I have never shed. I wonder if I shatter it, will those tears be spilled at last? I hold it to my eye and the world is transformed, all its straight edges curved, small things enlarged. I slip my wedding ring on to my finger. It is too big, even for my thumb. Soon *I* will be transformed.

Soon.

I will fly away.

I read Mistress Lanyer's dog-eared poem: *Rare Phoenix, whose fair feathers are your own.*

I feel my feathers sprouting in the prickle of gooseflesh about my shoulders.

I ring Geddon's little bell to take me back, but the bright chime puts me in a place I do not want to go, where my Scottish aunt's neck is hacked at like a piece of timber.

And there it is, that small traitor, hiding at the bottom of the bag. I pick up the Agnus Dei between the tips of my fingers, as if it might burn me, and fling it from the window.

It is four years now that I have been throwing it away. Each morning it is returned to the ledge. I am cursed by it. It whispers to me of the one true faith. Starkey tells me to resist it, that it is testing me.

The lieutenant, Wade, had found it amongst my things when I first arrived. He said it spoke of insurrection.

'I am no Catholic,' I told him.

'We shall see,' was his reply. He placed an elbow on the arm of his chair and cleared his throat. 'The Countess of Shrewsbury, your *Catholic* aunt, will be here within the day.'

'Aunt Mary has been arrested?'

'Indeed, *My Lady*' – he said it as if I didn't deserve the title – 'the aunt that would have put you at the heart of a papist plot.'

'You are not speaking the truth. My aunt never wanted anything more than to give me my liberty.'

'I fear you delude yourself, My Lady. It is what everyone says.'

'Everyone can be wrong.' I could see *he* wasn't a man who liked to be wrong. The up-pointing moustache, carefully curled, spoke of his vanity. Yes, he would be too beset with pride to like being proved in error. 'If she is coming here then I will ask her myself.'

'I'm afraid I cannot allow that. But *I* shall draw the truth out of her.' The way he said it made me crumple a little and think of all those others who had served me and might be having things drawn from them.

'Perhaps *she* will know why you have a trinket blessed by the Pope in your possession.' Lieutenant Wade was known for having drawn the truth out of the Powder Treason plotters. People said he had a nose for papist insurrection.

'What of my servants, Crompton, my women?' I imagined Bridget and Margaret somewhere working on that embroidered woodland scene they began in Barnet.

'They are being held elsewhere.'

'They have done nothing save what I demanded of them. They cannot be charged guilty of obedience.' I could not

439

bear to think that those I held dear, those who were loyal, had lost their freedom for me. I wanted to ask about my husband but my throat had become choked and the words would not form.

My harpies have returned and with them dear Doctor Moundford. He looks at me with a face so sad I would cry if I were the crying sort. But instead of bringing tears his look turns my insides out.

A sharp piece of me has broken off and is lacerating my guts.

Moundford drips his tincture into my mouth.

I drift.

The harpies recede. They watch me from their perch beyond the window. Is it they who return the Agnus Dei?

But I don't feel sure of anything.

'Just a sip of caudle,' Moundford is saying. He holds a cup and a spoon. It reeks of milk and nutmeg. I shake my head and shut my eyes; there is my Will, free. He smiles his impish smile and blows me a kiss before flying away.

Aunt Mary came to my rooms.

'I was told I could not see you.'

'I bribed the guards. There is always a way if you are resourceful.' She was dishevelled as usual, and smiling, which reassured me.

'Oh God!' was all I could find to say. I was so very pleased to see her but not pleased she was in this place with me.

'Come, sweeting.' She opened her arms and I fell into them, a child once more.

'Where is Will?' My voice was muffled. I didn't feel able to let her go, wanted to keep my face pressed into her shoulder with its scent of powder and musk.

'His escape succeeded. He is with friends abroad.'

'Thank God.' I had an image of him mounted, galloping into the distance. He looked well on a horse, straight-backed, poised, manly.

'The King is ailing,' she said.

Deep in my heart I sinned by wishing him dead. I knew, had long known, that if Henry Frederick came to the throne I would be released – I would have all I ever wanted.

'Listen,' she said in the faintest of whispers. 'Don't lose hope. There are people who will liberate you from here. I can arrange it.'

'What people?'

'You don't need to know, sweeting.'

My gentlewoman puts a plate of bread and ham on the small table beside the window.

'Doctor Moundford says I must try and encourage you to eat.'

I pretend I haven't heard and say, 'Do you know, Nan, that your husband used to wear my glove in his hat?'

'I do know,' she replies.

'A long time ago.'

'He still has that glove. It is a family treasure.'

I wonder if she can be trusted. She takes her food and begins to eat, spreading the bread thickly with butter, folding the ham inside it, stuffing it into her mouth as if she is starving. My stomach turns. When she isn't looking I peel strips of ham and drop them from the open window, where my harpies sit waiting. They make me think of the dogs beneath the table at Hardwick.

It takes all the force I have.

'Nan, can you tell me what became of Bridget and Margaret. Were they released?'

'Long ago,' she replies, as if I have asked that question countless times, which perhaps I have.

'You've been writing again, I see.' She speaks with her mouth full and I have to avert my eyes.

'I have written myself into existence.'

I must have said it out loud for she says, 'Yes, yes,' like someone humouring a lunatic. I have given up trying to prove I am not mad.

Mary came again. It was just after we heard of Prince Henry Frederick's death. We both wore black sashes. 'They are saying he was poisoned.' Mary's expression was indecipherable, a calculation that would never be solved.

'Who would do such a thing? He was so well loved.' I thought of that glittering boy, bursting with life, the hope of England. I wished in that dark part of me that I could have exchanged myself for him, imagined making a pact with God that allowed him to live and me to die in his place. I was not afraid of death, for I knew Starkey was waiting for me, and all my hope had withered away with the end of that glittering boy.

'That family has many enemies.' Again, that puzzling look.

'What do you mean?' I asked. 'It is my family too.'

'His death puts you closer to the throne, sweeting.'

I would rather have not thought of that, for surely it made my freedom less likely than ever.

'Just that sickly, lame boy Charles and Princess Elizabeth lie in your way now.'

'Stop it.'

'The Princess Elizabeth's nuptials will still go ahead in February, despite her brother's death,' she said. 'I feel it in my bones that the King will grant you a pardon. Isn't it a tradition for the King to grant pardons at a royal wedding?'

My dead hope shifted slightly and I began to mull over what I could sell to raise the money for a dress – for dresses.

I still had those paltry pearls; they would be worth *something*. I would need to look the part on my return to court.

'It will be a *Protestant* wedding.' Aunt Mary's disapproval was visible in every fibre of her being.

'What do you mean by that? Of course it will be a Protestant wedding.'

She doesn't elucidate. 'It's time we do what needs to be done.'

It was as if she spoke in a language I had never come across before. 'Do what?'

She picked up the Agnus Dei from the window ledge and, taking my hand, unfolding the fingers, placed it in my palm. 'Let's not pretend any more . . . It is the only path to the Kingdom of Heaven.'

My breath was loud in my head. I had heard those words before. It was the Scottish Queen who spoke them and this: *I will be up there watching over you and your Catholic England.*

'No,' I said. My voice came out more forcefully than I expected. 'You've got it wrong.'

The Agnus Dei was still in my palm; a circle of red. It reminded me of that sailor's bullet wound or – the thought shocked me – a holy stigma. I remembered hearing of nuns who manifested stigmata at Easter time.

'But you want to be free.'

'There is no such thing as freedom.' Only as the words left my mouth did I understand their meaning as an intrinsic truth.

'You become increasingly opaque,' she said, before she got up, kissed me on the forehead with the words, 'Think about it,' and left.

The gun salute in celebration of the royal wedding caused plaster to drop from the ceiling of my room. The church bells rang and there were fireworks. I made Nan put my new dresses away in the trunk so they wouldn't mock me. In the night I'd heard them talking about me, whispering into their frilled sleeves.

I had asked to be moved. There was a new lieutenant, Elwes, who questioned why I should want to leave the best rooms in the Tower. I didn't tell him it was to get away from Aunt Mary, who could see into my window from her balcony. I didn't want to be part of her scheming – all those stories and secrets weaving back far into the past, back to the Scottish Queen.

My new chamber was round, with deep-set window alcoves and a view of the river far below. Escape would be impossible from such a room. I would be safe from Aunt Mary. She sent letters hidden in my food but I threw them on the fire without reading them.

All that time, all my life, I'd believed her to be something other than she was. I was nothing but a cause to her. If I thought too hard about it I might truly have become cracked in the head, as they said I was. I heard the talk, even shut in that place gossip found its way in.

Wedding fireworks lit up the sky in the distance towards Whitehall. A whisper went round that someone in the Tower had been pardoned. It was not me.

'These rooms housed Lady Katherine Grey, long ago, when she was here,' the lieutenant had said when he showed me to my new quarters, smiling as if he thought the fact would please me.

'I know Lady Katherine.' He looked at me strangely when I said that and I didn't think it worth explaining.

Tap, tap, tap.

'Nan,' I say. 'When will they stop hammering down there?'

'They stopped a month ago. Listen, it is silent.' I can see the concern on her face. She can hardly bear to look at me.

444

'But I hear it.'

I am very weak; it takes a supreme effort to lift my fingers from the bed to my cheek. Pain echoes through me perpetually.

'Do you?' She says it like someone talking to an infant.

I stroke the side of my face; a down has sprouted there. Perhaps I am finally becoming the boy my family once wished I had been.

She pulls back the covers and, averting her gaze, deftly removes my soiled shift, moving my body easily, as if I am a puppet. I am reminded of Margaret, deep in the past, who was able to take off her shift without undoing her gown. It used to make us laugh. It is a long time since I laughed.

Nan replaces the shift with a clean one. It smells of grass. I suppose it is summer and everything has been laid out on the lawn to dry. The scent takes me back to Hardwick and that miniature queen with the wooden stump beneath her skirts, the first great disappointment of my childhood.

'In heaven's name, I wish I could persuade you to eat something.' Nan's eyes are dewy and bloodshot. I feel her hand cradling my own.

'Shhh,' I say. 'Don't cry, Nan. It is what I want – what God wants.'

A harpy is perched near the window. Black feathers, red lips, sharp teeth, black eye. I watch it through the cracked pane. My vision is blurred but I can see it clearly in my mind's eye. It moves towards the place where the window is ajar and drops something from its mouth on to the sill, then opens its vast wings, momentarily blocking out the day, before soaring up and away.

I squeeze Nan's hand. 'My body is not my *self*.' She looks baffled, as if I am speaking in Greek.

Starkey is beside me. *Do you remember when I asked you, years ago, what kind of queen you intended to be?*

'Of course I do. "A just queen," is what I replied.'

You may not be Queen of England but you are queen over the realm of your body. You have the power to mete justice to your soul and set it free.

Nan is talking in murmurs with Doctor Moundford. They are trying to find ways to save me but their efforts are futile, for I have already won this battle.

Despite the frailty of my body my mind is robust.

If you give yourself liberty you also set your husband free.

Very quietly, I whisper to Starkey, 'I know what is right.'

I have that image of Will galloping into the distance. He rides Dorcas. It makes a flower of elation blossom in my breast.

Doctor Moundford and Nan loom over me. A hand covers her mouth but it can't hide her grief. I want to tell her that I am setting myself free, that it is an occasion for joy, that I am taking my life back, but I find I can no longer speak.

They retreat. I hear their footsteps recede.

I feel Starkey's hand slip beneath my pillow for my bag of treasures. He takes something from it then reaches for Moundford's pestle and mortar. The glass tear clinks as it falls into the bowl.

He brings the pestle down hard, several times, shattering it prettily into a million sparkling pieces. All the tears I have never shed.

I feel my own fate in my hands – it is substantial, real – raw, like a cut of meat. It is mine.

He drops the fragments one by one into my open mouth, wide-open like a ravenous cuckoo. I feel them pass into my throat.

If you count back far enough you reach infinity, he says.

Arbella is perched up by the ceiling, wings tucked up neatly. She can see people come and go below.

Nan is kneeling beside her empty body, clutching her bag of treasures; she is weeping.

Doctor Moundford explains something to two men Arbella has never seen before. 'She was unable to ingest anything at all,' he is saying. She notices his use of *unable* rather than *refused* – loyal to her even now, when it no longer matters.

Aunt Mary is there, furious, tearful. 'She is . . .' – her voice breaks – 'was . . . my niece. I should have been made aware. I could have comforted her at the end.'

Or tried to convert me, Arbella thinks. Mary looks up, suddenly, as if she heard the thought.

'She asked that you not be admitted, My Lady.' It is the lieutenant who tells her this. 'I was obliged to do her bidding.'

Arbella sees everything. She sees Aunt Mary's dismay on hearing that. She watches her aunt pick up the Agnus Dei from the window ledge and slip it into her glove.

A pair of servants is sorting through her possessions, unhooking the hangings, folding them carefully, collecting up her bits and pieces, her almost-empty jewel box. One of them pilfers a brooch; he is not aware it is made of glass and worth pennies.

The lieutenant surveys the chamber, lifting things to look beneath them, inspecting Arbella's collection of books, occasionally choosing one and flicking through its pages. He turns Plato on its side to decipher her marginalia, but fails to understand what she has written. He is more stupid than he thinks.

He picks up the stack of written papers on the table, reading passages randomly, rolling his eyes, before taking a fresh sheet of paper and writing something on it: *The Lady Arbella – TO BE DISCARDED*. She can hear his thoughts. He thinks her scribblings are the outpourings of a lunatic.

Taking a length of frayed ribbon, which she has worn sometimes in her hair, he ties the sheaf of papers and tosses it to one side with the other detritus that is of no use to anyone.

'This lot can be got rid of,' he says.

She feels Starkey's presence as a breeze, lifting her, carrying her along, up, away, until she spreads open her wings and flies out into the open expanse of sky.

Clerkenwell

Ami is crying, great racking sobs. She is running with tears, a sea of grief, partially obliterating what she has written.

'What is it?' asks Joyce. 'What's the matter?'

'They are the tears of another.' Ami replies, taking the handkerchief the girl holds out and wiping her face, blowing her nose. Joyce looks baffled by her answer but is too polite, too tactful to ask for an explanation. 'It is a curse to be unable to cry.'

'I s'pose it is.' The girl goes quietly back to her book and Ami reads for the thousandth time those final fragments, hoping against hope that she will find herself there. Her absence screams out. Perhaps, she tells herself, as she has told herself many times before, she is in a part that is lost.

Taking up her pen, she turns to her verse, allowing words to drift towards her from nowhere, inky marks writing themselves into a perfect final couplet:

> For although her tongue is gravely still,
> Sweet Philomel's song the air doth fill.

The door bursts open and Hal appears with a man, a ghost from the past.

'Goodness, Mister Seymour!' Ami gets up from the table.

'Mistress Lanyer.'

They stand in silence looking at each other, like men preparing to fight. She can't help but think of the last time she saw him, the absurd beard, his seething rage: *I will never forgive you*. But he is there, before her, older, a little lined and a smile opens over his face, that same elfin smile she remembers so well.

Neither of them seems to know what to say to the other but Hal makes introductions and produces a jug of wine, handing round cups.

'You must find us very meanly housed, Mister Seymour,' she says, making talk to ease the awkwardness, 'but our fortunes took a tumble. They are on the rise once more, though. Has Hal told you about the school I plan to open?'

'He has. I think it a wonderful project and I was hoping you would accept my sponsorship.'

'I don't know what to say. That is a very kind offer.' He has wrong-footed her with his generosity. 'I am most grateful, but I have no need. I have ample funds.' She likes the idea of the school being entirely hers, of not being beholden to anyone. 'I'm setting it up in your wife's honour.'

Now she has brought Lady Arbella into the room the atmosphere is in suspension, like the quiet that comes before turbulent weather. Hal, always tactful, has led Joyce over to the hearth, where they are talking very softly. She can see Will Seymour's sorrow. Those sad grey eyes, so vividly described by Lady Arbella's pen, show that his loss has not faded and she wishes he would shout at her, be angry as he was before, for she deserves it.

'I'm sorry,' she says. 'So very sorry.'

He holds up a hand to stop her. 'It is I who should apologize.'

'I don't understand.'

He is holding a worn leaf of paper. It is a letter. 'I cannot give it to you to read, for it is a last letter to me, found amongst her things, and contains passages of great intimacy that I cannot share. But in it she asks me to convey to you her deep and heartfelt gratitude for the great risk you took on our account.' He hesitates, the paper quivering in his fingers. 'She wanted you to know that, although she may not have put it into words, she always considered you as a dear and precious friend and that thoughts of you and your poems gave her great comfort, even' – his voice breaks slightly – 'even in her final days.'

Ami feels something shift, deep in her mind, like the unpicking of a lock or the untying of a tight knot.

'She has taught me,' he continues, 'that you cannot condemn a person for a single frailty.' He stops, looking down and then up again, directly at her. 'I beg your forgiveness, Mistress Lanyer.'

'You have it, unequivocally.' The thicket of shame she has been tangled in for so long now opens, unravelling.

She looks over at Joyce and Hal, seeing how they, red-cheeked, stealthily unclasp their hands when they notice she is beckoning them over. A smile spreads over her, inside and out.

Then, raising her cup, she says, 'Let's drink to forgiveness!'

Author's note

The Girl in the Glass Tower is a work of fiction, though one which is largely based in fact. Arbella Stuart, Aemilia Lanyer and almost all the characters surrounding them in the novel are historical figures but they also exist in the world of the novel as my own inventions. Through the filter of my fictional scheme the events of Arbella's life are, in the main, accurately depicted, but of course there is much of her story that lies outside my text. To anyone interested in reading her full biography I wholeheartedly recommend Sarah Gristwood's meticulously researched and wonderfully readable *Arbella: England's Lost Queen*.

Like many women of her time, Arbella was a prolific letter writer and, because of her political significance, many of her letters still exist, which offered me a unique perspective on her complex inner world. To see her writing veering from a perfectly regimented italic to an almost illegible scrawl, sometimes in a single letter, and to read her meandering thoughts allowed me to understand something of her state of mind during particular periods of her life. The content of her letters often exposed her intimate voice, from which I was able to excavate the quirks and tics of her character that were to form the basis of the Arbella of my novel.

Of course, the found manuscript in the novel is my own fabrication. I did not seek to create a pastiche of early modern women's life writing, the few examples of which are nothing like Arbella's autobiography as I have imagined it. But it was a means by which I was able to explore the theme of storytelling and the invisibility of early modern women's lives – a constant personal preoccupation.

My characterization of Aemilia Lanyer, an English female poet of some significance, although very little known nowadays, was different. I wanted to bring her into the light, and in doing so she became an ideal cipher to carry the motif of women, voice and silence in the novel. I had little to go on in terms of the biography of her later life but her published poetry offered insights and helped form my depiction of her. I chose to ignore the theories that she was the 'dark lady' of Shakespeare's sonnets as there is no hard evidence to support this. Her published work and the few facts we know of her life can be found in *The Poems of Aemilia Lanyer*, edited by Susanne Woods

Ami's story is interwoven with Arbella's as a way to support the thematic aims of my novel rather than with an eye to historical veracity, and the passages in which she helps William Seymour escape from the Tower are entirely imagined. The aspersions of witchcraft are also fictional, though such suspicions abounded in the period and were often directed at lone women who didn't conform.

She was, however, orphaned and taken into the household of the Countess of Kent and under the wing of the Countess of Cumberland and, aged only eighteen, became the mistress of Queen Elizabeth's first cousin, Henry Lord Hunsdon, who was some forty years her senior. She was married to Alphonso Lanyer when she became pregnant with Hunsdon's son. Alphonso left her in debt but she eventually acquired the means to open a school in St Giles-in-the-Fields. Another truth is that her son Henry married a girl named Joyce Mansfield.

The only firm link I have found between the two women is Aemilia's poem dedicated to Arbella and the fact that they would both have been amongst Queen Anna's coterie simultaneously; but they sit side by side in *The Girl in the Glass Tower* because their stories chime together.

Elizabeth Fremantle, November 2015

Acknowledgements

There are two women without whom *The Girl in the Glass Tower* would not exist: my agent Jane Gregory and my editor Maxine Hitchcock. I am truly grateful for their unerring support and wisdom. Both are surrounded by a host of talented individuals who work together to turn an almost incoherent stack of written pages into a novel on the shelves of bookshops. Thank you to the team at Jane Gregory and Company, in particular Stephanie Glencross, and also to the team at Penguin: amongst others, Louise Moore, Liz Smith, Francesca Russell, Clare Parker, Kimberly Atkins, Eve Hall, Tim Broughton, Claire Bush, Emma Brown, Chantal Noel and the rights team, Martin Higgins and Isabel Coburn, as well as Lee Motley and Gill Heeley, who continue to surprise and delight me with their cover designs. My hawk-eyed copyeditor Trevor Horwood also has my unreserved appreciation. Lastly, I must thank Katy Green for helping me understand what I ought to already know.